✳ ✳ ✳ ✳ ✳ ✳

CHARLES

✳ ✳ ✳ ✳ ✳ ✳

CHARLES

A NOVEL BY

Victoria Lincoln

Little, Brown and Company · Boston · Toronto

*Published simultaneously in Canada
by Little, Brown & Company (Canada) Limited*

Contents

Preface

THIS IS a biographical novel, not a biography. This does not mean that I haven't tried to avoid pulling my facts about, but only that I have not chosen from my facts in the same way that a biographer chooses from his. Let me explain.

Every life contains many stories, many of them lived simultaneously; the simplest of us is not so simple as we sometimes think. But when a biographer has chosen a subject, he climbs to a lookout point, takes in the whole birth-to-death complexity of a man's life, and sets himself to record everything that does not show, in the over-all perspective, as too trivial to be worth the telling. The novelist, however, walks into his accumulated knowledge as we walk into our own fields of latent memory. He wanders about his borrowed life until he finds the strand of it to which his borrowed mind would be likeliest to return as he lay upon his deathbed. He sights along it for the beginning and end of a tale (one of many possible true tales) and he snaps the shears twice. Then he tries to forget what is irrelevant to his purpose, so far as he may without falsifying what remains.

If you want a biography, don't read this. Read Edgar Johnson's *Charles Dickens, His Triumph and Tragedy*. It is a superb book and superbly indexed; I have blessed that index often when I wanted to be sure that I was remembering events in their proper order.

Johnson's Charles is not quite mine, but few of Charles's friends could have agreed about him, either. There was a lot of him, and for each friend he pulled out only the relevant handful. In one sense, it was only his public who knew him, for in his books the whole crowd of him could have their say. His long love affair with the Audience was based on a sound instinct.

But fortunately for us, Charles was also a born telephone-talker who lived before the telephone. He wrote letters continually, to be posted or carried around the corner by messenger. And people kept them. A six-volume edition is due shortly, I believe. The Nonesuch Edition alone, now out of print, alas, holds as many words as would make nine books the size of this one, and not a dull word in the torrent.

To be sure, Charles seldom told a story twice in exactly the same way, but he told a good story often. If you know something about the people to whom he wrote those thousands of letters, add or subtract accordingly as you read, and then go through the novels again in their light, you will have your own Charles — not mine or Johnson's or the Charles that any one of his friends knew. Oh, yes, I'm convinced that I know him better than anyone else ever did, but so, I expect, was everyone who loved him.

What's more, you will know things about him that he did not know, consciously, about himself. He didn't need to, when he could splinter his heart into that multitude of dancing simplicities who have so much more vitality for us, as we read, than many better-rounded creations of genius self-aware.

He could also, despite all that talk, be most efficiently secretive when he chose. After he died, his friend John Forster and his daughter Mamie wrote little books which reveal a good bit, inadvertently, about themselves, but next to nothing about him. His daughter Katey could have done far better, and would not. As she put it, he was not a good man, but he was wonderful, and half a truth is worse than nothing.

She was thinking, primarily of his relationship with Ellen Ternan, who came into his life less than a year after the point at which this book ends. Katey could have written that story better than it will ever be written, I think, after their last long talk together on the night before Charles died; but to her, a young Victorian matron, the tale was unprintable. To me, it is simply another story. And after I had wandered about for a long time in that complex life which holds so many possible novels, I found that the story I most wanted to tell was that of how Charles got to be the Dickens of the great middle-period.

We leave him midway through the great invective of *Little Dorrit*, with the sunlit realism of *Great Expectations* still waiting for him just around the corner from the end of this book. Try not to feel cheated. Middle-aged men go to bed with young actresses every day and many novels follow them there, but it is rarely in the history of any planet that a novelist like Charles finds his full stature.

Furthermore, since Charles was so very Charles, the story was both more predictable and less central to his life than one might expect. You, his blessed Audience, were his deepest love, and though he died in — and for — your embrace, few artists would deny that his was a story with a happy ending.

So, I hope that you will laugh at him sometimes, and sometimes cry for him; but close this book with quiet hearts, as he always wanted his own readers to do.

I have acknowledged my debt to Johnson. In closing I should like to thank another contemporary, *Staphylococcus aureus*, the onlie begetter of this book. I was housed, deaf in both ears, and with nothing new to read. I was never a Dickens fan, I shall never know why I took down the first volume of that shelf-long set, but I did, and I was hooked. I read straight through to the last sentence of *Edwin Drood* that Charles lived to write.

Then I found those thousands of letters, and books about friends and relations that made them yet more revelatory at the second reading, and the third. I could hear by that time, but I could no longer pay attention; another voice was distracting me.

I did not work like a scholar; I am not a scholar. I did not even know that I was getting ready to write a book, only that I was having a wonderful time. That was three years ago. Throughout the last year of those three I dreamed about this book every night; and when I retired the notes and ever-shortening drafts of my manuscript to the attic, I dropped the box off on the bathroom scales, halfway, and was taken aback to find that it all weighed forty pounds.

And now I have been back for six weeks in the twentieth century. I even begin to feel that I lived with Charles a long time ago. But I remember him vividly, I assure you. I expect that I always shall.

✻ ✻ ✻ ✻ ✻ ✻

BOOK I

Little Charles

✻ ✻ ✻ ✻ ✻ ✻

He was what they called an old-fashioned little boy, by which they used to mean, in those days, a little boy with odd, grown-up thoughts. His eyes, deep blue and brilliant, were too large for his face; and his clothes, bought hopefully for him to grow into, had a way of stubbornly remaining too small for his body. A bout of kidney trouble when he was four or so had hung on, flaring up from time to time still.

But his skin was so fair and bright and his whole look so full of life that strangers took him for a sturdy boy of seven or eight, rather than a sickly child of nine.

And he was likable; he had an inborn genius for being himself and still fitting in. Despite their natural herd distaste for the ailing or the too-clever one, the other boys approved of him. His feeble cricketing was outweighed by his wild enthusiasm on the sidelines. And his cleverness and fancies, far from making him the odd outsider, were their cherished common property.

"It's raining. Get little Dickens to tell a story."

"Come on, let's play Dick's game 'bout Rod'rick Random."

And in winter, when the toy pasteboard theaters came out, he was invaluable. Writer, director, stage manager, and publicity man, he could be everywhere at once, and still keep everyone feeling important and central to the enterprise.

"Make sure you keep your broom working sharply up and down the canvas all through the murder bit, Collinson. A deal depends on it, you know. The whole awfulness is lost without that sound of the wind."

"How was it last time, Dick?"

"Perfect, splendid. Rogers, how low can you turn that lamp without risking it will go out entirely?"

They were not children playing with a toy theater because the weather was bad. They were Drury Lane professionals.

And more than that. Indeed, fully as it ever hung on a cricket match, the whole honor of the school would somehow take to depending on the performance's coming off in what Dick himself would pronounce a slap-up job.

Mr. Giles's school, its students would have assured you, was the best in Chatham. They called themselves Giles's Cats and wore white top hats to distinguish themselves from the lower orders who studied at inferior establishments. Charles was highly sensible of his rank as one of Giles's Cats.

He and his pretty dark-eyed sister Fanny, in truth, were both most pleasantly aware of being the children of gentlefolks, a fact which their mother frequently mentioned to them. She was also given to referring with a trembling sigh to their "present limited circumstances." But that, they knew, was only her indirect reference to the home she had left when she married — a home, they gathered, of phenomenal splendor.

Money was no concern of theirs. Even when they moved from the middle-class comfort of Ordnance Terrace to the shabbier, smaller place at "the Brook," it was only moving to another house in a world where everything was still a size bigger and brighter than life.

Their mother, despite the fact that she never stopped talking and seldom made sense, was an exiled princess; their father, with his vast collars, vaster vocabulary, and perpetual air of being midway through a banquet toast to a guest of honor, was a Brummell and a Lord Chesterfield. The Navy Pay Office clerkship which he held was a position of trust with the government.

Chatham was the center of the universe; and it had the largest and finest town clock in the world, to boot. And the Brook had simply replaced Ordnance Terrace as the center of Chatham. Charles found it a little sad at first to live no longer next door to the peach-colored Lucy whom he had once kissed under her dining-room table; but even she was rapidly supplanted by a black-eyed Henrietta, four doors away. He was already, so far as a pretty face was concerned, exquisitely susceptible.

It was in his third-floor bedroom at the Brook that he had found the books. They were in a large wooden box, and nobody knew or cared where they had come from. Left behind by a previous tenant, his father suggested with lack of interest. But the new servant followed him up to his room, eyed them, felt the bindings, and said, "Who'd of forgot them or left them when they'd fetch so much to sell?"

She was an extremely small servant, and her little sharp eyes peered out from under the flounce of her cap like the eyes of a fox at the mouth of its burrow. She was a charity girl from Chatham workhouse, bound out to work for keep, and she had replaced Mary Anne Weller, who expected wages and was getting married anyway.

Mary Anne told delightful horror stories that made Fan sick and gave him nightmares; Charles had been sincerely sorry to see her go. But even as the dream of Henrietta was fast replacing the dream of Lucy, he had found a new enchantment in this new servant who was either so small for her years or so old for her age. Nor was the least potent of her charms the fact that she did not know her own name: because, as she explained, she was "a orfling."

The stories that she told were factual, nor did she even know that they were stories. Fan would not listen to them; she said that the Orfling was low. But for Charles they were more fascinating and disturbing than all of Mary Anne's man-sized rats and gory murderers put together. For they were about a world strange and different as Africa; and still they were about Chatham, the real place where he lived and had lived for as long as he could remember.

Afterwards there would be conversations.

"Why didn't those children's father take a position and make money, then?"

"Weren't none. Not for him."

"Because he drank so much gin?"

"You've got it hind-end-beforemost."

He thought about that one for a long time; then he said, "They don't say so in sermons."

Under the overhanging flounce of the huge cap the little black eyes changed. They lost their shrewdness. They were, for once, neither the eyes of a wary animal nor of a little old woman, but of a child; they puzzled like his own.

"It's not for a orfling that can't read to ask questions," she said at last, slowly, "but did it ever strike you odd, how different He sounds in the stories they read out from the book about Him, and when they just tell it out of their heads?"

He thought for a while in silence.

"It hadn't struck me before," he said at last in his most old-fashioned manner. "But it is odd. It's . . . it's worth considering."

It was quite a moment: for him, for literature, and for the English social structure.

The Orfling, however, only said, "I'll get below before the Missis skins me alive."

They nodded together gravely. And then, for no reason he could lay his hand on, he broke into a schoolyard shout of laughter which she joined in a brittle, unaccustomed-sounding little cackle.

But now he looked at her, fingering the books and making her pronouncement, and for once she had shocked him.

"Sell them?" he said. "Sell these? Nobody who owned these would sell them. You can't think what the stories are like."

But she clattered her brush against her pan and walked from the room. As she reached the head of the stair he heard her speak, though whether to him or to herself he did not know.

"There's a deal that others can't think," she said, "and some of 'em, I'd like to watch 'em learning, and some, well, I hope they'll never know. Master Charlie being among them I named last."

He wondered if he had offended her, and how. But not for long, as almost at once he fell to reading and was lost.

That miraculous windfall was a wonder that never wore thin; his books, his secret world, his power. *Humphrey Clinker, Tom Jones, Roderick Random; Don Quixote, Robinson Crusoe, The Arabian Nights.* After the bad kidney gave him a bout of pain, he would lie convalescent and happy on the bed under the sloping eaves, holding the book in the golden shaft of afternoon light that made ripples on the page and on the wall behind him. And through the window, less real than the world of his story, he would hear the children in the churchyard over the way, playing at hide-and-seek behind the tomb-stones.

It was incomprehensible to him that though they liked to hear the stories from his mouth and play games about them, nobody else wanted to read them for himself.

"Why don't you, Fan?" he asked once.

"They're too hard. They're dull."

"But you like me to tell them to you."

"You only tell the good parts."

"No I don't. I tell any part."

"You make them different."

He looked at her. She wore a dress of dark crimson merino, and her hair, newly washed, was shiny. They had always been very close. Letty and Frederick were late-comers who did not count in at all the same way. Letty, the elder of the two, was only five.

"You're pretty, Fan," he said abruptly. "You look very old, too, for only a year older than me."

She laughed and tossed her head, like a young lady at a party.

"You silly. I'm hideous."

"You are, though. It's hard to tell at her age, but I don't think Letty will ever be pretty like you. Her chin goes backwards, like Mama's."

"You shouldn't say things like that. It's wicked."

"I daresay." And he looked so grave that she laughed again.

"You are wicked, though. You don't love Mama as you ought. You love me better, don't you?"

"Fan, don't tease me."

But her eyes sparkled with the zest of the game.

"You do. And it's because I've nothing better to do than listen to you all the time, that's why. Because you can't bear it not to have somebody always listening. You've always got to be directly in the middle or else stuck off all alone pretending, the one or the other."

He dreaded her teasing. Big as he was, she could still make him cry. She always knew how, every time. He was going to now.

"Ha, ha. Now the waterworks. Shall you cry like a girl your whole life long? I should love to have your precious Cats see you now."

"Fanny, please. Please stop teasing, Fanny."

She pulled a handkerchief from her pocket.

"Here, don't use your sleeves like that. Oh, mercy, everybody loves you, silly. You're fun, and you think of games, and . . ."

"And what, Fan?"

"And, Tom Thumb, your eyes would fit a giant and they're blue as oceans. And they're why I tease you."

"No, they're not."

"But they are. It's such a lark to see them get all full of such huge, tremendous passions over nothing."

She began to laugh again, but in the other way, the warm way. Suddenly he was giggling with her. He dabbed at imaginary collars with his fingertips.

"Fanny, you are the delight of my life and my intollyerable—er, in a word — pig!"

They fell into one another's arms, shrieking with laughter. He did not wonder, then or later, why Fan could make him feel wicked over saying that Mother had a receding chin, when he could mimic his father with such careless ease.

[6]

The fact was that he loved and admired his father intensely. And those who laugh where they most love are fortunate; they can also, in the hour of need, laugh at themselves.

✻   2   ✻

So THERE you have him at nine, in the golden time that he would always remember through the eyes of a child, with everything a little bigger and brighter than life.

He was a gentleman's son, in a world where everyone had a money tree except for the dwellers in that strange country about which he learned from the Orfling. His maternal grandparents were so fine that they now lived abroad, and his widowed Grandmother Dickens, a calm, pink-faced old lady who always wore black, was recently retired from some unspecified position of trust and confidence which she had long held with a certain Lady Crewe. From his own experience of her quality, Charles imagined the post to have been that of combined taleteller, social director, and household soothsayer.

He was almost twelve when he woke in the night after the party that had appeared to confirm his whole picture of life, and heard the · quarrel that destroyed it.

It is curious that so shrewd and penetrating a child should not have known it all before. On the other hand, children tend to take their parents and their way of life pretty much for granted, and it was only with Fan and the Orfling that Charles ever really talked at home. His vital interests were bound up exclusively with Giles's Cats.

The party had been, like all his father's parties, delightful. The company took a great deal of that refreshment to which his father referred as "the rosy"; mysteriously, as it was made of water, lemons, and the contents of square bottles. It made them gay.

There was laughter, there were quadrilles. His mother wore a June rose in her hair and looked almost young, though not really pretty. And Fan played the piano, and was duly applauded. And finally, as always, his father swung him onto a table, and the limelight was his.

His father's parties, from beginning to end, were a never-failing heady excitement. The talk, rising from its first genteel murmurings to a noisy babble as the rosy worked its charm; the laughing, the dancing, the ladies' elegant dresses, and the gentlemen's stupendous cravats — it was the beau monde, society at play.

But the best moment, the one most eagerly awaited since he had first tasted its sweet, when at the age of four he mastered his first comic song, was the moment of silence when he looked down from his table and drew his breath, to take them all into his hand.

Usually, he sang. This time he had given them a recitation: "The Vision of Sennacherib." And the applause made that which had followed Fanny's effort sound like the merest genteel pattering.

He could hear the company, still laughing below, as he got into his third-floor bed.

The nightmare that woke him was the old one, the worst one, about the poisoned murderer who swelled until he burst.

It generally made him feel sick; but this time, though he was sweaty and shaking, he was hungry. He decided to slip down and see whether there were any bits from the party that Mother had forgotten to lock up before she went to bed.

When he got to the second-floor landing, he froze still, hearing the voices. Their door was ajar, they were both shouting, and his mother was also crying. She often whined, and occasionally indulged in lady-like hysterics; his father sometimes withdrew into a noble and melancholy silence; but strangely enough, Charles had never in his life heard them really quarreling before.

" 'Smooth out!' " It was his mother. " 'It will all smooth out!' You'll sing another tune the night you come home and find a bailiff with a writ sitting on the rosewood sofa!"

"You can scarcely be complaining of the refreshments. They were skimpy enough to occasion me the gravest embarrassment. Perhaps you object to the money you spent to get yourself a new gown for the occasion?"

"So you want me to go in rags, while you run up bills that a lord couldn't face?"

"Keep to the subject for once, if you can. Decent hospitality is necessary for appearances, whether you care about your friends, which I doubt, or not. If we once let our situation show, every creditor in Chelsea would be on me like a hawk, and if you weren't born a fool, you'd know it."

Creditors? Did they owe money they didn't have? And were these brawling strangers his mimsy-mild mother, his courtly father?

Charles shivered, barefoot in the dark hall, and the sickness which the nightmare had so unwontedly failed to bring rose in his throat, acid raw.

But now his mother's voice changed; changed so that although he could not see her he knew quite well how she had struck an attitude and was now apostrophizing the ceiling.

"A born fool? Does he speak like this to a lady and the wife of his bosom? It was of this that my mother warned me on her very knees, when I married the son of servants despite all she would urge — deaf, headstrong girl that I was. The son of a footman risen to be a butler, and a scullery maid who worked her way up to be a housekeeper at Crewe!"

There was a moment of dead silence.

Then his father said, quite flatly and with an extraordinary absence of his usual verbiage: "You think it better to be the child of an embezzler? A common thief, hiding on the Continent from English law?"

At which his mother shrieked, and his father said in a small, sad, oddly bewildered voice: "I am truly sorry, my dear. I am—er, in a word — astonished at my own lack of sensibility. I can only say that the occasion was—er—great."

The shriek turned to a keening wail.

"Control yourself, my dear. You'll wake the children. Don't let our sorrows—er—burden their innocent years. Sorrows, I may add in closing, which came upon us largely through my being disappointed of those preferments that your father had promised me before he was—er—forced so precipitately to leave the government employ."

The wail became once more a shriek.

And once more the small, bewildered, sorrowing voice that was so unlike the normal, orotund fullness which always seemed to savor its own timbre so pleasantly:

"I am truly sorry, Elizabeh. Once I've—er—brought the subject up I don't seem to know how to drop it."

It was at that point that Charles began to cry. He got back up the stairs without being heard and cried in his bed for quite a long time; not for himself but for his father. It was impersonal weeping, of the kind one does in a theater.

Not until it was done, and he had blown his nose on a corner of the bottom sheet and tucked it back again, did the hard, personal shock of all he had learned come upon him.

They were in debt. His father was not a gentleman, but a servant's son. His mother was not an exiled princess, but the child of a hunted thief. In a book, that last would have been exciting; in the fact, it was ugly and horrible.

At least, they would never know that he knew. And Fan would never have to know it at all.

❊   3   ❊

NOBODY EVER treasured the quality of openness more intensely than Charles Dickens, or felt a more urgent need to be known. And no man ever had more friends, or loved them more, or told them less. The weeping, laughing, cheering crowds that faced his little red reading-table under the flaring gaslight knew him better than his closest companion did, or his dearest love.

However, I suspect that most novelists of stature draw their driving force from that same mingling of compulsive self-revelation and compulsive secrecy. Though their talk be open to the point of indiscretion, the openness is illusory; the true communication is only through print and with multitudes.

Perhaps the nightmare from which the child woke, the unexpected hunger, were a stroke of fortune. In any event, he lay awake for a long time that night after he had got back into his bed in the little room under the eaves. A long time, while he struggled with all he must realize, and hide, and, so far as possible, forget.

And the next morning was a Sunday, a sunny Sunday in June.

He slept late and came downstairs unwillingly. He had already managed to put the midnight behind him at considerable remove. Nonetheless, at the pit of his stomach, he expected to find change, ugliness. At the very least he would see strained faces and angry eyes.

There was no change.

Mother was fussing with Letty's hair and demanding of her why she couldn't have had a natural wave like Fan and Charlie.

Fan was playing a hymn on the piano and singing:

> "I wish they'd get this nasty thing
> Tuned up as it should be."

[10]

The windows were open, and through them he could see his father, walking in the little back garden. He was wearing his best suit, and from time to time he made a sweeping gesture with one hand, as if he punctuated an imaginary conversation. He looked very smart and wholly at one with the universe.

Charles looked at them, one by one. His diaphragm relaxed. For a single flick of time he felt, senselessly, as if he were going to cry.

Then he saw the French clock on the mantelpiece and laughed, instead.

"How did I oversleep myself like that!" he said.

Shortly after dinner, his father, who had been in abounding spirits through the meal, suggested a walk. A fine, long walk, with tea along the way.

"Where shall it be, my boy?"

The choice, seeing that it rested with Charles, was a foregone conclusion.

"Oh, to Rochester, Father, if you please. To the Cathedral and then Gad's Hill."

It was June, the month for which England waits through all the rest of the year. They set out under a sky of azure and came home under a sky of gold like clear glass. The air was soft and moving, the colors of the world were fresh and lively.

"A fine day," said his father. "A *very* fine day."

He walked at a swinging pace, his gray top hat set over one eye, and his smile approved the day as if he had just made it; or, more accurately, as if he had just purchased it at considerable expense.

"The finest I ever saw," said Charles. And from the infection of his father's manner he said it gratefully, as if he were receiving it from him as a present.

The proud white topper of a Giles's Cat so exaggerated the angle of his father's that he could scarcely see out of his left eye, and his short legs were put to it, keeping abreast; yet they managed, and with a lively swing and swagger.

"The ladies, bless them," said his father, "provide us with another world of delight; but on such a day as this a man wants—er, in a word — only the society of other men."

He nodded at his son, who nodded back with the air of a Casanova on vacation.

"That's true, Father. It's very true."

There had been no midnight wakening. It was a June afternoon without beginning or end, a timeless slice of lovely eternity.

They walked, much of the time, in happy silence. Sometimes they discussed the theater, which they both frequented as often as provincial opportunity and the family purse would allow. From time to time his father delivered himself of capsule lectures, elegantly worded, on letters, travel, history, and the current political scene. Charles heard them with pleasure, proud of the scope and brilliance of his father's learning.

And his father, susceptible as Charles himself to a good audience, smiled often and said, "You are a keen boy, Charles. I believe that I do not overestimate your capacities when I predict that you will go —er—far."

It was a good day, a day to keep alive and in the forefront of memory even before it came to its unforgettable climax.

They had left the Cathedral — "this historic Pile, this fragment of a—er—greater past"; the Cathedral, with its wonderful smell of cool, dark earth, its high-arching dusk shot with long rays from the living day outside. They had gone up the small rise of Gad's Hill and he had seen *it*: the house to which he was so unaccountably drawn, the house which in his mind he always called his.

A very old house, large, and somehow perfect. In the afternoon light, that day, the soft ocher of its bricks had a warm shine that made it look alive.

But they had not stayed to admire it long, right then, because they were both hungry. They went to the tavern across the way, where they had a princely tea. Charles washed his down with a small beer, and his father, with a brandy-and-water.

He was surprised but not disturbed when his father, a fairly abstemious man, sighed after his first glass and remarked, as he beckoned the waiter back, "I begin to feel myself. Late hours, gay companions, and the rosy, Charles — they create an—er—a vicious circle."

"Didn't you feel well, Father?"

"A certain weariness. No more, thanks to this holy restorative, as my own dear father used to name it."

A flicker, then. A flicker from the midnight that had never been. He tried to disregard it, but it persisted: a small, black, fluttering wind under the breastbone.

He spoke in a voice that was nearly as casual as he meant it to be, only wavering a little.

"Was he like you, Father? Were you very fond of him?"

"To your first question, no. He was a serious man who looked askance at ebullient spirits. To your second, yes. Yes, I was."

"What did he do?" The question, unpremeditated, shot out in a sort of italicized whisper.

"He was the steward at Crewe House, my boy. A fact which your mother would like to forget. And, of course, with some reason, in this world where opportunity's golden smile so often waits upon—er—the preservation of appearances."

A moment's silence, the glass drained and waved toward the waiter. Then a smile, and the ruffle of the shirt front swelling outwards, as if it were crisping up and acquiring fresh starch.

"Yes, my boy, ours was a family of fallen fortunes which your grandfather endeavored in his lifetime to better by honest toil. And after his death, I acquired with Lady Crewe's generous assistance that education which has enabled me to—er—press forward on the same path. Fallen fortunes. But I have recently come upon our original coat of arms, Dickens. I have not yet had our claim to it proved, but there is no doubt that we have the right to bear it. A lion, couchant, bearing a Maltese cross in its dexter paw. Yes."

"And Grandfather Barrow?"

A long swallow from the glass freshly filled.

"Uncongenial to me. But a man of great parts, and of family. Unfortunately, the victim of—er—financial misunderstandings. Certain careless transactions of which many — even I, alas, on occasion — have taken an unsympathetic view."

And he drew a half crown from his pocket and laid it regally on the table in the bowing waiter's sight.

Yes, some things might be hard for strangers to understand; but how different is warm and living truth from shallow fact! Charles eyed the half crown, tossed down with such careless affluence. He had nothing to forget, because there had, indeed, been nothing to forget.

He drew a deep, luxurious sigh.

But the unforgettable climax, the peak of the day was yet to come.

They were standing in the road, his father waiting while Charles turned one last, yearning, loverlike gaze upon the beautiful old house in its beautiful old gardens. The slow June sun still bathed it in full light, the ocher bricks gave off their shine of living gold.

His father was now feeling most expansive.

"Ah, yes, a noble old residence," he said. "The splendor of bygone days interexplicably entwined—er—inextricably intertwined — with the simple charm of a lowly cot."

"I'll tell you something," said Charles suddenly. "I've always pretended that it belongs to me, Father. I pretend it's mine. That's stupid, at my age, isn't it?"

"Stupid?" said his father. "Stupid, in one who stands, filled with the heady wine of youth, at the foot of young ambition's ladder?"

He swayed, obviously full of strong emotion. He removed his hat, gazed for a moment into its depths, and then drew himself up very tall, replacing it at an angle which mocked gravitation.

"My dear son," he said, his voice deeper than its wont by half an octave, "my dear, dear son, do not, I beg of you, take my words for the undue confidence of a devoted father, but as sober" — he swayed again, and righted himself even more proudly — "sober truth. There is no reason, in this age of dawning opportunity, this age when hith . . . ahem . . . hitherto impregnable barriers now crumble before the onslaughts of financial enterprise—er, in a word, there is no reason why, if you plug away at your books and keep your eye on the mark, you shouldn't be able to buy this house for your own, one day, and no pretending about it."

Somehow, it was the abrupt change in style, the sudden shift upwards to the normal register of his speaking voice that brought the conviction.

"Me?" whispered Charles. "I? Really?"

But it was not a question. It was a grateful, a reverent acceptance. *Gad's Hill Place, home of Charles Dickens, the wealthy ironmaster . . . barrister . . . actor . . .*

He turned from his father to the house. He faced it as if it were a long-reluctant beautiful woman who had suddenly leaned toward him, her young lover, and said, "Oh, my dear, my dearest."

He was alone with it, kissing it with his eyes. Work? Giles's Cats barely knew the meaning of the word. Ah, he would show them . . . he would show the world.

The light had softened, not dimmed; it was golden clear. A lark shrilled from the zenith, and cuckoos answered in laughing shouts. The air stirred, soft and yet lively-fresh.

He drew a sigh again, from the very soles of his feet; a sigh of pure happiness. He turned back toward the road, and walked forward, into the promise.

He said, "I say, Father, hasn't this been a really slap-up day!"

❋ 4 ❋

THAT SUNDAY AFTERNOON came almost at the end of the golden time — the time of which he would tell, with loving embellishments, when his children asked him about his boyhood. He told nobody, ever, about the black time except for that once when, a young man in his twenties, he described it all, on an odd wave of impulse, to his friend Forster.

And even then, with the old wounds opening as he spoke, he told of it under the ban of secrecy, as if it were a shameful confidence. And he told of it, too, curiously enough, with embellishments; pulling it about, saying that he was ten, not twelve, when he worked at Warren's Blacking, 30 Strand; making the six months that his father spent in debtors' prison sound a far longer time than that.

However, he had not changed the story as he felt it. He told it staring out of a child's wretched eyes, as he spoke, across the vacant lot of nettles behind the house in Camden Town toward the distant dome of St. Paul's where it shone in a bright evening mist that veiled the sun without hiding it.

They had moved to London, and his father's affairs had gone rapidly from bad to worse. In those days, Camden Town was not an urban slum, but a poor suburb. They lived in a shabby street of slapped-together cottages, with open fields behind them. It would not have been a bad place, actually, if there had been friends to play with. But the neighborhood children were not of the sort with whom a gentleman's son is allowed to associate, and he was unfitted for loneliness.

He spent hours with his little cardboard theater; but without Giles's Cats it was an empty business. It puzzled him why it should be so easy to pretend a whole play, to see imaginary gaslight flare and the cutout actors come alive; and so hard, so impossible, to pretend the full pit, the murmurs of delight and terror, the thundering applause when the curtain fell.

[15]

And Fan had become different there, sometimes pettish, sometimes sad, but strangely apart from him, not even teasing him any more. The younger children just played together like puppies; dingy-coated puppies, nowadays, for the only active gesture that his mother seemed to make toward any of them was to shift the new baby, Alfred, from one side to the other. He could not recall that she had suckled the others so incessantly, and so much in public.

In that tiny, crowded house, he could not so much as have any more real talk with the Orfling. For it had always been a forbidden pleasure; it was called "encouraging her to forget her place." Sometimes it seemed that there was nothing much to do for hours on end but to stand staring out across those nettle fields at the dome of St. Paul's. Then he would think about Chatham, its wharves with their smell of tar and piracy, its wonderful town clock. He would think of Giles's Cats, of Rogers and Collinson and all his friends.

But of one thing he tried, always, not to think: of the Sunday walk to Rochester, when he had looked at Gad's Hill Place, smiling in its gardens, golden and alive, and had known that one day it would be his.

It would not be his. For his education had stopped, and his parents had simply forgotten him. His mother now talked almost exclusively in monologues; incoherent monologues about her past splendors and present downfall. And when his father came home, he avoided the children and talked to her about something called the Deed.

It was, apparently, a paper that he had unwisely signed. When he spoke of it, his face got smaller and his shirt looked limp, as if it wanted washing; he was like a stranger, a dull, sick-looking, unattractive stranger.

Charles knew, of course, that somehow they had become poor, and that schools cost money. But surely they could have managed if they cared. At the very least, they could have set him lessons themselves.

Yet they did not, even when his mother conceived the notion of starting a school of her own and they moved to the bigger house on Gower Street where she put the brass sign on the door: MRS. DICKENS'S ESTABLISHMENT. Not that anyone ever came to it.

They remembered Fanny, though; they got her a scholarship at the Academy of Music, and she went away. She got three new dresses and left, radiant, to come home no more except on Sundays until she should be a real, proper pianist who could play at concerts.

Charles could not keep the tears back when she left. But it did not matter, after all, for Mother and Father and Fan herself thought that he shed them because they had always been so close, and would miss her.

For her own good, her departure could not have been better timed. His mother's uncharacteristic burst of imaginative energy, which resulted in the bigger house and the meaningless brass plate on the door, was, in fact, the last blow to their financial difficulties.

The butcher would no longer give them credit for so much as a stewing bone; the baker wanted hard, visible pennies for every crust and crumb. Pennies which had to come from selling things.

Charles took them to sell. He was small enough and shabby enough to excite no notice going into the pawnbroker's; if his father or mother had been seen at that door, it could have got back to the landlord. The Orfling, clearly, could have driven a shrewder bargain. But in a sibilant whisper that was clearly audible all over the first floor, his mother asked him, Dear me, what was he thinking of: let a servant know their private business?

Charles, watching the small, sharp eyes under the dingy flounce of cap, as they questioned each new empty space on the mantelpiece or the parlor table, thought of a good many things to say to his mother, and said none of them.

Confusingly, the man who bought the things was even poorer than they. He was often drunk, sprawled on his tumbled bed in the room behind the shop when the bargaining took place. When the price was arranged he would feel through all his pockets with shaking, dirty hands for the sixpences and pennies, and cry when he could not find them.

But his wife always had enough hidden on her to settle the bargain, in whispers, on the outside stair.

After the knicknacks were gone, they began to sell things like the saucepan that was not used as much as the other one. And finally his mother remembered his books, in their box under the bed that he now shared with Frederick.

Don Quixote went last. It was bound in morocco, with gold stampings, and Mrs. Dickens fingered it with the most hopeful satisfaction before she smiled and sent him off with it. Later, the Orfling found him in a broom closet, hidden to cry.

She did not remind him, as she might well have done, of a past conversation that they both remembered. She only whispered: "Now, then, you got the insides of it safe in your head, anyways"; and shut the door on him again softly.

That same evening, his father came home looking happier than he had done for a long time.

"I have fine news for you, Charles. Your cousin James Lamert, now connected in a business way with Warren's Blacking, 30 Strand, has found you an excellent position there at six shillings a week. You will label bottles, to start; but it is your first step on the ladder of—er —enterprise. He has arranged that you will work apart, and not in the front window with the other lads, who are of—er—inferior origins, and he has even kindly consented to set you lessons which you may study at your dinnertime."

His face glowed as if he were announcing the offer of a scholarship to Eton.

The lessons, however, were forgotten at the start. It was almost immediately discovered that the front window was the only place where a boy could be efficiently employed. And twelve days later his father was arrested for debt. The rest of them lived a little longer on selling the furniture, and then the whole family, Orfling included, moved with him into the cozy shame of the Marshalsea.

All but Fan, at her Academy; and Charles. The Marshalsea, they said, was too far from 30 Strand. They lodged him with a Mrs. Roylance, who took children in — by the dirty bedful. They left him in her black, chilly house that smelled of overcooked cauliflower, and went away together.

Pride, which had prevented him from so much as hinting about the school or the lessons that they would not think of for themselves, kept him silent for a few weeks. It was on a Sunday almost a month later, when he had gone to the prison with Fan, that he began to cry.

His father was sincerely distressed.

"Why, my boy, of course you shall be nearer us if you want it. We shall seek some place, without these tragic walls, not at too great remove from your place of employment nor from your unfortunate family, so that we may breakfast together daily."

And so they found him the little garret room that faced the timber yard. The only washing was at the yard pump, which sometimes froze. He was dirty, often hungry, and his clothes were far from warm; but he loved that room. It was high and private, and his first proper place of his own. He could move its few poor sticks of furniture about and keep it all neat and shipshape, though he had to be so untidy and ill washed himself.

It restored his sense of status. And so, in an odd way, did those breakfasts with Father in the prison.

For once more, bewilderingly, Father was himself. After that first terrible day, on which he went down like a shrunken balloon and told the bailiff, with clearly final heartbreak, that the sun had set on him forever, he became almost overnight the social arbiter of the Marshalsea. He was a former and a director of committees, a gentleman temporarily embarrassed. The shabby, defeated stranger had vanished; the kingly light of golden Chatham was reborn.

Only, beyond the breakfasts there stretched out the long, sad shame of the days at Warren's Blacking. Days whose only comfort lay in the company of a boy, Bob Fagin, from whom he learned all manner of absorbing facts about streetwalkers and thieves and receivers and policemen; Bob Fagin, who alone of the boys did not mock his fallen gentility but, rather, treasured it.

They were, indeed, a precious pair of snobs.

"You're a sort of connection of Mr. Lamert's, aren't you? I mean, that's how you come to be workin' here?"

"Yes, Bob." Kindly. "If you're going in business you should learn to get a living young. It sharpens your wits, you know."

"But how about the schooling?"

"Oh, I went to a very good school until last year, and I shall go back to another after a bit."

"Ah."

"But we mustn't talk about it, Bob. You see, the whole good of it is for me to be no different from any of you. In clothes, or pocket money, or anything."

Was there doubt in the quick glance? He had a face like a rat, Bob Fagin, a sickly rat; but intelligent. And friendly.

"That's why it was decided for me not to work up in the office alone, as I did at first."

"Ah."

"On the other hand, I might decide that business wouldn't suit me at all. As a career, I mean."

"When I'm old enough, I shall go for a soldier."

And the boy with the runniest nose and the filthiest hands said, "Wot you two mumblin' about?"

" 'Bout soldiers. Push the gluepot over, will you, Sloppy?"

"Grab for it yourself. Or let the Gentleman."

They laughed at that. The myth, so necessary to Charles, so curiously valuable to Bob, never took them in.

Paul Green — pronounced Poll — had until Charles's arrival been the Count D'Orsay of the group. His father was fireman at the Drury Lane Theater, and his little sister had already entered the theatrical profession; she played imps in the Christmas pantomimes. He was, moreover — except where he, himself, was concerned — a boy of strong egalitarian principles.

He had a fight over them with Bob, one noon just as Charles was starting off to lay out the pennies apportioned to that day on the cup of coffee and slice of pudding which would be his dinner, eaten, as befitted his station, alone.

(Six paper packets he would separate his wages into each week, so that no fierce temptation of stale pastry set out for sale at half price should leave him penniless until another payday. And still, even such prudence did not always avail and he would spend the dinner hour wandering about the Adelphi, looking at the pineapples on the coster-mongers' carts, tasting them in his spittle that flowed so free at the sight. It was hard, then, to come back looking superior and well fed.)

The fight had been going on at the bench for some time, in angry whispers. But not until Poll and Bob left their work and walked out into the yard did it flare up loud, for all to hear.

"So, Mr. Lamert 'ad connections as married beneath 'em. So, not to let blood kin starve, 'e gives one of them the chanst to earn a bit. Only this one, 'e can't be content to take it like the rest of us, 'e 'as to make 'imself fine. For two pins, Bob, I'd beat you up, you and your little Gentleman both. As much of a gentleman as my grandmother's backside!"

And Bob carefully removed his tall paper cap, and drew a circle in the dust with his toe.

"We've been good friends afore this day, Poll, and trusting we'll become so again, I'd like to hear you say that over. Seeing as Charles goes out of 'is way to make 'imself one of us, and eats alone for no reason but that it's no more than proper."

Poll said it over, Bob gave him a bloody nose, and they shook hands.

There was no overt difference in the way the boys treated Charles after that. He was still as poor, as hungry, and as dirty; he still worked his seventy-two-hour week for his six shillings. So far as he knew, his world had ended. His books had been sold one by one, and he was forgetting all that he had learned with Giles's Cats. But something was saved, and Bob Fagin had saved it for him. A gentleman of fallen fortunes is still a gentleman; he was not a slum child, but a gentleman's son.

Yes, he owed a debt to Bob. And he was, his life long, a man who honored his debts; it was strange that he told nothing about Bob to his friend Forster, on that evening he told him so much. Doubly strange, as it was also a good story.

Far easier to understand why, when he wanted at the time so much to tell Fan about Bob, he never could.

He met her each Sunday at the Academy, and they went to the Marshalsea together. She would come down the Academy steps, far from smartly dressed to be sure, but still always so clean, so ladylike. She would look at him with her warm, laughing eyes; and immediately the single important thing in the world would be that she was Fan, who had once been tenderly close; Fan, of whom he must not, could never be jealous because she was happy and getting an education.

So he could tell her nothing about Bob and Poll; or about the temptations of stale pastry, or the recurrent spasms of pain that were frightening to him, alone in the night, even alone in the tidy shipshape garret that was all his own.

He could only listen, and ask questions, and try to be glad that she was going to be a concert pianist and famous. And they would go to the prison and watch Father being grand, and the Orfling eying him, and the children tumbling all over; and listen to Mother babbling about her departed splendors.

The week, devoted to the pretense of gentility; the week end, to the pretense of knowing no ugly jealousy. And how, in week or week end, could he have said where truth left off and deceit began? For indeed wasn't he *very nearly* what he wanted Bob so much to think him? And *very little* jealous of Fan?

The pain came only at night until shortly before the blackest time ended. Then one day it struck him so cruelly while he was at the bench that he was terrified, and sure that he was going to die.

They did not call for a doctor. But they let Bob leave his work and take care of him, on a sofa in the countinghouse. Bob filled empty blacking bottles with water and kept them coming, always hot.

" 'Ere, 'old that tight to the pain. That'll ease you. Now pass the other back, it's 'alf cold already."

He was kind, tirelessly kind, through the whole long day.

By eight in the evening, when the place shut down, the cramp had slackened so that Charles could stand and even walk. He still felt weak, but he was determined to go home alone.

"You could to take faint, like. I'll fetch you back to them, Charlie. You can't go by yourself."

"Oh, no indeed, Bob. I'd liefer, truly. For an hour or more I've felt quite well, really I have. I only lay here so that you needn't go back to work when we could be away from it together, having a lark."

"Quite the little bantam cock, ain't you? And still all white to the gills. The rest have left, they'll never know and say you was a baby that couldn't get home alone with his little bellyache. Ah, that was it, weren't it? Fess up. Here, it will be our secret, and Gord strike me dead if it ain't; but I'm a-taking you to your own door."

No. Not to his garret near the prison. It was impossible.

He knew that even if Bob learned where he lived and guessed why, he would not taunt him; that he would be as good a friend to him as ever, and perhaps better.

But he knew, too, that they would both lose something of value; both of them, the gentleman and the gentleman's toady. Sham or real, they would lose a bulwark against hopelessness; against the stinking, festering, dead-end hopelessness of poverty.

Nor was he bound by a wholly meaningless vanity, or foolish cowardice. Between the fashion of kissing lepers and the fashion of the income tax, poverty slowly acquired a quality of its own. Its sickness, dirt, hunger, crime, were only what had always been; but its shame, in that world of the Veneerings, and the Merdles, and the Gradgrinds, was something new in history.

A small child could feel that shame without analyzing it.

"All right, then, Bob. You're very good. But it would worry my parents, you know, if you came quite to the door, and then I'd have to put up with doctors and dosings and such a fuss. Because, I don't want to sound rude, Bob, but I should have to explain your being with me, shouldn't I? So perhaps you'll just see me near to the door and run out of sight, and then I'll ring."

They walked to the Southward Bridge on the Surrey side. And at the nice-looking doorway of a house that was not too grand to be plausible, but not at all poor, he stopped and shook Bob's hand.

"Thank you, Bob. You were very kind to me today. I shan't forget it."

"Ah, gammon. Like you said, it was larks, getting off of the work. Sure that pain's gone?"

"Quite sure."

Shaking hands, man and man; but still not quite as equals, because that would have meant giving up a hope that somewhere, at the end of that black alley, there was a way out.

Just as Bob loped out of sight on the bridge, he rang the bell. When the woman opened the door he felt a wild, incomprehensible desire to laugh and laugh until he should have to fall on the steps with laughing.

"Pardon me, ma'am," he said politely, "but does a Mr. Robert Fagin live here?"

"Nobody of that name," said the woman, and slammed the door in his face.

He stood against the house in the shadows, catching against the pain in his side with one elbow and laughing until he was quite weak. He stood so, laughing and catching at the pain, until he was quite sure that Bob was safely away and he could make it safely to the ship-shape loft with the view of the timber yard; make it at the slow, bent walk for which his body had been crying out since the moment when he strode erect, and always one pace in the lead, from Warren's Blacking, 30 Strand, humoring the overcautious friend.

❊   5   ❊

ONLY SIX MONTHS his father was imprisoned. But a child's six months is a long time; long enough to establish itself as the whole pattern of reality. Those six months, when they had almost ended, stretched back behind Charles until he almost believed that he had only dreamed the bright world of Chatham. They piled up, a massive dam across the flood of time; there was no happier past and no future to mock him with vainglorious promises; there were only yesterday, today, and tomorrow, all alike.

He had been fond of Grandmother Dickens, but he was not ashamed to learn of her death with unalloyed, incredulous joy. She had always saved her wages and set her face firm against lending a penny; it had occasioned past resentment, but they could forgive her prudence gladly, now. For her little capital paid John Dickens's debts, and the whole family moved, rejoicing, from the Marshalsea to yet another squalid cottage, this time in Somers Town.

It was even sadder in smell and appearance than the other houses had been; yet in that first joyful surprise, Charles took it for granted that things were quite changed, his father's debts paid and a new life starting. Now, he thought, he would go back to school.

The difference, however, was only that he had lost his tidy, private garret and took a few scraps of food to work in a bowl tied over with a handkerchief, so that his shillings could find their way home.

The release when it came was from another quarter.

He was at his bench in the front window when a clerk from upstairs thrust his head through the inner door.

"Dickens boy wanted by Mr. Lamert."

Could somebody at home be ill? He pushed back his chair and hurried up the steps to Cousin James's office at an anxious trot.

"Cousin James?"

Little by little through those months he had been coming to think of Cousin James as a stranger; to regard him, like the other boys, as an employer, remote and apart. But in the golden time, James Lamert had boarded with them for a year, and taken him to the play and made him the first of his pasteboard theaters.

Charles had liked him. He smiled at him hesitantly now, the old affection mixed with the new shyness. But he was unprepared for the look that fixed itself, not upon him, but upon the air directly beside him as if another boy and a troublesome, unpleasant one, stood there.

"Charles, have you complained to your father about working in the window? About not being hidden as if you were ashamed to get your living?"

He was too surprised to do anything but stare and shake his head for "no."

A smile, swift and lean yet certainly one of approval, flashed and vanished at once. But it was lightning before thunder.

"I thought as much!" Square fist hitting the table, square face now fronting him directly, the eyes hot, the jaw pushed forward. "Charles, your father is a born beggar and a fool. No cadging shames him if he can only call every dole a 'temporary loan.' His son may help support him, if he is kept hidden away. Nothing wrong with the work or the wages; but the window, ah, that's a disgrace. Did you hear him discuss this precious letter with your mother?"

And the large fist snapped open, snatched a paper from the desk and waved it before him. A paper covered in the large flourishes of his father's unmistakable hand.

Charles saw it. He looked at Cousin James, at the flushed forehead, the hot, angry stare, the tight mouth. His own mouth quivered, the soft, gently molded lips trembling as they worked together. Only for an instant, though; then a short spine stiffened and two large eyes fixed themselves in steady blue accusal.

"I don't know of any letter. But I won't hear you talk so."

Cousin James blinked and looked vaguely about him like a man who has mislaid his spectacles. Then he spoke in his own familiar friendly voice.

"I ask your pardon, Charlie. Heartily. I've always liked you, and now I hope you won't cry over what I've got to say. You've earned your wages here, every penny; since you worked with the other boys, that is. The man who oversees you has told me how well and quietly you keep at it. Yes. But I've borne all I can. I will not help your father or your mother any more. They are incurable."

And he began to tear the letter up into small pieces, whispering under his breath as he did it.

" 'Low companions,' " Charlie heard. " 'According to our initial understanding.' My God."

It was frightening, and in a funny way. Frightening because Cousin James was not angry with him, but with his father; because he was not being thrown out for his own fault, but because of the letter.

And still, the fact remained that he was set free; he would never have to come back to Warren's Blacking, 30 Strand.

He walked out of the building stunned with that release. It was so intense that it stifled him. His breath hurt in his chest as he walked through the streets, incredibly in midmorning of a weekday. From time to time he forced himself to run a few steps, to kick a stone in the gutter: trying to believe in his freedom, his escape. He was halfway home before he remembered that he had gone off without saying goodbye to Bob Fagin.

He stopped short, then; he half turned as if he would go back. He thought of Poll Green's bloody nose, and the blacking bottles full of hot water. He saw the pinched, sharp face under the tall white cap, the watery eyes, pale and bright, with their strange, mixed look of keenness and gullibility, of patronage and respect, of hunger and of being fed.

He walked on. What they had both lost that morning, he and Bob Fagin, they had lost for good. He could not go back.

After he had walked for some minutes he spoke aloud; quite suddenly, and unconscious that several people turned and stared curiously at him as they passed.

"Poor Bob," he said. "I hope he does well. It's hard for a boy circumstanced like that to keep out of trouble, it is indeed. Poor Bob."

He spoke the words in a firm, kind, benevolent voice; much, in fact, as Cousin James might have spoken them. Then he began to run, and ran until his chest hurt again.

Some things are too frightening and some too puzzling to stay long in conscious memory. Long before he had reached the fields that lay between Camden Town and Somers Town, he had stopped thinking about Bob Fagin; he had almost forgotten what Cousin James said about Father.

The heavy fog that had lain all over the town at dawn was lifted; a light wind pushed rifts here and there through the smoke pall, and rays like long silvery searchlights played down from the sky, lighting the wet rooftops.

The air was damp and raw; it would have been a more pleasant day for one who owned a greatcoat. But the boy was not conscious of that. He had begun at last to believe in what had happened. He walked on steadily in that large, heavy consciousness of freedom, of escape.

A thing that should never have been, no longer was. It did not matter how it had either begun or ended. It was over, over. There was no past or future; only the present moment, heavy and light at once: relief beyond anything he had ever felt. And light on the wet rooftops.

He was still heavy and light at once with that realization, intensely aware and yet dazed, remote, when he opened his door.

Frederick was playing on the floor. Charles stepped over him, vaguely, like an abstracted man stepping over a dog. He walked into the front room where his mother sat by the grate, holding Alfred. He spoke to her from a distance, out of the large, strange dream.

"I lost my situation."

She shrieked, handed Alfred to the Orfling, and fell into hysterical weeping.

Charles drew a short, gasping breath, like someone startled from sleep. Then his face began to work, like a much younger child's. He turned it aside, hiding it from her; unnecessarily, since her own, as usual in such moments, was lifted to the ceiling.

He turned it blindly; and found that he had turned to face the Orfling. She had prudently backed against the wall, having learned that shrieks may be followed by cuffs. She held Alfred in extended arms, strategically placed between herself and the room. But under the edge of the dingy cap-flounce her eyes met his, and they were bright, not with animal shrewdness, but with the tears of human pity.

And after a moment's hesitation she laid Alfred on the floor, walked to the small, brisk fire in a wholly transparent pretense of being about to stir it up, and grasping the poker like a weapon she leaned close to him and whispered.

"Leave her scream herself down. You wasn't built nor raised to be wore out for six shillings, nohow. And, listen, there's new bread and the larder's unlocked. Postman come when she had it open and she went off and clean forgot."

She struck the grate, laid down her weapon of offense, picked Alfred up again, and was back against the wall even before his mother could catch her breath for the wail which invariably, at such times, came between the shriek and the declamation.

Charles got into the little dark pantry room. The larder *was* unlocked, and the bread fresh, crusty outside and moist at the heart. He wolfed a great deal of it down, between sobs; undone by the love not given and the love so bravely offered.

He would learn to laugh, even with a certain affection, at his mother; he would forget the Orfling until, before the eyes of his imagination, the little Marchioness sat faithfully by poor Dick Swiveller's sickbed. But now he stood in the dark, and ate as much as he could hold of the forbidden loaf, and wept.

The next day his mother went to Cousin James and persuaded him to relent. She came home triumphant, waving a letter in which he had given Charles "a good character."

". . . For he had nothing but praise for you, it was only the preposterous letter which your father took it upon himself to send off that did it, and when he found I had gone the whole way afoot he was shocked at my not hiring a conveyance though he knows how I have always sacrificed myself, nor had it escaped his attention, you may be sure, that when he visited your father in the Marshalsea he was entertaining half the inmates like a lord on not only porter but wine, though how he obtained the credit for it or how he expected to meet such obligations dear only knows, so on my promise that not one more word will be spoken about windows or lessons or any such nonsense he'll be glad to take you back at the same wages and starting tomorrow, and I trust you're properly thankful to him, not that I expect anyone to give the remotest thanks to me for all I have been put to."

What would his father have done next if his vanity had not been assaulted? Charles would never know, nor would he ever allow himself to ask.

On the past evening, John Dickens had, in fact, had little opportunity to say anything. Mrs. Dickens held the floor. But now he waited until his wife had quite run down, drew himself up magnificently tall, and cleared his throat.

"Rhnph. Ahem." Then he smiled. He let his eyes travel slowly all over his wife, from the insecure bonnet which she had forgotten to remove down to the muddied hem of her quite visible petticoats. He thrust one hand into his bosom, and extended the other palm uppermost.

Mrs. Dickens opened her mouth again, but she was too late. The round tones of her husband's best after-dinner voice filled the room.

"My son's education," he said, "has been interrupted overlong already. You have, my dear—er—exceeded yourself needlessly. I have laid quite other plans, plans which should have borne fruit long since had the immediate pressures of business not lain so heavy on me since my return from—er—this enforced absence. Indeed, I am at this moment inquiring into the relative merits of several schools. You cannot, I trust, wish to—er, in a word — prejudice your eldest son's future? You or your—er—officious cousin?"

And Charles looked at him, loving him from his heart and believing in him as fully as he had on that golden Sunday afternoon when they stood together looking at Gad's Hill Place, the beautiful house that would one day be his, his own.

He wished that his father had taken him earlier into his confidence; it would have eased the past weeks. But he supposed that he had wanted to save it for a glorious surprise. Charles looked at him, and at his mother. What he felt about her at that moment he would pray earnestly, for some weeks thereafter, to forget.

And, to a large degree, his prayer was answered.

✿   6   ✿

WELLINGTON HOUSE ACADEMY, at which Charles spent his next two years, was a poor, ridiculous shambles of a school, in which by all the rules of taletelling a sensitive, ambitious boy should have been utterly miserable.

He loved every minute of it, except the whackings; and day boys didn't get whacked anything like so much as boarding-in boys, anyway. Mr. Jones, the headmaster, despite his fondness for the ferrule, had a certain caution. Day boys can tell tales at home.

It was a school; that was what counted. A school, to which one went in clean, whole clothes; a school, with friends. Boys like Giles's Cats; equals.

He was a schoolboy, like any other. He'd been ill and at home, he'd missed work and had some catching up to do in his books, but nobody thought the worse of him for that; particularly as, even so, he managed to find as much time as the best of them for thinking of ways to break the rules and avoid the ferrule. For being avidly, continually, the life of the party.

They kept white mice in their desks and tried to teach them to do tricks. He fetched his pasteboard theater there for the boarding-in boys, and the plays he put on were very fine and the audience was continually stamping and whistling and groaning and applauding. They played outrageous, brutal tricks upon one another; they engaged in long, earnest discussions about politics, sex, and religion.

It was Giles's Cats all over; only better, more urban, more mature.

He had crowds of friends, but Daniel was the closest. They loved to walk the city streets together, looking at people and guessing at what they were like and how they earned their livings. On those walks they would talk to each other in an extraordinary pig-Latin of their own invention, which not only safeguarded their secrets but made everyone take them for foreigners.

And another game of deceit was even more of a lark. One of them would make himself small and shuffle just behind some woman, begging, hand outstretched and voice quavering in a Cockney whine:

"And our Guv'nor, 'e fell off a ladder and may never walk proper again, and the little ones all got sores on their legs, and coffing and feverish . . . Oh, please, lady, please, mum, just a penny . . ."

Then when the victim reached for her purse the two would take off shouting with laughter, two obviously well-to-do schoolboys, gentlemen's sons.

When Fan came home on Sundays now, it was he who did the talking and she the listening.

"You used to be such a mousy little thing," she said to him once, "and you've grown into such a brag and bounce!"

"Well, I was always having those awful pains, you remember, Fan. That's odd, come to think of it. I've not had one since . . . since I've been at Wellington House."

"You've almost grown up to your eyes, too. Do you remember how I used to call you Tom Thumb and make you cry?"

"No, did you? Do you know what I remember, Fan? The two of us, very small, after dark in a little garden somewhere with the lights lit inside the house . . . and we were eating something, and looking at a star, a big one."

"I don't recall that."

"It was long ago . . . even before Chatham, I think. In Portsmouth."

"You zany, you can't remember Portsmouth. You were only two."

"I do, though. It was cold and dark, and there was a window behind us, lighted. It was a bread we were eating. And the star was enormous. And I was feeling very fond of you."

"Do you know, I think I remember that myself."

"I daresay." But he had already lost interest. "Fan, do you think Daniel will ever go far?"

"Far? How?"

"Far. You know, in the world. I'm fond of him, but it often strikes me that he isn't very ambitious."

"Are you? You never take a prize at school."

He laughed. "If their prizes came in good, hard, chinking bits of the ever-needful, I should fast enough. Mark me, Fan, I intend to be rich."

"Like Papa?"

He looked at her until she flushed and fumbled uneasily at the neck of her dress. His eyes that had just now been dancing with blue fire were hard blue ice.

When he spoke at last, his head was very high.

"If a man of parts, Fan, is held back by the best qualities of his nature, his generosity and, well, hopefulness even, I should say that only a pretty small person would try to make jokes about it. Aside from how you should feel about your own father."

But the flush had died away, and she ran her fingers, carelessly but with affection, through the natural glossy curls of her short side-hair.

"Oh, mercy, you preachy prig! You used to laugh and mimic him enough when you were small. Not that you're so big now, in anything but your opinion of yourself!"

He ignored the irrelevant addendum.

"That was different."

She only shrugged, and then smiled. A curious, secret smile.

"What are you thinking, Fan?"

The smile deepened, quivered at the corners. She laughed aloud. Then, still laughing, she bent with a quick, impulsive swoop and kissed him, hugging him up close as she had not done since they went away from Chatham.

"If you will know," she said, "I was thinking, 'Heaven pity your wife.' "

"My what, you lunatic? What do you mean?"

"Do you always have to be in the right, Charlie? Shall you always have to be in the right?"

At the kiss, however, he had not only forgotten her error of taste and breach of daughterly love; he had also become bored and a little restive. By Wellington House standards a sister of fifteen was, after all, pretty dull company.

Politely, he stifled a yawn.

"I haven't the remotest idea of what you're going on about, Fan. And in any event, I must be off. Daniel is waiting."

✽　✽　✽　✽　✽　✽　✽　✽

BOOK II

Charles and Maria

✽　✽　✽　✽　✽　✽　✽　✽

FIRST LOVE is the passion which we remember with tears and recount with laughter. Perhaps only the moment of death provides us with another experience so private, so singular, and so wholly commonplace. Young Charles Dickens's love for Maria Beadnell was not a burning glass for his ambition, as he later liked to remember it; he had needed none. It was the garden variety of adolescent tragicomedy, distinguished if at all by sheer duration: from seventeen to twenty-one is a long span, and remarkably long for a boy wide open to every pretty face since his seventh year and first kiss, beneath the peach-cheeked Lucy's dining-room table.

Yet it is true that the heart's first full amazement comes most strongly to those who, in another sense, were born in love. The gardener who has sat thumbing his seed catalogues by the winter fire sees the first snowdrop break the cold earth with a sharpened wonder; and Romeo walks on our stage sighing for a certain Rosaline. They are both ready.

Charles was ready, as his friend Potter could have assured you with a most knowing lift of the left eyebrow.

For two years after Charles left Wellington House Academy, Potter replaced Daniel as the *fidus Achates* and boon companion. Charles was fifteen and Potter a year older when they entered the firm of Ellis and Blackmore, Attorneys, as clerks at thirteen shillings a week. It was a sum upon which it took some contriving to be men-about-town. Yet they managed; handsomely, too, on quarter day, with chops and kidneys and cigars and Scotch. Sometimes one or the other of them was forced to seek the air rather abruptly, by preference in a retired alley; but this inconvenience, with dedicated courage, they both ignored.

Potter had dash. True, his figure was squat and his complexion somewhat lardy. But his waistcoats were dazzling, his smile knowledgeable, and before his ears he had a most enviable growth of glossy black whisker. Charles found his appearance both mature and slightly Continental.

They went often to the play, after curtain time when the unsold seats dropped to half price; and next day at work they would discuss the plot, dwelling long on the questions of carnal passion and pure love. Potter regarded the latter with a jaundiced eye.

"Are you really a cynic, Potter, or only afraid to suffer?"

"I like to see things as they are."

"Perhaps you're wise, but don't you ever feel an emptiness in your life?"

"Only in my pockets."

The conversation, exquisitely flattering to them both, would continue until Mr. Grimble, the senior clerk, came back into the room.

Mr. Grimble, though neither of them was old enough to perceive it, was a disappointed man. Until his fortieth birthday he had nourished a quite unfounded hope that he would one day be called to the bar. In this hope, and fed on a diet which, from financial necessity, leaned more upon starch and malt than flesh and grape, he had developed a manner and figure of magisterial amplitude. Now, as he approached, he gave Potter a glance of distrust and Charles a benign nod. Young Dickens, he would have told you, was a *solid* lad.

Potter, eying young Dickens, began to suffer a twitching in the face. Young Dickens was swelling; his slight body took on poundage, his features thickened. His manner, as he held out the book of double entry, was at once pompous and insecure; his voice both worried and unctuous.

"Oh, sir. Will you glance this over, sir? I've double-checked for errors, sir."

A sound of strangling from Potter, which he attempted to smother in a pocket handkerchief.

"Ah. Ah. Quite in order. Taking a cold, Potter?"

"Only . . ." a gasp and a swallow ". . . only a frog in my throat, sir."

"Then stop dawdling, Potter, and get back to work."

Mr. Grimble was unpleasantly aware that, for some reason or other, Potter found him amusing.

Potter, as the door closed, lowered the handkerchief with a gasp.

"Dick, if you take him off like that one more time it'll be too much for me, and then we'll both be out of a position."

Charles rose, smiling and bowing from the waist.

"No, I mean it! Why doesn't the old donkey ever take you up on it himself?"

"How could he? Voice the perfect mixture of sand and oil, not a drop or grain too much; thumb and forefinger set so exactly in that lovely gesture of helping yourself to another fellow's snuff . . . Ah, genius, Potter, sheer genius!"

"Good Lord! There you sit, ticking him off to the life, and . . ."

"And he recognizes an indefinable something in me that inspires his confidence. As my own dear father would say, he is sensible of a bond."

"Oh, you're mad. Be the old woman that sold us the cherries again, would you?"

"Another time, Kettlepots. Something tells me that a certain eye now rests upon us."

Long silence, two quills whipping sharply down the columns of double entry.

At last, Potter, *sotto voce:* "A natural complexion, Dick, a lovely form, a pair of legs — does it take a cynic to ask no more?"

A shrug. "If you're wise, Kettlepots, you'll ask at least one thing more."

"A fine head of hair."

"No, a willing disposition."

"I bow, romantic dreamer, for once you make sense."

Almost sixteen and almost seventeen. Polished, weary-wise men-about-town.

The law, however, was in itself a depressant. There was little to envy in the lots of Mr. Ellis and Mr. Blackmore themselves, aside from their income. Moreover, a raise of two-and-six in two years was less than dramatic.

"We could do better than laugh at poor Grimble," Charles said one day, abruptly. "Forty years could go faster than we think for and shift the joke a notch down."

And after work he walked home fast, alone.

His silence at table that night passed unnoticed. In a family group of six children, a mother given to soliloquy and a father who embraced any gathering as occasion for oratory, one voice less was scarcely observable.

"I didn't spill it, you spilled it."

"And then I said to her, Fan, 'You're a silly to talk of having lovers at your age,' and do you know what she said then?"

". . . not that I expect any notice or consideration for the sacrifice, my dear mother always said you are too generous for your own good my dear child and outside your own proper sphere you will not find the delicate attentions to which you are accustomed, sit straighter Letitia or you will never find a lover at any age, as I was saying this Mrs. Wyland in spite of that diamond brooch which she wears at the most unsuitable occasions . . ."

"A precept which none of you is too young to grasp, yes, and lay to his heart; neither you, Frederick, nor Alfred, no, nor even you, Augustus, who are the — let us hope — final gem in that diadem of motherhood which . . ."

And over it all (the Orfling having found love in the person of an extremely small and hoarse carter and been granted her freedom) the voice of the new servant, which was always both extremely loud and extremely apologetic: "The pudding looks someways *odd* in the middle and should I serve it up anyways?"

Charles, quiet and alone as he could not have been with Potter, watched his father and thought; thought hard.

John Dickens, these days, was looking wonderfully well. His linens were a marvel of gloss and crispness, and he had taken to wearing an eyeglass on a broad ribbon, purely as an ornament and to enhance his gestures. Having been dropped from the Navy Pay Office he had somehow, somewhere, managed to raise a loan which enabled him to study shorthand, and he was now reporting for Parliament at fifteen guineas a week.

Reporting for Parliament. Hearing debates, speeches, about things that were alive and mattered. Associating with keen, wide-awake, go-ahead people. And pocketing, from the start, mind you, fifteen guineas a week.

Yes, fifteen guineas and a boundless future. No shadow of Mr. Grimble touched the Strangers' Gallery, that high, bright heaven of competitive mind where the reporters gathered in glory. The Mr. Grimbles were crowded out immediately; they could not dangle on until hope deferred had transformed them from whiskered, smart-waistcoated ambition to the figure of fun, the nightmare warning.

Charles's hands, which had been loosely spread on the cloth, one at each side of his place, came together. His lips moved, forming soundless words.

Suppose a fellow bought a book, started to teach himself . . .

The large blue eyes that Charles had turned courteously toward his father's face as the peroration swelled, blazed, brilliant and unseeing. His head continued to nod in automatic show of grave attention long after his father had done speaking. Then, with a start, he realized that the others had risen from the table and left them alone.

"Father. What's the best book for studying shorthand?"

"Why, Gurney's *Brachygraphy*, indubitably. Not a tome to yield its meat to one who has not at his side a patient and skilled instructor. Indeed, there are none such, or my present profession would be less profitable than I have found it. But under those circumstances, it is compendious, a model of clarity and—er, in a word, handy."

"Where's yours, Father? Your copy?"

"I found it unnecessary to purchase one, dear boy. The volume which I employed was let me for the term of my study by the gentleman who initiated me into its mysteries."

"I've been thinking that I could learn . . ."

"My boy! With your costly education, your enviable prospects, you would not grieve me by displaying a wavering purpose? Once you have lifted your eyes to those heights which might be crowned with a seat upon the woolsack—er, a little infelicitously phrased, 'crowned with a seat,' but you take my meaning . . ."

"I shouldn't quit my position until I had a better, Father, if that's what you wanted to warn me of."

The sudden frank, lean, almost boyish smile that was John Dickens's most endearing attribute flicked across his lips.

"Precisely, dear lad. And if I were more amply blessed with this world's goods, if I could afford you instruction — not to mention the necessary hiatus in your present earnings — be sure I should. Albeit with some disappointment, I confess, for the law is a noble taskmistress, I should not say you nay."

"But now I know the book, I can teach myself."

"Alas, it could be but wasted effort. I, Charles, flatter myself that I have a gift of quickness in such arts, yet I should have been lost without professional — and excellent — direction. Not to mention my having the always inspiring motive of an—er—full quiver."

He sighed, flicked at his collars and gave his wristbands a twitch. "No, Charles, rather persist in your chosen way. For those who mount that ladder high, you know, Justice, too, wears a golden smile."

"Yes, sir." The blue eyes wide, remote. "By the bye, how many words can you take in a minute?"

He found the book at second hand on a stall during the next day's dinner hour. Potter returned to the office and found him sitting with it open before him, silent upon a peak in Darien.

He would have to equal his father's rate. Better it, double it. He would have to be the fastest shorthand reporter in London.

"Look at this, Kettlepots. Our key to the prison door and money to burn. What do you say to our learning it together?"

Potter looked at a page and shuddered.

"Simplicity itself, Pottsibus. Only dots and flies' legs. There's a box at Doctors' Commons where the shorthand writers wait about until a lawyer engages them. You work there, you see, being paid all the time you're gathering speed, and you end up a reporter with a life fit for a king."

"You could never get on with it, Dick. Ugh. It must take a born knack."

"Do you want to wager that this day year I'll be pocketing four times our earnings?"

"I want to wager that this day week you'll be blind or mad or both."

That cinched it. If Potter had taken him up, sharing the enthusiasm, they might have wound up by sharing the boredom and discouragement, too, and in the end laughing it all away. But Potter laughed; and Charles was alone in the desert with Gurney's *Brachygraphy*.

He wrestled with it as Jacob with his angel. He dreamed dots and flies' legs. They obtruded themselves between his eyes and the columns of double entry. They fogged the footlights at Drury Lane, and danced like motes in the sun over Hampstead Heath. Again and again he left Potter, saying that he must be home early, to walk about London half the night fixing their elusive combinations in his mind: *excessive, recessive, recession, decision* . . . the little devils crowd each other out, you've got one and the last is gone . . .

He was superbly, perfectly happy. He had found for the first time in his life that obsessive, drunken single-mindedness of purpose to which he would always refer mildly, from then on, as "having something in hand."

Potter was baffled.

"But, Dick, what's the point? You could learn it as well bit by bit, you know, and still have the time to enjoy your life."

Charles looked at him and did not know how to answer. He looked at the flattish, pale face framed in the knowing black sideburns, the face of his best friend, his so lately admired model. As one looks at the faded photograph, the letter in the half-forgotten handwriting, he looked with that same stir of affection and sense of inexorable separation in time.

"I don't know, Kettlepots," he said at last. "I seem to be the sort that enjoys doing things hand over fist, that's all. Shall we go to the play and make a night of it?"

His voice had the forced, bright enthusiasm of one saying to the convalescent child, "How's for a game of checkers? You won the last, but this time I'll get you for fair!"

Still, he enjoyed the play, once he was at it. More than that, he forgot the moment of separation almost as soon as it was gone. He was always oddly ungifted at self-examination. Indeed, he was quite sincere when he said, some thirty years later, "I have never lost a friend."

He often missed Potter, once he had started taking shorthand for Doctors' Commons. Now that he saw him seldom, he remembered a wider sympathy than they had actually enjoyed, and felt, quite incorrectly, that he and his fellow clerk could have found great comfort of shared laughter over that outdated monument of muddle which in 1829 still dealt with litigations which concerned churches, shipping, and private inheritance.

On the other hand, by the end of the year he was quite as often glad that he was seldom thrown in with Potter any more. For aside from the fact that he would, so clearly, have been an outsider in the Beadnell background, Potter knew both too much and too little about love.

Potter could never have understood about Maria.

❄ *2* ❄

BUT COULD ANYONE else have understood about Maria? Maria, beautiful with a beauty created for his eyes alone to see in its full astonishment, his heart alone to know in its full, compelling wonder? And was he, Charles, that same half-awakened fool who had paced the dark of his room in years gone by, murmuring syllables of no meaning — Rose Fowler, Amelia Banks — when all his life should have been a waiting silence, readying itself to speak that hymn of hymns: *Maria. Maria Beadnell. Maria.*

It was his sister Fanny who first took him to Lombard Street.

"Mr. Beadnell's a banker, you know, so dress your best."

She said it to tease him, for his concern with clothes and his meticulous tidiness was a family joke. But he only nodded, and went out gravely to buy a new stock.

Once he had worn the proud white topper of Giles's Cats, and all eyes had marked him for a moneyed pupil, a gentleman's son. Once, dirty and tattered, he had walked the Adelphi to feed his eyes on pineapples when he could offer no such service to his belly, and costermongers had bidden him sharply to stand over a bit there, or move on. He had stood on Sundays in his slum child's clothes, waiting for Fan, the neat, ladylike girl on a scholarship, to come down the steps of her Academy and walk with him to their debtor father's prison. He knew the importance of dress as she could not.

The shop to which he went was so superior that he hesitated for ten minutes, pretending to examine its window and the windows on each side of it before he could nerve himself to go in.

The clerk behind the counter, however, was most respectfully attentive, even suggesting a waistcoat as well.

"Only feel this material, sir. We could make you up something most attractive."

And though the stock was far too high to be comfortable, and its price had been a staggerer, it spread its richness over his whole appearance, right down to the toes of his nicely shined boots.

He touched it from time to time as he walked by Fanny's side

toward Lombard Street. The gesture was unconscious; his mind was
in rehearsal for the moment when, faced by the liveried man and the
extended silver salver, he should fumble in his pockets and discover
to his annoyance that he must have left his cards at home.

The door, however, was opened by a plump, motherly woman in a
cap and apron.

"Give me your mantle, Miss Dickens, while I fetch Miss Anne."

"Thank you, Sarah. What ails you, Charlie? You look as if you'd
lost a shilling and found sixpence."

"I don't know what you mean." Stiffly.

Before she could answer, a girl with auburn hair had come into the
hall.

"I'm Anne Beadnell, Mr. Dickens. It's so nice you could come."
She put her arm about Fanny's waist and gestured him to follow.
At once, the brief moment of letdown was forgotten.

The drawing room that opened before him was a very perfection of
taste and opulence. There were velvet draperies and rich carpets,
there were handsome paintings of ruins, gorges and waterfalls, and a
marble statue on a pedestal. The rosewood furniture was so richly
grained and whorled, the brocades of sofas and chair seats looked so
brilliantly, spankingly new that the whole room shimmered in
splendid witness to Mr. Beadnell's solvency. Another maid — this
one with streamers on her cap — was replenishing the already
lively fire in the grate; and before it, unmistakably, stood Mr. and
Mrs. Beadnell themselves, the banker and his wife, substance personi-
fied. And all around them, modish and gay, swirled the young crowd.

It was an intoxicating sight. Charles's hand went once, quickly, to
the new stock, made sure in one swift dab that his hair swept forward properly on the left temple. Then, with his wide eyes flashing
confidence he stepped forward into the world that was waiting for
him: the world of fashion, of wealth.

In other words, he walked into the cozily ornate little parlor that
was loud with its pleasant, young, middle-class company; into the
Beadnells' tidy little world of satisfied mediocrity. And it danced and
glimmered on his sight as once the golden town of Chatham had
shone the center of the universe. Charles Dickens's eyes would never
wholly lose their vulgar innocence; but not the fantastic splendors of
Bulwer's Knebworth, nor Devonshire House, no, nor Windsor itself
ever quite came up to the golden revelation of Lombard Street that
night.

And then, with no more than three steps taken into the glory, he saw Maria.

She was standing by a harp, as if she had just done playing. Her dress was crimson, trimmed with black velvet. She was small and exquisitely proportioned, and her hair, knotted high at the back and cut short at the sides, fell in loose, dark ringlets against her cheeks. Her wide-set eyes were soft and dark, her mouth sweet and petulant. She was, in fact, the heroine of the early Victorian novel made flesh.

In a dream, Charles bowed to Mrs. Beadnell and heard her say, "Delighted I am sure, Mr. Dickin." In a dream he bowed to the eldest Miss Beadnell, staring over her shoulder all the while at the vision.

Maria was one of the last in the room to whom he was presented. All through the bows and polite automatic phrases he kept his eyes upon her. He saw her tip her head back to laugh; saw how, when she looked grave, she pressed three outstretched fingers to her cheek, holding the little one curled in and resting at the corner of her lips.

And at long last, he was near enough to hear her voice. It was not as he had imagined it, but higher and lighter, a childish voice that babbled like quick water running over stones; and that, too, was enchantment.

"Oh, you dreadful person," she was saying. "You wicked, flattering creature."

A fat white spaniel lay at her feet. She stooped and caught it up in her arms, laying her cheek against its head.

"Dearest Daphne sees through such nonsense, doesn't she? Dearest Daphne would never say such silly things to her own Missie, would she?"

Dearest Daphne, lying in Paradise and knowing it not, yawned and tried to struggle free.

At Charles's side, the soft-faced, auburn-haired Miss Anne laughed.

"Put that silly dog down, Maria, and let me present to you Fanny's brother, Mr. Dickens."

Time caught its breath. Two astounding dark eyes lifted to his, a thousand secret sorrows and laughters trembling in their depths. Daphne, who had yawned in heaven, was cast aside. The whitest, most delicate, most divinely useless hand in the world lay in his own.

"Oh, Mr. Dickens, why has that wretched Fanny been such a time bringing you here?"

Maria Beadnell was a flirt. Even an absurdly cravatted, blushing seventeen-year-old was worth her care; art is its own reward. She was, moreover, exceptionally pretty, and her airs of gaiety and petulance, of innocence and naughty knowingness were all in the high style of the period.

Charles looked at her and knew that he would love her forever.

"You . . . you play the harp?"

His throat was tight. The words jumped embarrassingly between a baritone and a high contralto.

"Oh, I pretend to. But you mustn't expect me to be really gifted, you know, like your wonderful sister."

Whoever loved that loved not at first sight?

His eyes prayed. He did not know whether he was happier or more miserable than he had ever been before in his life. With a desperate effort he caught upon the lowest register of his voice.

"When a lovely woman plays the harp, Miss Beadnell, men can only hear with their eyes."

She laughed, her head swaying until the sweet, loose ringlets swung against her cheek.

"Oh, Mr. Dickens, why are all you gentlemen so dreadfully insincere?"

He was accepted; he knew it. In that crowd of amusing, smart, mature men around her, not one of them awkward or ill dressed, scarcely one of them, surely, younger than twenty, she saw nothing out of place in his presence.

The evening took on the quality of his most pleasant recurrent dream: the one in which he would take two jumps, the second from the crest of the first, and then fly around the ceiling a bit at the urgent request of the company; fly, protesting all the time through the applause that it was nothing, that any one of them, really, could do it as well.

So dreamlike it all passed, in fact, that afterwards he could recall no detail of it except that in the game of forfeits he sang them "The Dandy Dog's-Meat Man" and it went down very well.

Nor could he have said whether he had felt most happy or wretched, or whether the greater part of the evening had been spent in the troughs of tongue-tied self-consciousness or on the alternating waves of a tipsy, spinning freedom like nothing he had ever felt before.

But his life had taken a direction that it would hold, unwavering, for nearly four years.

※ *3* ※

THERE ARE boys and girls who leap almost overnight from childhood to full sexual awareness. They have never been the legitimate stuff of farce, and few in any period have so conceived them. But it has remained for our own canon of taste — whose archangel, pity, has the biased outlook of most archangels — to make them the sole proper source for any story of adolescent love.

And yet there remains more truth in the now despised tale of William Sylvanus Baxter at seventeen than is dreamed of in our critics' philosophy. We do not grow by rule; Miranda, given an unfortunate break, could have been another (and more heartrending) Juliet; no amount of star-crossing could have qualified Rosalind or Celia. Indeed, if either of them suffered a broken heart soon after the curtain fell, so much the better. Otherwise, they married too young.

Charles, with his hairless, fresh girl's cheeks and slender body and unpredictable voice, need hardly have looked back in wonder from his later years at the purity of his passion for Maria Beadnell. One may well wonder at the stubborn endurance of a dream so loosely rooted in warm earth, or that the shattering of an illusion so childishly self-created could have left a genuine scar on the mature life. But there is nothing else to wonder over in a story that we have all lived, unless we have been cheated of our spring.

In the day after he met her, he bought a pair of pumps like those which, even in that delirium, his quick eyes had observed to be the mode among the men present. They were wickedly small and pointed at the toe, and in them he limped, time after time, to Lombard Street, glorying in the pain like a martyr on his rack.

Sometimes he could see her only in the crowded drawing room. Sometimes — oh, days of holy wonder — she received him alone in her little garden, chaperoned only by Daphne, and, of course, by the open windows and a family at home directly behind them.

He carried her paper-frilled pyramids of rosebuds and mignonette. In exchange, she smiled, or scolded, or made him run errands; and even so much notice was all the heaven he asked. The day that she gave him a bit of blue stuff and sent him to buy gloves to match it was a day of sober exaltation and sacred trust.

He was her toy, her fool, and what of that? Save your pity for those who cannot remember what it was like when we dreamed so much and asked so little.

It was no trouble to Maria to keep him as humble as Daphne, and as content. And though she laughed, she was touched and flattered, too. She was glad that her group all liked him, young as he was.

He made them like him, with all his genuine warmth and all his skill for picking up a tune. His unfeigned admiration gave each one of them a pleasant sense of being his especial patron; his enthusiasm brought a freshness to all their amusements. He was a spirited if clumsy dancer, he was clever at guessing games, and invaluable at charades.

Surprisingly, too, he had the wit to keep his devotion from becoming a bore to the company. He engaged in a continual mock flirtation with the sole predestined spinster of the group, a sallow, lashless, sharp-tongued girl called Mary Anne Leigh.

Marianne, she preferred to be called. She was, by her frequent profession, Maria's bosom friend; and perhaps the sole doubt that he entertained of Maria's integrity was a tolerant guess that so much beauty might enjoy a foil of such excessive plainness.

"Poor Marianne," Fanny said to him one night as they were walking home. "Do you know, Charlie, she really thinks that you pretend to flirt with stupid Maria so that the rest of us shan't know how you two clever ones are heart in heart!"

Charles laughed. "Oh, Fan, you dolt, she's ugly, but she's not a fool! Besides, she doesn't really care for men at all. It's written all over her, don't you see?" And at once, with no thought of changing the subject, with only a spontaneous leap from a dull subject to an interesting one: "I say, did you happen to overhear any of the talk that we men were having with Henry Austin over the rotten boroughs?"

Austin, a young reporter for Parliament who was rather in love with Maria himself, had become the new friend; a friend beside whom Potter faded into the limbo that held Daniel and poor Bob Fagin. He was a sensitive, civilized young man, who returned Charles's affection warmly, enjoying the role of mentor.

"A dear, good little chap," he would say of Charles in his absence, "and keen, I swear it, as a fellow of twenty."

Maria laughed at that.

"But how should you know otherwise, Mr. Austin? I declare that all men are great babies, with nothing to choose between them!"

And still her laughter held more satisfaction than mockery. Those grave blue eyes of worship gave Maria a pleasure beyond any that she took from her looking glass; which is saying a good deal. It suited her to have Charles accepted.

Mr. and Mrs. Beadnell alone had reservations. They both considered him too clever, and Mrs. Beadnell said that when they all got to playing at charades he made her downright nervous. She often spoke of it to her husband in the privacy of their bedroom, while she was unloosening her stays and letting her complexion subside from the bright purple of its public appearance to the comfortable china pink of more secluded hours.

She was unusually troubled on the evening when Charles had accepted a challenge to do them a one-man charade of his own, and made the whole room laugh, weep, and eventually cheer with a rapid fire presentation of the word *osculate*; in which, changing his very appearance before her unimaginative and indignant eyes, he had been a little Cockney stableman, a nervous young understudy faced with her first public performance, a tardy, much embarrassed guest at a ceremonial banquet, and finally, with all stops drawn, the dying Nelson: "Kiss me, Hardy."

That evening Mrs. Beadnell fumbled her knotted laces for some time in silence before she said darkly, "You'd think he was an *actor*."

Mr. Beadnell, who disliked drafts, undressed under his nightshirt. There was a moment of silence before his woolens fell to the floor; a moment followed by a sigh, as he also rather disliked Mrs. Beadnell. Reluctantly, nonetheless, in this instance he saw her point.

As his head came through the neck of the shirt he sighed again, and restored his whiskers to order with the silver-backed brushes on the dresser. "Ah, well, just a boy. Not, I admit, a steady sort of boy. Makes you wonder about the family."

"*Miss* Dickin is sensible and ladylike enough. But it upsets me to have that young fellow always in and out and *looking* at Maria so. Why, at the rate they humor him, it might keep on until she *liked* him."

At that, however, Mr. Beadnell only snorted.

[*47*]

"*Baby?* Baby, with all her swains and her airs? Why, aside from money and those odd, excitable ways of his, he's just a child. My love, you are too — shall I say — free from coquetry to understand Baby."

"I daresay you're right. She was always a shrewd little minx. But I still say that he upsets my nerves."

The girlish complexion that Charles so regretted was, in fact, his high good fortune through more than two years. What he lacked in comprehensibility, by Beadnell standards, was outweighed by his patent harmlessness.

They were years in which, outside the realm of emotion, he grew up fast.

At eighteen he got admission to the reading room of the British Museum; it became his University. His avidity for print outweighed his lack of direction. He read with unslakable greed, and continually better. Austin, too, fired his mind with current politics. They went together on tremendous nighttime walks over London, talking, talking in spate. And from Austin, too, he learned, as much as he ever would, the difference between a friend and a captive audience.

Most restfully, he had no need with Austin to pretend to either more or less sexual urgency or knowledge than he possessed. Early in their acquaintance he could admit, with curious release, to both his inexperience and his indifference. Later, with the changing fact, he could tell of his first experiment and find reassurance after a hurried, unwashed girl and a bed with bugs in it had left him impotent. And when a streetwalker ("a fallen woman," he would still have called her) would accost them on the Embankment, he could open his heart to his friend in a way that would have moved Potter to obscene mockery, sure that Austin, too, felt much the same mingling of angry desire and fastidious distaste and awful pity.

His cheeks kept their girlish smoothness; Mr. and Mrs. Beadnell remained irked but fundamentally unworried by his presence. But he was growing up, and to more percipient eyes it showed.

He was nineteen when Maria, much against her will, fell briefly in love with him.

She was desperately ashamed of herself. She, Mr. Beadnell's daughter, and with more eligible suitors than any girl she knew!

To Anne she said, "That Dickens boy is getting tiresome. Two years and more of cow's eyes and dismal little bouquets, and no encouragement!"

Anne only smiled.

"Don't smirk! Since you got engaged to Kolle you think you know everything."

"Don't I?"

"Anne!"

"Very well. But the only cow with eyes like little Dickens is the one that jumped over the moon. What's more, you'd encourage the lamppost if it came indoors. You can't help it."

"You hateful . . . hateful . . ."

Anne eyed her calmly. "Does he know you're in love with him?"

A shocked stare and a flood of tears.

"Oh, Anne, of course not! Oh, Anne, if anybody guessed, I should die of mortification!"

The laughter went out of Anne's face. It filled, instead, with a look of tender pity.

But what she said was, "Poor Charles. Oh, dear. Poor boy."

Charles knew that evening.

Maria told him abruptly, almost fretfully, to come to the dining room while she saw that the table was ready for the supper that would close their evening. From the odd, nervous edge to her voice and the impatient way she thrust out of the room ahead of him, he believed that somehow he had offended her.

He followed anxiously, and stood behind her while she fiddled the silverware at a corner of the table. They were hidden by a screen from the door to the hall.

"Miss Beadnell? Have I — vexed you?"

She kept her back to him, but he saw her push the loose ringlets back from one cheek with an uncharacteristic, awkward gesture. Then both her hands fell at her sides, open. At that instant his heart turned over in its incredible understanding.

"Miss Beadnell? Maria?"

She turned, her eyes lifted, wide and unhappy. And gently, as if he were the older, the practiced one, he touched her cheek and the side of her neck.

"Oh," she whispered, "I can't think why I'm acting so."

He answered her out of a strangely mature, accepting percipience which he would never find again. "Don't be afraid. Nobody shall

[49]

know until I've bettered myself so that they shan't laugh at you."

The troubled dark eyes and the eyes that were filled with blue noontide stillness came together, searching, clinging. Their eyes had kissed deeply and long before the lips of a reverent boy and a flirtatious prude brushed together in the small, irrelevant anticlimax.

Then Maria said, very softly, "We'd best go back," and moved away from him toward the open door, and the company. He followed her in happiness sharp as physical pain, intense as heartbreak.

The happiness of those next few weeks was indeed very like heartbreak. It was the happiness which gives to first love its human importance, for we know only once that season when the heart strains like a seed in spring earth to burst apart and release the waking life.

He gave Maria a little brooch. She told her mother that she had taken a fancy to it in a shop, and she wore it constantly. She worked a fob for his watch, with a flowered wreath encircling his initials in tiny needlepoint. At night he laid it on his pillow and slept with his cheek pressed against it.

They could not snatch many minutes alone, but those they had were always the same: the eyes voyaging, discovering, kissing long and deep before the light touch of the meeting lips.

How much it all satisfied a girl of twenty-one is anybody's guess. For Charles, those weeks were a timeless heaven, without past or future. He was too happy to desire more or to remember that he had ever had less.

Then, one afternoon, he came to Lombard Street and found the family out, and Maria alone with Daphne in the little garden.

They sat on the stone bench, apart, and an awkwardness possessed them both. As if they were afraid to be silent they plunged, together, into parlor inanities. He paid her flowery compliments, and she refuted them with those coy appeals to Daphne which he had once found so enchanting.

Sarah and Maude of the streamered cap were both doubtless belowstairs with Cook over the teapot; the house behind them was to all intents and purposes empty. The thought of the empty house obsessed him. The timeless happiness was gone; the minutes dragged while still his voice, and hers, babbled on in rushing haste.

When they both fell silent, it was abruptly. They sat empty-faced, avoiding each other's eyes.

"Please let's stop," he said at last, out of the frightening silence. "Please, let's never be anything but ourselves, alone together."

An odd sound came from her lips. It was the first note of a little automatic peal of parlor laughter, choked off before it was fully sounded. Her small fingers went to her lips, and for an instant she only stared before her, expressionless as if she had not heard him, or forgotten that he was there.

Then she stood up.

"Mama will be home soon," she said. "Just for this little bit, come into the house where we shan't be seen."

They stood in the dusk of the hall. They wasted no time on the long, preliminary look, nor were their meeting lips those of a reverent boy and a flirtatious prude. Maria was twenty-one and Charles not twenty; yet in that kiss she learned more than she taught.

So did he. Each learning, each teaching, they clung together, eyelids closed and still, lips parted, moving. Learning, teaching. Her hands were quiet, but his hands moved, learning and teaching, down the soft curve from waist to thigh, up, unrebuked, to the deep square neck of the soft mull dress to discover and cup a more amazing softness, delicate wonder of touch. His discovering hand, their joined, discovering, teaching, learning lips were one inseparable voyaging.

It was the click of the latchkey which woke them, jerked them apart.

Mr. Beadnell said, "Dear me. Dear me. Well."

Mrs. Beadnell said, "Good afternoon, Mr. Dickin."

Her voice partook equally of the drill sergeant's authority and the high tragedy of Lucrece's mother.

It was too abrupt. That singular education of touch, that flowering dark, and without transition the jangle of broad farce. An older man might have done badly under the circumstances. For Charles it was utter confusion.

He made three undirected little bows, snatched up his hat from a chair, and attempted to thrust a hand into the wrong glove.

He said, "How do you do? I mean, I happened to be passing. I mean . . ."

He rushed blindly through the door which still stood open. He was nearly home before it came on him that he had run away and left Maria to handle things alone.

Maria, however, was a girl of quick reflexes. As the door shut upon Charles she burst into tears.

"Oh," she cried, "I'm so vexed and upset! Mama, he even tried to kiss me!"

She had, to be sure, neither hope nor intent to deceive; she was merely relieving the situation as much as possible for everyone concerned. And prudently her parents accepted the gesture.

The fact remained, however, that they had seen what they had seen; and before they went to bed that night they had decided that Maria's French and music still needed polishing. A year abroad would do nicely to finish her education.

"And," Mrs. Beadnell concluded, "you needn't trouble to say a word either to her or that dreadful little Mr. Dickin. You know Maria, my dear. Out of sight will be out of mind, and when she comes home there'll be no trouble at all."

✻ 4 ✻

A YEAR, AN ENDLESS YEAR.

Charles marveled at Maria's courage as she told him.

"We shouldn't write often. The time will go fast if we don't mope."

"Oh, my own lovely, my brave girl. It will be all different when you come home, I'm determined it shall. Somehow I'll manage so that they will be glad because nothing could change you."

She gave his hand a light pat. She whispered, "They're watching. Please, go and talk to Kolle or Anne. Anyone."

They had no opportunity to kiss again but once, and that was for goodbye. It was a snatched, hasty kiss as he had known it must be. Yet even so his lips found hers strangely cold, almost perfunctory. He was troubled and unsatisfied until he had nearly reached his own house.

He had swung about the last corner with no slackening of his swift, nervous pace when, quite abruptly, he stood still, catching in his breath and lifting his face, while the sensation of belated understanding flooded his heart. His eyes filled, and his full, vulnerable lips quivered.

She wanted to spare us both, he thought; she wanted to spare us all the pain she could. My love, my gentle love.

No young man indeed ever put all his eggs in one pretty basket with more unquestioning trust. He was incapable of doubts. The angel of his soul had been sent away, but she would come back; and neither of them could ever change.

The infrequency and reserve of her little notes told him of the watchfulness that surrounded her, told him that they must be patient, cautious. And they told him no more. Maria would come back, and he must be ready.

"I shall be twenty in a matter of weeks," he said to Austin. "And as things stand, I'm wasting my life. If I could only once get into the Strangers' Gallery with you, good Lord, nothing could hold me back."

Austin's long, narrow lips twitched at the corners; he covered them quickly with one hand, in a gesture of careful reflection.

"Of course we, your friends, know your capabilities, old boy. But you're young, and — pardon me — you look younger. Have you worked hard on your uncle?"

John Barrow, Mrs. Dickens's brother, edited the *Mirror of Parliament*.

Charles's face colored. "I sent him a note. No answer."

"Well, push it, next time you see him."

"There are reasons I'd rather not."

Austin had often met John Dickens, liked him, and was altogether capable of guessing at those reasons. He had liked him so much, in fact, that at their last meeting he had parted quite open-eyed with a pound note. ("Dear me, I seem to have miscounted my wealth before I left our humble domicile — would you be inconvenienced for a day or so, my dear fellow?")

He had noticed more than once, too, how Charles avoided any talk of his childhood, and how, when he spoke of his father it was affectionately and still with an odd suggestion of — of what? Protectiveness? Perhaps self-protection? In any event he was both proud and loyal, and the subject of maternal connections clearly was not one to be pursued.

"No answer, eh?" said Austin. "Oh, I daresay you'll hear from him in a bit. Busy man. Meanwhile I'll remind Beard and Mitton and a few of the others to keep their eyes cocked for an opening."

"For God's sake do, Austin. It means more to me than you can imagine."

And once more Austin maintained a gentle restraint.

Poor little devil, he thought. He'll find her out when the time comes. He may as well live in his fancies now.

But though it never entered Charles's head to doubt his angel's constancy, he was wretchedly and continually aware of the passage of time. Days became weeks, weeks months, and every hour of them he felt for a reproach. For she would come back, and she must, must find him ready.

The inspiration, in its beautiful simplicity, took him amidships. It was a slack week in Doctors' Commons, the waiting-box full, and as he sat in it he had been restlessly whittling down a pen, shorter and shorter, until nothing but the feather remained in his hand.

"Well," he remarked vaguely to the young man sitting beside him, "haven't left much of this one, have I?" and before he could reply Charles had shouted, "My God! Of course! What have I been thinking of?" and rushed from the box and the building.

He walked the streets for the rest of the day, dazed with the simple perfection of *the answer*.

What was he best at, always? What did people coax him for, laugh at, weep over? The theater, the theater! For what else was he made and how had he been a blind fool so long?

That night he sat alone in the pit, hands clenched on hatbrim, eyes blazing, as he watched Charles Mathews, the idol of playgoing London. Yes, yes, he was superb. But let him wait for company.

In his business, when a rocket goes up it goes fast and high.

He determined to take nobody into his confidence but Fan until he should be well under way. She was a musician, a public performer. She would, he knew, be all quick understanding, quick enthusiasm. He felt closer to her in the prospect than he had felt since they were children together in Chatham.

She was, in point of fact, appalled.

"I can't believe it of you!" she exclaimed. "It's worse than poor mother with that brass plate on the door, thinking it would fetch her a school and the sense to run one, too. I thought you were the one practical person in this house besides me. Don't you realize that acting is a *profession*? Like music? One doesn't just walk in."

"I know that, Fan."

"Well, then?"

"I shall find a successful actor who is willing to take me for a pupil. I can, and make the money to pay for it, if I eat at home and do without everything else."

"But why, Charlie? Why?"

"It's what I should have been at all along, that's why."

She stared at him. Then she began to laugh.

"Oh, oh, it's too ridiculous. Oh, I don't want to be heartless, but I can't help it. Aren't I right, Charlie, aren't you doing this in the hopes of making a splash with Maria Beadnell when she gets home?"

"I am doing it to get ahead in the way I'm suited for."

He could control his voice, but not his eyes or the color of his face. Fanny looked at him, and doubled forward again, shaking help-lessly.

"Oh, poor Charlie, really, really I wish I could stop laughing, it's not actually at all funny. But please, please listen. Don't you know that she's rich, she's spoiled, she's twenty-one, and the worst flirt that ever lived?"

The baseless mockery hurt him almost as much as the slander of his dear. But he would not betray Maria's secret heart to save his pride.

"I know that she is twenty-one. And rich."

"But, Charlie, stop and think. Even if you succeeded, which of course you wouldn't, think. The Beadnells? The theater? Haven't you any sense?"

"I understand your point, yes. But real success is respected in any field, Fan. The Beadnells may not all be so clever as I used to think, but you must admit they know the value of money."

"Oh, mercy," said Fan. "Oh, heaven help us."

But despite herself she found that she was curiously stirred by the electric excitement of his face. Of course it was all nonsense. But what if it wasn't? What if it wasn't at all?

He kept the secret even from Austin, and not for any fear of even-tual humiliation but simply out of a pure, childish anticipation of that stunning moment when he should knock the whole world back on its heels at one swipe.

"I think little Dick's in love again," Austin said to Kolle, "but don't chaff him about it, will you? It's embarrassing to admit you're cured of a girl when you're his age, you know. But he's got a new one, I'd swear to it. I never meet him these days but he's riding the crest."

Charles was indeed riding the crest. Since he had pursued the dots and flies' legs of Gurney's *Brachygraphy* all over London he had not felt so wonderfully alive.

"You're running yourself mad," Fanny said to him once.

He laughed. "That's the one thing a woman can never understand, Fan — how it agrees with a man to have something in hand."

And, not in the least to his surprise, the sheer drive of his excitement melted all obstacles down before it.

Robert Keeler was playing a successful season, he taught unwillingly even when he was at liberty, and since he got to the top he had never taught for the sort of money that Charles could scrape up. He opened his mouth for the courteous refusal, found his eyes fixed by those eyes of blue fire, and heard himself say, "Twice a week, then. And you've got everything to learn, you understand."

"Good Lord, yes. Everything!" Not humble, not determined, simply exultant. "Everything!"

Everything. Voice, gesture. Three, four, sometimes five hours at a time merely getting up from a chair and crossing the room, again and again. Hours in the theater, staring, analyzing. Systems for getting parts by heart, one after the other. Whole Sundays spent on Hampstead Heath, tramping and declaiming them to the sky.

Indeed, Austin's guess had not been far from the truth. Through those days he was as little conscious of Maria as we are of the air we breathe. Only at night as he went to bed, that air stirred. Then he would detach the fob from his watch, finger the tiny stitches, and kneeling beside his bed pray soberly for God's blessing on her and on the work he had entered for the sake of their love.

But the prayers, though grave, were wholly confident. He knew that he could not fail, any more than he had failed with Gurney's *Brachygraphy*. And when at last Keeler told him with a smile that Charles Mathews was about to start casting for a new season and that it could do no harm if Charles wrote to ask for an audition — "and mention my name if you like" — the excitement, the glory were, somehow, no less intense for their being only what he had expected all along.

His hand was steady as he dropped the note in the pillar box, and he walked home with his head high.

The answer came promptly. The manager of the Lyceum would be happy to hear Mr. Dickens read. Mr. Mathews would also be present, and the time was set for Wednesday week at four.

And Ate Dea treading soft observed the weather, the incidence of the common cold, and smiled. On the Wednesday that was to re-mold his life, Charles Dickens woke with a face rigid and swollen as if he had the mumps, and a voice that no desperation of hot gargles, pastilles, or passionate will could raise above a whisper.

Fanny brought a kind letter back from the Lyceum. Next year, with the new season, perhaps Mr. Dickens would try again. And Mr. Dickens took it from her hand, read it through, shut the door of his room upon her, lay face down upon his bed, and wept.

Maria would come home in a few months. She would come home, and only to go on suffering her hopeless, humiliating love for a short-hand writer in Doctors' Commons.

❊   5   ❊

LIKE MOST OF US, Charles had taken the wrong thing to cry about. Maria came home to find him reporting, not on one paper but two, earning double pay, and surging ahead; and she couldn't have cared less.

His swollen face had scarcely subsided to its normal shape when the despaired-of offer from John Barrow came and put him in the Strangers' Gallery, paper on knee and pen flying. His speed and accuracy made, in his own delighted words, quite a splash. And within a week, the new connections had led to a simultaneous job of general reporting for the *True Sun*.

It was a leap into life. Through those first weeks he felt younger and became in fact more mature than he had ever been. And he was made mature not as we commonly imagine the process, by difficulty and overcoming, but by sheer enjoyment.

The dismal futilities of Doctors' Commons still droned on, but he need hear them no more. The theater was once more simply a place where one went with friends for an evening's fun. Went with new friends, keen and sound as Austin, and relishing with Charles their ringside seats at the making of a new world.

Not that one didn't take down a stunning lot of futility and muddle even there, in the Strangers' Gallery. Yet all those words, whether they came from wrong heads or cold hearts, were still about things that mattered. One could steam out from an addlepated debate in which the proposed Poor Law, with all its bland denial of our common humanity, was witlessly laid bare, and pound the tables for a whole evening with Austin and Mitton and Beard, in magnificent quarrel. There was even satisfaction in the warm hate that Lord Grey inspired as he stood with that maddening tip of his head, advocating live reforms with such gentlemanly deadness of spirit.

Charles himself managed in those days to be simultaneously a Benthamite Radical, a Christian Utopian, and a firm believer in laissez-faire enterprise.

"There's a new conscience wakening in the world," he said to Austin. "The rich will not remain mindless of the poor."

Austin grinned. "The needle's eye will scrape off the spiritual dross and leave the shekels intact, eh?"

"Don't laugh, Austin. What's needed, and what's coming, is a wakening of the heart. That's what maddens me about Lord Grey; he's of our side but with no real understanding of the hell that poor men live in."

"And you have?"

"When I was a child I used to talk for hours with one of our servants, a young girl, an orphan, who had seen people starve. Later I — I had a close friend whose father lost his money and went to prison. The boy's education ended, he was doomed to a life of want and ignorance. And I — we had been very close friends. I have never gone through a slum since without — without understanding and a kind of horror."

"What's your remedy?"

"I don't know, yet. But at the very least, Austin — don't laugh at this, it's possible — at the very least every child in England should have the opportunity to learn elementary reading and arithmetic. The means of a step up, if he can take it."

"Nice thought. Shall you do it by taxing the rich, or converting them, or both?"

"I don't know, Austin. I only read and sit in the Gallery and listen, and worry. And hate Lord Grey because he's always on the right side and still holding his head at that damned superior angle."

Austin laughed again, and then said, "I'm not laughing at you, Dick."

The whole thing was at once a sharp waking to reality and an intoxication. Charles was knife-sharp and whirling at the same time with the discovery of his radicalism, his first real perception of the part that government and economics play in private lives, and his unquestioning faith that the bad Good Old Times were being overwhelmed by a present which would at least face up to the facts of any walk through London streets: to ignorance, to want. He was sharpened and drunk together with his sense that a world was changing and he was in on the start.

"You can grow up with a bang, can't you," he said to Beard. "I feel I've spent my whole life, to now, shut in a box."

As the time for Maria's return drew near, he looked forward almost as avidly to enlarging her horizons as to kissing her again. How they would both look back in laughter at the dull little cage from which he had set her free!

Maria came home, and sent him no word. Fanny, back from a call on Anne, evaded his questions with a troubled face. He knew, however, that Kolle had surely let her parents learn of his new status. He gave them a little time for the information to permeate them thoroughly, but he did not wait for them to let his captive dear communicate with him again. He realized how slowly a man of Mr. Beadnell's age and a woman of Mrs. Beadnell's disposition could bring themselves to acknowledge their error in evaluating his prospects.

He only waited for the evening which heart and shrewd sense alike assured him to be the predestined time for him, for Maria, and for her parents, too; and he accompanied Fanny, uninvited, to Lombard Street.

From the first coy smile, the first prettily welcoming extension of the remembered little hand, he knew what had happened.

He would not know, quite simply because he could not bear it. Tides do not one day arbitrarily cease to ebb and flow; the sun does not just take a notion to leave off shining. The love that could not change was unchanged.

It was his good fortune that Mr. Beadnell bowed but did not speak when Charles approached him, and that Mrs. Beadnell's eyes followed him about the room in much the same way that a fastidious lady might regard a cockroach on the tablecloth. He could see them and know, yes, know that Maria was forced to dissemble.

He at least, he told himself, had no need to dissemble. He looked at Maria with his heart in his eyes. She was lovelier than ever.

And he was a year less innocent. Yet he could admit to the hard, specific desires that her beauty created as little as he could admit to the knowledge that he had lost her. As he followed at her side while she moved restlessly from group to group, his eyes were set and his face white with the inner force of the total denial. His love was all tenderness and purity; in her heart nothing was changed.

"Fan tells me you're making quite a stir in the world, Mr. Dickens," she said. "Isn't that nice."

He excused himself as quickly and inconspicuously as he could, to walk half the night through the streets.

Kolle and Anne were to be married in a few weeks. He met them together one day in Regent's Park, and they were very kind to him, so kind that he was able, at last, to break down and admit his first doubt.

"You must know," he said to Anne. "You must surely know how she feels about me."

But Anne only said, "My dear Charles, I am the last to understand Maria or her affections."

On the next day he met Sarah, who had opened the door when he first came, in the new stock, to Lombard Street.

"Fetch her a note? To be sure, and gladly. Oh, no, Mr. Dickens, please keep your money, sir, do you think I'm too old to recall my own days gone by?"

Perhaps Maria was not after all quite sure of her heart. Certainly she had a taste for intrigue and a pleasure in flouting parental interference. For a little, Charles met Sarah on the same corner twice a week, waiting with a little note in her basket: a cautious little note, always, but neither mocking nor cold.

And then the notes stopped, and Sarah did not come again. Charles tried at last, and tried hard, to make himself believe the obvious truth: that Maria had merely played one more little game, until it bored her.

Agonizingly, as they still knew many of the same people, they continued to meet on occasion at parties. But they were never alone. Mary Anne Leigh, now more obtrusively than ever the bosom friend, was always present too; by Maria's side if he approached, following him when he wandered off, discouraged, trying to corner and engage him in one of those mock-love duels of the old time. And slyly, continually, she would invite his confidence, her lashless eyelids making coy play with each artless little question.

"Are you really still in love with that naughty Maria of ours? She won't tell me anything, you know. Not a thing!"

"Ah, Miss Leigh, I know that really you ladies are all as open with each other as you are willful mysteries to us!"

A bow over her hand in his best theater manner, and a quick escape. He was confident, of course, that whether he had lost Maria's heart or no, she would keep secret all that had ever passed between them; keep it secret with the innocent dignity of her woman's pride. Yet he wished that it were possible to warn her against the probing malice that he saw behind the arch flutter of those lashless lids.

"That Mary Anne," he said to Fanny after one such evening, "is a vixen."

"That and more," said Fanny. Her hand tightened on his arm and she walked for a moment in silence before she spoke again. "Forget the tiresome thing, Charlie. At least we needn't ask her to your ball."

The ball would celebrate his twenty-first birthday. And the Misses Beadnell were invited.

". . . which I hope will satisfy you, Fanny," said his mother, "for I assure you I disliked penning an invitation to the daughters of that common, conceited woman who never so much as returned my call considering herself so much finer than we no doubt though I was bred to a style of life in which she would dear me find herself totally at a loss I am sure and it is only one of the smaller banks besides her total deficiency in any refinement of speech or manner though I must grant you that Anne is a natural lady, so attentive and kind on those few occasions when we have met, of course as a general thing I could hardly expect your friends to gather here when they admire such ostentation as the Beadnell's home displays, those who are accustomed to wealth think much less of it to be sure . . ."

She had, Charles was confident, written no invitation with deeper satisfaction. The party would be one in the eye for any who had ever felt a doubt about the solvency or social standing of Mrs. John Dickens.

"An eldest son's coming-of-age," his father had observed frequently and with eloquent variations through the past weeks, "is an occasion of proud and tender emotion in the hearts of those whose nurturing care now achieves its—er—result. Therefore" — the throat invariably cleared at this point, and the eyeglass on its broad ribbon waved forward — "therefore, restricted though our means and humble our dwelling, my dearest Charles, I have determined that the celebration of this proud event shall want for no elegance which, er, the amplest means could not procure."

And at the decision upon each new elegance, Charles did rapid, uncomfortable sums in his head. A supper fetched in: "lobsters, and, er, pheasant, yes, I think we should certainly order pheasant." Champagne. Hired glass and silverware. Hired waiters. Hired small gilt chairs. A small orchestra. Oh, Lord, and add the interest on the loan!

Once or twice as some new opulent touch was suggested, he opened his mouth to protest. But he was always too touched, in the end, and too tender. Besides, he had inherited all of his father's pleasure in spending money; the difference was only that he could not enjoy spending money that he did not have.

So, swallowing the discomfort, he said, each time, "I'm very grateful, Father. That will make it an absolutely slap-up affair."

Nor did the prudence which once separated a week's lean pennies into six little paper packets keep him from being glad and proud that his coming-of-age would be so nobly celebrated.

And Maria accepted. He would see her, and without Mary Anne Leigh. He tried, when he thought of it, to hold his fancy back, to tell himself that she no longer loved him and that the mere fact of their being alone together on the glorious evening of his majority could make no difference to a story already ended.

And still, he could not. Despite the admonitions of his angry common sense, every new arrangement that his father made, every excited anticipatory word that the children spoke right down to the squeals of little Shrimp, who had been given leave to stay up until the dancing began, yes, and even every article of his own carefully planned clothes, including the new underwear which he intended to put on after his bath (no rags of the past for manhood's splendid dawn), confirmed his irrational, unshakable conviction that Maria, too, would bring to that evening a kindness, an eagerness, a newness to match the whole aura that surrounded the coming occasion.

[62]

"My God," he said to Fanny, half an hour before the guests began to arrive, "you'll have to tie my stock over for me. My hands are shaking so I can't manage."

"You ninny, one would think you'd never had a twenty-first birthday before." And her laughter was one more tender, unquenchable assurance that Maria would be kind. "And how do I look myself, Charlie? Will I suit?"

"Wonderfully pretty," he said. But he did not see her. He saw not one of the first guests who came in, laughing and taking his hand. He saw nobody until he saw Maria.

She came into the room two steps ahead of her sisters, her face lifted and smiling as she stepped forward alone, like the star who advances, at the final curtain, from the supporting cast to take her bow, all gentle, humble gratitude — and quenchless self-assurance.

She wore a dress of delicate sea-green, with slippers and gloves to match, and just above the fall of side ringlets a white rose was fastened in her hair. Her eyes had never looked so large and dark, her complexion so brilliant and delicate.

He took a step forward from his place beside his parents, and she approached him quickly, directly, her hand held out in a pretty, innocent, open gesture.

"Your twenty-first birthday!" she said.

And immediately she was paying her courtesies to his mother and his father with exactly the same warm, open, innocent grace.

He was the host, and a born host, too. He could not dog her steps all through the long evening. And he had forgotten, somehow, in the anticipation, how very full of people two smallish rooms can be. Still she was continually in his sight; and whenever their eyes met, her glance was radiant and gentle, gay and confiding — as radiant, gentle, gay, confiding, and utterly open as the glances she gave to every other creature in the room.

The evening had already worn shabby, the party, which had been elegant and gay beyond his father's warmest hopes or his mother's headiest ambitions, was at last starting to give at the seams before Charles could manage a word with Maria alone.

The opportunity came abruptly. A little group which a matter of seconds before had been all intertwining chaff and laughter melted abruptly away, and left her standing by herself. The rose in her hair had begun to droop, the heat of the room had given a childish shine to her nose. She stood by herself, her shoulders dropped. The hand that held her bouquet hung at her side, loose and awkward.

She looked tired, uncertain. Charles stared at her. He felt his heart turn and stop and start again, while he stood seeing her face, for the only time he would ever see it so, truly open: the mask down and the life bare.

He had himself, a few minutes earlier, been part of one of those now abruptly dissolving groups. He, too, was alone. He took a few steps toward her and caught her hand. Before she could smile again, arm herself again, he had maneuvered her behind a half-open door where they stood together, hidden from the room.

"Oh, Maria," he said.

He caught her against him with hands that were not pleading but protective; hands that were all confident, protecting, possessing love.

The evening had been long and Maria had been playing her game with the dedicated abandon of the champion. Now, a moment in the little break between sets, she had felt her fatigue; he had seen no more than the fatigue and concomitant uncertainty which even the best player must sometimes feel toward the end of the tournament.

But Charles was not only very much in love; he had taken a good deal of the champagne. As he held her — and she did not protest — the unquenchable, irrational hopes of the past week leapt up to a towering assurance.

His hands upon her cheek, her neck, her soft, bare shoulder took up a story that they had not forgotten; took it up as if they had never been interrupted by the click of a key and the abrupt opening of a front-hall door. And his words, when they came, were all confidence, protection: not a pleading, but the giving of comfort, of reassurance.

"Oh, my darling," he said, "don't be sad. You must not let them frighten you any more. They were right when they sent you away, I was nothing. Now it's changed, I'm of age, I have two positions, the best prospects. They'll have to hear us now, my poor little love, my beautiful!"

Perhaps his eyes, those extraordinary fires of love and trust and champagne, disturbed her judgment for the moment. Perhaps she, too, remembered a dark hallway and a few minutes more delicious and illuminating than commonly fall to the lot of a well-chaperoned young lady.

In any event, she did not avert her face, and the kiss, the kiss of protecting, overmastering, all-confident love lasted for quite a long time before she shrugged herself away and began, with the vexed, dabbing gestures of one made untidy by a bothersome wind, to push back the wilting rose and smooth the sea-green gloves up her arms.

"Oh, please," she said, "let's not start all that again, Charles. Please don't be tiresome. Can't you realize that you're just a boy?"

He stared at her without sight, out of a face gone dead. The word, the destroying word, scorched in his brain.

Boy. A Boy.

His lips worked, they parted and closed again without sound. He made a bow and turned away.

Guests were beginning to leave. The dishes that still lay on the table looked hired and messy, and the waiter who was tidying them off looked hired and messy too. So did the company, both those on whom the champagne was beginning to wear off, and those who had taken excellent pains lest it should. Only his father was fresh as a daisy, standing before the burnt-out grate and gesticulating, the eye-glass on its broad ribbon in one hand and a superfluous glass of the rosy in the other, as his rolling periods enchained a limp-shouldered handful before him.

Charles stared about him. He stared, first half-seeing and then seeing with intolerable sharpness. He turned slowly, taking in the whole room with his eyes. They came to rest at last upon his friend Tom Beard, who was standing with Mitton near the door.

Beard's voice, loud, harsh and warm, sounded out over the nearer babble: "It's an utter sham, I tell you. Wait until you hear Lord Grey get up tomorrow, damn it, wait!"

"Beard! You!" Charles shouted as if he called across an open square and ran up laughing. "You and Mitton, the evening's about to start! Where's Austin? This show'll be done in just a bit, and then we'll smash the town. How often does a fellow come of age?"

The hangover with which Charles entered upon his majority was monumentally worthy of its occasion.

✻ *6* ✻

UNFORTUNATELY, life lacks the dramatist's sense of timing. It was in February that Charles came of age, and May before he wrote Maria the last letter relinquishing the last hope.

His friends, during that time lag, were more fortunate than they ever knew. If pity had not been so distasteful to him from the day he turned his back on the shabby nettle fields of Somers Town to embrace Wellington House Academy and the successful life; if he had not from that time forth been so possessed to exhibit, at every leanest opportunity, his health, wealth, and deliberate happiness, those three months would have made him depressing company.

As it was, he carried it off. Carried it off so well that Fan, one day, said, "Mercy, Charlie, I'm glad you're through with that love nonsense. I really ached for you when that little wretch was making such sport of you. I couldn't bear to tell you about it, then. Not that her precious Mary Anne wasn't worse, with the way she'd make us laugh with everything she knew. Some of it so silly that I'm sure she made it up, besides!"

He said, "I didn't realize that, Fan. Tell me more." Quietly. So quietly that Fanny Dickens never guessed what she had seen her brother lose.

She told him. Charles listened quietly. He learned that Maria's memory of every tender word he had spoken to her was as accurate as his own. He learned that half his acquaintance had laughed to hear them delivered by that excellent mimic and most retentive listener, Mary Anne.

Once earlier he had found nothing, where he had still believed beyond belief that there was love. But this time no Orfling was by, with full, percipient eyes and whispers of new-baked bread. Nor, in any event, could a young man have been comforted like a child.

"And you knew, Fan, all along and didn't tell me?"

But he said it with so little emphasis that she giggled as she answered, "Truly, Charlie, I was too sorry for you, so head over heels with that little fraud!"

"I shall never forgive you, Fan," he said. But once more he spoke quietly, with no emphasis.

Indeed, he had spoken so quietly that later she said to Anne, "Of course I was silly, but after I'd told him I was still afraid he'd make a fuss. You know, just out of conceit."

But that was not, after all, quite the end. Fanny's promised escort had come down with a cold, and she had persuaded Charles to take her for one last time to Lombard Street. He went unwillingly and wondering why he went.

It was a dull party. Perhaps Maria felt bored and wanted amusement. In any event, she said that the room was close and asked him out into the garden.

Immediately he forgot everything that he had known he should never forget.

"You must love me," he said. "Oh, Maria, look at me. It's not possible to love anyone so and not have them love you in return. Maria."

But he was too intense. As she told Mary Anne, he unsettled her. She averted her face and brought her hands together sharply.

"Oh, please," she said, "please let's not be tedious."

And she walked quickly back toward the house.

He wrapped the little hand-worked fob in a bit of silk paper, and set it aside to be carried to her with his letter.

"Our meetings of late," he wrote, "have been little more than so many displays of heartless indifference on the one side, while on the other they have never failed to prove a source of wretchedness and misery . . ."

It was a long letter, and typical of its kind even up to that sentence in which the wounded pride gathers itself up for the final words of magnanimous nobility: "If you are happy as I hope you may be, you will indeed possess every blessing that this world can afford."

The difference lay only in what followed it. For Charles did not conform, at that point, by writing poems to read to himself in secret, nor did he start a diary or even — which goes deeper — did he enjoy that common luxury of the long, heart-to-heart talks and long, understanding silences with the friend who has also suffered.

On the contrary, he kept on the run.

The speed, the accuracy of his transcriptions became a marvel in the Gallery; the *True World* was delighted by his pursuit of the scoop, his tireless energy. Night after night he had his friends up to dawn arguing religion, economics, politics. Beard's legs, Mitton's, Austin's, and Kolle's were half lamed by the walks he took them over nighttime London, and over the Sunday countryside.

And still time hung on his hands.

"I say," he urged, "why don't we get up some theatricals?"

Clari, or the Maid of Milan was produced in May, to cheers. Charles, as producer, director, star, stage manager, carpenter, and odd-jobs man, had brought off, as he promised throughout, a slap-up performance.

"Well, we've lived through it," Austin said to Kolle after the final curtain. "How's your strength, old boy?"

"My God," said Kolle.

Maria came to the play with Mary Anne, who clung to him like a leech once it was over. Strangely, Maria seemed uneasy, and a few days later she asked him to Lombard Street. There in the garden, large-eyed and with lips that trembled prettily, she accused him of telling their secrets to "that wicked, gossiping Mary Anne."

He did not understand women well enough to know how few can rest content if they suspect that even the most insignificant of former worshipers has found reason to believe her less worthy of worship. He only saw that for some reason wholly ulterior to her affections she was readying for another little game. He looked at her lovely face with horror and got away as soon as he might with courtesy.

Once home, he wrote her a note that began, "Really, Miss Beadnell . . ."

But a day later, weeping shamelessly, he wrote again.

"I have no guide to ascertain your present feelings, and I have, God knows, no means of influencing them. I have never loved and I can never love any creature breathing but yourself . . ."

Kolle fetched it to her. She smiled, her face gentle and satisfied, and she said that there was no answer.

"I'm truly sorry," said Kolle when he came back. "From my heart, you know, and so is Anne."

"Oh, for God's sake," said Charles, "let's forget it, shall we?"

A door had shut.

Pride, however, cannot stifle the heart's consuming need to be known, and loved for what is known. When that door shut, did another open to show the small red reading-table, waiting, in the flaring gaslight? In any event, late in that December Charles walked to the pillar box, his heart racing, and with a hand that shook uncontrollably he posted a love letter of another kind. It was an unsolicited contribution to the *Monthly Magazine*.

The *Monthly* did not pay for material it had not ordered, or notify its volunteer contributors whether or not they would achieve the glory of print. On publication day Charles entered the bookshop with hands that trembled again.

He had fumbled the new issue of the *Monthly* twice over before he found it: *A Dinner at Poplar Walk, by Boz*. They had changed the title.

He paid for the copy, and walked out into his London. He strode down Whitehall, his head high, and his face pale. As he neared Westminster Hall he felt his eyes running over, and he fled into its sheltering dusk. He was there a long time, pacing its flagged floor, before he had mastered the joy enough to risk getting home without crying in the street and making a show of himself.

Nonetheless, when the *Monthly*, having seen a few more sketches, wrote Mr. Dickens suggesting a series, he had so far mastered joy and trembling that he could reply in an admirably firm hand that Mr. Dickens had countless ideas which he would be more than glad to work up for adequate remuneration.

That night, as he walked through the Adelphi with Mitton, he wore a new blue cape with velvet facings. One side of it was rakishly swung back over a shoulder, and a new soft hat with a touch of the brigand to it was set over the left eye.

He had bought a bag of cherries, and as he talked he kept popping them, one by one, into the mouth of a bemused baby who dangled over the shoulder of a workman directly before them. It was a game of which he was fond; he had often played it before.

"So I told them, Mitton," he said, "that I'd gladly deliver, as soon as they came through with the ever-needful. Fame's a fine thing, but fame and money are finer yet, eh?"

Mitton grinned. But he only said, "You'll have that brat full of cherry stones."

His eyes remote and enormous, Charles popped another cherry into the open mouth.

"And they'll pay up," he said. "This 'ere laborer name of C. Dickens, 'e's worthy of 'is hire."

Boz was on his way.

❄ ❄ ❄ ❄ ❄ ❄ ❄ ❄ ❄

BOOK III
Charles Takes a Wife

❄ ❄ ❄ ❄ ❄ ❄ ❄ ❄ ❄

Boz was on his way, and prancing along it. Above his flashing blue
eyes, the broad-brimmed bandit's hat rode at an angle which his
father's topper had never bettered in its most gallant days. The new
velvet-faced cape streamed back from his shoulder like a flag of
triumph.

There was, as he remarked often and joyfully, no end to his
notions. The sketches flowed like beer from a bunghole, people
laughed, and the *Monthly* paid. Not that he considered chucking the
Morning Chronicle and turning Grub Street hack. He had stuck with
double entry for Bradbury and Evans until he knew for a fact that he
could do better in the shorthand box at Doctors' Commons. He
would have hung on to the parliamentary reporting if it had been
drab slavery; and it was, in fact, slap-up sport.

The *Chronicle* and the *London Times* were neck-and-neck com-
petitors. The rivalry called for sharp wits and unspared energies. It
called for wild night rides in jolting coaches, one knee for a desk, and
a spattering candle gripped in the left fist to guide the scrawling pen.
It called above all for zest, and Charles had it to spare.

So had his friend Tom Beard: Beard, with his horse sense and
angry idealism, his good health, good nature, and quick, wild roar of
laughter. Between them, they made a team hard to beat. Usually they
were sent out on an out-of-town story together.

Separated, they wrote letters, Beard's terse, Charles's voluble over
every triumph or absurd misadventure alike — "a thing that could
only have happened to me." And often, by the same post, Charles
would repeat his newest tale for their mutual friend Tom Mitton;
repeat it with new touches and embellishments — for though he
rarely, in his whole lifetime, wrote a letter with intent to deceive, he
seldom managed to tell a story twice the same way.

Charles and Beard and Mitton, a young lawyer, were now a solid
triumvirate. Kolle and Henry Austin somehow had begun to drift out
of the picture. Kolle had become excessively married, of course, and

Austin was absorbed in paying court to — of all people — Letty. Not Fan, but amiable, dim little Letty. Moreover, Charles had an indefinable yet nonetheless oppressive feeling that they both — dear fellows as they were — belonged to another chapter. To the Maria business, in fact, so completely behind him.

The feeling, however, was vague and never fully verbalized. Charles was not given to self-examination. He simply took it for granted that Beard and Mitton were his closest friends.

And Ainsworth was his patron.

Charles had met Harrison Ainsworth at the *Chronicle* office. He was dazzled when the author of *Rookwood* asked him to dine. He was humbly amazed when Ainsworth, with a wave of his small, jeweled fingers, remarked that Charles should meet his publisher, Macrone, one day.

"For, at the rate you turn these things off, they'll soon make a book."

That night Charles walked home with his hat set straight, and his cape hanging down before on both sides, as if to disarm the gods. A *book*. A *book by Boz*. Young writers traditionally starve and struggle; they don't simply pick up a pen and waltz between cloth bindings. The cape hung down; the face beneath the broad hatbrim was awed, vulnerable. Charles walked delicately.

Yet the next day, as he raced to tell Beard, the cape flew back from his shoulder once more, a flag of triumph.

"And he meant it, Beard, what's more. He's really the soul of kindness. By the Lord, the way things open up these days I'd feel I had a charmed life if . . . if only . . ."

He broke off.

"What's up? Something wrong?"

He shrugged. "Everybody has something wrong." And he changed the subject.

He was not being courageous, or restrained. He had, simply, no stomach for discussing the black shadow that lay athwart his bright present. Whenever he could, he looked the other way. The shadow, however, remained. It was an undeniable fact that his father was once more in heady flirtation with the Marshalsea.

The pattern was sickeningly familiar. The Barrow uncles had given him the sack. Touched for one loan too many, probably, as John Dickens was an adequate reporter. Still, he had picked up a not-too-bad position with the *Herald*. He could still have managed and made do.

John Dickens, however, had no gift for managing, or making do. He lent what he did not possess as readily as he borrowed what he could not repay; he exuded hospitality. And Charles, in an odd, ineducable way, not only loved his father but admired him. Behind the shored-up memory of the black time, the light of golden Chatham still shone. Charles was torn between a child's panic fear and a child's pride. He averted his eyes. He cocked his hat to one side, and kept on the run.

Or, as he put it to himself, he knew that the Governor was sailing too close to the wind, it was damned depressing, but keeping active is a sovereign cure for the blues. So he bustled, and pranced; and one day he pranced home, hung hat and cape on the rack, touched his hair with a gesture directly inherited from his father, and opened the parlor door.

For a single flash of time, his heart clogged, and his nostrils flared to a hallucinatory smell of chill mold and overboiled cauliflower. He felt his legs ache with the heavy trudge from shame to shame, Warren's Blacking, 30 Strand, and Mrs. Roylance's grubby hell of exile for the unwanted.

Immediately, the sick shock of memory gave way to a mad, impersonal detachment. His eyes caressed the room as if it were a stage and he the director on his opening night. Yes, yes. All in order, all superbly, hilariously right.

His mother was upon the sofa, her eyes rolled up to show the whites, one hand pressed to her bosom. A bottle of *sal volatile* lay upon the floor where she had let it drop. Except that her color was high, the effect was reminiscent of Hogarth's "Death of the Countess." Fan and Letty, in tears and curlpapers, bent above her.

Frederick lounged against the mantel. At fourteen, it was clear that his face would always remain snub-featured. Yet, despite its limitations, it now managed, quite creditably, a hawklike brooding. Alfred showed less talent. He merely stood front center and staring about as if he had been overcome with stagefright during a nursery production of *The Babes in the Wood*.

Apart, in the draftiest corner of the room — what signifies a draft to one who reaps the whirlwind? — stood his father. Mrs. Dickens herself could not have bettered his posture. A hand was clapped to his brow, a closed fist pressed his breast, and his eyes were fixed upon a crack in the ceiling. And on a straight chair just behind him sat a very pale, small man with a very red, large nose. He, also, was motionless except that his hands were locked in a curious tug-of-war upon the brim of his battered white hat.

It was only a second or two before Charles's body gave a waking start. Then his head lifted, and he walked into the room.

"Well, how much is it for?"

Except for the small bailiff, the tableau remained fixed. He, however, leaned forward with a look of pathetic gratitude.

"Burr, creditor," he said hoarsely. "Four pun seven, amount, and if you ain't got it would you ask the gentleman to come along with me as they've been like this until I feels more of a waxworks than human."

And a frightened little voice from nowhere said, "Oh, Charlie!"

"Shrimp? Where in the world are you?"

A small streaky face peered around the far corner of the sofa. Charles looked at it, and a spasm of pain caught his left side.

"Take Mother upstairs, Fan," he said. "Run along, Letty. Everything's in hand."

But Mrs. Dickens had a strong feeling of her central role. She shrieked. She uttered a peal of strange laughter. Charles looked at her, and at Shrimp. He dug an elbow in against the pain. "Fan, take her upstairs."

He had cracked out the order like a drill sergeant. At once he turned to his father.

"Don't take it so hard, Father," he said. "We'll manage."

His elbow dug his side, his voice was heavily hearty, heavily casual. *Oh, God, and now Mother's disposed of, here comes the oration.*

But John Dickens only stood with sagging shoulders, and there was no stagecraft in the gesture with which the unsteady hand sought the unsteady mouth.

"I'm sorry," he said. "I thought they'd give me another week."

Charles bowed his head. He wanted to apologize, though for what he did not know. He began to talk briskly.

"Four pounds. Now let's see. I get paid Saturday, and Mitton's flush. Fred, you and Shrimpington run over to Tom Mitton's lodgings with a note, will you? And while the bailiff waits, how's for a drop of cheer all around?"

The tug-of-war on the hatbrim became frenzied.

[75]

"What do you say? Give it a name, Mr.—er—"

Left hand won over right. Right sought forelock, remembered authority of law, dropped hastily.

"Fish, the name, and anything acceptable, but rum-and-luke the preference."

Blessed, necessary Mr. Fish. Thank God for Mr. Fish.

"Cheer up, Father. Come on up to the fire, both of you. Rum-and-luke's the word."

The pain in Charles's side had gone away.

Of course, though Mr. Dickens had neglected to mention it, Burr, four pounds seven, was not the whole story. When he went for a walk with young Alfred the next day, Alfred came home alone. Mr. Dickens had been picked up and detained at Sloman's sponging house on Cursitor Street until a much larger bill should be settled with Sloane and Maxwell, wine merchants.

Charles mortgaged his salary. He found cheaper lodgings for his mother, the girls, and the small children. He took a small suite, top floor back, at Furnival's Inn, and set up bachelor's quarters with Frederick. And he borrowed another fiver from Mitton; the Governor needed something in his pocket to keep up his spirits in that hole.

It meant trouble; and still, except for the painful visits to Sloman's it was all oddly pleasant, nor was he whistling in the dark when he wrote to Beard, "We have more cause for cheerfulness than despondency, after all."

He enjoyed bustling through second-hand shops to find a proper table-lamp, a trivet for doing chops, bargain curtains to make the shabby suite at Furnival's Inn look like something. Amazing, how curtains and a good rub-over with French polish can smarten a place!

He enjoyed setting Fred lessons. Really, he should have started in on the boy long since, drummed some notion of neatness and punctuality and the value of money into him.

"He's a dear little chap," he said to Mitton. "He only wants waking up."

After a week or so, he even ceased to dread the trips to Cursitor Street.

"Now you mustn't fret, Governor," he would say. "I've got it all in hand."

And as he spoke, the wide blue eyes blazed with their innocent self-esteem, their total faith in the power of human will.

Nonetheless, he had sustained a loss. He was too busy to notice it; but though his tenderness for his father was unchanged, the light of golden Chatham had gone out forever.

❋   2   ❋

THE TOO KEEN, too firm young face impressed the publisher Macrone enormously. He had called at Furnival's Inn to oblige Ainsworth. He climbed the three flights of stairs grudgingly, but as he came down he was thinking hard.

Mr. Willis, the American who had come along with him, chattered on.

"Dirt poor, I'd guess, and rushed to blazes with work, but didn't it beat time how he had that place shined up? Like the most persnickety housekeeper this side of kingdom come!"

"I didn't notice. Quite a face, eh?"

"Very sharp. God, I can still see him, yanking on that coat, hustling the liquor out! A real publisher, right out of the blue! He must have thought he was dreaming."

"Mm," said Macrone. It was an answer that satisfied him, being both courteous and effortless. He had, however, a highly developed sense of business, and a good fencing-arm judges another quite well through the first light touch of steel on steel.

"Mm," he said again; and this time the sound was one of pleasure. Most writers want money, but few know how it is made. Of course, the sketches did not amount to enough yet in sheer bulk to be worth a serious discussion. Still, Macrone had a distinct feeling that he was getting into a good thing, and on the ground floor.

Ainsworth was delighted that the meeting had gone so well. He was a dandified small creature, and something of a poseur, but his enthusiasms were genuine. He liked young Boz, both for himself and for being, so clearly, a comer. The boy fitted in. Poor though he was, he kept himself dressed up to the knocker; and he was a good talker, he had that most invaluable of social assets, the quick ear. He was, briefly, a born dinner guest.

Ainsworth was glad of that — for himself, and, generously, for

[77]

Charles. He delighted in giving little dinners for big names —
Bulwer, Disraeli, the witty Father Prout — and their gratification was
enhanced as he watched the easy manners and blazing eyes of his
young protégé.

Yet, though Charles also found those dinners a heady delight, he
tended to avoid rather than seek them. For Ainsworth's group would
not, clearly, have been quite at ease eating chops done over a grate.
As his father would have put it, one could not, in a word, offer them
a suitable exchange of hospitality.

This attitude, so very middle-class, was paradoxically central to
Charles's nature. With the poor and the gently bred, he could always be at his ease and sure of acceptance; but it was to the Beadnells, the rejecting Beadnells of this world, that he was own kin.

Perhaps the chief seduction of the Hogarth ménage lay in its being so like the Beadnells', and still so welcoming.

George Hogarth was music critic on the *Evening Chronicle*. He
met young Boz to engage a series of sketches for his paper, and
liked him at once. And Charles, from his first visit to the small house
in Chelsea, felt himself utterly at home.

Hogarth was fiftyish, a solid, self-effacing man, and the author of a
history of music. In his Edinburgh boyhood, he had more than once
met Sir Walter Scott. ("An intimate friend of Sir Walter Scott,"
Charles would say, when his bond with the household grew closer.)

Mrs. Hogarth had a pinched nose, an opulent bosom, and a
manner which narrowly skirted the overgenteel. Nonetheless, it was
pleasantly clear from the start that Charles fell into her category of
"suitable" young men.

Robert was a nice boy. Charles offered at once to give him shorthand lessons. Edward and George were pleasant, too, in a negative
way. He was charmed by the little girl Georgina — Georgy — a
sharped-eyed nine-year-old with the air and the tongue of an ap-
prentice witch. The baby, Helen, was inconsiderable. Mary, a
straight-haired, straight-featured child of fourteen he scarcely noticed
on his first visit; it was at the second, or the third, that he observed
her gray eyes, so direct and aware, and caught the fact that her
laughter rang out first, and sometimes alone, when he was funny.

But as for Catherine, who could describe her? On that first night,
Charles could only look, and marvel.

In truth, the expression that Catherine Hogarth most commonly awoke in the faces of young men was that of a wistful gluttony. Her glossy dark-auburn hair, caught up in a heavy knot behind her head, fell at the sides in three smooth curls against each cheek. One saw it, and imagined it as falling back upon a pillow. Her eyes were drowsy, and of the violet-blue so dear to romantic fiction. Her skin was velvet-thick and white, and the moist redness of her lips was startling in contrast. And though her waist yielded gently to the corset, all above and below was pleasing softness. Another pound or two would have made her plump, but that pound or two was yet to come.

She did not flirt, nor did she need to. She said, "How do you do?" shyly, and as she crossed the room by his side, she tripped over an ottoman and blushed. "Oh, dear, I'm the awkwardest thing that ever was!"

And at once, along with the delicious lust, Charles was filled with a protective tenderness. His lips parted for the conventional protest, the conventional compliment. And softly, gently, as if he were speaking to a child, he heard himself say, "Never mind. It's all right. Never mind."

"Thank you." The words almost whispered. "Thank you, Mr. Dickens."

She took his offered arm.

She did not speak more than a few words for the rest of the evening, but Charles did not notice that. He was too absorbed in looking at her.

There was a heavy fall of snow outside the house, but as Charles walked the long way back to Furnival's Inn, he was warm, and treading on daisies.

There are men who must always be in love or feel, somehow, less than themselves. Though Charles spoke from his heart when he told Maria Beadnell that he could never love another, he had, in hard fact, been waiting; and almost from the moment he broke with her. A pair of dark eyes in Norwich had been a pleasant temporary distraction, but no more than that. He came to the Hogarths' house like the quarry yearning for the hunter's shaft. And he had returned only a few times before he could scarcely recall the discomfort of being, as some call it, heart-whole.

Charles could never quite remember just how and when he became engaged to Catherine. They told the family in May, but they had understood each other — as the phrase went then — long before. There was no drama of declaration, no time of mutual trial and doubt. They drifted together so gently that his first use of her given name, even their first kiss, were less like a daring, a newness of ecstasy, than like the sweet, familiar custom of long habit.

It could not have come about otherwise. Never until he was old enough to know better would Charles again be able to lay himself open to the risk of hurt, as he had opened himself to Maria. And Catherine Hogarth lacked both the spirit to be passionate and the intelligence to be coy.

The first lack Charles treasured, thinking of it as her purity. The second he was too bemused to recognize until after their engagement was announced, and then he perceived it affectionately. It was restful that her mind, like her lovely body, moved softly and clumsily. It made him feel strong and central to her well-being. Nor was he moved by any impatient haste for that future in which, as he put it to himself, "her woman's mind would wake."

"Mary's going to be so clever," she once said wistfully. "Always reading. And I'm such a ninny."

He stroked her soft, heavy hair.

"When we're married," he promised, "I will read to you. Not hard books. Beautiful books that you will love."

Her cheek was on his shoulder, her arm about his neck.

"I like a nice novel when it's read aloud."

He loved the weight of her arm. He loved the innocent, incurious mind that he would form.

"My dear little Tatie. Little Tatie Wig-Pig."

They talked an excessive amount of baby talk.

She was also utterly lacking in humor. The unexpected phrase that made young Mary's grave, thin face light with its sudden laughter, that even sent small Georgy into shrill, shrewd witch cackles, left the drowsy sweetness of Catherine's eyes unchanged; yet Charles was never conscious of disappointment.

Rather, he found it somehow touching; and he was touched, too, when she would produce a labored, pointless pun, repeating it with innocent pride to make sure that it had been missed by nobody? "It was *Candid. Candied*, like sweets. Do you see?"

It used to make the family laugh at her, and she always laughed with them, guilelessly and hardest of them all, gasping out the so successful jest again, as often as she could get her breath. Sometimes she laughed until her cheeks were flushed, and her eyes wet violets, and a comb would drop from her hair or one of her bracelets perform their curious trick of unclasping themselves and falling from her arm. Then Mary always got up, kissed her, and put her to rights. "Now, Kate. Now, now."

That, too, Charles found charming: the devotion between the gentle, spinsterish girl and her lovely sister. Eyes less in love might have found something disturbing in the sight of a relationship so like that of a mother to an overdependent child. Charles was only touched and enchanted with them both.

"You take great care of Kate, don't you?" he once said to Mary, smiling.

She glanced about, as if to make sure that they were alone. Then she lifted her neat little head.

"We care for each other," she said, with odd, old-fashioned dignity. She paused, the clear gray eyes warmed, and the crisp little voice softened. "And I never seem to vex her. Do you know, she's never *once* that I can remember been cross with me?"

In the gentle pride of her love she had laid an unerring finger on the single flaw that Charles could yet perceive in his lovely Kate. There was no denying those occasional little flares of fretfulness, so out of key with the quiescent, waiting sweet of her essential nature.

He was startled, and a little vexed himself, that the child mentioned it so casually, so acceptingly. He held the vexation back. He put his arm about the hard little shoulders and gave them a brotherly squeeze.

"Teach me your secret, Mistress Mary Uncontrary."

He spoke lightly, teasingly. But the child was grave; a middle-aged furrow cut between her eyes as she felt out her answering words.

"It's hard to explain, Charles. You see, you're wonderfully clever, and perhaps — perhaps you think that people who aren't clever like you are, well, weaker in their feelings, too. They aren't, you know. And Kate — Kate has strong feelings. And she worries over not being clever, and a little awkward — as if it could matter when she's so pretty! When she starts to be cross, one must just humor her a bit — because, you see, it only comes from her feeling timid, or — or perplexed."

"I see," he said. "Thank you, dear." And he brushed his cheek across the sleek little head. He was too fond of the child to deflate her sober small moment of self-importance. Otherwise he would have pointed out the really unkind folly of overindulging those we love.

The interchange, however, was not without its effect, though the effect was not at all what poor confused little Mary had sought. Charles felt his mind oddly relieved and clarified by it. He had, he realized, been trying to ignore a situation which, in simple kindness to Kate herself, demanded the undelaying use of a firm hand.

And when, a week later, he found her in another of her sorry, sulky moods, he easily, even pleasantly, prepared to cope.

"Now, come," he said. "Give me a kiss, and show me my beauty's lovely smile."

But she made sad and ostentatious application of the handkerchief.

"No, you bad, cruel boy. You needn't have neglected me so this whole week, and you know it quite well. Papa works on a paper, too, and he has time enough for those he loves! No, I shan't kiss you for leaving your Tatie-Mouse all alone and sad, while you rush about looking for more things to be busy, busy, busy about!"

He wasted no time, as he always had before, on protests, attempted explanations, attempted caresses. He stood up and walked a little away from her. Then he turned, speaking gravely but, he hoped, without sharpness.

"I'm not a boy, Kate. I am a man, with a man's full responsibilities. Your father has a grown family, an established position, and no outside cares. I have heavy cares and my way to make. If you are unable to trust my love, or accept my circumstances, please say so at once. I do love you, whether you choose to believe it or not. But heartbreak is better than a life of niggling, distrustful misery."

He had no sooner spoken the words than he was terrified. Her face had gone oddly vacant as he spoke, he believed for one awful minute that she was readying herself to send him away, and forever. If she had kept her silence for more than a second or two, he would surely have cast himself at her knees in abject weeping.

But at once she leaned forward, reaching out her hands like a child as her voice came, sweet but trembling a little in its gentle flood of apologies and baby talk.

"Oh, dear, dear, my boy mustn't be so stern and frighten his own Tatie-Mouse so. Oh, I was most wicked to be all scoldy and c'oss. Oh, kiss your Tatie-Mouse and tell her that she's all forgiven and her own dear boy isn't one tiny bit angry with her any more!"

He forgot that he had been afraid. He comforted her, laughing between the tender, comforting kisses until she laughed, too. And in the upshot, they spent the happiest evening imaginable.

Yes, he told himself, it had been unpleasant to wound her; but clearly, it was folly and unkind folly to let her go on in ways that could only bring them both pain. He owed, yes *owed* her help in controlling her little moods, in understanding that happiness, as much as any other virtue, is largely a matter of will and effort.

✳   3   ✳

THE LESSON had gone well. Yet the memory of it filled Charles with a vague sense of unease, and he was glad that it had to be renewed so seldom in the months that followed, and never so harshly. And Kate had, indeed, when he came to think of it, a lonely time in comparison with most engaged girls.

"Never mind, my Mouse, my own Piggy-Wig," he would say, kissing her. "When we're married it will be quite different."

One evening, after a particularly crowded fortnight, he found her looking so forlorn and smiling so determinedly that he was quite unmanned. The next day he walked about Chelsea until he had found a room to rent only around the corner from her house. He could use it when the long trip from Furnival's Inn and back felt like the insuperable last straw.

Realistically, of course, it only put off the day that they could be married. He told her of it in a voice of brusque apology.

"I daresay it's a fool's waste. But when I can't see you for days, I'm wretched. I feel as if I'd only dreamed that you love me or that we'll ever be married."

He was amazed at the light that filled her face.

"Oh!" she cried. "Oh, do you feel like that truly?"

"Why, my darling, you know that I do."

She hung her head. "Please don't be angry, Charles, but sometimes it's hard to see how anybody could be as dreadfully busy as you if — if he badly wanted not to be."

He shook his head. "My Tatie-Mouse must have the same faith in my love that I have in hers."

[83]

And instantly he was shamed by the sight of her humbled face that had been filled with such a light of joy. We are not aware of our faults of taste when they are common to our period, and Charles moreover was, at best, not self-critical. But he was, at worst, wholly alive. He blushed for the pompous cheapness of his words, his nobly-rebuking voice, his absurd shake of the head; blushed, even while he shrank from himself to see how he had extinguished that light, how her face was so humbled, and dulled.

He did the best, the only thing he could have done. He began to kiss her, and continued, wordlessly, to do so until they were both quite free of any other preoccupation.

Though their time alone was spent almost exclusively in kissing, Charles never kissed Catherine as he had learned to kiss Maria. He was intoxicated with her innocence. It moved him near to tears when sometimes, between their kisses, she laughed like a triumphant child, imagining herself both wise and abandoned, possessed already of the whole knowledge of love, and love's delight. On many nights after he had left her, he himself lay wretchedly awake, possessed by her sweet, soft flesh, her fragrant hair, her heavy-lidded eyes — all, all so purposefully created. Yet even in the sharpest discomfort of his longing, the thought of her utter innocence would flood him with tender pride of possession like an ecstasy.

Now, in the doorway of the parlor, with the family abovestairs, he kissed her until they were both lost in their kissing. But at last she bent back in his arms, the amazing light almost wholly come back into her face.

"Oh," she cried, "let me go. I must tell Mary about your getting that room — I must tell them all!"

He looked at that light, that joy, and he spoke to it directly, from a curious, uncharacteristic, simple humility.

"Oh, darling, I'm glad that you're so glad."

They would never in their lives be quite so close again.

Summer turned to winter. That was a period in which long engagements were taken for granted, but had they been the exception rather than the common lot, Charles's life would have allowed him little time to fret. In fact, he had never felt time go faster.

And though the room around the corner had worked no miracle, and lovely Kate still had her occasional moods and sulks, there was, when he came to think of it, a flattery in them as well as a vexation.

"You must remember, my darling," he said often, "that you are always at the center of my heart. It's for us that I work so hard, you know. Only for us."

He spoke sincerely. And the words had a certain factual, objective truth. Kate was indeed at the center of his heart; except when the dashing quill moved as if it took down dictation and his own sentences made him laugh until he cried. Except when he was all a destroying fire at the sight of want, ignorance, injustice, pharisaical religiosity. Except when he was dashing with Beard by coach, in a mad rapture of scooping the *Times*. Except when he was lecturing Frederick on neatness, or punctuality, or financial realism. Except when he was wolfing the heart out of the British Museum reading room, or teaching himself French, or meeting more of Ainsworth's brilliant, invaluable circle, or building the friendship with Macrone which would so obviously be a lifetime source of personal delight and mutual benefit to them both. (A curiously unselfconscious expression of that genuine if complex warmth was the letter which condoled with Macrone on the sudden death of his infant son, closing with gentle sympathy for Mrs. Macrone and the cheering news that Cruikshank expected to have the illustrations of *the book* finished by Christmas.)

For the book was sold. A hundred and fifty pounds outright for the copyright, and a top-ranking illustrator to give it the final touch. Two volumes, cloth, at 21s. Oh, glory, glory.

In December, a better suite was to let at Furnival's Inn, at the front and a floor down. He took it for three years.

"Perhaps the lease won't be up before we can get married," he told Catherine, "but we could hardly afford a house in any event. And meantime I need it, you see, with the book coming out."

Catherine looked puzzled. "The book?"

He smiled at her feminine slowness. "You see, Tatie darling, a fellow must look decently prosperous to be in good bargaining position. And, of course, one book leads to more."

But he could not spend much time, that evening, on explainings or kissings either. The *Chronicle* staff were on strike, and he was heading up the protest for them.

And January passed, and the publication date was just around the corner.

It meant a deal to be seen to. There must be inscribed copies with covering letters for relatives, friends — for every acquaintance whose word might carry weight. One had to sift out memory, to be sure that nobody was forgotten. Lord Stanley, for example, would recall that slap-up job of reporting the Irish Disturbance Bill; a copy must certainly go to him. And the letters that went out with review copies, of course, needed a particular twist.

Macrone was amused. Behind Charles's back he told Ainsworth that Boz had missed his trade: he should be selling patent medicines. Nonetheless, he enjoyed the young enthusiasm, and was realistically grateful for it.

The book came out in February, on Charles's birthday. He celebrated twice, with his family, and with Catherine's.

At home, the children shrieked. "Charlie's a author! Charlie's a famous!" His mother delivered a monologue which was singular, even for her, in its length and intricacy, intertwining her bygone splendors, her present humiliations (". . . though, as you know, no word of complaint has ever passed my lips, I am too proud, and, I trust, too kind to add to the sufferings of my dear ones . . .") and her unwavering confidence in her son's literary gifts from the moment he had downed his first swallow at the maternal font. And the Governor, once more restored to the family circle, poured glasses of the rosy all around, with his face, between the flying collars, radiant as a cherub's framed in its wings.

"My dear, dear son," he said, "as we gather on this auspicious occasion—er—doubly, as one might say, your birthday, I—er—well, in point of fact, words fail me."

He drained off the glass at a swallow and held out his hand. Charles grasped it, and they both used their handkerchiefs.

Then, profligate with triumph, Charles took a cab for Chelsea, and triumph's crown. The family were converging from all directions as Kate opened the door.

"Goodness," she said, "we thought you'd never get here!" And she lifted her lovely face for his kiss.

Mrs. Hogarth advanced, her nose pinched tighter than ever, and her bosom downright overwhelming; yet Charles regarded both phenomena with a kind of affection, they so obviously indicated her sense of the occasion. "Charles, we are proud of you."

Mr. Hogarth smiled quietly, and handed him a copy of the review which he had written for the *Evening Chronicle*. Charles had feared that Mr. Hogarth's natural modesty might restrain any puff he felt inclined to give one who would so soon be a part of the family; but the fear had been unfounded. Indeed, it was hard to believe that the whole subscription list of the *Evening Chronicle* would not be shortly speeding to the nearest bookseller, twenty-one shillings in hand, to acquaint themselves with this new light who combined the gay ease of Washington Irving with the social indignation of Victor Hugo.

"Oh, sir," Charles said, "I am grateful."

"Quite sincere." The voice dry and quiet, the smile affectionate. "I'm not merely pushing private trade."

But Charles had begun to laugh. "Georgy, you're staring at me as if I had three eyes!"

The small witch-face remained solemn. "It's *odd*, Charles. Of course I knew that ordinary people like Papa write books about things that are really *so*, teaching books. But I always thought that people who wrote the *other* kind were different. I mean that they were nobody one would ever meet."

He hugged her, delighted. "Georgy, that's precisely how I felt when I met Mr. Ainsworth!" Then he glanced around him. "But where's Mary?"

"Paying you the supreme compliment," said Mr. Hogarth. "Up in her room, with the book."

But as he spoke, Mary came down the stairs. She was looking very small and erect, with the book in her hands. Her wide, shining stare was like sun on gray oceans.

"Oh, Charles," she said, "I've almost finished. It's so much more wonderful than reading them one at a time."

Charles looked at her. A sweet, aching tightness filled his throat. *She is like me*, he thought. *My sisters, my friends are strangers. This child is like me.* Wordless, he nodded at her, while the light from their eyes mingled. His heart was a brimming glass. He remembered his father's pride, the radiant cherub head framed in those gallant wings. His fingers worked affectionately on the manuscript of Mr. Hogarth's splendid review. Reluctantly, as if the moment were too sweet to break, he turned his eyes from the gray shining eyes, from the child, the dear child who would be his sister.

He turned to his lovely Kate, holding her in the circle of his arm, bending his face down to her uplifted face.

"And you? Are you happy too, my darling?"

She smiled her softest smile, the smile of a sleeper in a delightful dream.

"Oh, yes!" she said. "You'll have so much more time now that all this vexation is done with, won't you?"

He knew, of course he knew, that she had no skill to show her heart in words. Even as he felt the ugly physical sensation of a sharp drop, the ground gone from under his feet, he knew that it was a senseless reaction and one to be ashamed of.

It was wholly without his volition that his voice jerked out hard, with a cutting edge. "Is that all?"

He saw fear in her eyes as she caught at one of her bracelets and fumbled the clasp.

"Oh, please, your Tatie-Mouse isn't clever, but don't believe she isn't 'cited to bits of her Charles, writing books and everything."

He was ashamed of his exasperation at their dear, private baby talk. He was ashamed of the dead drop, the chill. She was a child, his lovely child. His greed for empty, wordy praise, his vanity, had made him speak like a fool.

He spoke again, his voice careful in gentleness. "You must remember, love, that your husband will always be writing books and having what you call vexation."

She sighed, but the gentle voice had reassured her. She leaned her cheek on his shoulder. "Only we needn't think of that today! Your birthday, and all!"

Before he could answer, Mary had slipped her arm between them, drawing Kate away.

"Of course we needn't, darling," she said. "Tonight we'll have fun."

He knew that he had been rebuked, yet, strangely, he did not resent it.

He said, intending it as a joke, "Mary, when we're married you should live with us."

But Mary, for once, did not laugh at the right moment. And Kate cried, "Oh, Charles, I was afraid to ask you. I was afraid you wouldn't like the idea."

It was, by contemporary standards, a commonplace suggestion. Outside the bedroom, privacy played no part in the current picture of domestic bliss. Charles could not understand why he recoiled from the notion in a kind of shock.

But he remembered that it was a day for happiness, a day of triumph for all who loved him. He made himself laugh.

"It's worth considering," he said. "Come, Georgy-Witch, into the drawing room and play us your most bacchanalian polka. And don't thump it, wooden fingers. Let it whoosh, whoosh, with a *boom*-zip-boom! Come, all of you, let's celebrate!"

He caught Kate's waist and swept her off as he sang the tune. He swept her in circles, laughing when she stumbled to keep up with his own clumsy gallop. He loved to dance and had not the faintest notion that he was a bad dancer.

"No, Kate, no, darling," he cried, "loosen up! Let it swing. Whoosh, whoosh, and a boom-zip-boom."

Many things had happened in a very few minutes. As usual, however, Charles preferred not to pause and examine them.

❅ 4 ❅

THE BOOK got excellent notices and moved rapidly. Charles was a hundred and fifty pounds in pocket, and every paper in London had given his name free advertising. The mortgage on his salary was nearly paid off, and the Governor was back on the *Morning Herald*.

On the other hand, marriage was going to mean three to clothe and four to feed, from the very start. And only God knew when Father would need a hand again. A week after the book came out he had called at Furnival's Inn and kept Charles up until two with his highly specialized financial reasoning.

"For you see, my dear boy, though it was a bargain at ten pounds, I recalled that I had—er—been recently rebuked by circumstances, so, regretfully, I let the opportunity go. However, I'm as well pleased now; for ten pounds saved is ten pounds earned, and it only needs a fiver to make up this necessary fifteen which you shall have back in a few days — a few weeks at most."

"But you didn't have the ten pounds in the first place, Governor."

"Dear boy, that's precisely my point. I realized that fully, and *saved* it to make up this fifteen now."

It wasn't the money. Five pounds was a pinch, but Charles was ready to hand it over, and with a good heart. It was the singular argument which backed the request that kept him pleading elementary logic until, at two, from sheer exhaustion, he had to fetch out his purse.

And still, despite the weariness and vexation, his smile was affectionate as he held the door open at last.

"Good night, Governor. Sure you won't have another drop of the rosy to go home on?"

He was nearly undressed for bed when the spasm started in his left side. It was like the worst seizures that he remembered from his childhood, like the attacks which used to frighten him, alone in his shipshape garret above the timber lot. Though he was not one to coddle his body, it kept him from work all the next day.

Mitton dropped in that evening. Charles, still angry, tender, and laughing, told him about it.

Mitton drew a sharp breath and slapped his hands on his thighs. "But why, for the love of God, do you encourage it, Charles? Why should you shell out? For matter of that, who made you your father's keeper?"

A blank blue stare was followed by a peal of laughter. "You had me on, Tom. For a second, there, I thought you meant it."

Mitton gave up.

In a week, Charles had quite forgotten the pain and its occasion. In any event, prospects were brightening. Fan was engaged to a good chap, Henry Burnett, a singer. When Austin married Letty, the girls would both be off the Governor's hands. Keeping Frederick was no great expense. And since his father's only vices were optimism and hospitality, his troubles always mounted slowly; one need only keep watch, and dip down a firm oar at the right time.

Charles, in fact, felt well. He got to work with the French polish, he bought a nice, almost new carpet and a few proper wineglasses. The second floor looked downright elegant. He slapped Frederick on the shoulder as he eyed it, his eyes bright with the zest of stagecraft.

"A neat bachelor's establishment, eh, Fred?"

Frederick's snub nose wrinkled. He arched his black brows and gave his small, well-oiled chuckle. "I'd say we're living in style."

The set was just prepared when Mr. Hall came.

A tiny, bird-boned little man, he tapped at the door one evening just as Charles — having first made Frederick clean his nails over again and set him his lessons — was brushing his hair and his suit before he set out for Chelsea.

The opened door showed a fresh-faced, well-groomed young man, and a pleasant room which glowed with firelight and French polish.

"Mr. Dickens?" A flash of quick eyes, and a card extended. "I'm Hall, of Chapman and Hall."

But instead of inspecting the card, the young man seized the hand that held it, stared into his face, and pulled him, with a shout, over the threshold.

"Come in, come in! This is incredible! Oh, my brother Fred, Mr. Hall. But this is fantastic! Fred, take Mr. Hall's hat and fetch the Madeira. Mr. Hall, this is a meeting of splendid omen!"

Mr. Hall, understandably, looked somewhat like a wind-blown and uncertain sparrow. The startling young man now stepped back and stood, an accusing forefinger leveled at him, for all the world like a magistrate delivering his charge.

"Sir, in the shop under your offices in the Strand you sometimes take over the duty of a clerk?"

Mr. Hall moved back slightly before the blaze of blue eyes, the extended finger.

"Why—ah—yes, I do."

The young man's voice dropped a full octave. "Sir, I sent my first contribution to the *Monthly*, and I came into your shop to find if they'd used it. And you — I'd know you anywhere — *you* changed my half crown!"

"By the Lord! You're the boy who snatched a *Monthly* and pawed it through backwards and forwards and tore off like a lunatic. I remember perfectly, I remember wondering what the blazes ailed you."

"It occurs to me, sir, that you must have been wondering the same thing only now."

They both began to laugh. Charles snapped his fingers. "Fred, wake up, boy. The Madeira!"

The matter of the twice-cleaned fingernails had been rankling when Mr. Hall's knock came at the door. Now, at that cavalier snap of the fingers, it returned in full bitterness. Fred sniffed. "You're already late to Catherine's. You told me so twenty times."

"You misunderstood me, Fred. Here, I'll take care of the wine. You may go back to your lessons."

He drew the cork neatly, with a flourish he had picked up from Ainsworth.

Mr. Hall sat down. Though he was a trifle winded, still, he had begun to like this enthusiastic, hospitable young man. He cleared his throat.

"Mr. Dickens, have you any binding arrangements with Macrone in the immediate future?"

"No. Oh, I've promised him another book, but there's no time set."

"Excellent." Mr. Hall, twirling his glass, did not observe that the open young face had become a cautious mask through which the blue eyes flared. "What I'd in mind was this. You know how popular Seymour's hunting pictures are, these days. Now it occurred to us that they'd do well in a monthly shilling issue — adventures of the Nimrod Club, a lot of Cockneys who consider themselves hunters. Some silly mishap in each sketch, and a text alongside. Lively, like your sketches. Of course, as you wouldn't have to think of ideas it shouldn't take much of your time."

The light behind the mask had gone out. The proposal was not at all what Charles had expected from this meeting of good omen, this remarkable coincidence. He tried to conceal the disappointment as he answered, slowly.

"I have no lack of ideas, Mr. Hall. But I know nothing of hunting and care less. To be honest, I think you've come to the wrong man."

Mr. Hall looked up. He saw the disappointment behind the courteous mask, and felt some surprise that his own disappointment was so disproportionate. After all, it would be easy to find someone else. He leaned forward, silent for a moment, wondering whether to urge it or let it drop. There was no mistaking the sincerity of that hesitation. Nor was it surprising. The offer was one of hack work, if you came out with the plain term, and Boz was obviously in a more solid financial position than he had been led to believe. His clothes, his unpretentious, agreeable, well-kept quarters showed that, plainly enough. He cleared his throat again.

And before he could speak, the courteous mask broke, in a smile of dazzling frankness; the blue eyes danced alive, became simultaneously shrewd and disarming, like the eyes of a schoolboy swapping marbles.

"On the other hand," said Boz, "what would you pay?"

Mr. Hall, veteran man of business, drew a breath. Then crisply, without hesitation, he named that topmost figure upon which, in the unlikely event of bargaining, he and his partner had decided to settle.

"Fourteen guineas an issue," he said. "It will run for a guaranteed two years."

There was another moment of silence — a brief one in which Charles sat still, his lips compressed and his eyes doing rapid sums. Abruptly, he stood up and raised his glass.

"To the Nimrod Club," he said, "and to my bride immediately-to-be."

No sooner was the toast drunk than Charles was in a fever to be off to Chelsea with the news. But he gave no least indication of his impatience. He drew Mr. Hall on and allowed himself to be drawn in turn with every appearance of leisurely enjoyment.

Mr. Hall himself was now wholly disposed to take his ease. Young Boz was excellent company, he liked him more at every minute. He was a pusher and a bit of a name dropper; but ambition is a good quality, and the names he dropped were first-rate names. It was impressive that the boy had made so many valuable, and genuine, friendships. Nor did he try to blow a chance meeting into something else.

"I don't really know Disraeli, sir. I've met him several times at Ainsworth's, but I don't like him and I doubt he knows I exist."

"If he ever does, your politics will hardly draw you closer. Tell me, how does Bulwer impress you?"

"Bulwer?" Charles smiled, stroking the stem of the new, proper wineglass. "A thoroughly *satin* character. But the best satin." The line pleased him as he spoke it. It was one that he would use, as he used all his best lines, more than once. As Hall laughed, he refilled his glass. "In spite of which, or because of it, I like him. In fact, I like and admire him enormously."

And he kept himself, with fierce determination, from glancing at the clock on the mantel.

However, by the grace of God, Mr. Hall kept early hours. Charles bowed him out, and rushed to the bedroom door. "I'm sleeping in Chelsea, Fred. Sorry I was short with you. But this was business."

He tore down the stairs and took the four blocks to the nearest livery at a run. "Get me to Chelsea, and as fast as you can."

The liveryman smiled. "Your first, I'll be bound," he said. "When you got six of 'em, like me, to eat you out of 'ouse and 'ome, you'll scarcely notice another no more than as if the dog was a-goin' to pup."

"Hurry, for God's sake!"

He felt no disproportion in his haste. Rather, whirling through the dark to Chelsea, he thought with bewilderment, with incredulity, of the matter-of-fact calm in which he and his Kate had endured so much time of waiting.

"Kate," he whispered, over and over. "My wife, my wife."

And once, before the end of the journey, he wept, with an odd, loose, almost womanish weeping, the pleasurable weeping of an unexamined release, relief. "Oh, God," he wept, "I love her so much, I want her so much. I didn't dare let myself know until now. It was too far ahead, there was too much chance that it could all go wrong."

He had paid off the cabby and sent him away before he realized that the house was dark.

"Nah, then, chirk up," the man had said, driving away. "It'll be all right. Until you start to pay for it."

The house was dark. He couldn't wake them, even Kate would think he was a fool. As he was, he cried out against himself, as he was. Not now, standing there crazed with his haste to see her, touch her, tell her that the waiting time was over, over. Not now, but as he had been with Hall, playing the prize catch, the game to be bagged, as if his future depended on anything but pen and paper and human emotion.

He pulled his eyes from the dark house and started to walk away in the direction the hack had taken. When he had gone a few yards he wheeled and ran back, ringing the bell and beating on the door with a closed fist.

Mr. Hogarth opened it, in his nightshirt. For a blank moment he stared, the candle in his hand held high. Then he set it down on the seat of the hall rack and leaned forward, whispering, a conspirator.

"Run around the corner to your room, that's a good boy, and sober up. I'll just say someone found the wrong house. Quick, now, or we'll never hear the end of it!"

"Is Kate abed? Can't she throw on a wrapper? Oh, sir, I must tell her tonight, tell her myself. Hall's just come through with fourteen pounds a month for the next two years, over and above the rest. We can be married immediately!"

Mr. Hogarth seized both his hands. "Of course you may tell her, of course you needn't wait for morning!"

"God bless you! God bless you!"

But in the same moment, Kate herself came down the stairs clutching her flying wrapper. "I heard, oh, Charles, I heard."

They clung together, mouth to mouth. Her soft body, free of its corset, lay beneath his hands. Giggles and low whisperings sounded from the upper hall, and Mr. Hogarth picked up the candle.

"Come back in the morning," he said, quietly. "Come back to breakfast. I'm very happy, happy for you both."

Charles and Kate did not hear him. Mr. Hogarth took Kate's shoulder, drawing her away. "Come now, dear. Joy or no joy, what will Mother say?"

But Catherine, in the immodesty of flannel nightgown and wrapper, still leaned on Charles with all her full, sweet weight. "She sleeps like a pig," calmly, "you only hear the girls. Oh, Charles, good night. Good night."

Once more, in the dim light, she lifted her lovely face. She closed her eyes, the rich quietude of her lips waiting, unflurried, for their lover's kiss.

Around the corner, in the hired room, Charles knelt by his bed. "Oh, God, thank You. Make me worthy. Thank You."

And when he had stretched out his body in bed, resting his cheek on the pillow as if he rested it on Catherine's soft breast, he whispered again, "Thank You."

The waiting time was over, the time — as he had already, in such short space, begun to remember it — of anguished impatience, of weary pain. A great, calm flood of happiness swept him quickly to the edge of sleep. He did not even remember that he had cried on the road to Chelsea with another sort of happiness altogether. He fell asleep unaware of how vast a part of that happiness sprang from the discovery that he was now, in very truth, impatient, eager, desperately in love.

His distaste for doubts was so great that he would seldom recognize the happiness of a doubt resolved.

❊   5   ❊

But Mrs. Hogarth had her own ideas of what, in propriety, was indicated by the phrase "getting married at once."

At the outset, Charles simply refused to take her seriously. "Seven weeks! But, Mrs. Hogarth, that's absurd. I can get my first number dashed off for Hall and be perfectly free in one week!"

And he held Kate against him, laughing alike at her mother's protests and at hers.

Mrs. Hogarth, however, knew her motherly rights, and Mrs. Dickens supported her. Think of the clothes, the linens to be sewed! And was Charles truly ignorant enough to imagine his bachelor's quarters ready to house those mysterious rites to which they both, with reverent voices, referred as proper housekeeping?

(It was a singular tribute to Catherine Hogarth's beauty that Charles, lover of shipshape tidiness and French polish, had not noticed, until Mrs. Hogarth herself made solemn mention of the art, that her housekeeping was, indeed, almost as vague as his own mother's.)

Mrs. Dickens and Mrs. Hogarth, up to that time, had met infrequently and with marked reserve on both sides. The imminence of the wedding, however, made them wholly at one.

"I shall see to covering the sofa, my dear Mrs. Hogarth. Indeed, I'll oversee the whole arrangement of the little nest, for you've enough on your hands as it is."

"How kind. But isn't it a pity that they're so set on such a plain, tiny wedding? Nothing, really, for my Kate to look back upon."

"Oh, Mrs. Hogarth, how clearly I remember my own. To be sure, my parents' circumstances . . ."

They were in power. Seven weeks it would be.

Seven interminable weeks. Charles had told Kate for a year that she was at the center of his life; told her, and believed it. Now it was true. He resented every moment that kept him from her side.

Even the love-making was changed. Little by little, kisses softened to the inner lip, little by little his hands made desire more explicit. And each new advance met, always, the same shy shrinking, the quivering moment of doubt, and the final childlike acceptance. Yet she never took the initiative, or seduced him beyond the present moment. She was only docile, trusting. Looking into her eyes of soft assent he sometimes felt a delight, sharp as a stab in the flesh, from the knowledge that she was wholly innocent of what they promised.

Oddly enough, he was not far from the truth. Kate Hogarth was a girl of strangely incurious mind.

Nonetheless, she enjoyed the new kind of kissing, and the memory of it was dimly reassuring to her on the evening when Mrs. Hogarth, her nose phenomenally pinched, took it upon herself to explain, though with a modest shrinking from detail, the ultimate humiliation of womanhood.

And Charles, surprised by joy, impatient as the wind, loved Kate more with every breath he drew.

Life, however, demands business as usual. And the habit of work can no more be overthrown by happiness than by trouble. It was on the day after Charles danced on clouds of glory to breakfast with his Kate, and received Mrs. Hogarth's fantastic ultimatum, that — as he put it, long after, in those small words — he "thought of Mr. Pickwick." And by the end of the fortnight, he was writing triumphantly to Hall, "Pickwick is begun in all his might and glory."

For he had thought not only of Mr. Pickwick, but of Mr. Snodgrass, Mr. Tupman, and Mr. Winkle; thought of them, indeed, with such affection that Mr. Winkle's being the only sportsman of the lot appeared to him as no breach of contract, but, rather, as its sole proper fulfillment.

"You see," he explained to Beard, "this gives leeway for variety. Seymour will welcome that, once he's thought it over. He's popular now with this hunting stuff, but, my God, two years of it and people would be bored stiff! Enough sameness to know what you're buying, enough variety to perk up your appetite, that's what people want, and if they don't get it they'll go to another shop."

Beard, who had been a Seymour fan for a good many years, looked at his friend; looked curiously, as if he saw the young, flashing, so certain face for the first time. He was a kind man; he had never taken satisfaction in watching an overconfident rider thrown from his high horse. He started to speak, checked himself, and, instead, took a long, slow swig from his unfinished beer.

No, he thought, let Seymour and the publishers show him where he gets down. That way, he'll be able to tell himself that he simply changed his own mind.

Charles leaned forward, tapping his arm. "Woolgathering? Or don't you agree?"

Beard set down the mug. "I'm a journalist. This humor trade is Greek to me." But he found himself staring once more at the face before him, so searching and yet so certain, so quick with vulnerable life, and still so shrewdly firm.

Suddenly, to his own surprise, he broke into one of his great roars of laughter. "I only 'opes" — he struggled for breath and then started in again — "I only 'opes poor Seymour don't like it too 'ard."

Charles glowed. It had quite slipped his mind that he was hired simply to provide Seymour's pictures with a running text.

The glow persisted through the walk to Chatham that evening. He would have saved time by riding, but Mr. Pickwick needed walking out. He had fetched the first few "slips," the long manuscript sheets in which a sketch went to the printer; he always loved to read aloud his work in progress, and the Hogarths were a gratifying audience.

Little Georgy always sat eying him as if he were a parlor magician whose tricks she was bound to unravel. Mr. Hogarth would nurse his chin, nodding at every touch that had pleased Charles himself most highly. Mary, dear child (and how could one believe that she was now nearly sixteen?), sat perfectly still, always with her hands clasped upon her lap; but straight before her lay a changing scene, and the gray eyes laughed, pitied, wondered in such a miracle of total response that Charles sometimes caught his breath with the sheer pleasure of seeing it. And Kate, although she never laughed unless she caught the infection of the room's laughter, sighed, invariably, when the reading was done and said, "Oh, Charles, that was so nice."

He knew, as he hurried through the early dark, that she would find Mr. Pickwick very nice, and he gave an occasional friendly slap to the bulky folded slips in his hip pocket.

But as soon as he came to the house, he forgot them. They went on the seat of the hatrack, and lay there until it was time for him to go.

Kate opened the door, and she had never been more beautiful. Her hair, newly washed, was shining, soft to the touch, fragrant. She wore a while mull dress, cut deep and square over her lovely bosom, and her face was sweet and calm although she had surely waited for him a full hour past his promised time.

"Oh, Kate," he whispered. "Kate."

She lifted her mouth for his kiss, and that kiss became the sole reality.

Until the next. And the next. The family were really kind, they had left them alone and together far longer than he realized before they all came in, friendly and gregarious as sparrows.

Georgy had invented a new guessing game, and they played it. Mr. Hogarth was seized by a spate of reminiscent anecdote, wholly out of character for him; and Charles listened courteously, and said from time to time, "How interesting, sir." Mrs. Hogarth, her nose like a chisel and her bosom enormous, read him a list of household linens, and Charles, writing his name in the dust on the mantel with his fingertip, said, "You take too much trouble for us."

And it was late, really late. Clearly, they were waiting for him to go, and clearly, he would have no more time with Kate alone.

His abrupt outcry, when it came, startled him more than it appeared to startle anyone else.

"Oh, Mrs. Hogarth, must we bear five weeks more of this nonsense? Forget me, if you must, but ask yourself, as you love Kate, how you justify this senseless delay?"

Mrs. Hogarth sniffed. "Senseless? When a short time ago you were both prepared to wait for months, possibly years? I scarcely feel that I'm the senseless person."

It was Kate who answered for him, her lifted face earnest and innocent as the unexpected, earnest, innocent rush of her soft voice. "Oh, Mama, don't you remember? Back when you were small, how Christmas didn't even seem real in October or November? But, oh, a few weeks, a few days before, it seemed that it would never come!"

The soft, rich pallor of her cheeks had turned to a delicate flushing; her wide, unsubtle eyes were awake, intense. A startling went through Charles's body as he looked at her.

Mrs. Hogarth sniffed again. "Precisely," she said. "The attitude of a child."

"Oh, come, now, my dears," said Mr. Hogarth. He took his watch from his pocket and compared it, pointedly, with the mantel clock. "Hm. Hrm."

Charles heard them both as if they spoke from a distance. He heard his own automatic response, the good-humored laugh, the quizzical reply: "Oh, well, Mrs. Hogarth, you know, 'Unless ye become, ye shall by no means enter . . .'"

He was still seeing Kate.

He saw her still as he walked back through the fog to Furnival's Inn. As his light, swift stride ate the miles, the city grew about him: that nighttime London which always worked so intensely upon his imagination. A drunkard staggered along before him, trailed by his sorry drab. He caught up on them and passed them unseeing. His eyes were still upon Kate: Kate standing before her mother, the lovely sleepwalker's face come so suddenly awake, the violet eyes wide, the cheeks flushed like a child's.

"Christmas didn't matter in October or November . . ."

Once more he fingered the fresh, so simple words in his mind, as his full lips, smiling, quivered with the extremity of his tenderness. His step slackened. He spoke aloud, neither hearing his own voice or attending to the words it had made, as they still hung in his mind, meaningless as the sounds of nature, of wind or of water, once they were spoken.

"She might have been Mary. She might have been Mary's own dear little self."

He walked on through the night, smiling, a young man deeply in love.

❊   6   ❊

AND FAR from being too long, the five resented weeks turned out to be scarcely enough, if he were to arrange seven days of complete freedom for the honeymoon. Parliament was in session, and there was out-of-town reporting as well. There was a sketch to be done each week, he was turning one of the more successful sketches into a farce, and in one way or another he and John Hullah, a composer friend of Fanny's fiancé, had got themselves up to the neck with work on an operetta, *The Village Coquettes*.

Furthermore, the second *Pickwick* was due. The first had not made the splash he expected, but now he had found his villain — and such a villain! At every wild word that jerked from the inspired mouth of Alfred Jingle, Charles himself was moved to such convulsive laughter that his sides ached. And still, strangely, the piece grew more slowly than any piece of writing he had ever turned out.

Nor could one just go at it whenever one had the time. To get Jingle talking, one's own spirits must first be screwed up to top party pitch. Indeed, the further Charles went on with the number, the more he was forced to accept an inexplicable fact: this fourteen pounds monthly, this easy extra money was turning, somehow or other, into the hardest money he had ever earned.

It was really fortunate that he had on hand that good unsold story, "The Dying Clown." It could be told to the Club by some strolling player at an inn. A month's free pay, it would amount to, and right in the good old picaresque tradition as the whole show was shaping up.

But even that comforting prospect had its vexatious side; for Seymour would need even more managing than ever, seeing that a good, telling, dramatic plate of the dying man would be needed. Hall would help bring him around, to be sure; still, the bringing around would be in itself one more job. It was excessively odd, when you came to think of it, that such a nervous, moody chap as Seymour should be so set on comic shootings as the end-all of graphic art.

However, Hall could manage. It had turned out a blessing in disguise, really, to have had that story rejected. Kate could never have understood if he'd had to work during their honeymoon. Even the constant, reassuring little notes of these last weeks ("My mouse . . . I should love to have you by me so much . . . a million, million kisses") did not always ensure him the serene, soft welcome that he so wanted, needed, when he could get to her at last.

And for the past week, to top it all, he had been housed with a foul cold and a swollen face. Now that he was free to get back to Chelsea at last, he could only hope that little Mary, with her odd, instinctive understanding of a man's alien world and a man's work, Mary, with her quaint, motherly knack of lifting Kate's spirits, had managed to keep that lovely face serene, to help his dear girl keep those sorry moods at bay.

He gave a final, dubious dab to his still swollen nose, and brushed his hair and his suit before the glass. At least, he comforted himself, it would not be long before his dear had the pride and responsibility of her own little establishment to keep her occupied and happy as a lark the livelong day.

He set out for Chelsea tender with anticipation, eager with longing; yet prepared, if need be, to set the evening on its course with a kind, firm hand.

There was no need. He knew it, from her first kiss.

She said, "Oh, wicked boy, to take a cold!" And standing with her arms about him and her cheek rested on his shoulder, she laughed with the sweet, aimless laughter of a child. "Oh, Charles," she said, "I've missed you so." But there was no rebuke, no sorry sulking in her voice; only the gaiety of a child who cries, "No school today! No horrid old school today!"

Her gaiety made her beauty breathtaking. Her face was lovely in quietness, but now, flushed with that unusual brilliance, that holiday excitement of a birthday child, it was beauty beyond beauty, an amazement.

Perhaps his own face, responding to that beauty, mirrored a little of it. For, between the long, long kisses, she would stare into his face as he into hers, and whisper in a voice small as breath, "Oh, Charles, you are so very handsome."

The hour alone that the family granted them was a timeless eternity of wonder, and it was a fleeting instant. When it was done, and the family trooped in upon them, they could only stare about for the first moments with faces empty and confused, too suddenly wakened, dazed by light.

Dazed, yet even in that first moment, unresentful. Almost at once Kate was laughing again, the charming, undirected laughter of a happy child. And Charles, after his first stunned, waking pause, felt a surge of affection that even embraced Mrs. Hogarth.

"Welcome me with bells and cannon, I feel like Lazarus. Better — I'll be bound he didn't have to keep honking his nose in the tomb. Never mind, I've risen, and Kate says that a swollen nose is just what my manly beauty needs to set it off."

The violet eyes became completely round, the red, sweet lips dropped ajar. "Why, that's a *story*."

The dear, the lovely, lovely ridiculous dear! "What shall we play? Twenty Questions? Up, Jenkins? Georgy, choose for us!"

And the evening, set aswing, was gay as a Christmas. Kate had never been so merry. She romped through every game, clumsy and sweet as a newborn colt in pasture. She made one pun after another, each more laborious and meaningless than the last, and when they laughed at her absurdity she laughed the hardest of all, intoxicated with her success.

At the peak of the evening, Charles had never seen her in such spirits. She was a birthday child, wild with the day's triumph, a spring lamb at play, a tipsy bacchante. It was delightful. Charles urged her on, with clowning, with jokes pitched at the level which Shrimp found most hilarious, until she gasped for breath and showered combs and bracelets, the rare, bright flush on her rosy cheeks and her eyes brilliant and brimming.

And Mary spoiled it. Gentle, quick-laughing little Mary started abruptly to her feet and ran across the room. "Kate! Stop it! Kate!"

The small, straight features were pinched, the clear, light voice rang shrill, almost shrewish. "Kate! Stop it, Kate!" The gray eyes were not sun on oceans now. They were frozen; more incomprehensibly yet, one would have sworn, if the thought had made any sense at all, that they were frozen with fear.

Charles was most unpleasantly baffled and vexed. The very fact that he was baffled vexed him beyond endurance, for it was, somehow, counter to all the rules. Quite aside from his own quick insights, a wordless communication existed between him and this child not yet sixteen — a communication closer than he had ever felt for any friend.

What did she think she was at? What ailed her? There was not one drop of jealousy in her nature; he would have staked his life on it. Yet now — there was no other word for it — she was making a scene.

And when Kate was so happy, too! Why, she had been so teary and low at his last visit that he had — yes, he could admit it now — dreaded this evening almost as much as he looked forward to it. It was too bad, really it was! From whatever nonsensical child's notion it sprang, it must not be encouraged.

His head jerked up, and his lips worked nervously. He took two sharp steps to their side.

"Let Kate enjoy herself, Mary." He had given an order, and in an angrier voice than he intended. At once he was sorry. For now there would be Mary's tears, and the knowledge that he had caused them.

He said, "I'm sorry," in a voice that came out, to his helpless surprise, still angrier; and he stared at the carpet.

However, it was Kate, not Mary, who suddenly started to cry.

"Why, my Tatie! Oh, my darling Mouse!"

The tears stopped almost as soon as they had begun, but the violet eyes, opening, wandered past him as if he had not spoken. She looked at Mary, and spoke to her, as if the two were quite alone.

"I'm not excited now," she said.

Like a child she held out her hand to Mary, who took it and stroked it.

Charles stared at them, and then about the room. Only Mrs. Hogarth looked interested; and she was smiling.

"Dear Catherine," she remarked to nobody in particular. "So easily overwrought, so sensitive. My own girlhood, re-embodied before my eyes."

It all made absolutely no sense. He looked at Kate, who now smiled back at him, drowsily, serenely. At his Kate, his lovely, waiting sleeper; Kate whose greatest range of emotion, beyond that deep sweet bond between them, was no more than the reach between a child's merriment and the childish, silly little moods that she was learning so nicely to overcome. Like a man who has got out of the wrong side of his bed in the dark, and finds the familiar become madly unfamiliar — *What did I stumble on? What in God's name is this?* — his mind blundered in the frightening, infuriating dark that had been, only a few moments past, such a jolly evening.

And Mary, dear little Mary, Mary, upon whose responsive face he had come to depend as if it housed his own soul made new, Mary was the strangest part of it all. She came close to him now. She smiled. Her gray eyes lifted directly to his face, sad as the eyes of a mother who smiles encouragement at the child who will not get well. She spoke, her voice easy and light: the mother's voice, tenderly controlled. "We haven't had a game of charades for a long time."

He hated questions with no swift, clear answers. He hated confusion. The boy with his shipshape garret, the man who filled Gad's Hill with mirrors to flood every room with the light of reflected suns, lived as we all live, in symbols. He had not yet learned how to splinter life's terrible complexities into that host of other lives which generations would love, as he loved them, for their blessed simplicity.

He hung his head, like a sulky child. He spoke without hearing how the words came out so thinly voiced, pettish.

"I don't mind."

Yet once they had chosen sides, he was all invention and energy. Indeed, when he and Robert and Georgy had done their word, the others refused to compete.

"You outdid yourself, Charles," said Mr. Hogarth, still laughing. "The contrast would be too depressing. Let's go back to Twenty Questions."

Charles wiped his forehead. "I'm played out. I couldn't even guess one of Kate's questions."

The charade had served its purpose. The brief, unhappy, puzzling episode had been forced so completely out of mind that he did not even recall it when, once more in that evening, Mary proved oddly vexing.

The conversation had turned to the final wedding plans. Charles sat beside Kate on the sofa. Her hand was on his knee and he traced its outline as he listened.

"I still say that it's a pity to have no guests," said Mrs. Hogarth. "Our Catherine will be such a lovely bride."

Kate yawned. "Oh, Mama. I only wish funny little Fred was big enough to be best man, the way Mary's attending me. Even one outsider is more than Charles and I really want."

"Oh, Tatie pet, that reminds me." His hand closed on hers for emphasis. "Do take care that you never let it slip to Beard that he was our second choice. He wouldn't be *hurt*, you know, but he's happier as it is. I must say that I still think it's nonsense, our not having Macrone. Why must a best man be a bachelor?"

"Why, it's the rule."

"Oh, Lord. Ah, well, I daresay Macrone will appreciate being the only guest."

And Mary spoke. "Isn't Mr. Beard your best friend?"

"One of them, certainly. Why?" He glanced toward her as he spoke and saw a face like a disappointed child's. "Why, what's the matter, dear?"

She looked away. "I suppose you like Mr. Macrone?"

"He's the best of chaps, Mary. Why do you ask?"

"I only wondered."

Bewildered, unpleasantly bewildered, he persisted. "But you see, child, the important thing is that we owe him such a deal."

And her face remained oddly bereft, defenseless. "I see."

"It doesn't really change the plans, Mary. One lone guest isn't a crowd. I couldn't ask a fellow to be best man and then exclude him outright when the ladies pronounced him ineligible."

"You're overtired, Mary," said Mrs. Hogarth crisply. "Of course it would be highly injudicious to exclude Mr. Macrone!" And she favored Charles with a smile.

The smile, however, was as confusing as Mary's sad gray stare. It was not merely an approving smile; it was shrewd, confidential. It said that Mrs. Hogarth and her son-in-law knew what they were at better than most.

Charles looked from the one face to the other. Mary flushed, and bent her head over her embroidery ring. Her needle moved in sharp, rapid little flashes. Kate leaned upon his arm and yawned again, an unashamed, luxurious yawn. "Aa-uh! Mercy!"

He looked at his watch, and laughed aloud. "Good heavens! You should have sent me packing an hour ago. No wonder poor little Kate is yawning and Mr. Hogarth is yawning and Mary's looking like a mute at a funeral!"

He stood up, drawing Kate with him. "Come, love, and say good night to me properly."

In the hall he held her against him. "It's been such a happy evening, my Tatie. It was so good to see the bright little face that knew how sad I'd been, missing my love so many days."

"Thank you." The words spoken scarcely above a whisper, grateful, a child receiving praise.

"My Kate. My sweet."

He kissed her, pushing back the heavy curls from the smooth, soft cheek. And still, before the kiss was ended, he felt a heavy rush of weariness, and wondered that such a happy evening should have left him so tired at the end of it.

She leaned upon him with all that full sweet weight that he loved, and he loved it still, in its trustful repose; only, because he was so tired, it did not make him feel strong tonight. She was whispering, and he bent his head to hear.

"Not even a week."

"Yes, yes. No more good nights, my sweet. And when I have to work, I can look up and see my angel, sewing or reading, right there by my side."

"Oh, yes. Yes."

It occurred to neither of them that Kate did not care for reading or sewing either. They clung together once more, mouth to mouth. He smelled the fragrance of her skin, her hair. His hands loved her.

"Good night, little wife. Little wife."

He walked back to Furnival's Inn, because it was necessary for him to be at the *Chronicle* office in the morning. The walk felt extremely long and he told himself that he was not yet properly over his cold.

He was dropping off to sleep when he saw, in the bright, floating images that came, always, between waking memory and dream, Mary and Mrs. Hogarth, side by side. He saw the smile that said, "We know which side our bread is buttered on, don't we?" He saw the sad gray eyes.

He started up. He lit the lamp and walked restlessly about the room until the anger born of the abrupt understanding should have a chance to subside.

Did they think that he had forgotten good old Beard, that he was using, *using* Macrone? Could Mary, pure-hearted little Mary think that? Mrs. Hogarth, of course. But Mary? Damn it, the dearest children are prigs, doubtless he'd been a fine one himself once, but when it came to misunderstanding a gesture of simple gratitude . . . It was too ugly, too ridiculous. And there was nothing one could say, with any dignity, to make her *see*.

He walked about the room for some time until he said, in an easy, casual voice, "Good Lord, what a stew over nothing. How can I be such a fool? What earthly difference does it make? The poor child, the poor, silly little dear."

He blew out the light and got into bed. When he had been asleep for an hour he woke, sweating from a nightmare. The dark streets kept turning into blind alleys, it was late at night and he had only got halfway to Somers Town when he remembered, and had to start back to Warren's Blacking, 30 Strand. But he could not find the way, he blundered against walls and into dark courts, crying.

The sound of his own voice woke him, before the door pushed open and Frederick stood beside him.

"For heaven's sake, wake up. Are you awake?"

"What, what?"

The familiar, oily little chuckle brought him to himself.

"Sorry, old boy. Lobster for supper. Get back to bed."

"Tell me first though, who's Bob Fagin?"

"Who?"

"That's who you were yelling for. Bob Fagin."

Charles, fully awake, laughed. "I knew him when I wasn't much older than Alfred. Just another boy."

"Well, sleep on your stomach," said Frederick. "You gave me the creeps."

❋   7   ❋

By MORNING he had forgotten the dream. He had not, however, forgotten Mrs. Hogarth's smile or Mary's sorrowing eyes, and a rage of furious self-justification mounted hourly.

A rage of self-justification, and of loss. Startling loss, for he had not realized before how much he valued the child's unqualified love, her unquestioning trust. Yet she was a child; he could not storm down upon her because she had, in effect, called him a toady — implied that such talent as he had and all the grueling work he did were not enough to let him stand on his own merits; that he could only advance by using — by God — *using* his friends.

Thank God, Mr. Hogarth, true gentleman that he was, had no such base notions. Thank God that his high-minded Kate was so far removed by her own nature from such ugliness that she had seen nothing, nothing of what lay before her very eyes.

He had not any time to spare and he knew it. Nonetheless, early in that afternoon he started back to Chelsea. He would see his own high-minded Kate. And, somehow or other, kindly, he would set poor little Mary right.

Not Kate or the servant, but Mary opened the door to him. She looked very tidy and pale; she also looked smaller, younger than the picture his unhappy anger had been making. She had not expected him, of course. Her small face startled, seeing him, and at once she gave a quick, cautious glance behind her. She leaned forward, speaking rapidly and low.

"Everyone's out but Kate. She's having a little nap. Charles, I was impertinent to you last night, and I want to apologize."

He looked at her, so inaccurately remembered; the child, the gentle child.

Her voice rushed on. "Those snippy, *hinting* little questions. But, Charles, they came out in spite of me. Because Mr. Beard and Mr. Mitton both are such old friends, and you haven't known Mr. Macrone long, and only through his being your publisher . . ."

She broke off, working her fingertips together, staring at them. She did not see the dangerous blaze shoot up in the blue eyes before her. She went on as if she had not noticed her own brief silence or his.

"As if, you see, even with something like getting married, something that's really private and — and holy, you were still thinking about all those things you do think about so much. Money, and, oh, getting well known and all. And I hated it because — because it was a puzzle to me. Not being the way I'd always thought you were — and, you see, many people sometimes puzzle me . . . but never you. Never before."

The blue fire was frozen; the impotent fury of self-justification, the irrational, anguishing sense of loss made his eyes like eyes in a remarkable painting of a man in rage. They stared, unmoving, across the child's sleek, bowed head.

And the light voice went on, warming, leaping, the quaint, formal speech and the strong inner joy making an effect for which — since he was unfamiliar with the music of Mozart — he could find no parallel.

"Oh, and then, Charles, I saw! I was in bed, and I couldn't sleep for puzzling still. And all suddenly I remembered how quickly you and I got to be friends, real friends, though I'm only young, and a girl, and ignorant. I remembered how you look at people, really look, and of how you talk to everyone of us differently, and still not pretending — all out of your own real self, only fetching out the different parts to suit. Oh, Charles, I *saw!*"

The ice was thawed, the fire gone out. The blue eyes, limpid with the gentled self-love, the healing wonder, bent to the girl's face. Her head was still bowed in the intense effort of articulate thought. He could see only her smooth forehead and her eyelids, blue-white and fragile like the eyelids of a sleeping child. He touched the sleek bound hair, the cool, still cheek with delicate fingertips.

His voice came low, the humble, soft voice of prayer.

"What did you see?"

"Oh, Charles, how stupid I've been! Why, it can make no difference to you whether a person can help you or not. He's still the same person, he's only another person you've *seen* — really seen. If you wanted Mr. Macrone for your best man, it was only because you'd grown fond of him quickly just as you did with me. And so — oh, Kate is coming, that was her door! — Charles, now that you understand why I was so foolish and hateful will you please, please excuse me?"

Charles shut his eyes. He trembled in himself, and not only with the restored self-esteem, but with all his integrity, humbly. Mary, speaking from the blind love of a child, had still come closer to his truth than one life often comes to another's. *My child*, he thought. *My child.*

Yet the repeated words were not joyful, but like a foreboding. They sounded in his mind as if they expressed the knowledge that such true insight and blind faith were qualities of youth, doomed to short life like the earliest loveliness of spring. His lips formed the words: *my child.* And they were like a wish that the child need never come to maturity's bluntings and confusions, that she might walk out of life still so full of pure, true insight and blind, gentle faith.

The wish, born not only of self-love but of the writer's unending impulse to check the fluid, continual changes of the living world, passed through him like an underwater shock; too cruel, too tender, too shocking to be recognized for what it was. Yet he felt it, and disowned it in one awful instant, before he leaped to the top, top surface of his life like a drowning man forcing his way up to the blessed air.

He caught her against him with a brother's arm. He kissed the top of her tidy little head.

"Dear child," he said, "I was a great baby to have my feelings hurt and you were another, to trouble for me so."

And at once he had released her and was bounding up the stairs to meet Kate coming down.

They went into the drawing room with their arms about each other's waists. His left hand patted Mary's lean little rib cage, his right pressed upon Kate's intoxicating softness.

"My little household," he said. "We three, and Fred. What a good little family!"

[110]

Six days later, Charles and Kate were married in the parish church near her house. As he waited on the church steps with Beard, Charles was shaking. He laughed as he held out his hand, to show the tremor. "I only 'opes as I makes a good end. 'Angman better make it nippy, or I'll jump before the drop's pulled."

But his color was high and his eyes were brilliant. When the Hogarths' carriage drew up he ran to it. "Oh, dear God, Kate, you're so lovely."

"Don't swear, naughty Charles. And oh, mind, don't crush my beautiful dress beforehand!"

She wore a crown of white roses, and her face was timid, and triumphant. As Charles looked, the trembling left him and he stood straight, with his head high.

As he went into the church with Beard, as he took his place at the foot of the altar steps, he gave the impression of being a far taller young man than he actually was.

Kate, too, was standing tall as she approached, her crowned head proudly high, her lovely face composed. Yet her measured step was slower than the step she had rehearsed. She advanced with proud head and timid feet, and as she came close Charles saw that her fingers had nipped up a bit of her father's coat-sleeve and pinched it close.

A tender smile touched his mouth. Woman, crowned queen, timid child, she came to him; and with every step she took he stood taller, felt quieter, more strong. He was not even disturbed when she stumbled at the first little stair of the sanctuary and had to clutch both hands on her father's arm, with a gasp of embarrassment. No, in that moment he even loved her for stumbling, loved the flushed, exquisite, vulnerable face lifted to beg his forgiveness when there was nothing to forgive. He looked back at her as if his eyes would pour that superabundant strength he felt into her own. His lips formed the soundless, absurd words of consolation: "Nobody noticed." They moved together, and the clergyman stood before them.

"Dearly beloved, we are gathered together here in the sight of God, and in the face of this company . . ."

What words are more moving, more evocative, except perhaps those others: *Man that is born of woman* . . . ? Charles heard the words and loved them. He saw Kate and loved her. His emotional heart dedicated itself gravely to its unexamined God and to the years before him and Catherine, his wife.

And his strong actor's voice, placed low, full without vibrato, filled the church, in the perfect control that gives each row in a theater the illusion that it is the last which hears without effort. His heart all unselfconscious dedication, his voice delighting in its superb skill, he gave the holy words all that he had: "I, Charles, take thee, Catherine, to my wedded wife . . . for better, for worse, for richer, for poorer, in sickness and in health . . ."

One clause of that vow, at least, was never put to test.

It was a sunny morning. As they came back to the house for the wedding breakfast, a lark was shouting high over the orchard across the way. Except for Kate's dress, the champagne, and the shining faces, it might have been any simple family party, Beard and Macrone the familiar, well-liked guests.

There were few toasts, and none of them wordy. "Happy years." "Charles and Catherine, bless them." Toward the end of the meal, Charles's father got up, with his wave of the eyeglass that portended oratory. However, he only said, "Dear children, as you set out upon the path that is strewn with roses and their thorns, may you find—er —in a word, may you be happy."

And he blew his nose, while everyone clapped.

Then Kate went upstairs to change to her traveling dress and the women went with her. The men avoided sentiment, argued politics, and finished off the champagne. As the voices on the stair told them that the bride was coming back, an odd self-conscious silence fell on them all.

Fan came first into the room. She had grown thin in the last year, but it became her. Her dark eyes looked strikingly large in her narrow face. Charles went up to her quickly and took her hand, speaking low.

"Once I said that I'd never forgive you, Fan. I hope you've forgotten. It wasn't so."

She threw her arms about his neck. "Oh, Charlie, I . . . I'm glad it turned out for the best."

"Dear Fan." They had been small, in a dark garden, looking at an enormous star. And long, long after, he stood in the nipping wind and waited by the Academy stairs. He and Fan, wholly changed, and unchanged. "Dear Fan."

But she spoiled the moment. Her eyes became wet with the tears that women weep at weddings, and she whispered, "Charlie, always *try* to be kind to her."

He tried to cover his annoyance with a smile. He spoke in the tone of their bygone mutual teasing. "Fan, where's your theater sense? You've stolen Mrs. Hogarth's line."

He turned away quickly. Kate was standing in the door. He went to her and circled her with his arm. He lifted his head, held up his free hand for attention.

"Thank you, my dears, all of you, for your love. My thanks to God and to her parents for my wife, my lovely girl. God bless you all. And now, as you fetch out the rice and old shoes and whatever else is wanted, do save the sniffles until we're gone, my dears, keep the scene gay, and remember that Chalk is not the Antipodes and we'll be back in a week's time, not much aged or changed, to keep on loving you just as we do now."

For the fraction of a second's silence, his lifted head and his hand continued to hold them still. He looked at the Governor, at Mary, at small Georgy; at Fan, at good old Beard, at kind Macrone. With total inconsistency he drew out his handkerchief, wiped his eyes, and blew his nose. Then he nodded and tossed out his hand before him, the director's hand: *Places, please. Curtain.*

The kisses, the few inevitable tears, the babble of affectionate words, jests, blessings, began. He bent his head.

"Come, darling. Now, with the tide still rising and the sun out full. This is the time."

No member of that wedding party ever forgot the happiness in his face and in Kate's as he handed her into the carriage that was to drive them away.

※ *8* ※

THE RAIN STARTED before they reached Chalk. They had left the Mail at Rochester and taken a closed carriage. Charles let the side window down.

"Oh, this will be good to walk in. Wait until we smell it mixed with the sea. Nothing brings the ocean alive like rain. It makes it better than a crowd, than a street full of faces."

Kate shivered in the wet draft. "Do you want that window? It's so cold."

"Here, come in the tent." He spread his cape and wrapped it about them both.

"You're mussing me most dreadfully."

"Slip down lower. So. You just took a vow at God's holy alter, dear girl, to be mussed both dreadfully and interminably."

"Charles! Let me sit properly. Suppose the coachman looked in?"

"Do you want to make him think I married you for your money?"

Her face was a sweet blank.

"He won't look, dear. He knows a bridal pair at sight and he wants his tip."

"Are you sure?"

"Perfectly sure. See, love, now we have the good air and you're warm. Kiss me, my own dear."

His mouth covered her mouth. Under the cape his hands found their treasure. A quiver went through the soft body and he moved back his head a little. He saw the heavy eyelids flown wide open, and the violet eyes were not the eyes of imagined virginal innocence, but full of ignorance and fear. They stared as the small girl stares, unwillingly, at the exhibitionist who has cornered her in the little grove behind the school. The fear was infectious. For an answering moment Charles, too, was uncertain. Not over the petticoated, corseted, constricted sweet of the present, so limited by the decencies; it was to the arrival that his doubt leapt ahead — to the night.

His voice shook. "Tatie-Mouse. Dear Kate, dear wife. It's all right."

The fear went out of her eyes. A blank, violet acquiescence came in its place. The sleepy lids dropped once more, the moist red lips lifted.

"Oh, Kate, my love."

They huddled together in the sheltering cloak. They did not feel the driving rain as it freshened and blew in across their faces. Their eyes shut, their lips engaged, they clung together in the initiating rapture that he had so often imagined. Their kisses were wonder in themselves, and, in their promise, peace.

It was highly unfortunate that the functions of Kate's body had always been unpredictable, and more unfortunate that Charles believed the twenty-eight-day cycle to be as fixed in woman as the waxing and waning of the moon. Before they were fully unpacked, Kate withdrew, and when she came back her cheeks were flushed and her eyes averted.

She said, "I have a headache."

Charles stared, utterly incredulous. At once he was filled with murderous fury against Mrs. Hogarth. The woman had known, when she set her precious, arbitrary date. While she mewed about proper housekeeping and the dust gathered on her mantelpiece, she had known.

"Charles, you look so strange. Are you angry?"

"Dear love, with you?"

Nor was he angry with her. What little Mrs Hogarth had seen fit to tell her child had doubtless been saved for the last minute. Kate was only the other victim.

"Lie down and rest, dear," he said, "while I get this place livably shipshape."

It was, nonetheless, peculiarly unfortunate that Charles, who had never known what it was to be bored, should have learned so much about boredom in the first five days of his marriage.

The wind and the rain kept on, delightful, filled with the live, salt smell of the tidal flats. However, he discovered, Kate did not care much for walking, even in fine weather; and she had inflexible ideas about nice days and horrid days. She submitted with obvious reluctance to being read to, and when he suggested a game instead she sighed and said that she was not clever enough for games that were made up for just two people alone. The conversations, one-sided, were heavily stillborn; yet when he went out to stretch his legs and get a breath of the good live air she was fretful and lachrymose.

"You've been such a time, I thought you'd never come back. How slowly time goes here, doesn't it?"

Still, he bore almost three days of it before he bought pens and paper in the village and fetched out the manuscript of *The Village Coquettes*, which, thank God, he had thrust into his valise at the last moment.

She interrupted him aimlessly but continually, and the bits he read to her sounded even flatter in the reading-aloud than they had when he set them down, which was saying a good deal. One can work in company, or in solitude; but not, Charles now discovered, in a room where there is neither the one or the other.

Continually, he heard himself making the sort of suggestions that a wearied mother makes to a convalescent child.

"Wouldn't you like me to buy you a length of cloth and some needles and thread? Have we enough dusters, for instance?"

And the loose little hands would pick fretfully at the gray skirt.

"Oh, Charles, you're so restless. Of course Mama has provided us with dusters."

The clock had a loud, creaky tick. The room was too hot near the fire, and musty away from it. He told himself that she was lovely. He told himself that he was amused and enchanted to discover that she used curlpapers to produce those soft, lustrous ringlets. It was, in fact, disillusioning; and he would gladly have exchanged a face that gathered into itself all the beauty of womankind from the dawn of time for the sound of one hearty laugh from the ugliest girl alive.

Worst of all, a self-conscious chill was upon even the daytime love-making.

Toward the last, Charles was too wretched to wish the time over or believe that it would ever end. Like hell, it was not an everlast-ingness but the one awful, changeless moment of eternity, without beginning or end. He had never been free, they would never return to Furnival's Inn; there had never been and never would be anything but the hideous inactive boredom of *now*.

He was quite hopeless on that final morning of his misery. He woke early and took a long, stiff walk along the cliffs before breakfast, to get his necessary exercise and still avoid the moping that would come if he took it after Kate awoke. He walked hard, with his face lifted, but he did not even notice that the rain had given place to a light, blowing fog and that southwest, over the brightening water, the sky was clearing.

As he came back into their room he bore down hard on the knob to quiet the turning of the latch, praying that Kate would still be asleep. She slept late — and heavily, breathing through her mouth.

But she was at the dressing table, still in her full white nightgown. The six ugly twists of paper were gone, and she was stroking her brush around a curl on a forefinger. She turned to him with a timid, eager smile.

"You went for a walk. Was it nice?"

"Just a short walk. I thought you'd still be asleep."

"It's clearing, isn't it? We can go out together today."

"Why, so it is. That's odd. I hadn't noticed."

He glanced back from the window to her face and started. Had it been like this from the first moment he came back to the room? Had he really not seen this, either?

"Why, Charles, what is it? What are you staring so about?"

"Kate, you look so beautiful. You always do, but not so — so *damned* beautiful."

And she laughed aloud, filling the room with the sound of blessed, full, spontaneous laughter. "Oh, wicked, cursing Charles."

Yet Charles himself did not laugh. He could only go on staring at her with eyes that grew more brilliant by the second. At last he made an odd, questioning little gesture, his hands thrust forward, palms uppermost. "Kate?"

She blushed and looked away.

"How . . . how do you feel, darling?"

Her answer was a whisper. "Oh, quite well. I . . . that nasty old headache is all gone."

Charles, to his total consternation, burst into tears.

"Oh, Kate, my love, my loveliest. Oh, God, have I been unbearable these last days, have I been very hard to live with? Never mind now, dear. Never mind. Stand up. So. So. Yes."

And Kate, too, wept. "I hope you didn't think . . . I . . . oh, dear, I don't even know how much unmarried men know or what it's proper to say . . . but, you see, there are girls who just can't plan . . . count on . . . Oh, Charles, you've not been angry with me? You do love me, truly, truly?"

He said, "Don't cry, dear. It's all back of us. Don't cry. Look up, my Kate. Show me your lovely eyes."

She was all, and more, than the waiting time had imagined. The innocent wonder, the acquiescence, the astonishment of touch all, all leaped far beyond simple fulfillment of the dream. And he was strong and sure in himself as he had prayed to be.

He was gentle, too. Before the full tide of passion had swept him away, he got up from her side. He wanted all the light that was in the room, he longed to see her lying in that light, bathed in it; and yet he knew that it would make her afraid.

He went to the windows, and with hands that shook a little he closed the shutters, making the room dark as earliest dawn, almost as dark as night.

❊ 9 ❊

THERE WERE no backward glances. A flaw of character can sometimes act as a virtue; and Charles, at least, would never spoil a present joy with probing and questioning.

They did not become better acquainted. They had indeed, little time for anything but love-making. Nonetheless, what time was left passed gaily, and in that tender laughter for the lack of which he had recently been so lost to himself.

They hired a gig and tooled about the country lanes, with Charles, an absurdly incapable driver, wholly at the mercy of a wild little nag whose sense of fun rivaled his own. Though Kate could tremble and weep at a disapproving glance, she had a curious courage that was almost phlegm in the face of physical danger. As the addlepated pony darted from left-hand hedge to right, and switched them around corners on two wheels, she and Charles laughed like children on a carnival roundabout.

The sun shone, the villagers stared, Charles waved his hat and Kate her handkerchief. They risked their lives so for three afternoons, and each was more delightful than the last.

They drove to Rochester and found, in a shop, a game of tiddledy-winks, at which they both proved to be phenomenally clumsy and well matched. When they were not being whirled in their gig around the outer edge of extinction, or eating, or making love, they played at tiddledywinks — Kate grave, Charles hilarious, and the neatly annotated score sheet, never weighted more than a game or two on the one side or the other, lying between them.

"Now for the clash of skill," he would cry. "Will Charles be champion of Chalk? Will Kate keep the crown? Hold your breaths, here comes the play!"

He had quite forgotten that the waking and forming of his lovely Catherine's mind had ever played a part in his dream of love's fulfillment. He was happy as people seldom are in a lifetime. Sometimes as he looked up, across the little table with its red and blue counters, its glass cup, and saw Kate's face, his laughter died away in a hush of pure happiness that was like prayer.

Perhaps only those who can, on occasion, live completely in the present ever know such happiness. Perhaps it always comes too high. In any event, Charles did not look ahead, or wonder if the small rooms at Furnival's Inn might not be better fitted to further that beginning union of flesh and heart, and the laughter and the love-making flourish better, if he sent Fred back to the Governor and suggested that, for a bit, they could do without Mary.

In the end, alas, they also left the set of tiddledywinks below-stairs for the night, in their landlady's parlor, and quite forgot it as they packed to go away.

In London, they found the door of his suite locked and there was no answer to his knock and cry, "Hallo, there, Fred! We're home."

He fumbled the key from his pocket. "I hate to think how things will look if Fred's been back from his stay with Father for any time."

"Oh, I'll tidy it!"

He swung their valises through the opened door and turned back to her. "Put your arms around my neck, Tatie, and hold fast. We must do things properly."

But Kate was not slender, and all Charles's strength was in his wiry walker's legs. He was gasping and laughing at once as he lifted her over the threshold, in mock exhaustion.

"I couldn't spare an ounce, sweet, but if you will let me be a shade coarse, you're an easier bedful than armful."

"Charles! What a thing to say!"

But his eyes were already policing the room sharply.

"Amazing! Neat as a pin. The devoted mamas must have been in fierce competition."

Then he saw the note upon the table. Such tidy, precise little writing, like the small voice itself made visible. "For you Kate, from Mary."

She read it through with a smile. "Mama had to bring her here early, and she's walking about with Fred until they find us back. She says she's got chops to do for our supper."

She crumpled it a bit and tossed it toward the grate, where it fell short. She untied her bonnet and let it drop on the nearest chair. She gave an odd, short sigh. "Why, I needn't tidy, or shop, or anything, need I?" she said. "It's all done."

Absently, Charles picked up the hat.

It was a devastating little bonnet, trimmed with a white silk rose and trailing black velvet ribbons to tie beneath the chin. He was still turning it in his hands, when the laughter sounded on the outside stair: Mary's clear peal, and Fred's oily chuckle.

He opened the door. "We're home, dears, safe and sound." And Kate, beside him, said, "Oh, Mary, we've had the *nicest* holiday!"

"Kate, darling Kate, you look so wonderful. All . . . oh! . . . all *shiny!*" The light voice so tender, so full of love.

Was it possible that for a single instant, just as he had started to lift his Kate over their threshold, he had fancied that perhaps they would be happier without Fred, without Mary; that even Kate herself would be better pleased if they were to start out alone? Why, the very suggestion would have broken Kate's poor little heart.

Without noticing what he did, Charles dropped the bonnet back onto the same chair from which he had just tidied it away. He seized Fred's hand. "Did you keep at those lessons like a good fellow without me by to prod you? To be sure you did!" He extended his left to Mary. "And you, dear child, how you've shined our house. And chops, too! It's capital, we must have a drop of wine with them for this first evening we're all together."

Yet though the arrangement was, in actual fact, new, and to be celebrated, recognized with a drop of wine, it felt to Charles, even in that moment, sweetly familiar. It was as if he and Kate had only come home, after a week's absence, to the good little household that was theirs of long custom.

"Mary," he said impulsively, "you know, you've always lived here with us."

She smiled, her thin child's smile. "I know it. Isn't it funny, and nice?"

The still gray eyes and the blue eyes met, smiling.

Kate said, "What in the world are you talking about? We've just this minute got here."

Charles looked away to her and laughed. He put his arm about her and held her close, caressing her shoulder. His hand loved her, even while, once more, his eyes found their way home.

✳ ✳ ✳ ✳ ✳ ✳ ✳ ✳

BOOK IV
Charles and Mary

✳ ✳ ✳ ✳ ✳ ✳ ✳ ✳

Tom Beard, alone of Charles's friends, was at all surprised by the new domestic arrangements. About a week after the honeymoon, he leaned both elbows on a chophouse table and eyed Charles with wonder.

"But, for God's sake," he said, "where do you *write?*"

Charles laughed. "By the fire. Happy company helps any work, Tom. Ignore the words and enjoy the tune — that's all the trick it takes."

"God forbid," said Beard, piously.

Charles reached across the table and gave Beard's shoulder an encouraging slap.

"You're young, yet," he said. "Cheer up, Tom, bless you, you'll fall in love yourself, one day."

One fell in love, one married, and established a good little household: it was as simple as that.

Nonetheless, there was a single evening, near the start, when Charles wondered if it was all as simple as that.

Mary had gone to spend a few days with her parents. As Charles walked home that evening, he fully expected to find things in rather a mess. Mary's knack for housekeeping was unobtrusive, but Charles was far too fond of shipshape, spanking tidiness to take it for granted where he found it; nor was he fool enough to impute the delightful orderly shine upon Furnival's Inn to his sweet, disorganized Kate.

Yet when one realized that it had all been made in a few hours, the clutter upon which he opened the door was astounding. Charles ran forward and snatched the smoking frying-pan off the fire. The kettle had also boiled dry; he set it on the hearth, smudging his good new gloves. He picked up the two potatoes that lay beside it. They were raw and unwashed. He stared at them, in a sudden leaping of terror.

"Kate! Fred! They're not here! My God! Kate!"

Before Charles could reach the bedroom door, Kate stumbled through it. She had a washcloth in her hand, her dress was unbuttoned, and her hair hung limp and sorry. Her cheeks were streaked with tears and soot.

Charles snatched her against him. "Love, love. Oh, thank God you're safe and sound."

"I'm not, I'm not! I mean, oh, dear, I spoiled the chops, and look at me, and I wanted things to be so nice . . ."

"There, there, my Tatie-Mouse, my sweet."

He took the cloth from her hand and wiped her face clean. He did up her buttons. "There, love, there . . ." He kissed her, smoothing her hair. "There, love, there, little pet, it doesn't matter now."

She snuffled wetly, like a child being comforted. She gave a long, shuddering sigh.

Charles was hungry.

He began to move about, to clear a small oasis of order, to forage, while he continued to soothe. "Bread fresh today! Who wants potatoes too? Why, love, don't cry, we'll make a splendid meal."

"Oh, and the kettle boiled away!"

"We'll be grand and open a bottle of wine."

There were clean plates, at least. Mary had washed up before she left. But the chops, surprisingly, were not only burnt outside but purply raw within. Charles ate with a determined show of appetite. The wine helped, but scarcely enough.

"I lunched with Beard."

"Oh?"

It was hard to make conversation, too. However, at last he could wipe his lips and lean back with a pleasant, well-fed sigh.

"Where's Fred, dear? Gone to Father's?"

She answered in a dead, flat voice that startled him upright.

"He found it dull without Mary, I daresay."

She was looking past him, her violet eyes lusterless. Her cheeks sagged in a strange, heavy look of age. For one shocking instant, she did not look like his Kate at all, but a fat, defeated old woman.

Then, to his infinite relief, her hands, which were too large for her tiny wrists, clenched and fell limply open, and she began to cry. "And now you'll find me dull, too, and I spoiled your dinner, and my hair looks ugly, and . . . and . . ."

"Oh, sweetest, silly Mouse, oh, foolish Piggy-Wig!"

Charles had jumped to his feet, pulling her up to stand against him, feeling her softness, wiping her tears. Except for a lingering weakness in the calves of his legs, he might never have had that glimpse of possibility, that sip of damnation. He held her hand to his mouth, kissing the soft palm and the clumsy fingers.

He drew her toward the sofa. He brushed aside a bronzed kid slipper, a teacup, and a pair of scissors to make room. He sat down, drawing her into his lap. She hugged herself to herself, weeping; her weight was awkward and heavy as a sack of coals, but he did not care. She was his Kate, his love, his lovely girl.

"Sweet, sweet . . . there . . . there . . ."

"Oh, Charles, we were so happy in Chalk . . ."

He turned her face to his. The untidy hair was soft, her neck was warm.

"Darling, all these tears for two burnt chops? Don't you know that I love you more each day you live?"

"Really, Charles? Really?"

He kissed her mouth. She shifted her body and her weight was disposed sweetly. Charles's arms and thighs felt suddenly rested, full of an easy strength. They kissed for a long time.

"Now," Kate said at last, "you must do your writing or we'll never get to bed."

She stood up, stretching. She wandered toward the uncleared table, regarded it absently, sighed, and turned away. She sat down by the fire.

Charles went to his desk. The disorder of the room fidgeted him badly, but he could think of no tactful way to start setting it to rights. The silence, too, was obtrusive. He sharpened a pen. He riffled pages and pushed them about.

"Charles." A very small voice. "Charles if you're not going to write, I shouldn't much mind if you wanted to read me a book."

Charles started. He looked up at her.

Sometimes, in the street, Charles saw a stranger's face as if the whole life were naked in it; saw it so, and afterwards wondered whether he had been moved by insight or fancy. Now, in his own house, he looked at his wife's face, a mask of gentle emptiness become transparent, showing love that was urgent and helpless and frightened by its own inadequacy of means. He saw it and felt his heart fill with pity and guilt.

"Let's not read," he said. "Let us sit on the sofa as we used to do in Chelsea, and kiss, and long for the time when we can afford to marry."

Her eyes widened. "You mean, to *pretend?*"

"Only long enough to give us the pleasure of remembering the facts and acting on them."

Her face was always most beautiful in unsmiling happiness. She looked at him gravely. "That sounds . . . nice."

He started at that lovely face. With a struggle which took him by surprise, since he could not have guessed that it would be so intense, he faced his dear Kate's truth as he believed that he saw it.

"Oh, my Kate, don't ever be afraid that you are not all I need. Oh, Kate, I love you so."

Her eyes puzzled. "Why, Charles, what is it?"

That was when Charles came to a fork in the road.

He was quiet for a long, waiting pause. Then he said, "Shall we tell Mary that she need not come back? Mary and Fred, too? Kate, don't cry for Chalk. We can be alone here, too. Just as close, just as quiet, learning each other's hearts."

Kate started. Charles believed that her face was wiped so blank by the shock of gratitude. Even when she hid her hands in her face and began to cry, he believed that she wept for joy. He had never loved her as he did in that moment.

"I should have seen it all before," he said. "But we'll not think of that, dear love. It will all come right now."

Her voice came in a long, heartbroken wail. "Oh, can't you ever understand anything? The bad part of Chalk was the lonesomeness. The good part was having no cookery to go wrong and things!"

Charles's breath went out of his body as if a boxing glove had taken him in the diaphragm. He caught it back and shouted.

"Stop that noise!"

Her sobbing ceased at once. The prompt obedience was shameful, and the shame involved them both.

Charles clasped his hands and stared down at them.

"I'm sorry. I didn't mean to shout."

"Oh, never mind. I knew you'd be nervous and vexed tonight if I couldn't have things perfectly right, like Mary. That was what muddled me and made everything go wrong."

He tried once more.

"Oh, darling, no. You're all I want, just as you are. Let us send them away. Let us be happy and alone together."

He saw how she held her eyes wide, trying to control the tears that might displease him. And still they overflowed.

"I never thought that you'd turn on her and be vexed that she helps me," she said. "I knew you'd be vexed with me, but I didn't think that you'd turn on her, too."

Charles flexed his hands once or twice, helplessly.

"What a droll little muddle," he said at last. "I only wanted you to feel the unimportance of your poor little accidents, dear. I love our Mary. She belongs to us both."

Kate was used to confusions, and used to letting others solve them for her. She laughed, a little trembling laugh.

"I see," she said. "How could we have got so mixed up? Never mind, it's over now, isn't it?"

Charles took her hand.

He felt a singular, pure upwelling of thankfulness, of happiness that he did not trouble to examine.

He said, "Still, it is pleasant to have this one night all to ourselves, isn't it? Shall we leave the clearing away and washing up for tomorrow, and let it be just like Chalk for this one time?"

Surprisingly, sweetly, she lifted their two joined hands to her cheek and turned her head to one side, kissing the backs of his fingers. Then she looked up at him and smiled.

The promise of the night filled the room.

✳   2   ✳

AND THE PROMISE was richly fulfilled. Kate was passive — or, as Charles would have put it, pure — but she was beautiful and docile. More than that, although she had little idea of how to go about it, Kate wanted to be a good wife.

Given time, a double bed, and no distractions, enduring marriages have been built on no more.

And indeed, considering how neatly most of us manage to live within our bulwarks of imagined possibility, it is likely that Charles's affection for young Mary Hogarth might not, in fact, have come to be a distraction of any significance if Seymour, the comic illustrator, had been a less unstable sort of man.

Hall brought Seymour to Furnival's Inn on the evening after Mary came back from Chelsea. Charles, as he waited for them, gave the little household a last-minute coaching. He was edgier than he liked to admit.

For, as he put it to himself, the trouble was not in the way Seymour still gagged upon his poor old notion of the Nimrod Club, like a fishbone of vanity that he could neither spit out nor swallow down. *Pickwick* was a comic draftsman's paradise, and sooner or later Seymour would see it. The hitch, the immediate problem came from poor Seymour's downright obsessive, pitiful, self-narrowing conviction that he was *only* a comic artist, and nothing else. When he read the new number which contained the story "The Dying Clown," he had rushed in upon Hall insisting that he *could* not illustrate it.

"Of course he'll do it in the end," Charles repeated as he walked about the room. "Chapman and Hall have made him see that the issue must come out. Our task, you understand, is only to make him happy about it. To show him how a tale with tragic power like that enables him to use his gifts as he never has before."

He wanted to believe it very much. A certain look that had been in Seymour's face, an odd, unhappy mingling of pride and discouragement, kept coming before him as he talked.

"You see," he said, "it really gives him a superb new sort of opportunity."

"And besides," Kate said, "he should realize that you needed time for your honeymoon and using up that story was the only way you could get it."

It was not the right answer.

Charles smiled at her brilliantly. "Remember, dear, you must leave all the talk to me. Just toss in a word now and then to keep the atmosphere easy and homelike. Seymour only wants encouragement, poor chap. He came by success late, you see, and somehow he's afraid to trust it."

He checked his pacing and gave them all his warmest actor-manager's smile of confidence, encouragement.

Only Kate smiled back. Fred was shining his boots on his trouser legs, and Mary looked uncomfortable.

For a second Charles hesitated. He was always sensitive, even when he was most actively selling himself a bill of goods. But almost at once the swing of the performance had caught him up again.

"Ah, but I've made it all sound too serious," he said. "Now, wait and you'll see the transformation scene. Ah, once our Seymour has this evening with two pretty girls smiling at him, and Boz's own gin-and-lemon particular flowing free, he'll be ready to fly at that delicious, heart-rending, belly-churning deathbed scene like a fighting cock!"

And the evening went well, Charles could have sworn it. Hall did what unpleasant insisting still had to be done, Seymour agreed, and Charles had only to be heartening. He spent himself tremendously on the task, but it was altogether self-rewarding. As he called out his last hearty good night, Charles's straight back was an embodied triumph, and his eyes, as he faced about to the little household, were blazing blue suns.

"Whoof!" He mopped his brow in comic exaggeration. "Told you we'd 'earten 'im! I 'aven't talked so fast or delightful since I gave over selling Bott's Curative Elixir for Man and Beast!"

Nobody answered. Charles gave his head a shake, like a diver coming up into the air, and stared in complete bewilderment at the group before him. Fred was cleaning his nails on his teeth, Mary was looking at her shoes, and Kate, lolled to one side on the sofa, had shut her eyes. None of them so much as seemed to hear him.

"Dear me," he said, "are we all worn out together?"

But the jocular tone was lame.

Kate sighed. "What a nervous, depressing man."

Fred pulled his round face down long, working his mouth in a spasmodic, one-sided twitch. His excellent mimic's voice came out in a weary bleat: "But, Hall, it's not what we planned. The whole thing's shaping up altogether unlike our *plan*."

Complete silence followed his effort. It was, in fact, the perfect tribute, but Fred did not know it. He looked hopefully toward Mary. She was sitting straight, her gray eyes large and fixed and her lips compressed.

It is painful at any age to expect laughter and get that unmistakable silence which follows on a breach of taste. In the vulnerable teens, it is agony.

"And what ails *you?*" said Fred. His voice sounded like a sob of fury.

Mary did not look at him. Instead she made a gentle, vague little outward gesture.

"I'm sorry, Fred. It was very good, very like. Only — only, you see, unhappiness isn't funny to begin with."

Charles looked at them both. He looked at Kate, who was pushing herself upright once more with a gesture of fretful weariness.

"I don't understand," he said. "What are you talking about, Mary. Everything went so *well.*"

He sounded even younger than Fred, thin-voiced and querulous as a disappointed child.

Mary turned her head.

"You were very entertaining all evening, Charles. And . . . and encouraging. I . . . you tried, that is. Only, you see, he is such a frightened person."

"Nonsense," said Charles. A sharp twinge came in his side and he dug his elbow in upon it hard. "Nonsense! To be sure he needed heartening when he came, I warned you of that beforehand. But he left in splendid fettle."

Mary moistened her lips. "You may be right," she said. "I know that I imagine things about people, sometimes. Oh, I hope that you're right."

Charles squeezed the pain tighter and it went away.

Kate yawned. "Gracious, Mary, are you taking a cold? You sound morbid."

Fred felt better. He snickered. He mopped his eyes with an imaginary handkerchief. "She's in love. Mary's in love with Mr. Seymour."

Charles snapped at him. "Fred, be still! Mary, so you imply that except for, well, the agreement, I made a failure of this evening?"

Once more, Mary made a little outward gesture with her hands. Her narrow forehead and high cheeks were sharply defined between the deep side-loopings of her hair. She looked both younger and older than her years, spinsterish and immature.

"He is oldish," she said. "And worried . . . and seeing you so sure of things, and handsome, and young, and, oh, with everything just beginning . . ."

"Dear child!" He began to laugh. "We're all tired, I'm far more tired than I knew. Do you know, I was afraid that you were about to tell me that I'd said something stupid, something that might have depressed that poor fellow. 'Just beginning!' Bless you, child, now Seymour will be just beginning, too. Don't you see, we've given him pluck to try out powers he never knew he had!"

"For mercy's sake," Kate said, "must we sit half the night and talk about that disagreeable man? Do bank the fire, Charles. I'm tired to death."

The news of Robert Seymour's suicide reached the office of the *Chronicle* two days later.

Charles said, "Oh, God, God, no! Oh, God, his wife, his poor children!" He snatched up his cape. "Oh, God, poor Hall, he cared for him, his friend . . . he wanted to be kind . . ."

He ran the whole way to Hall's office, down the Strand, his mouth open and dry with his laboring breath.

Hall, too, had been shocked at the news. In the same breath he had exclaimed, "Oh, poor, poor devil, God forgive him, God forgive us all!" and, "So that's the end of our fine new series, Chapman."

As Charles stumbled in upon him, gasping for breath, he got to his feet, even more frail and birdlike than usual, an elderly canary in moult. He had expected the boy to be upset, but the extreme pallor and the fixed blue stare were truly disturbing.

Dear me, Hall thought. Never dreamed he needed the money so much. And only just married, too. We must manage something . . . a little loan . . .

Before Charles could speak, he found himself being supported with the utmost filial tenderness.

"I'm winded, I ran, I wanted to be with you as soon as I heard. You've known him so long — the shock, the grief — I couldn't bear to think that you'd have any worry as well. Please know that all my time is yours, all of it, until I've found some artist who can take his place for you. I'll comb the town, work at it, spare you every bit of effort that I can. And don't, don't thank me, you've been so kind to me that I could not do less. You shan't lose one issue by this awful tragedy — that, at least I can promise you."

"Dear me," said Mr. Hall. "Ah. Thank you very much."

"Don't thank me, don't. Oh, God, poor Seymour, his poor family. Oh, what a wretched, cruel world this can be. If there's anything I can do for his widow, anything . . . I feel so helpless."

Mr. Hall was at a total loss. He saw the shocking pallor of the young face, he heard the anguished voice, he felt the tenderness in the gentle, supporting hand. And it was not an act, it was no piece of desperate, vulgar, last-minute brazening. Mr. Hall was old and shrewd; absurd and unlikely as the circumstances made it, he was being offered pure, disinterested sympathy, and he knew it.

With considerable unhappiness, he parted his lips to explain to this bewildering young man, as gently as possible, that their business connection had just been brought to an abrupt but necessary end.

And instead he found himself spinning into the most profitable decision of his life.

"Dear me," he said. "Well. Most kind of you, Mr. Dickens. Yes, indeed."

"No, no, that's the horror of it. There's no real way in which one can be kind, there's nothing adequate one can do. What, is that clock right? I lost track of the time, I've a friend waiting now to meet me. Lunch. You'll hear from me again shortly, sir. Oh, God bless you. Goodbye."

When he had rushed from the room, Mr. Hall stared for some minutes at the empty doorway. He shook his head as if to clarify his thoughts.

"Dear me," he said. He shook his head again. "Dear me."

He gave a little tug to each of his cuffs.

He thought, Now, how in the world shall I explain it to Chapman?

Charles, on the other hand, forgot Hall the moment he left him. He pushed through the crowds blindly, hurrying as if Beard lay on a deathbed at which he might arrive too late. He thought, This is mad, why am I rushing like this? He checked the run to a restless stride, and immediately found himself running again.

Beard, already at their accustomed table, laid down his newspaper with a start.

"My God, are you ill? Has there been an accident?"

"Oh, Beard, poor Seymour's dead. He shot himself."

Beard was a sympathetic man, but Charles's face had — to put it mildly — overprepared him. He slapped his napkin open in a gesture at once angry and shrinking. Tenderness and distaste for histrionics struggled in his face, and burst from him in the form of a coarse, rallying good humor.

"Now, *look*," he said. "It's an 'ard world, mate. Sit down. Buck up."

But Charles, across the table, went right on looking like a corpse with two glass eyes, and Beard was taken with a shocking fear that he might even — right there in a chophouse, my God — begin to cry.

"Beard, he was cutting a plate for a picture. They found it, botched up, and a note to his wife asking her to forgive him. Saying that it was nobody's fault but his own."

The waiter was hovering like a vulture. His fascination was only too comprehensible, yet Beard found some relief in turning on him with a roar. "Chops and kidneys for two. Porter and a brandy. Clear off, and make it nippy!" He turned back to the table and added in a low voice of truly remarkable restraint, "And do, Charles, stop making a holy show."

"He spent Tuesday evening with us. This Tuesday. It . . . it was a pleasant evening. The pleasantest imaginable."

Quarreled. So that's it. And now he has to act as if he were in the dock at the Bailey. Lord!

"He'd got rid of all his doubts about that picture."

"What picture?"

"For a tragic interlude in *Pickwick*. Very powerful. It . . . he quite saw how it gave him a new kind of opportunity."

"I see."

And Beard, with a painful stir of pity, did indeed begin to see. The pity was more embarrassing than anything he had yet been forced to bear. He examined his fingernails minutely.

"Certainly my note couldn't have depressed him. I had to write to him about the sketch he turned out the next day. It didn't do at all, the dying man wasn't pathetic, only repulsive. But I put it as encouragingly as I could. I told him that he'd depicted the furniture of the room *admirably*."

The undesired percipience was complete. Beard, however, though a loud man, was fundamentally reticent; and, quite suddenly he knew that he had had as much as he could take. He slammed his fist down on the table. He roared.

"Oh, come off it! You don't know what Seymour's trouble was, and neither do I. I hate to spoil your fun, but the credit for the suicide isn't yours. Now, for God's sake, here comes our food, and do let's talk of something more pleasant while we eat — bedbugs, for instance."

"I'm sorry." The words were clipped. "You wholly misunderstood me. I knew him, Beard, after all. Naturally I felt shock — and sympathy, and interest."

But even before he had done speaking, Charles's color began to come back.

He'll manage, Beard told himself. Poor bastard. And poor Seymour.

He said, "Sorry I shouted. Been odd and edgy all day, I don't know why." He paused briefly to admire the falsehood, like a bad golfer who has just shot a hole in one. "And now, let's put it by, for our stomachs' sake."

It did not occur to him until after they had parted that it was altogether natural for Charles to have been upset, in view of the grim and obvious fact that he'd just lost the income he married on. He was amazed at his own impracticality.

Strangely enough, Charles, always so practical, had not yet thought of those fourteen guineas a month at all. He did not feel much better after seeing Beard, but he told himself that he had been bluntly and properly rebuked for letting his sympathies run away with him so. Luxuriating. Womanish.

He went back to the *Chronicle* office and kept himself very busy.

He did not precisely put off going home, but he was not all anxious to get there. He walked slowly up the outside stair, rehearsing. He must tell them carefully. Nothing, at first, of the death's being suicide. *I heard a sad thing today.* The important thing was not to upset Kate. He must not upset Kate.

The three were sitting by the fire when he came in. They were all laughing, their faces turned together. They had not heard the door open.

Charles stared at them. He wet his lips.

"I heard . . . I heard . . ." And, without warning, he began to cry, with helpless, blubbering sobs, the tears pouring over his face. "Oh, Kate, Kate, Seymour's dead. He shot himself. He was working on that damned picture, and he shot himself."

Through his tears he saw them turn to him, the three faces gone empty. He caught his breath. He said, in a remote, impersonal voice, "I can't stop crying," and began to sob again.

"Good Lord," said Fred.

Mary looked away. "I am very sorry." The words delivered like a small formality. "I am very sorry."

But to his wonder, to his anguish of gratitude, gentle, vulnerable Kate whom he had planned so carefully to keep from shock, Kate, his wife, stumbled to her feet and ran to him. She clasped his body tight to her own soft body, weeping with him, loving him, supporting him.

Charles pressed her to him. In wonder, he felt her softness support him even as it clung to him for support. He felt the need to weep go out of him in the presence of her compassionate weeping, her perfect, answering tears.

He thought, But she loves me and I knew it. Why did I run like a fool to Hall, to poor old Beard, and not to her? And at once he knew why he had run at all. The knowledge ran through him like a fierce kind of joy. It was by my fault. I can let myself know it now. It was by my fault that Seymour killed himself.

His hands tightened on Kate in an ecstasy. His lips formed words without sound. "My love, my loving love. My strength, my love."

And Kate's wail rose, shrill and trembling. "Oh, Charles, how dreadful! Oh, how in the world will we manage for money now?"

Charles's arms dropped.

He did not know whether only one moment or several passed before he spoke, and he listened to his own words with an odd detached interest. Their tone was cheerful and only slightly flat.

"Why, Kate, don't distress yourself so. We'll have to find another artist, but Hall has no thought of dropping the series. I talked with him this morning."

He took off his cape and hung it away. He walked to the fire and stood facing it.

Fred was still staring, his face very round.

"He shot himself? Mr. Seymour *shot* himself?"

"Be still," said Mary. "Let Charles rest and try to eat."

Out of the dour, narrow mask of her face, her gray eyes lifted to Charles's averted head. They yearned upon him and turned away again, gray, arctic oceans, empty of life.

※ *3* ※

A week and a half later, Mitton dined with Beard.

"Do you know why Seymour shot himself? I asked Dick, and he looked as if he were about to be sick in the gutter and changed the subject."

"I wish you'd seen him the day it happened. Seems they'd had some difference, and you know how he has to squeeze everything for the last drop. I swear, he was dead set on grabbing the full blame for himself."

"Oh, you fancied it. He's not a fool."

"At all events, he's forgotten it now, with Sir Andrew's Sunday Bill up before the Parliament again. No bakeshops and excursions for his blessed poor, God you should hear him froth. He's writing a pamphlet and he thinks of nothing else from breakfast to bed."

On the same day, Chapman said to Hall, "I'm glad we kept on with it. Hablôt Browne's a good draftsman, and this new issue is the best we've had."

"Boz is no hack," said Hall. "He puts his whole heart into this Pickwick thing."

Macrone was also happy; Boz was in top form, absolutely boiling over with notions for new sketches. And Braham, the producer, rubbed his hands when he spoke of his forthcoming operetta: "Hullah, and that Boz feller. At it day and night, both of them."

On the other hand, Ainsworth was deploring Charles's idleness. "Bulwer, a boy with his gifts shouldn't waste his time at charming his betters. Not that he doesn't do it well. The Golden Virgin, the triple-fortuned Angela Coutts had him to tea this week. They discussed their duty to the poor, apparently."

Bulwer stretched his long legs and yawned. "Better than you've done, old fellow."

"I haven't given it such dedicated effort," Ainsworth said, waspishly.

"Why do you rush about so, these days?" said Kate.

"I put too many irons in the fire and they all got hot together. It happens. Come, give your whirling dervish a restful kiss."

It was a very restful kiss. Indeed, for the last ten days, Charles had been wonderfully content with Kate. There are times when we can ask no greater gift from love than that of a total inattention.

The kiss could not be protracted, however. It was a Sunday afternoon, and Mary and Fred were in the way. Charles put it to himself in just those words.

"Good Lord," he exclaimed suddenly, "how can you all frowst about so, doing nothing? Let's take a walk."

Kate moaned. "Charles, can't you ever be quiet?"

Fred shrugged and grinned. "Not I. I know your walks!"

Mary alone jumped up.

She went to the bedroom and came back at once, tying her bonnet strings. It was a black and white bonnet, spinsterish and unbecoming.

Charles said, "Oh, Fred, Kate, up with you! A stroll."

Mary laughed. "Oh, Charles, let them suit themselves. Come, while the sunshine lasts."

And, when he thought about it, Charles could really find no reason for that odd reluctance to go without them. Mary was a dear child and he always thoroughly enjoyed her company.

He caught up his hat and laughed. "They're off! The Boundin' Wonder takes the lead. No more bets, gents, sorry, no more bets!"

Mary ran after him. "Don't disgrace me, you zany!"

She was laughing, too, as she tucked her hand under his arm. He knew that the persistent, edgy feeling made no sense at all. Mary was a dear little thing, he was fond of her, enormously.

"Lord," he said, "the week I've put in."

"I know."

"How did I get involved with so much at one time? The *Chronicle*, *Pickwick*, Macrone's sketches, the operetta, people, people . . ."

"I wonder. Sometimes, Charles, when I . . ."

At once, as if personal conversation were a reef to be skirted at all costs, Charles was plunging through a torrent of anecdote. About Angela Coutts, her vast wealth and touching anxiety to use it for the world's good. About the Ainsworth circle. About Hablôt Browne, Hullah. He imitated Braham, singing the score of *The Village Coquettes*. "Straight through, with expression, like a lovesick hippopotamus!" The tide of his words rushed on; he walked, turned corners aimlessly, talking, until at last for sheer lack of wind he fell silent.

"Where are we, Charles?"

"Ah? Why, dear me, child, how long have I been walking you through such shabby streets?"

"For some time."

"Poor child, we'll find a cheerier part at once! You sound quite glum!"

"I . . . I hoped you'd come on purpose. To show me, you know, where the people live that you're troubling over in that pamphlet."

He laughed. "And I'd only lost my way while I tried to entertain you."

"I see. This is a sad-looking street, isn't it?"

"Yes."

"I wonder whether the people who live here find it sad, or only ordinary."

The street, in point of fact, was very like that in which Mrs. Roylance used to live. Mrs. Roylance, who "took in children."

Charles stopped still, and looked.

"They find a good many hard things ordinary, in a street like this. It is ordinary to go hungry before payday. To go dirty when the outside pump freezes. It is ordinary for children who live here to come home from their long, underpaid hours of work so tired that they ache for bed . . . a filthy, crowded bed with bugs in it."

Too much emotion had got into his voice. He knew it even before he felt Mary's fingers quiver and tighten on his arm. He finished carefully. "I lived not far from a street like this when we first came to London. I was ten. I . . . I learned about these houses, and the people who live in them, by going into them."

His eyes were fixed before him as he spoke. He did not suspect that they were naked in the mask of his face, nor did he see Mary's brief, startled stare of intelligence. But he began to talk again, very fast.

"Yes, it is not a slum, but this place is also a part of the London that comfortable people prefer to forget. Look about you, child. It is Sunday, the Sunday that Sir Andrew Agnew is bent upon destroying for these people who long for it all through the long, sorry week. May God forgive him, as I cannot. Look at that open bakeshop, smell it, like a hungry child's dream of Heaven! Twoscore families fetched their bit of meat to be roasted there today for their one decent dinner in seven. Today a little family may have left this street on an excursion, to look at trees and water and such rare wonders. Look, over there, a tavern, and two old men sitting over their pots of ale, free as lords, because it is Sunday, and they are not poor old machines, wearing out, but human souls. Mary, is Jesus of Nazareth displeased at this?"

It was a good speech. Charles himself was quite swept away by it. When he glanced down he was not surprised to see the little black and white bonnet lifted, and the narrow face so firmly intent.

"You are right," he said. "The shock in your eyes is reverent as you recoil from such blasphemy."

And Mary said, "Oh, Charles, stop."

He stared at her, utterly incredulous.

She said, "I'm glad you're writing the pamphlet. I know that you want to help these people. I know how you . . . remember those children you used to know. But I assure you that if you write it in the way you were going on now, sounding all fancy and *holy*, everyone will be too vexed to care, one way or the other."

Charles pulled his arm from her hand. He felt nothing but anger; so much, such disproportionate anger that his face was blank with it, and his voice when he spoke was perfectly flat.

"I have many faults, Mary, but self-righteousness is not one of them."

Her lips were tightly compressed. Her cheeks were narrowed. She looked thirty years old, ugly and spinsterish.

Two women passed them.

"Fightin'," said one.

"Too bad. Married too young, like our Jen. Married too young."

Charles and Mary did not see or hear them.

"Well? Be just, Mary. Is it?"

She looked away. She swallowed. "Only . . . only when you've done something that you wish you'd not. So much that you . . . don't want to think of it."

"I believe that I'm quick as the next man to acknowledge a fault."

"No." The thin face still turned away. "But only because you're so sorry, Charles."

She hesitated, and suddenly she looked at him square; and her face was not spinsterish, or childish, but beautiful with a mature, clear look of love that took away his breath.

"People do things they wish they hadn't," she said. "Never mind. I never knew anyone, Charles, as really good as you."

Occasionally life brings a moment of exaltation or of grief so intense that it is like a splinter of eternity, something that never began and can never end.

So, for a moment, Charles saw Mary Hogarth. He closed his eyes, not as if he would shut her face out but as if he would enclose it so and keep it safe from time.

She took his hand.

"I still think of how you cried when you came home that night," she said. "I've prayed very hard for a chance to tell you how sorry I am. I didn't intend to sound rude, just now. Only I've known so — horribly, what it must be like for you, thinking over and over that perhaps, if we'd only noticed more on that night he came, it — it might not have happened."

He heard her in a strange, almost impersonal wonder. Her words came laboriously, her voice thin, as if she spoke from a tight throat, but he was not aware of that. He listened with his mind to her mind, speaking. He opened his eyes again and saw that almost frightening beauty of pure acceptance still in her face.

"Only I knew," she said, "that it could not have been as hard for me as it is for you, because I am not really so kind or so good as you are. So very good."

He began to cry.

"Oh, Charles," she said gently, "not out in the street."

He wept. "You don't understand, Mary. You see goodness in me, because, oh, God, everyone sees what he looks for in me. I never knew before how terribly that's true, but it is. I change, not in pretense, not in trying to please people, but in myself. I feel like them. That night, I felt like Hall. Oh, God, I could never make you understand it, you of all people, Mary . . ."

She said, "But, Charles, I've always noticed that."

He stared at her.

"But there's a part of you that stays itself, too," she said. "It's . . . it's what the people who love you love."

He bowed his head. He had never felt anything like the amazing sensation of lightness and quietness that was flooding his whole body.

He whispered, "God bless you, Mary."

But the emotion was too intense. Mary gave an odd little shake to her shoulders, as if she were shrugging off a heavy cape.

"Mercy!" she said. "In another minute we'll have a crowd about us waiting for the hymn!"

He looked up. He saw her everyday, sensible, sweet little face with a sense of awful loss, and of exquisite relief.

"My dear little sister," he said. "My dearest little friend."

The absolution that Kate had denied him, and that Mary gave, was real. His perception of Mary's understanding love was real. And they were a size too big; he had to wrap them up.

He spoke the right, serviceable, vulgarizing, necessary words, and everything came back into place; the pattern held.

He smiled at Mary, his little sister, his dear little friend.

"Hadn't we best start towards home? It's getting late."

It might almost be said that nothing was changed.

And still, something was changed.

❉   *4*   ❉

IT WAS KATE who came nearest to expressing in words that new quality which had come into the little household.

She had gone to Chelsea for the day. She sat with her mother, and her face was proud and serene, for she had just confided that she was "almost quite sure that a little stranger" — yes, she put it so — "was coming by January."

"You'll be badly pressed for space," Mrs. Hogarth said, "with Mary and that boy."

"Oh, no, Mama. Fred's so droll we'd miss him sadly. And of course we couldn't do without Mary."

Mrs. Hogarth, to do her credit, had always tried to overcome her partiality for Kate, the beauty. She had little intelligence herself and distrusted it in other women; despite herself, she felt that both Mary and little Georgy were too clever by half. Moreover, Mrs. Hogarth had a thwarted genius for jealousy; nature had created her for the role of Medea, and her husband's contented domesticity cramped her at every turn. Kate's marriage was, in a way, her second chance.

Now, though she could never have admitted to herself that Mama did not love all her children just the same, far less to any notion still more base, she looked at the violet vagueness of her favorite's eyes and drew a breath which pinched her nose and swelled her bosom phenomenally.

Kate, lost in an unwonted effort at self-expression, did not notice. "About Mary, Mama," she said. "All along I've felt that I couldn't do without her. But, when we first got back from Chalk — it was ridiculous, but once or twice I found myself thinking, what if Charles should start to draw comparisons. You know, about her housekeeping, and being clever and reading books, and all. And there was a night when I spoiled some chops . . ."

"Ah," said Mrs. Hogarth. The word was a sigh; a protracted, brooding, and still curiously relishing sigh.

Kate, however, cut its pleasure short. She laughed, softly.

"So ridiculous. For, in fact, it's precisely the other way about. Having her there makes all the difference. Not only things like cookery and tidying, though he could be very difficult about them, I'm afraid. But when we all chat in the evening, or play at games, or he wants someone to listen to rather confusing jokes, or to hear about politics. You see, it keeps him in spirits and never dull or anything until . . . until it's time for us to be alone."

And she broke off, blushing wonderfully.

"Hmm," said Mrs. Hogarth. "At least, she's a scrawny little thing and behind her years in many ways."

Kate nodded, and replied in perfect innocence, "Yes, I can't help being glad for that. Perhaps we can keep her for a long, long time. She doesn't even care particularly for dancing, as yet."

Kate was right. After that Sunday walk, Charles wanted nothing from her that she could not give him. And all that Mary gave he could accept without question, since every day ended in night, and night gave him Kate's loveliness.

Surely there has seldom been so chaste a bigamy.

Charles, however, had no time to think about it. Chiefly, in those days, he thought about money. The news of Kate's pregnancy stirred him with sentimental awe; and it also sounded through his blood like a challenge of trumpets. He lost no time in setting off at once to see Mr. Hall.

Mr. Hall, as it happened, had been, most unhappily, intending shortly to see Mr. Dickens. The Pickwick venture was, after all, turning out to have been a bad guess. Even with Seymour living, the sales had wavered between four and five hundred copies a month, and now, despite his hopes, they had sagged still more.

When Charles's card was brought in, he pushed it across the table to his partner and remarked, sadly, "Oh, dear, I daresay this might as well be our time to break the news."

Charles entered with a buoyant step, but his mouth was set gravely firm.

"I hope you won't feel that I've no right to interfere," he said, "but I feel a duty to you as well as to myself. *Pickwick* as it stands hasn't a chance."

Mr. Hall's jaw dropped.

Charles shook his head. "I appreciate your confidence. But wait. Let me explain."

He explained, with masterly precision. Respectfully, but with underlying sternness, he made it clear that they had sustained an irreparable loss in Seymour; that a younger artist, however good in his own right, could not measure up as a drawing card.

"We can't escape it," he said. "It's not the pictures that must sell *Pickwick* now."

Briskly, he outlined the only possible course. They must advertise that they were improving their format, and thereupon cut down from four pictures to two, adding eight pages of text, enough, that is, to satisfy a reader's appetite for entertainment.

"Try to believe me," he ended. "As we're handling it now, it's hopeless."

There was a long moment of silence. Mr. Hall swallowed. He avoided his partner's eyes. He stood, extending his hand. His voice, as he spoke, was that of one who says, "God helping me, I can do no other."

The actual words were less impressive.

"I quite agree. I'm glad you spoke out."

Charles wrung the frail hand in a grip of iron.

"So, on to victory! What would you think a fair figure for my extra work? Shall we say, from now on, twenty a month?"

And it was not the suggestible Mr. Hall who answered. Before he could speak, Chapman, thick-skinned, hard-headed Chapman, said in a voice bemused: "Twenty . . . that's just to both sides, I should say."

Charles left them warmed through with both partners' quick good sense and his own helpfulness. For now, it was certain, *Pickwick* would catch on like a house afire.

Unfortunately, it did not catch on. The issue in the new format lay on the bookstalls in the same sad, undiminishing little piles as before. And as if a contagion had spread from its failure, Braham became evasive about the operetta and talked about tight schedules and bad seasons.

Charles developed a cold that he could not shake off. The Melbourne-Norton trial was depressing, too.

Indeed, it was an ugly mess. Lord Melbourne was Charles's political idol, and his wife had not gained in sense what she had lost in looks since the days of her girlhood when, with watering ruby lips she had proclaimed Lord Byron mad, bad, and dangerous to know. Nor was there reason to suppose that she had learned discretion over the years. Nonetheless, the suit for divorce had clearly been precipitated by some very small last straw.

Charles sat in the courtroom, and blew his nose, and heard servants' babblings and letters that were absurdly unincriminating even when they were quoted, *molto appassionato*, by the prosecution.

"It knocks all the laughter out of one," he said.

He tried to blame the cold and the trial for his depression. He could not admit to the inadmissible, subterranean swellings of fear that he had lost the touch, the golden touch.

He worked desperately on the June *Pickwick*. Kate laughed heartily at it. She said, "Oh, that's the drollest yet. The jokes are so nice and easy to see."

Charles recognized the kiss of death. He was prepared when Hall sent for him to say that unless he could work for ten guineas a month, *Pickwick* would have to go.

Being prepared, he could shake Hall's frail little claw firmly, and leave the office with his head up.

But as he reached the street, his shoulders hunched and he caught his lower lip between his teeth.

For the good little household was threatened. He could not keep two, let alone four, properly on four guineas a month less than he had married with.

It could not be threatened. Utterly and completely, he refused to let it go. He lifted his head. While his body still fought the undertow of fear, he began to think fast, in words.

"Macrone. Of late I've let myself neglect him. Kate should call on his wife. We must make that tour of Bedlam together, as he wished. This week, perhaps. It would be a good time to push ahead my notion for a novel about the Gordon Riots. Or, perhaps at his office, quietly. I can make him see that we should get at it quickly."

He made no effort to control the underrushing fear. He only ignored it and let it flow, as a thing apart. But mercifully, Charles was self-suggestible. By the time he drew near the *Chronicle* office, he felt almost easy, almost confident.

And it was at that moment that he met his father.

John Dickens's hat was to one side, both his hands were flung out, and his face radiated paternal benevolence.

"Dear boy, what a delight!"

"Father."

"Only now I was in the very act of promising myself a visit to your little nest! How have I let the press of affairs keep me away so long! How's Fred? And the sweet bride and her modest young companion?"

"All well, thanks. I've been intending to see you and Mother, too."

"How well I understand, dear boy! The turbulent stream, each of us swept along by his manifold obligations!" The eyeglass, extended on its ribbon, described a semicircle and appeared to check its flight in mid-air. It wavered delicately. "Yes, I have been absorbed in duties and—er—by a little temporary problem which I am loath to mention . . ."

A pause, a clearing of the throat were followed by a quick touch to the hatbrim. The hat sat straight, transformed by that sleight-of-hand from rakish elegance to a very churchwarden's grave sobriety.

Charles looked at it. He hesitated and glanced about. He spoke low and fast.

"Governor, I'm sorry. Please don't let this out, it would do me no good, but I'm hard up myself. I've just come from Hall. *Pickwick's* not going well, and I've agreed to take half of what I've been getting."

At his very first words he could see the confident, well-staged approach begin to crumble. Shockingly, before his eyes, a new and far more genuine transformation was taking place. The Governor's fine-cut lips lost their senatorial gravity; they loosened in a nervous quivering. The Governor's eyes, which, a moment since, had been at once so benign and so expectant, appeared to wither at the lids. They were old, frightened eyes, workhouse eyes; Marshalsea eyes.

Charles stared at them, and at the face gone so small. He stared at the linen shirt ruffle that drooped, visibly loosing its starch, second by second. For a brief, bad moment as he stared he was filled with a dreadful sense of helplessness, of interior cold. It was curiously laced with a smell of overboiled cauliflower. The hall at Mrs. Roylance's was black . . .

Almost at once, he heard himself begin to speak again, each word incisive as a snap of shears, severing the frayed, unsightly edge from the bolt of time.

"So I can't be of much help until I've arranged with Macrone about a new novel I'm starting. Historical background, wonderfully dramatic. *Gabriel Varden, the Locksmith of London.* Bad luck we're both cramped at the same time, Governor. Would a fiver help?"

And blessedly, miraculously, the ruffled bosom regained its starch. The pearl-gray topper came back with a flourish to its accustomed angle. John Dickens's bearing was so proud and his smile so benign in the moment when outstretched hand met outstretched hand that no passing stranger could have guessed which of the two bestowed and which received the benefit.

Indeed, in that moment, neither Charles nor Mr. Dickens was quite clear on the subject either.

"We'll meet again soon, dear boy. Goodbye, goodbye."

"Goodbye, Governor. My love to the family."

On the stair to the office Charles met Beard, who eyed him affectionately and grinned.

"What's the good news? Your horse just come in first?"

Charles, to his surprise and Beard's, began to laugh, in wild strangling whoops of laughter that went on and on. He leaned against the wall, laughing until he was weak with it. From time to time he tried to speak, waved a helpless hand, and was off again.

At length he caught his breath, wiped his eyes, and straightened up.

"Oh, Lord." He took another breath and spoke carefully for fear of another onset of laughter. "Not so funny, really, it only struck me so.

When you said 'horse.' Because I was — oh, Lord, here I go again — I was just about to touch you for a quid until payday."

Luckily, Beard's sense of humor was on the primitive side. Even more luckily, he was flush. He laughed almost as hard as Charles had done as he handed over the loan.

Charles asked Macrone for an advance with as much show of confidence as he could manage, but all the time he was speaking he knew that the show was pathetically transparent, and he was overwhelmed when Macrone nodded and said, "Sounds like a good thing. Two hundred pounds and you'll start it now, eh?"

"Immediately." But Charles's voice broke and he had to feign a cough. He raised an imaginary glass, "Well, Gabriel Varden, 'ere's to you!"

He hired a cab to get him back to Furnival's Inn. The news could not wait. Between sentences he kissed Kate's mouth and Mary's cheek and slapped Fred on the back.

"I hadn't told you, but Chapman's having troubles and he asked me to cut back for a month or so. This is a godsend. It's good I write so quickly, did I tell you that he wants it by November?"

"A *book* by November?" said Mary. "All of it?"

Charles laughed. "Five whole months for a tale that will fairly write itself?"

He looked about the room and drew a deep sigh. He should have known that nothing could go wrong. Things so good are somehow protected by their own goodness, they cannot go wrong.

Nonetheless, when the sigh had fully exhaled itself, Charles went to his writing table and sat down. A friendly, confirming letter to Macrone was in order. While there was no chance that he might change his mind, the terms of their agreement should still be set down, without delay, in good, enduring old black and white.

✳   5   ✳

SOME WRITERS work their best with the wolf slavering on the threshold. Charles was not one of them. The lump sum of two hundred pounds was a wellspring.

Joyfully, Charles set *Gabriel Varden* at the back of his mind — to gather incident, as he explained — and began to write. A sketch that had hung fire for weeks wrote itself in slap-up style. New lyrics for the operetta popped into his head as he walked to the *Chronicle* office. Parliamentary reporting ceased to be a weary task and became a delightful exercise in satire.

Best of all, he could write the July *Pickwick* simply for the pleasure of the thing. With two hundred pounds in hand, he could afford to amuse himself, for once, without sweating.

When it was done, he liked it. Sam Weller was no such hilarious creation as Mrs. Leo Hunter with her "Ode on an Expiring Frog," but he had a quality. Mary would laugh.

However, when Charles read it aloud, it was Fred who laughed. Kate looked puzzled and Mary's face grew increasingly remote.

Charles turned to her as he laid the last page down.

"Woolgathering?" He intended to sound teasing, but the unexpected disappointment made his voice sharp.

Mary lifted one hand, palm outward, in the gesture with which one deeply absorbed in some task staves off an interruption.

"It's the boots," she said. "Sam Weller. Droll and yet *sensible*, a person you can feel like. That's what makes all the difference. When there's one you can feel like, you aren't only laughing about some ridiculous people, you're *there*, with them."

Charles shrugged. "It didn't make you laugh."

"Mmm," she said. Once more her face was remote. "Mmm," she said again.

It was only Mary who felt no surprise when the July *Pickwick* ran away.

"Incredible," said Chapman. "The new printing gone almost before it was on the stands. Orders for back numbers from Birmingham, Edinburgh . . . Incredible!"

"Hardly that," said Hall. "But gratifying. Ah, yes indeed."

And still the sales mounted with that runaway exuberance which comes only from the one kind of promotion that cannot be bought.

"*I assure you, my dear, it's delightful.*"

"*Know wot you needs? A larf, and I knows where you can get it.*"

"I told you," Mary cried, inaccurately, "I *told* you!"

Charles sent a note to Macrone, in block letters: "PICKWICK TRIUMPHANT."

In Hall's office, Chapman shook his head. "They'll all be after him now."

"He's ours so long as we play fair with him."

"Yes, we must restore the previous terms."

"Restore it! Hall, we must double it!"

"Do as you like. It appears that you had better sense than I thought for."

Mr. Hall settled his hair and his lapels. "Twenty-five," he said. "For the present, twenty-five."

But though he spoke in his most brittle manner, a wild and bird-like glitter did not leave his eye.

When Charles was told of the decision, he stood so tall that he appeared to look down with affectionate eyes even upon Chapman, who topped him by a good four inches.

"I cannot tell you," he said, "how it moves me to meet with conduct so spontaneously honorable."

He left them quickly, with his face still grave and his head held high.

"Didn't thank us much," said Chapman.

But Hall hugged his elbows. "Mark me, Chapman, conceit like that goes with *staying power*."

But it was with the utmost effort that Charles had taken the news with such dignified calm. He went back to Furnival's Inn with a bouquet in each hand and a bottle under each arm, capering like Harlequin, and pausing only to bow from left to right, occasionally, as people stared.

And he opened his door with a shout.

"We're rich, we're rich! A toast to the world, and may all their ships come in at once! Kate, Kate, give me a kiss!"

Charles had always known that nothing succeeds like success. Still, he was intoxicated by the attentions, the invitations, the requests for pieces that flowed in from every side. It startled and hurt him when Macrone asked him to lunch and said, in a manner that one could only call grudging, "Don't get your head turned. You know our novel won't leave you much time for the social whirl."

However, he tried to keep his voice patient as he replied, "You know, that's a book that needs time and thought, Macrone. We'll both profit if you push the publication forward a bit."

And he was glad that he had been so forbearing, for Macrone, though he was not the sort to apologize, made amends at once.

"Perhaps you're right," he said, "but let's not push too hard."

The words were clipped; clearly he was embarrassed by having betrayed his lack of faith and generosity. But Charles smiled at him with immediate forgiveness.

In the full, rushing weeks that followed, Charles was glad that he and Macrone had had that talk. Indeed, when November came around, *Gabriel Varden* was still at the back of his mind, gathering incident.

"No," he said, one night by the fire, "a contract's a contract, and Macrone's book is as good as written in my head, I'll do it shortly. But the present day is where a real novel lies, a living tale that could do some living good. The new law for example — what a tale one could hang upon *that* piece of iniquity."

Kate fingered her lips. "But people don't like to read of horrid things, do they? Unless they happened long ago?"

She was looking very pretty. He smiled at her.

"People are timid, Kate, but they're good. Catch their attention, and you'll further the Kingdom. For they'll hear anything, this I'm sure of, anything, so long as it's part of a tale that stirs them, so long as it makes them laugh and cry."

"They will?" said Kate.

Mary hugged her. "To be sure they will! Oh, Charles, how splendid, Mr. Macrone will like this notion every bit as well as the other, I'm sure of it!"

"Dear, that's not quite . . ." But Charles broke off. He did not know how to put the difficulty into words.

Kate did it for him. She shook back her shining curls and smiled at Mary like a tender mother. "You little ninny, Charles can't do that after he's spent the money for the other and told Mr. Macrone so much about how good it will be! Why, Mr. Macrone wouldn't know what to think!"

Charles was startled by the conciseness with which one so habitually vague had hit the nail on the head. Yet, somehow, he was not grateful. He spread out his palms and studied them as he spoke.

"More than that, I've done a great deal on *Gabriel Varden* already.

You know the bulk of a writer's work — his significant work — isn't done on paper."

"Never mind," said Mary, "you can write what you like when you've finished Mr. Macrone's."

Like Kate, she had spoken kindly. Charles did not know at all why he felt angry.

"Fred," he said abruptly, *"let me see your fingernails."*

He had, in fact, begun to write *Oliver Twist.*

He did not know it for some time. He walked the streets, watching people: pinched, too-knowing boys, drunken bravos and their trailing drabs. Once he saw a woman standing before a pawnshop, and he stood still, fitting words to the details of her poor dress and her un-washed, half-curled hair and her frightened face, until the shopowner came out and asked her, in a curious, whispering-sweet voice, if she had something to sell at a place used to handling the best. The man was an Old World, picturebook Jew, with sidelocks and a gown, but it was his voice that stayed in Charles's mind as he walked on. The voice, and the eyes, so coaxing and wary.

That voice and those eyes clinched it. There had been the nebu-lous, uneasy feeling that a novel should spring from a living concern. There had been the evening when Mary and Kate played shuttle-cock with that feeling in an oddly disturbing way. And then the voice, the eyes — the catalyst, and a story growing.

A taleteller's story, a street ballad; not allegory, not political satire, a story.

"I saw such a regular old out-and-outer today," he said that night, after a long staring silence. "Too good to waste. I must get him into a sketch . . ."

But when he started the sketch, irrelevant images came crowding out of the background, attaching themselves to that old out-and-outer, and to each other.

He pushed the unsatisfactory pages aside. He spoke in a voice utterly unlike the voice of strong emotion which had sounded so pleasantly in his own ears, a few nights back, as he declared his pur-pose to write a living novel, a novel that would do some living good. He spoke whiningly, peevishly, like a child housed with a cold when his brothers have all gone out to play.

"It will be gone before I can get to it. I couldn't take the time unpaid, and Macrone's advance is spent."

"Get to what?" said Kate.

"Nothing. A fancy, about people . . . Oh, the devil with everything, let's go to bed."

When Richard Bentley, editor, dropped out of the blue a day later, Charles could no more have imagined refusing his slap-up offer than a starving man would have rebuffed an angel with a platterful of manna. Bentley was florid, overhandsome, and dressed like a successful race-track tout, but Charles, looking at him, saw glory.

"Twenty a month to edit the new magazine." By a superhuman effort, Charles kept his voice reflective. "Twenty per issue extra for a novel to run through the first year at least . . . I'll consider it seriously, and let you know in a day or so, Mr. Bentley."

He made himself accept Mr. Bentley's cigar and smoke it through, though it was agony to delay the bliss of getting home with the news.

Fred crowed. He shouted. "Forty more each month! James, my carriage!"

Kate's cheeks flushed pink. Her eyes were altar lights. "Oh, Charles!"

Mary had sprung to her feet. "Oh, I can scarcely believe it! Oh, how wonderful! Didn't Mr. Macrone make a dreadful fuss at first?"

Charles was genuinely baffled. "Macrone?"

Mary looked baffled too. "Three books written *together*?"

Charles laughed. "No, bless you. Did I never tell you that months ago Macrone agreed to wait, if I'd rather? He can afford to be sensible, you know, with the last volume of Boz sketches coming out next month, and the others earning again, too, thanks to *Pickwick*."

Happily for the triumphant evening, Mary believed Charles quite as fully as he believed himself. He turned back to Kate.

"And what are you trying to say, my Tatie-Mouse?"

The altar lights flared, the caught breath was slowly exhaled in a sigh like a prayer. For once in her life, Kate Hogarth Dickens said precisely the right thing.

"Oh, Charles. Oh, Charles, you are so wonderful."

Clearly, the editor of a new magazine could not be a reporter, too. Charles felt real sympathy for Mr. Easthope in the loss of a working team like Dickens and Beard. He took pains over the letter that bore the sad news, and he posted it the instant that Mr. Bentley's contract was safely signed and pocketed. He felt that it was fair to the point of punctilio. His salary might expire immediately, and the sketches already paid for would be sent in as soon as they were due. It had been a trick to express his honest regret for Easthope's loss and yet avoid a tone of conceit; it pleased him that he had turned it off, and well.

The tone of Mr. Easthope's reply was less than tender. Charles broke two pens in answering it. When he and Mary took the Sunday walk that had become their weekly ritual, the hurt still rankled.

"Easthope rather surprised me," he began. As soon as he had spoken the words he knew that he had been waiting to be alone with the child, to get it all off his heart and receive the balm of her sympathy. He dropped her arm, he gestured as he talked. As the rush of angry eloquence grew he walked faster and faster, until Mary had to run to keep within earshot.

". . . nor even the most routine expression of gratitude for my years of effort. No, I owed him six pounds and sixpence. Six pounds and sixpence — though it was always I who was chosen when there was harassing and difficult duty to be performed, traveling at a few hours' notice hundreds of miles in the depths of winter, leaving hot, crowded rooms to travel all night in a damp chaise, tearing along and writing under every possible difficulty. And my reward, at the last, a fear lest I had received six guineas too much!"

Gasping a little, Mary overtook him and caught at his arm. He felt the clutch of the hard, narrow hand, and he covered it with his own, gratefully. His steps slackened, and he turned his head to see the righteous anger, the pity; to see the face of healing.

Mary was pale; she often became pale when she had to run. The cool, gray look that she gave him was quite detached.

"So that's what you wrote him?" she said.

He blurted like a schoolboy, "What do you mean?"

"Oh, mercy, Charles, your reading-aloud voice is always the same, even when you're running!"

He could not believe it. "You're of Easthope's side?"

Her face worked. "I feel as you do, Charles, I daresay. That it would have been — better — to talk about it to Mr. Easthope at the start. Even though Mr. Bentley might have changed his mind and you'd have had to stay with the paper after all."

He stopped dead in his tracks and stared at her. Her thin cheeks were set in their most dour and spinsterish lines, but her wide-held eyes were full of tears.

"To be sure his feelings were hurt that you didn't," she said, "after you'd worked for him so long. But you didn't intend it. Don't blame yourself so."

He shouted, "I don't blame myself!"

She bowed her head, as if she were struggling with some strong emotion. Then she said, "At all events, it's done with now. Let's not make a fuss."

Unexpectedly, shakily, he began to laugh. He said, "Oh, damn it, Mary, why are you always right?"

"I'm not. And I'm always interfering, and acting holy. Oh, Charles, I wish I could get over it."

He put his arm around her without knowing that he did so.

"Please don't ever. I need you as you are."

Unselfconsciously, almost absently, her own arm returned the embrace.

"No, Charles, you don't. I only get holy, and impatient."

"Dear."

Their arms dropped, their hands joined. They began to walk on.

They were silent for a little. Then Mary said, "It's getting dark."

"Yes. Winter. Such short days."

Another silence fell.

At last Charles said, "What are you thinking of, dear?"

"I don't know." Her voice was light and impersonal, like a sound in nature, a stir of summer leaves or a dropping of small rain. She spoke so lightly, so vaguely, that the words came into Charles's ears void of any meaning but the meaning of their natural music, pure sound, like stirring leaves or raindrops falling. "Days, so short," said the light, small voice. "I was thinking of winter. Days going by. Seasons, years. Time. I'm afraid of time."

A small voice, a sound in nature, companioning, impersonal. Charles smiled. Their hands, still loosely joined, hung between them, swinging, as they walked.

❋ ❋ ❋ ❋   PART II   ❋ ❋ ❋ ❋

❋   *1*   ❋

CHARLES WAS NOT afraid of time; indeed, when he was happy he lost all effectual belief in it.

Kate, now monumentally great with child and still beautiful, seemed to him not like one waiting, but as if pregnancy were her essential state of being. Mary would always be like those days of March that are not quite winter and not yet spring, a girl not quite a woman or a child. Fred, with his first paid position, had become a sort of never-aging Potter, full of worldly airs and knowing anecdote.

That winter was set out of time. And the timelessness was not wholly illusory. For Charles had found one joy that would not change, the joy of discovery. He was eager for money as he would always be, but he was no longer a showy young hack. Ulysses had set out on the voyage that is new from the morning it first slips hauser until it comes to the whirlpool at the end. A discoverer who still answered to the name of Boz had started edging out past the harbor light.

Not that life, that winter, lacked exasperations. For one thing, Charles was astounded to learn that Macrone had kept the careless note he had dashed off on that day when they made their first tentative, unrealistic plans about *Gabriel Varden*; kept it, and thought of it, what's more, as a binding legal document. He was also quite difficult about Charles's winding off the Boz series with one volume, not two, and far from understanding about the difficulties which kept Charles from delivering that volume precisely on time.

As Charles said, it is disturbing to realize that one has completely misjudged a trusted friend's character. He was glad that they were

[*154*]

now communicating only through the printer; otherwise he might have found himself saying things that he would later regret.

Still, it did not really matter. It did not even matter that the operetta died quietly almost as soon as it had opened to an enthusiastic, if padded, house.

The sense of timeless happiness not only lightened such exasperations; it gave a pleasant sense of easy custom to the fields of privilege, the invitations which came from every side for the young author of the successful *Pickwick*.

Kate's pregnancy, by the convention of her day, made her a stay-at-home. Charles was free to embrace the present and enter it as once he had entered the Beadnells' genteel and elegant drawing room untrammeled by a Potter who could not have picked up the tune.

On Christmas Day, that year, Charles visited the Governor — to eat the turkey and drink the numerous toasts that he had paid for, and his heart brimmed with tenderness for everyone at the table. He came home to another turkey, which Beard ate with them. It was a warm, good family time. Charles almost hated to leave it at the last, and set out for an evening party with Ainsworth at Kensal Lodge.

Yet it cannot be denied that he entered Ainsworth's drawing room with a heightened buoyancy, a sense of having more space to expand in. He crossed the room with his head lifted in the way which often made people remember him, quite incorrectly, as a tall young man. His color was high from the cold night outside, and his blue eyes shone.

"A merry Christmas to you, Ainsworth! Ah, what a slap-up finish for the best day of the year!" His look went eagerly around the room. "What a good party. Lord, Disraeli's waistcoat, it's blinding! Who's that huge youth behind him?"

"That's John Forster."

"Amazing. That hulking boy, the critic of the *Examiner?*"

"Your age, I think. How old are you, twenty-four?"

"It's surprising that I've not met him before."

"It is indeed," said Ainsworth, a little dryly. "Come and do it now."

It was surprising, for Forster was such a Boz enthusiast that he had even praised *The Village Coquettes*, and Charles was far from unaware of the value of the well-timed word of thanks. Ainsworth smiled, his hand on Charles's shoulder, while he waited to catch Forster's eye; for Forster, as usual, was pontificating. He smiled again, the introduction made, to see Forster bend down in flourishing

[155]

homage while little Dickens had to tip back his head. Ainsworth himself was half an inch shorter than Charles, but somehow he was never aware of it.

And now, he thought as he strolled away, Little Jack the Giant Charmer has a new friend at court.

Charles, however, was not being consciously charming. The brilliant smile that he lifted to John Forster's face meant, quite simply, that he liked it. It was an ugly, heavy-featured face, but it was full of goodness.

"You've written many kind things about me," he said. "Merry Christmas, and bless you."

Forster's large hand sought his bosom in an ornate gesture. He answered in a deep bass vibrato: "And permit me, sir, to wish you a merry Christmas in the name of those multitudes to whom you bring delight."

Charles controlled a slight twitch at the corners of his lips. He thought, What a show to get him together with the Governor.

But he liked John Forster.

In fact, that evening, two ambitious young men shortly forgot why they were there, and settled in a corner to talk the rest of the evening away. They were delightfully agreed on every literary question, and leaned forward, often to shake hands hard, laughing as they did so. They were delightfully disagreed on politics, and got equal pleasure from shouting each other down.

And when at last they realized that they had outstayed all the other guests, they walked the better part of their way home together.

They wrung each other's hands at parting.

"What a good, good talk," Charles said. "I feel that we've been friends for years."

He was whistling under his breath as he let himself in with the latchkey. He tiptoed into the bedroom and lit a candle. The quietness with which he moved was automatic; his mind was still elsewhere and having a lively time of it. When Kate spoke, he started.

"I thought you'd never come home."

"Eh? Why, Mousie, you're awake."

"Yes."

He laid his watch on the dresser and came quickly to the bed.

"Sweet, why couldn't you sleep?"

"I don't know."

She was lying on both pillows, her own and his. Her hair, which she had not put up in papers, flowed over them like a waterfall. He touched it, and touched the side of her neck. He felt desire like an angry twinge of pain, for she was getting near her time, and for a matter of weeks he had kept docilely to his own side of the bed.

He said, "Beautiful?" He told himself that she was going to have a baby; but still he did not believe it. She was Kate, inconveniently distended but painfully beautiful, and the time was present-without-end.

She put out her hand.

"Please don't stay out very late any more until it's — happened."

Her hand tightened on his, and she turned, moving her face clear of the shadow cast by the footboard.

"Darling, you're frightened!" he said; and, almost in the same breath, "Dear God, you're beautiful!"

She shook her head. "Please listen to me, Charles. I'm . . . I'm not good at telling of things."

He sat down on the edge of the bed and touched her hair again.

"When Mother came, today, she got to talking of things. Things that I didn't know could happen to women having babies. She did it to make me easy in my mind, to tell me that they wouldn't happen to me. In case I should be afraid, you see."

"I see."

"Don't be angry with her. Mary was angry. When she left she said, 'Oh, how can she! I daresay everyone worries and I shall too, when it's my own turn but' — this is what she said — 'but how foolish to be frightened of anything so ordinary!' "

"To be sure."

Kate shook her head in a strange little gesture, not like her; it was like someone wearily brushing aside an irrelevancy.

"Charles, it's the ordinary things that frighten people most. Dying's ordinary, too."

Charles stared at her, unable to speak. The gesture, the terse little sentences were out of character; her face, as she spoke, was a stranger's face, beautiful with tragic intelligence, wholly unfamiliar.

In the dim light, he looked at her face. He looked at the hillock of her distended belly under the covers. As he had seen it do often, it changed shape a little with the moving of the child. But this time it was different.

He started. He leaned forward, laying one hand on each side of her lovely face.

"My God," he said, as if it had just occurred to him, "we're going to have a baby!"

The lovely, urgent clarity left her eyes. She laughed, her own familiar, meaningless little laugh.

"There!" said Charles. "There, that's better. And Mousie's own boy is here now. Now she can sleep."

He was aware of no sense of loss, no difference. But he had left the place where time stands still and returned to the world of becoming and perishing.

As he shaved the next morning, he worried about his relations with Macrone. He thought of the money that he had lost on the operetta, and wondered if he had not been too hasty in leaving the *Chronicle*. The baby would crowd them; they should have a house, and they could not afford a house. How much depended on the second issue of *Bentley's* with the first installment of the new novel! Yes, God, whilst it is bettering the lot of London's poor, let us pray it will start close to home!

That day he asked Kate several times how she was feeling and if it weren't possible that the doctor had miscalculated the date.

He also said, "Do you really want your Mother to be here while it's happening? Won't she only get you upset?"

His voice broke on the question, and Kate and Mary both laughed at him.

Indeed, his return to the world of becoming and perishing, of fatal chance, was ridiculously complete.

❋　2　❋

KATE'S LABOR began at dawn on Twelfth Night. Mrs. Hogarth came in a hansom, and sent it off for Mrs. Dickens.

Far from hovering like a vulture, she positively exuded high spirits. When Mrs. Dickens arrived, she embraced her like a long-lost sister.

"Kate's doing splendidly, poor Charles is the one who wants nursing, ha, ha. Here, give me your mantle, we've a deal to see to!"

What they were seeing to was anyone's guess, but they bustled about in each other's way with the zest of two girls readying their house for an evening of quadrilles.

It was, in fact, Charles who did the hovering, as he urged Kate to lie down and assured her repeatedly, with a smile of deathbed cheer, that everything would go off in slap-up style.

He was completely taken aback when, at last, Kate said, "Oh, Charles, please let me be. Why don't you and Mary go for a walk? It will take your mind off your nerves."

"And do try to find a small, firm table," said Mrs. Hogarth. "There's nothing I can put by her bedside for the doctor's use."

Kate's face closed on a pain. Her hands made fists. She gasped, caught her breath, and spoke again.

"And do, if you can, let it match the bed and the dresser," she said.

Charles and Mary found themselves in the street.

So that day began to which Charles Dickens's heart came back, endlessly, until the day of his death. The day that he and Mary walked about and looked for a table. The day when he and Mary waited together for Charley to be born, and looked for a table.

Actually, they saw precisely the right table in the first shop window they looked into. It had folding flaps, two drawers with brass knobs, and nice stout legs. It matched the bed. Indeed, for the purposes of moral and aesthetic satisfaction, it was just such a table as should have ended a long day's search.

Mary pointed to it, laughing. "Done before we're begun. You're not too proud to carry it home yourself, are you?"

But Charles hesitated. "It looks to be an expensive shop."

Shortly before Christmas, he had bought a coat from Ainsworth's tailor. It was of gray broadcloth, with a velvet collar and a short cape at the shoulders. He wore it unbuttoned at the throat to show the new broad neckcloth, more fashionable that season than stock and ruffles. He had also begun to let his hair grow longer in a sort of artist-princeling style which became him vastly. He looked like a young Lord; or, more accurately, like a handsome young actor playing a lord.

Mary glanced at him and smiled broadly. "You look to be an expensive customer," she said.

"I couldn't afford this coat. Sometimes I show no more sense than the Governor."

"Ah, but it puts you in a position to haggle. The rich are wonderfully stingy, they tell me."

"One couldn't haggle in a shop like that. Besides that, I might be recognized."

"You mean, because of *Pickwick?* What difference could that make?"

"The point," he said, a trifle edgily, "is that I'd like to save a little money, if it's possible. Do you object to our looking a bit further?"

She took his hand. "It's really going well for her, our mothers would know if it weren't. Yes, let's look further, it will pass the time for us."

It did pass the time. They went to secondhand shops, where haggling is proper and expected. They examined dozens of tables, but all of them were too high or too wide or too weak or of the wrong sort of wood, except for one or two; and after minute inspection, even those one or two could be discovered to have some flaw: a faint, faint marking from a wet cup which would surely be hard to remove; a crack which proved that the veneer was about to blister.

They lost themselves in it. Once or twice Charles pulled out his watch, and Mary said, "It takes far longer to have a baby than one thinks, I'm sorry to say," and they went on hunting. They forgot to eat lunch. Once or twice, as the hours went on, Mary dropped into a chair as they entered a shop and said, "I'm half dead, aren't you?" But always, in a few minutes, she was up and back in the game, as set on it as he.

It was past midafternoon, and they had circled back nearly to their starting point when Charles said abruptly, "It must be happening now. Let's get back, Mary. Fred can go for that first table that we saw."

"Charles, that's precisely what I was about to say to you! Do you think that we both have second sight?"

As Charles opened his door, Mrs. Hogarth hurried out of the bedroom.

"Did you fetch the table?"

"I thought of sending Fred. Tell me, how is she?"

"Fred's gone for the doctor. Don't disturb Kate, Charles, she is trying to rest."

"My God, he's not here yet?"

He pushed past her, running into the bedroom. Kate was gasping for breath, her face contorted. He fell to his knees and caught at her hand.

"Dear, oh my dearest, how — how are you?"

The pain finished. She looked at him without interest.

"Where's my handkerchief? I want to wipe my face."

He wiped it with his own. His hand shook. Kate did not turn her head to him, and her face was now preoccupied, as if she were listening for a sound just beyond the normal range of feeling.

"You can feel them start to come," she said. "A sort of odd, tickly feeling before it really begins." She released her hand from his. "Why don't you take another little walk? I'm only now got properly started."

"Kate, don't you want me here?"

She drew a sigh. Her eyes, Delphic and remote, excluded him. She spoke in a small, weary voice.

"I don't want to sound impolite, Charles, but . . . I'd liefer not be distracted."

He got to his feet. He looked at her as if life and death were in the room, and Kate their priestess. He felt no personal rebuff, but rather a strange agony of embarrassment, as if he had stumbled through the wrong door in a church and found himself upon the steps of the altar at the moment of the Elevation.

Kate's hands grasped the covers, her lovely face began to twist in another pain. She caught one sharp breath and gasped as she let it out. She said, "Does the table match?"

As if, Charles thought, the pain were a secret. A holy, sacrificial rite that she must perform alone. She must not speak of it. "Does the table match?"

He choked on a sob. He said, "Perfectly, it couldn't be better, dear. Dear love. I'll only be away for a little, now. You're doing splendidly."

He fled the room.

Mary, still in her bonnet, was sitting on the edge of a chair.

"I just remembered that we didn't eat anything. Could we afford to go across the court to the hotel?"

He nodded, half hearing her. He walked down the outside stair, his face bowed.

He felt no hunger, himself, until the food was before him. Then he wolfed it down like a starving man. His plate was empty before Mary was half done with her own.

"I surprised myself," he said.

"Worrying often makes one hungry."

"You're not worried, are you?"

"Oh, Charles, you know quite well that we're both terrified."

"Kate is not. She . . . she is wonderful."

"But she's *doing* it. And we — oh, you know that we're both the kind that simply cannot let people do their own work, and particularly if it's hard. We go mad if we can't interfere."

"You don't interfere."

"Nonsense, I never stop." She turned her fork over and appeared to study it, front and back. "I've been half mad all day to jump right into Kate's bed and say, 'Here, let me do it!' Oh, I'm truly ridiculous. Not only today, but always, Charles. It's come on me sometimes that half the time I'm praying, I'm only trying to make God interfere, too! Like a great baby — hinting, you know, and coaxing. So ridiculous."

He reached across the table and took one of her hands.

"Do you pray a great deal? Are you praying now?"

The lean, boyish fingers clasped hard upon his own.

"Charles, dear, don't be so frightened. It's silly for us to be frightened, she's really doing perfectly. Our mothers aren't the least bit troubled. They know."

"I know it's absurd. But, Mary, I've been frightened ever since Christmas night. She was awake when I came home and . . ."

"Charles! It's only a baby."

"It came on me then. We've been so happy, we three. I mean, we four. As if it could never end. But things do end, Mary, they change for better or for worse, but they still change. Please pray."

He was ashamed of the outburst before it was done, yet he was relieved by it, too. He leaned forward, waiting with almost superstitious fervor for Mary, so good, so innocent, so surely possessed of some inside track if there were, possibly, an inside track, to say, "To be sure, I'm praying now. To be sure, I'll pray."

But Mary took her hand from his.

"I'm sorry," she said. "I've never told this to anyone before, but I can't pray the kind of prayers you mean. You see, I don't think they do any good."

He started. He looked at her incredulously, and was bewildered to see that her narrow face, though grave, was serene.

"I don't understand you," he said almost fretfully. "Prayers for those we love — what kind could do more good?"

She shook her head. "I can't pray for things to happen or not to happen. I mean, how can one see the way things are, the accidents that happen to quite good people and all, and think that God . . . Oh, don't you see?"

He was not only disturbed but shocked.

"Child, are you saying that God is not just?"

She flushed. She looked unhappy and confused. "I can't say it properly. I've never tried to say it even to myself, before this. But . . . but I've always thought that His justness is . . . is simply in how much of His love a person can feel."

"But God protects people He loves, child."

"In a way. But that's not the point." She broke off once more for an instant. Her face was puzzled, timid, tentative, and still behind the confusion there was a look like light. "The whole point is God, always there and yet — oh, this is difficult to explain — yet still wanting to be *more* there. And in a world where things can happen, you know, accidents and sadness, one remembers it. How much He needs to have us be *part* of Him, almost."

Charles sat perfectly still and looked at her.

But she's a saint, he thought. I know a saint.

She laughed, a vexed, apologetic sound as she might have laughed upon awkwardly upsetting a glass of water.

"Whatever took me with preaching so?" she said. "I set out to cheer you up, and I ended with being all holy and revolting."

"Oh, that's quite all right," Charles said.

They both looked at their plates.

Then Charles spoke again, stiffly. "Ordinarily I hate this sort of talk and the people who do it. Evangelism. Running about naked. Prayer should be private or confined to the decencies of the Church of England."

"I know. I was sickening."

"You weren't, strangely enough. And I want to ask you one more question while we're on the embarrassing subject."

"Oh, dear," she said. "Must you?"

"It's only this. When you pray for other people and don't ask God to interfere, as you said, what does that leave you? What do you pray?"

"What I try to pray is that people will find what they need most —
like being kinder, or braver, or whatever. I try not to imagine it, because one can't, seeing that we're all so different. Which is what
makes it important, all of us being *able* to be a kind of good that nobody else can be, and God can't do as well without."

She looked down and swallowed, and looked up again. She
smiled.

"Unfortunately," she said, in a changed, crisp little voice, "that's
precisely what I can't manage. Whenever I don't try to get God to
interfere I only try to do His imagining for Him instead, you see."

And Charles, his eyes full of emotional tears, leaned forward across
the table and took her hands.

"Oh, Mary," he said. "My God, Mary. Oh, I love you so."

She nodded quietly.

"Oh, Charles, aren't we absurd? Both so frightened, and getting
holier by the minute!"

The laughter, spontaneous and comfortable, released them both so
easily that neither of them was aware that there had been either
release or need for release.

With no sense of awkward transition, Charles said, "It can't be
much longer. Shall we buy that table now and fetch it home?"

"A boy!" Mrs. Hogarth cried, as they opened the door.

Charles ran past her, to Kate.

As he fell on his knees at her side, his mother hastily flung a sheet
over all remaining counterevidence to the bundle-from-heaven
hypothesis. Charles was blind to her presence, deaf to the un-
punctuated rushing of her voice as it hymned the entire Barrow and
Culliford lines from their illustrious beginnings up to this crowning
moment.

He did not even hear the wailing voice of his son; nor did he, in
fact, see Kate's face, sodden with weariness, though his eyes devoured
it, nor did he hear her voice, druggy with exhaustion, articulating
heavily: "What kept you so long? I'm . . . oh . . . tired . . ."

Charles only saw beauty and heard triumph. He lifted one soft,
lax hand to his mouth, and his lips moved against it, forming soundless words: "My love . . . my wonderful . . . thank God . . ."

"Boy," Kate whispered, barely audibly. "Big, healthy. Boy."

Charles knelt, a sentimental abstraction: worship, before the woman, before the beauty of triumphant life.

"Well," said Mrs. Hogarth, "aren't you going to look at the baby?"

He got to his feet, clumsily, unwillingly. He turned with resentment to the small, waiting fact that was thrust into his dream of reverent fatherhood and sacred beauty.

He turned, he looked.

His mouth widened, his eyes woke.

"So," he said. "Charley."

Suddenly he began to laugh. He pushed his hands past his mother's. His arms made a cradle; one hand, gentle and possessive, cupped the small, damp head.

"To be sure you know me, Phenomenon of Intelligence. To be sure, Phenomenon knows his own Papa. Yes, yes."

"So little," Mary whispered. "Oh, so little."

". . . but, alas," Mrs. Dickens continued, "as my dear mother so often said though I in those days dear me . . ."

Kate gave a sound between a moan and a yawn.

Charles looked down, his face wholly seeing, directed and composed in happiness. "There, ah, there," he crooned, swaying, "there, to be sure, Charley, Phenomenon. There . . ."

❊   3   ❊

IN TWO DAYS, Charles was urging all and sundry to call, to see the Phenomenon with their own eyes and enjoy a glass of mulled wine.

"Bless you, we're as quiet as if nothing had happened. Kate keeps to bed, but she's doing brilliantly."

The nurse was a stout, heavy-breathing woman who managed to smell of gin from the hour she came, each morning, until the hour she left, at night, despite the fact that the gin was kept under lock and key. Charles told her almost at once that she was not needed.

"Isn't it restful, not having her underfoot?" he said to Mary, happily. Before she could reply, he had kissed the top of her head, called a gay goodbye to his splendid Kate and hurried out, glowing.

He ran into Ainsworth at the Garrick and embraced him jubilantly. "Can't remember what it felt like to be childless," he said. "It's fortunate that our little Mary is a born nurse. I'm so pressed until we've got the first issue afloat that I couldn't have managed, otherwise. I daren't even think ahead to the second number, and *Oliver's* introduction to society, until this gamble's safe."

Yet the words were only a sop to fate, tossed out as an unsuperstitious person might toss a pinch of salt over his shoulder. Charles's euphoria in the days directly after Charley's birth was overwhelming. The wiseacres' dark predictions that *Bentley's Miscellany* would never live to see March ran off him like water off a duck's back.

And the prompt, exhausted sleep which overtook him each night as he tumbled into bed after a day of rushing, kept him from noticing that the temporary sleeping arrangements — Fred on the sofa and Charles on Fred's cot — were being protracted unduly.

He did sometimes frown when Kate would withdraw from the sofa to her bed at the sound of approaching guests. Afterwards he would say, "My lovely dear must try to believe that the way to feel all well and strong again is only to act so." And once or twice it struck him that Mary was less lively than usual of an evening, and he said, "Shall I help with the washing up?"

Occasionally, before he had drunk his morning tea, it even came to him that more new publishing ventures do, in fact, sink than float. Such moments were infrequent and brief, but they were bad, and not only because of the money involved. For the book, the still untitled book about the boy, Oliver, and the haunting old devil, Fagin, and the poor trull and her brutal lover — the book now so live and continually pushing, even under all the current rush of activity, would have to wait. If *Bentley's* failed, it would wait and go stale as that — that incubus, that rotting stillbirth of a notion about Gabriel Varden and the Gordon Riots.

"Fred!" he would shout at such moments. "Have you been using my razor *again?*"

But always, with the first cup of tea, he was restored. He was always smiling radiantly when he kissed his splendid Kate, and his competent little Mary, and marveled for a moment above the cradle of the Phenomenon, and set out, shoulders squared for the battle that could not be lost.

And *Bentley's Miscellany* was a sensation.

"Wot did I tell yer?" he crowed. "This little h'editor knows 'is public!"

Mrs. Hogarth came to call.

"Very gratifying, I'm sure," she said. "Now, perhaps things can be kept a bit more quiet for poor little Kate."

The venom in her tone bewildered Charles almost as much as it enraged him, and the rage was almost more than he could hold in check.

Yet he kept his tone even as he said, "Kate is doing wonderfully, Mrs. Hogarth. A convalescent, you know, wants encouragement, not its precise opposite."

Mrs. Hogarth's bosom swelled and her nose narrowed. Kate looked alarmed. She was frightened by quarrels. Abruptly Charles decided that since the old vulture was so clearly in a bad mood, Kate, poor child might bear her better alone than in his company.

"Get your bonnet, Mary," he said. "Your mother will be delighted to play at nurse for a bit, I know."

"Hmf," said Mrs. Hogarth.

In the streets the dirty snow had half melted and frozen again, but the air was crisp and the sloping January sunlight was clear and pale. Charles took a deep breath, lifting his face to the sky.

"Ah," he said, "one's a new person the moment he steps out of doors. How can people live, cooped in houses day after day?"

They walked in silence for a few minutes, both with faces raised to the light.

"Ah, how good! Mary, we've not had a walk since Charley came."

"It's a lovely day. Charles, were you sure as you seemed to be, about the magazine? That it would do so well?"

"In general."

"Do you ever feel that it's unlucky to be too sure of things? I kept having the most nonsensical feeling that it would be luckier for us to worry.

"Oh, speaking of worries, is Mr. Macrone still vexed?"

"Didn't I think to tell you? Ainsworth's handling him for me. If *Oliver* does well, we can buy back the copyrights and call Macrone an error of youthful judgment."

"But I thought that Mr. Ainsworth was a great friend to you both."

"To be sure. That's the beauty of it."

"If he manages to suit you both."

"Why shouldn't he?"

"I only . . . Then you shan't write that other book?"

"Oh, in time, for another publisher. At present little Charles continues *Pickwick*, launches *Oliver*, furthers the Kingdom and gets all these things added unto him. Namely sweet golden guineas."

"But considering the Poor Law, and all, you'd write it as you planned, wouldn't you, even if not so many people liked it as like *Pickwick?*"

He smiled, touched by her gravity. "You have a good little heart, dear, and I love it. But there's something I'm just beginning to find out. If a story's to have any real life of its own, for good or ill, it's got to catch the writer and his audience up together into a sort of love affair."

She dropped his arm and said, surprisingly, "There's love and love, you know."

He laughed. "I do, indeed, my dear elderly cynic. I'm talking of the sort of love where there's real understanding on both sides, and real trust, and affection."

To his amazement, she began to cry. Without words, without apology or explanation, she snatched a handkerchief out of her reticule and wept into it, walking ahead of him stiffly, her bonnet down.

"Why, Mary, child, what is it? What in the world?"

She kept her head turned from him. She answered in a dry, hard, tired voice that scarcely sounded like a girl's, let alone a weeping girl's.

"What do you know about understanding, you and your notions?"

"Mary, what troubles you? Child, don't you know how much I love you?"

He saw her thin shoulders contract sharply.

"Mary, dear," he said.

Without warning, her voice shrilled like the voice of a slum-bred shrew.

"Don't I, though! Don't I know how you love both Kate and me, your beautiful, splendid, happy, *healthy* wife, and her faultless, faultless little sister! Well, I'm not one of your notions and part of a book you made up and neither is she! I've plenty of faults, plenty of them, and she's felt feverish and wretched and longing for a little quiet and a little real notice ever since Charley was born, and we both get *tired!*"

She had stopped still and wheeled about on him in her fury.

Abruptly as it had come it was spent, and they stared at each other in shocked bewilderment.

Utter bewilderment: both of them hopelessly at a loss. For despite her strong, inborn streak of loving realism, Mary was not quite seventeen and as prone to romanticizing — or, in her own words, to notions — as Charles. And neither of them was old or wise enough to know that the outburst which had startled them both as if it were a demonic possession, was a common thing, springing from common causes; from fatigue, and that common, though rarely conscious jealousy, not for a rival of flesh but for the deadliest rival, the lover's fixed, inaccurate dream of the beloved's self.

Bone-tired, shrilling like a witch, Mary had made the most self-defeating of all demands — the lover's demand to be loved, not in a dream, but in angular, factual truth. And the demand had got what it usually gets.

Bereft, bewildered, Charles and Mary stared into each other's faces.

Where are you? cried their eyes. Where are you, Charles, flesh of my flesh and yet good and gifted as I am not? Where are you, my gentle, happy little sister, my angel with her finger pointing upward, my Mary, my other self?

They stared; anxious, lost eyes staring out of faces gone sharp and thin.

Mary turned her face away.

"I'm sorry," she said. "I can't think what got into me."

Charles spoke slowly. "Kate's not well? And you didn't tell me, speak out? Oh, Mary."

Slowly her face turned back to him. Slowly it lighted in a smile of such gratitude, such faith that his heart broke to see it even while his answering smile lit his own face with its mirror image.

The loss restored, they stood, face lifted to face, eyes in eyes kissing the necessary illusion, the dream given back.

"How cruelly thoughtless I have been," Charles said. "My poor little Kate, afraid to trouble me. Oh, child, dear heart, thank you for jolting me awake. Oh, the awful selfishness of a writer's business, when all his imaginary creatures walk about more real than life and life is only a hurry and a blur!"

"I might have told you quietly. I needn't have shouted."

"God bless you, dear, I don't know that at all. When Charley was born I walked clear out of the world, I see it now. I shouldn't have heard you. And I thought that I was being so tender, so loving . . ."

And Mary laughed.

"Aren't we a pair, both trying to get the blame? As if it mattered, now that it's over."

He put his arm about her. He was laughing, too.

"Dramatical, that's our Charles. But, to talk sense, do you think it would help if we went down to Chalk? We four, not Fred? To take her away to the good country air, close by the healing, good old ocean? And you'd rest too, and keep Kate in spirits when I had to be in town . . ."

He had begun to walk again, to walk so fast that it was hard for Mary to keep up with him, but he did not notice that.

He said, "Oh, Mary, dear girl, God sent you to make up for all my faults."

She answered breathlessly but with perfect faith, "I always feel that way about you."

❊ 4 ❊

KATE LOVED being in Chalk. They had two bedrooms and a little parlor to themselves, and Mrs. Nash, the landlady, took care of them. Kate spent her days by the fire, and while she spoke of the country air and the healing old ocean as "the damp" and "that dismal water in wintertime," she flourished withindoors like a conservatory rose.

Often, like one who had left the singly borne burden of a vast establishment, she said, "How pleasant not to be troubled with the care of a house!"

And on one day when Charles had just come back from a dash to London, and they were all together by the fire, she said with remarkable inexactitude, "This is so nice, it's like the first time we were here."

As she spoke, Charles was sitting with one hand held above the cradle; the Phenomenon liked to use his finger for a pacifier. His other hand hovered above a game of drafts, which Mary was close to winning.

He said, "Yes, darling, yes indeed."

He had not heard her words, yet it was a genuine response of pleasure to pleasure. His Kate was happy.

That night, as she was undressing under her nightgown, she glanced at the cot that had been set up for him in their room, and away from it quickly. She smiled, a hesitant, lovely smile. She said, "I feel so much stronger here than I did in London. I think that in another day or two I shall be quite well."

Once or twice, of late, Charles had found himself puzzling at an odd new docility, almost an indifference, with which he had begun to take his deprivation. He was busy, he went to bed tired, and still, should it be so easy? Kate was beautiful, and he was a man. Yet since the day they had thought of going to Chalk . . .

Whenever it came into his mind, Charles moved away from it restlessly and thought of something else.

But now, as Kate spoke and he saw her smile, his body vibrated like an E string sharply plucked. He said, "Oh, thank God, dear. Let it be soon."

That night he had insomnia, and welcomed it. Lying in the dark he felt a kind of joy in his harshly controlled, so urgent potency.

The next day brought the news of the second issue of the *Miscellany*, the issue that was launching *Oliver Twist*.

He kept his voice casual. "Ah, from Bentley. Now we'll see how we've done."

He made himself break the seal with deliberate, steady hands; he began to read, still with the smile of casual confidence.

He read it through, and he burst into tears.

Kate wrung her hands. "Oh, Charles, Charles, what is it? Oh, what's happened? Oh, dear, oh, dear!"

He spoke through sobs. "*Oliver* . . . tremendous success . . . oh, thank God, oh, read it, here . . . it's taken the town by storm!"

"What?" said Kate. "What?"

Mary ran to him and caught his hand with the letter in it.

"I knew!" she cried. "I tried not to, I tried like the other time, when it was only the magazine. But I couldn't. I still knew!"

Charles hugged her against him, laughing shakily. He drew her near to Kate, so that he could stand with an arm about each of them.

He said, "Not only the money. God knows that mattered, it mattered frightfully. But to know that I was right, that they'll hear me, that I needn't only play the jackanapes for them."

"What are you talking about?" said Kate. "Them? Who?"

Mary reached out and wove her fingers through the fingers of Kate's hand. She closed upon them hard, tenderly. She spoke low, like a mother comforting a confused child. "He's got famous for being droll. He didn't know whether people would like a book that was serious."

And Kate said, "Oh, dear, dear, did we need it so? I didn't guess! Oh, Charles, were we in debt?"

But Charles, though he embraced them both, had already leaped out of earshot and into glory.

"We'll buy a house," he said. "Did you notice, Mary, that I'd set my own name at the head of the manuscript? Charles Dickens, here he stands! Boz lived in chambers. Dickens will have a house."

He blew his nose and laughed.

"Now?" Kate cried. "Do you mean now, when we go back to town?"

She dropped Mary's hand and caught him in both arms, lifting the face of a child overwhelmed by the bounty beneath the Christmas tree. She had never looked lovelier than she did in that moment, so illuminated by innocent greed.

"Oh, love," Charles said. He kissed her. "Lovely love."

But when she moved back her head and looked up again, she had turned severe.

"You remember that I told you myself that it was not wise to write about poor people and depressing things. Why in the world did you say it was quite safe and take such a naughty risk, such a one that it even made you cry? Ah, well, it came out splendidly, but mercy me, it was really too bad of you, Charles! Now, wasn't it?"

He told himself that she was enchanting, like a child. And, indeed, in another moment she was enchanting again, as her delight swept back upon her.

She clapped her hands. "Enough money to buy a house! Oh, I must write at once, and tell Mama."

"A fine house, little Pet, in a fine street."

"Oh, Mary, fetch down my writing box!"

The satisfaction of composition had already begun behind her eyes. She held herself tall, a young woman of means, the mistress of a splendid house in town.

Charles kissed her again. "Lay it on good and 'eavy, my beautiful. The Dickenses is comin' h'up in the world, just you tell 'er."

His hearty, laughing tenderness was only slightly forced. Indeed, he was not really aware of his own sensation of letdown until Kate glanced at him quickly and spoke in an odd, apologetic, almost apprehensive voice.

"I hope that you know I'm really proud of you. I only said that about the riskiness because it . . . I mean to say, it would take something dreadful to make Papa cry and I never get used to . . . I only want to say that you are very clever, Charles, and I'm truly very proud."

Charles wanted to be grateful. He even believed himself to be grateful.

"I know, I know," he said. It was an irritable, almost pettish sound.

"I'll put a few more coals on the fire," he said, "and then you needn't trouble with it while I'm out."

Mary came back with the writing box as he was dusting his hands off on his handkerchief.

"I'm going out for a look at the ocean."

"Oh, wait. Charley's asleep and Kate wants to write her letter. I'll come, too."

As they turned into the road, Charles said, "This is our first walk since we left London."

"So it is. Since we came here we've seemed to go out by turns."

They walked apart, almost self-consciously. After a brief silence Charles said, "I expected that we'd walk often, here. It's curious how Kate dislikes being alone."

"Yes, isn't it?"

They both appeared to forget each other's presence. They strolled, apart, smiling absently at the gray sky.

"Shall we take the path down to the cliffs, Charles?"

"I always do."

"So do I. It's best on misty days like this."

The silence returned, but now it was not a separation. They came to the cliff, and purposefully, as if they had often come there together, they made for a shelving rock that was set back some yards from the edge of it. Mary brushed down her skirt. Their hands touched, and linked absently together.

[*173*]

Charles looked at her. Her eyes were fixed on the horizon; her face was sharp and clear with thought.

"What will it be like now?" she said. "As you get more famous and richer all the time . . . It's exciting and almost frightening, too, isn't it?"

He smiled. "Remember, child of faith, every trade has its ups and downs."

She shook her head. "No. There's a feeling I've got. The downs will scarcely count, and the ups will always come back greater and greater. No, it's begun."

He laughed. "Don't say it aloud. *They* might be listening."

"And pop us back into our four rooms, two flights up?"

"But we've been happy in Furnival's Inn. We'll always remember it, Mary."

"No we won't. We'll forget that the chimney ever smoked or that we were ever out of spirits. Oh, I wish we *could* remember it as it truly was. Keep it."

"Miser." Teasing, affectionate.

She sat a little more upright. She lifted her head as if she were try-ing to see over the horizon, over the curve of the world. Her face was quiet, intent upon distance. Unexpectedly, as if she were not speaking to him, she said, "In time I shall marry and bring up a family."

He was startled. "What?"

"I was reminding myself. I used to imagine it oftener, and I *should* do, you know, imagine it, if I'm not to end an old maid."

Charles smiled. "You've a year or two left before your charms begin to fade."

She drew her hand from his and clasped it with her other about her knees.

"I know," she said, in her most matter-of-fact little voice. "It's a thing none of us cares to think of. But we'll all get older, leaving Furnival's Inn makes me know it. And I should try to go back to imagining, about falling in love and marrying. So that when the time comes, I will."

He put his hands into his pockets. He told himself, as if it were a lesson that must be carefully memorized, that she was the quaintest little creature in the world, his Mary, his dear little friend whom he loved with all his heart, his dear little sister.

She turned her face full to him. "The strange thing," she said, "is to think that like as not he'll be quite commonplace. For that's really what it is to fall in love, isn't it? To have some quite ordinary, niceish person suddenly seem wonderful to you? More wonderful than anyone else, so that to you he's the whole world?"

Charles looked at her and could not say a word.

She smiled, her clear, small smile of impersonal thought. "In a way, it's a curious thing to want, isn't it? Like wanting to go out of your wits."

He made a tremendous effort and laughed. "Oh, Mary, let's make a pact. If you'll stay at seventeen forever, I'll stay at twenty-five and we'll let nothing go, we'll be misers together."

She leaned forward. She spoke in a low, quick voice that was earnest and vulnerable and altogether unlike her.

"Don't laugh at me yet, Charles. When I've done talking, yes, but not quite yet."

"Mary?"

"And . . . and don't answer what I'm about to say, either. It will make you want to laugh, I daresay, and I don't know what makes me say it, except that it's so quiet here . . . with the ocean . . ."

Charles swallowed on a nervous constriction in his throat. He had no notion of what she was about to say or of why he wanted so desperately to circumvent it, but he spoke with a loud, false heartiness.

"You look as serious as a judge. What's up, child?"

Her face, usually so responsive, did not change at all. The small, urgent sound of her voice went on as if it had only broken off to search for words.

"It's only this. I love you very much, Charles. Not in the way I was speaking of, not that way, but in every other."

He said, "I'm very touched."

The words came in a tight, dry voice, like that of one forcing himself to speak, past mortal pain, with some civilized remnant of courteous cheer. He heard his own voice, and refused to hear it, or to admit that the chill that went through his body was more than awareness that the February sun was sloping downward fast while they sat out of doors, unseasonably, on a stone by the sea.

And her voice began again, but now with a relentless calm; it was not like a child's voice, nor a woman's, but simply like one human soul speaking to another.

[175]

"So you see why I must go back to imagining about lovers as I used to do. For a time will surely come when I shall love someone in the same way that you love Kate. And since I already love you so in every other way, you can see what would be quite likely to happen to me. *Whereas* . . ."

She broke off on the curious, lawyerlike word, looking straight before her, setting the next words in order. And Charles shivered and his heart yawned open. Then she gestured outward with both hands.

"*Whereas*," she said, "if I imagine, and look for it, until I love someone else, fall in love, I mean, as one does, I shan't ever have to give up anything that I feel about you. I can love you always, just as I do now."

And her lips, firm and stern and still wholly serene, smiled as he had never imagined that anyone could smile.

"I don't know why I thought that it would be hard to say, or that you might not understand it," she said.

Charles bent his face on his clenched hands. He whispered, "Mary . . . Mary . . . Mary . . ." He did not hear himself nor did she appear to hear him. The sound might have been only one of the sounds of the earth around them, one with the hush of wind in the winter-dry grass and the reiterant statement of the incoming tide on the beach below.

Her hand touched his arm, lightly. For an instant they were both perfectly still.

Then, at the same moment, he lifted his face and she sprang to her feet.

"Why in the world did I feel I had to tell you all that nonsense? People aren't *intended* to know each other inside and out."

Charles stared down at the brown grass. His mind fumbled for the needful words: *her odd little fears . . . her trusting little heart.* None of them worked. The lid of the box would not shut.

Then Mary spoke again.

"Oh, Charles, I've bothered you. It was only talking, only talk about nothing, as people talk to themselves. It was absurd that I sounded so solemn over nothing."

He got to his feet and put his arm about her. He spoke gently.

"You didn't bother me, dear. Are you cold? We sat on that stone rather a long time."

"I am, a little."

"So am I. The walk home will warm us again."

That was all. Mary had been able to word a premature insight. Charles, less innocent, could not think about it any longer.

And still, in his own way, he, too, had made a confession and a renunciation.

They walked in Indian file along the cliff path, but when they reached the road they joined hands once more. For Mary was young, and she had eased her heart; and Charles had come back up to the surface. They walked at a stroll, though the wind had begun to freshen and the mist to turn into a heavy, blowing fog. They swung hands, they lifted their faces to the wet wind and breathed it with enjoyment.

As they came into the house, they were both laughing.

Kate had only that minute finished her letter and stamped down the seal.

※ 5 ※

CHARLES WAS a hard-working and brilliant editor, he was writing two best-selling novels at once, but the energy he put into finding and furnishing a new house was unbounded.

"House agents!" he cried. "And I thought I trusted the human race!"

But the relish in those outcries was unmistakable. The satisfaction with which Charles had once bought stale pastry at half price glowed in his eyes as he leaped into glad encounter with one agent after another. Prowling, tapping, questioning, he knew in no time flat whether a neighborhood had started to decline, or a new coat of paint hid a need for costly repairs. And after that came the joy of haggling. Every agent in town, apparently, had been tipped off that Mr. Dickens was Boz — a rich writer, innocent of the ways of business and created by benign Providence to be fleeced. Charles absolutely could not turn down a house, however unsuitable, until he had forced a sadly disillusioned man to admit its market value.

Yet in the end he spent more than he had intended or could afford, because 18 Doughty Street was so obviously the house he had been looking for.

It was built of warm, rosy brick that glowed in the afternoon light when he first saw it. Inside it had been kept superbly shipshape, sound from attics to cellars, with every one of its twelve rooms tastefully painted and papered, ready for moving into without the expense of another penny.

No, Charles had no regrets, though he had overspent himself so that furnishing those twelve rooms was a challenge. The secondhand dealers of London learned his eye and his mettle in the next few weeks as thoroughly as the house agents had done. Only the elegant front drawing room was all furnished new from the shop, yet before he was done, Charles — with the same abandon to the task in hand which the *Miscellany*, *Pickwick*, or *Oliver* each received in their turn — had coaxed every room of the twelve into looking tasteful and prosperous at wonderfully small outlay.

They moved in. They were settled, in surroundings which surpassed even Kate's eagerest dream. And almost at once, Hall sent Charles a bonus check for five hundred pounds, with an invitation to a banquet which should celebrate the first anniversary of *Pickwick*.

Kate fingered the check with incredulous awe. "Five hundred pounds *at once?*"

Mary said, "A year! Think, only a year, and so much to have happened in it."

"And blessings on Hall," Charles said, "and Chapman, too. I did sums today, and I'd almost begun to doubt as the Dickenses 'ad overreached themselves."

Yet almost at once they might have lived at 18 Doughty Street always.

Fred took up leaning against the mantelpiece in an attitude of aristocratic carelessness. Kate proved promptly that she could clutter twelve rooms as easily as four and sighed like an adept over the difficulty of finding good servants nowadays.

Sometimes Mary said, with a contented sigh, "It's really no different here at all, is it?"

It was almost anticlimax.

"We must give our parents a slap-up dinner," Charles said. "The proper wines, service, everything. A trial run for all the return entertainment I owe everywhere."

"I'd been wondering that we've not done it sooner," Mary said. "Your father must be so proud."

Charles smiled patiently. "Haven't my women remarked that I'm rather a busy man?"

"We're used to that," Kate said. "It's scarcely new."

He was baffled by the edge to her voice. He glanced toward Mary who was not, like Kate, given to little moods. But she was looking at Kate with an odd, sad look that was almost as baffling as Kate's ill-humor.

He said, "For God's sake do you both want me to sit about all day and chat?"

But before Kate could answer, Mary had begun planning. "You'll order the wines, won't you, Charles? I shouldn't know how."

The dinner was splendid. Mrs. Hogarth laughed often, in a high, artificial whinny and said, "Dear me, Kate, how fine you are, now, to be sure." Mrs. Dickens went into an ecstacy of tongues; she surpassed herself in showers of *non sequiturs* and the wild and whirling catalogue of her former splendors. George Hogarth said, "You've achieved astonishing things, Charles, for one of your years." Only the Governor seemed oddly quiet. Happy, yes, and wonderfully charming, quite the old courtier as he smiled and spoke occasional small compliments to Kate, or Mary.

Happy, at ease; what more did I want of him? Charles asked himself. I know how happy for me he is.

And still, he did want something more.

The port came on. The ladies, missing their cue, still sat at table.

John Dickens got to his feet. His glass was in one hand, the other flourished the eyeglass in the inimitable gesture.

And now, the oration, Charles thought, and smiled.

His father cleared his throat. "This evening—er—no evening, truly, but a dawn of a career—er—which Fortune's smile . . ."

And, abruptly, he had dropped the eyeglass, fumbled out a handkerchief, wiped his eyes, blown his nose, and gulped off the wine.

He said, "Oh, dear boy, bless you. Dear, dear boy."

He sat down.

"I'll not cry, too," Charles thought. "I'm damned if I will, and make a pair of us."

He reached for his own glass and rose, his face grave, classic, a hero returning a hero's toast.

"Thank you, Governor," he said. "I . . . Bless you. Thank you."

There was a moment of silence, and he saw that everyone else looked slightly embarrassed. He laughed, and threw back his head, lifting the glass high once more.

"Yes, yes," he cried. "Let us all drink to the Amazing Boz, and the glorious future, and the dear, good present! A toast, to me, and mine, and all my world!"

It made them laugh, as he had hoped it would.

The rest of the evening went off swimmingly.

Kate and Fred went up to bed as soon as they were gone. Mary walked about, straightening the chairs, putting out lamps.

"Your dear father," she said. "I know that your mother loves you too, and still, she'd be as — oh — uplifted, if Fred got to be a prosperous businessman. But he loves you. And would in the same way if you'd been less fortunate — like him. It's because you're alike, you know."

"Yes, I know. I forget, at times. I fall into hurrying. It came on me tonight that I've been in a rush ever since I was sure of *Oliver*. As if I must buy this house, furnish it, spend the money before it melted away."

She bent above the last lamp and blew it out. She walked out into the hall and stood in the light of the lamp on the newel post. Her head was lifted and she smiled, a shrewd, resigned little smile.

She said, "Charles, I become more convinced as I get older that people don't change as much as one would hope. I mean that people like Kate always have times when their spirits are low, and people like you always fall into fits of rushing and running, and people like me think too much about themselves and worry over nothing."

"Mary . . ."

"I mean to say that it doesn't signify, because the things that really count for most in us always come back — Kate's gentleness, and the way you understand people — and I know that I'm ordinarily very *sensible*, you know."

And Charles said, "Oh, Mary, do you know how much I love you?"

She closed her eyes for a moment. Then she opened them, and looked at him, smiling.

[*180*]

"To be sure I do," she said. "As much as I love you." She lifted her cheek for his customary good-night kiss, and started up the stairs. "Make sure you locked the door after them before you blow out the lamp," she called back. "I found it on the latch one day last week."

It had been a singular passage, and the most singular thing about it was that neither of them found it disturbing. Mary fell asleep smiling, and Charles, in his bedroom, said in a voice full of anticipation, "Kate, love, you looked so beautiful tonight."

And the next seven weeks were the happiest that Charles ever knew.

Throughout those weeks, Charles had never worked harder or with less sense of pressure. The fullest day still had the feel of leisure to it.

"This is a good house," he would say, "a fortunate house."

Sometimes as he let himself in at the door, he reached out and gave the bricks a pat, as if the house were alive. His eyes, in those days, had a look of easy confidence, and his full lips had a new, firm set. He had never swaggered less, and still his bearing said, "I am here because I determined upon it. Nothing is impossible to the dedicated will."

Such *hubris* in a very young man can be beautiful.

Kate said to Mary, "Do you ever feel that Charles is growing rather conceited?"

Mary kissed her and laughed. "He's sure of himself, and happy, yes. But after all, he's what he thinks, isn't he? That's not conceit, it's only common sense."

The party for Mr. Bentley would come off in the last week of April.

"You must have the finest gowns that can be made," Charles said. "Don't be afraid to be extravagant."

"Not we," said Mary. "We'll live up to the conservatory flowers and the champagne, never fear."

"That's the spirit, you'll make a stage manager yet."

She shook her head. "And only a year ago we were ready for a party by turning the cushions clean side foremost and buying some gin and lemons! Which makes me think, do let's ask Fan to come and to play and Mr. Burnett to sing, and we'll drop it about that they do it professionally at private entertainments. Then they can profit from it all, like us."

"Like us?"

"Why, like us while we're impressing Mr. Bentley."

The comment, so bald and cheerful, took Charles rather aback.

"The evening is in his honor, certainly," he said.

Kate sighed. "If only it weren't such a task. A man does not realize, Charles, how nursing saps one's vitality.

"Not at first hand," Charles said. "But in an academic way, one can scarcely complain of ignorance."

He had expected to sound amiably teasing, and he was startled by the edge to his voice.

Nor were his spirits bettered when Mary said, "Oh, men! Don't listen to him, Kate, when we're in our new gowns we'll be so gay that we won't know ourselves!"

And the evening, when it came, was a slap-up success. Kate had to leave it early, because of Charley's supper, but she was fresh as a girl while she stayed with the company. Her ball gown was of mauve satin; her hair, her eyes, her skin had never looked more enchanting, and the weight that she had begun to gain since Charley came was scarcely noticeable.

Pride cast a radiance upon her, too, pride in her house and her new position. She moved about with a charming, unaccustomed dignity. She did not talk, to be sure, but she listened, and her lovely blue-violet eyes created the illusion of response.

Charles told himself that she would make a superb hostess yet. And indeed, that evening, one would have had to know her very well to plumb the depths of inattention in that soft face which lifted so prettily to one guest's and another's.

"Indeed?" she said from time to time. Or, "Really?"

Several times as Charles glanced her way he thought in surprise, What can she be talking of? They look interested, actually interested!

Yet it was always to Mary that his eyes returned. And over and over he thought, with a sense of bewilderment that was almost like anger, She looks altogether changed. I shouldn't have known her.

She was not, in fact, changed. Even the white dress which bared her shoulders — not bony, as Charles had imagined them, but slender and straight — only heightened her everyday look of virginal freshness. Her hair was dressed no less severely than usual, and the Cape jasmine that she had set in the sleek loop at one side was a tidy, uncoquettish little bloom.

The effect was, rather, one of intensification. She looked precisely and movingly just what she was, a girl of seventeen. The smile, the charming look that Charles watched her raise to Ainsworth's face, to Bentley's, were her familiar smile, her listening, thinking, everyday look.

But I'm absurd, Charles thought. I want her to be loved. What troubles me?

At that moment, she turned her head and caught his eyes. She smiled and made a motion with her hand to signify, "Aren't things going nicely?"

Charles turned away, pretending that he had not seen.

But a white ball dress, only that, to make one see the life, and warmth, and grace, and peace, yes, peace, that one took for granted as part of his life, to make one see it as no part of his life, really, no private possession?

Charles nodded, much as he had seen Kate nod earlier that evening, at a faceless face before him. "Really? Indeed!"

He looked toward Mary again, in spite of himself.

He thought, I am turning into one of those fathers who never can admit that anyone is worthy of their treasure. I'm turning utterly possessive, the jealous father.

As soon as he had put it so, he felt better. He could laugh at himself. He could make the party swing.

The punch bowl was filled and refilled. The quadrilles began.

"Mary, will you stand up with me?"

"I'm promised to Mr. Bentley. Oh, Charles, isn't it going off perfectly?"

She was off, on Bentley's arm. The old fool's face was almost purple with wine and bouncing about.

"Fanny? Will Burnett let you honor me?"

From that first set, Mary was the belle. She danced badly, and nobody knew. She shone. Charles danced with Mrs. Bentley. With everyone who might otherwise feel neglected.

The evening was coming to an end when Mary came close to him again and touched his hand.

"Charles."

"Dear?"

She was pale, but her eyes were bright.

"It's perfect. Everyone talks of how wonderful you are. Everyone."

"Mary, you're white, are you tired?"

"I'm dead, and you must be too. But it's not been wasted. You were right, Charles, and everything they say makes me so proud!"

At once she was slipped away. He caught a glimpse of her across the room, a little later, smiling up into Bulwer's face.

Charles thought, She is tired, and she doesn't care. She wants it to be good for me. For me.

Nobody ever forgot Charles as he was at the end of that party, so gay, so electric with the atmosphere of success, so friendly, so madly clownish. His blue eyes swept the room like searchlights, as he proposed toast after toast.

Bentley was almost the last to leave.

"A stirrup cup," Charles cried. "Come, tempt him, Mary."

Bentley was half-seas over and a wave to spare. Mary took the glass from Charles and lifted it in both hands while she bent her head in a noble mock reverence.

"At the hand . . ." Bentley hiccuped and tried again. "At the hand of this Hebe, I cannot resist!"

There were cheers from the few last hangers-on. There were final farewells with much hand-wringing.

There was silence, Charles and Mary standing alone, their shoulders sagging and their faces drained.

"Where's Fred, Mary?"

"Don't scold him. Too much rosy. I saw before it got too obvious and sent him to bed. With bribes and threats."

"Lord. You were everywhere at once tonight."

"So were you."

"I expect I'll have to lay it on at being the heavy father tomorrow."

"He'll be sick enough to serve. Poor lamb. Ah, but wasn't it a wonderful evening? And think, Charles, only think, a year ago . . ."

She broke off, moving her hands outward. Her face was white and pinched with fatigue, her gray eyes were solemn and remote, but she smiled even while she gave her head a little, baffled shake.

Charles looked at her. Without warning, he felt his eyes sting and well over, his throat and chest tighten and his shoulders begin to shake.

"What is it? Charles, dear, what is it?"

"I don't know. Oh, God, yes, I do, and so do you. I saw you all the evening, I saw men's faces as they looked at you in that dress. I wanted to be glad, and I hated them. That day on the cliffs . . . the evening Father came . . . everything we both know and won't know, that we're so damned determined to have both ways . . ."

"Oh, Charles, please, dear, you . . . You're not making sense, you're tired, a little tipsy . . ."

He shuddered, hiding his face in his hands. "Oh, God, I'd be so glad to give up everything else, everything, to be back there in Furnival's Inn. A year ago, just as it was, safe, happy, never to change. Never . . ."

She shut her eyes.

"Oh, come," she said. "Don't be ridiculous."

He broke free of himself, by a tremendous effort. He blew his nose and smiled, a casual, rueful smile.

"Champagne. Wine is a mocker."

"To be sure. And the tiredness. We're both tired out."

"I expect so. Light a candle, dear. I'll put out the lamps."

"Yes."

They stood still, unmoving, looking at each other with tired, baffled eyes. After a long time, Charles held out his arms, in a helpless gesture. Mary went into them. He held her close, he felt her weight rest against him. The smell of the fading jasmine was in his nostrils.

He said, "Your damned flower smells like a funeral."

They were quiet again for at least a minute. Then she turned her head, hiding her face in his shoulder. Her outspread hands pressed harder on his back. He bent his own head over, awkwardly, until he could rest his cheek against her fine, smooth-parted hair.

At last she pushed herself away from him, with a gesture both heavy and matter-of-fact, like someone pulling herself reluctantly from a comfortable chair to get to bed.

"Carry the candle," she said. "I'm so sleepy I'd drop it."

She walked up the stairs before him, slowly. At the top landing she turned and touched his arm.

"It was a splendid evening, wasn't it?" she said. "I am so glad it all went off so well."

She walked away without a light into her own room and shut the door. It was the first time, since the day that Charles and Kate had come back from their honeymoon to the good little household, that he had not kissed Mary good night.

Yet, strangely, Charles did not think of that. He did not examine the sense of incredible reprieve that still trembled through him under the tiredness. He stood alone for a minute or two, with his head bowed. Then he turned to his own door and opened it very quietly, pressing down on the knob.

Kate had gone to sleep with the lamp still lit. She had not put up her curls, and her shining hair flowed out over the pillow. She was snoring, very slightly.

When Charles lay down in the dark, cautious not to waken her, he thought, I'm too tired for sleep, too tired to fall asleep.

He fell asleep almost at once.

✻   6   ✻

The first week of May it never rained except in the night. Day after day was bright and fresh, the light winds smelled clean-washed, and still one never saw the rain fall. It was the week when spring came in a rush, as it sometimes does, a season that has begun reluctantly, dubiously, leaping ahead of itself in a sudden confidence. Leaves and flowers whipped open like fans. Everyone talked about the weather. People in the streets forgot their hurry. They strolled to urgent appointments as if they had all the time in the world, and their faces were empty and foolishly happy with the sun and the air and the sudden rush of living green.

It was weather to invite the pathetic fallacy. It was a looking glass for the young and new in love; to those who sought to come to terms with death, it spoke the resurrection and the life. It was freedom to the poor, and innocence to the rich; for everyone with a minute to spare it had a kiss and a promise.

"Lovely weather," people said.

"Makes you want to go out into the country."

The costers' carts had baskets of primroses tucked in among the vegetables.

"I didn't walk to market today," Mary said. "I danced there and floated back, a good foot above everybody's heads. Ah, you should have seen them staring up at me!"

"You're getting to talk as oddly as Charles," Kate said. "You never used to be nonsensical."

"Poor love," said Mary, "do you begin to feel more comfortable today?"

Kate had rejected the weather by taking a heavy cold in her head.

"Pray the glory holds until Sunday," said Charles. "Mary, we'll have every walk that we've missed since we left Furnival's Inn all rolled into one."

"Oh, what a pity, don't you remember? I'll be visiting Mama from Friday to Monday."

"I had forgotten."

He was aware that his disappointment was disproportionate, but how absurdly so he did not realize until Fred broke into a shriek of laughter.

Kate blinked. "Did someone make a joke?"

Fred rolled up his eyes. "Don't you remember, I'm off to the Antipodes!"

"I didn't sound like that!" Mary's voice shook with anger.

Fred laughed more gleefully, delighted with the unexpected success of his teasing. He tuned his voice to the throbbing tenor from which alone he had expected to get his response. "And shall I never see thee more, alas?"

Charles held himself relaxed; he spoke, his voice carefully light.

"I did sound as if we get about one pleasant Sunday in a twelve-month, didn't I?"

He looked at Mary and she looked back at him. She spoke with equal calm and with equal lightness.

"Yes, but we should get back into the way of taking those Sunday strolls. They were always nice."

Fred shrugged and grinned. "Well, miss, you blew up fast and cooled off faster."

Mary shrugged too. "I hate to be mimicked. Now you've found me out my peace is gone."

Kate's eyes opened in guileless wonder. "I never knew that, Mary."

"You never tease, dear." The answer which was no answer at all appeared to satisfy everyone. Charles felt himself draw in a deep, fluttering breath.

He told himself that he did not in the least understand the passage which had just gone on. Its taste of complicity was strong and unpleasant in his mouth although he and Mary were involved in no complicity. They had just now acted together, he knew it, in a deliberate play of concealment; and it made no sense, for there was nothing to hide.

Nothing, it was senseless even to protest it to himself. It was lovely weather, rarely lovely. Since they came to Doughty Street, he and Mary had somehow been forgetting their Sunday walks. The lovely weather had brought them back to mind. For the moment he had forgotten Mary's plans and when he was reminded of them he had felt a childishly sharp disappointment. And Mary had been sorry that she could not enjoy her visit to her parents and have her stroll with him, both.

It was natural for Fred to have laughed at their childish chagrin. Why should they have joined together at once to conceal it? He, to be sure, was vain and capable of pulling things about to avoid being laughed at. But Mary was not troubled by such nonsense, and she, too, had deceived them for nothing.

For nothing . . . for nothing . . .

He jumped to his feet, pulling out his watch.

"The weather's addled my wits, I've an appointment with Bentley that I forgot."

He had no appointment. And that was lunatic, too, when he might quite as well have told the truth. That he wanted a good, hard walk; that he wanted to walk as he thought out the next installment of *Oliver*, walk and find his way into it properly.

He found his way into it, and the writing went well. Nevertheless, over that week end the house felt empty, and oppressively full of Fred's laugh and Kate's cold, both at the same time. Nothing looked tidy or shipshape. Nothing centered, somehow; even when he was at his writing, nothing centered until, blessedly, the Phenomenon got colic.

Charles held him against his shoulder, pacing the room with him, hour after hour, patting the small bottom, droning hymn tunes. Charley slept as long as Charles walked and sang and patted. Immediately he was laid down he woke, wailing.

And Charles, while he walked and sang and patted, did not feel the inadmissible emptiness and loneliness of the house, the inadmissible waiting and longing, or have to shut his mind upon it.

He did not need in the same way to shut his mind to the joy of her return. Everyone in the house loved Mary and was glad to have her come back. When he heard her voice in the hall he pushed aside his writing and ran down the stairs.

He caught her against him, laughing with happiness and untroubled by any need to hide it from himself. He kissed her, gladly, as if she were just come home from a long trip abroad.

"Oh, how good, how good to have you at home again! You don't know how we've missed you."

And Kate said, "Yes, truly, you couldn't have taken a worse time to go. Charley had the colic and we could scarcely do a thing with him. Poor Charles was half worn out."

"Oh, what a shame. And you, how's your cold?"

"It's gone, except for that depleted feeling they always leave one with."

"How splendid, we can go to the play after all. It's beautifully mild out of doors, and the fun is just what you need."

"Perhaps you are right."

Charles smiled, watching the struggle in Kate's face. It was always hard for her to relinquish an ailment but she dearly loved the theater.

She drew a little sigh and said again, "Yes, it is mild, today. Perhaps you are right."

They had tickets for a comedy at the St. James.

Kate and Mary wore the dresses that they had worn for Mr. Bentley's party. As they sat in their box, Charles could scarcely watch the stage for looking at them, at his Kate in all her soft, rich opulent beauty; at Mary, lovely as a young tree in flower.

That evening all that Charles felt for them both flowed sweetly in place once more, the chaste, impossible bigamy restored. He looked at Kate, his wife, his lovely love; he looked at Mary, his Mary, so newly beautiful in her girlhood's new young beauty and still forever changeless, the gentle child.

He loved them, loved them both. His happiness was complete and effortless. He was not even conscious of release. He was Charles, come back to the present-without-end.

When the play was over, all three of them were gay. They laughed over nothings all the way home. Even Kate laughed while she said, "How can you both be so nonsensical!"

The cabby shook his head as he drove away and remarked to the air, "You can't get around it, champagne goes better nor gin."

"Go into the drawing room," Charles said. "We're much too gay for sleep. I'll fetch us a bite and a sup."

Mary kissed Kate's cheek and his. "Not for me, dears. I'm dead on my feet."

She ran up the stairs, still laughing.

They heard her brief, strangling outcry as they stood in the hall. Charles, racing ahead of Kate, found her in her room, crumpled to the floor beside her bed.

He lifted her in his arms and laid her down. She gasped, her lips rigid with pain. "Sit me up. Can't breathe . . ."

Her face was small and white, sweating. It was a stranger's face, the face we always find most alien although sooner or later it will also be our own. It was only by the white dress and the smooth, delicate shoulders and the sleekly dressed hair that Charles could have known her.

He sat on the bed, holding her upright. He called, and even in that first awful urgency of terror he kept the fear from his voice, sheltering her with all the strength he had.

"Kate, dear, wake Fred and send him for a doctor. Mary feels ill."

He told Kate to send for her parents. When they came he took Mr. Hogarth's hand and said, "Make your wife see that it is Kate who needs her most. Mary is asleep most of the time. She should be with Kate, and make Kate rest."

Mr. Hogarth bowed his head.

He said, "I will tell her. I will wait downstairs. Call us quickly when . . . when she wakes, when she can know that we are here."

Charles said, "Thank you. It may help her if the room is quiet. Thank you."

He held her so through the night and until three the next afternoon. Once or twice, while the doctor was there, he moved aside to an armchair and drank a cup of tea.

It was in the afternoon that the pattern of Mary's breathing changed. A deep breath; then the next shallower and faster, and the next, until there was only a thin, incredibly rapid panting. Then a long quiet. Then a long breath again.

The doctor had come back. He stood by the bed. He heard the pattern through several times. He said, "I will speak to Mr. Hogarth. He can prepare his wife and Mrs. Dickens better than I."

Charles shifted his body and his arms, easing the pain in them. He heard the sound of the doctor's voice, and his mind refused its meaning. He heard the doctor go out of the room.

Mary lay in the compass of his left arm. He reached out his right and fumbled for the glass of brandy that her unconscious lips had refused so often.

"Darling. Mary, oh, God, dear Mary, take a sip of this. Just a sip. Oh, God, my Mary, my own Mary, please . . ."

Sleepless, in desperate prayer that had alternately lifted him into an overwhelming sense of present answer and dropped him back into despair, he had passed through hours that went like seconds and seconds that went like hours since her last waking. He made the gesture, he spoke the words in an empty automatism of despair.

Her eyes opened. She took a sip or two from the glass.

She spoke, in a whisper but not with any laboring of breath. "You'll make me tipsy." And then, in a whisper so light that he could barely hear it, "Dear Charles. Dear."

The eyelids closed. She was better, she had fallen into a natural sleep, her breath so soft that he could not hear it at all. The doctor came back into the room, looked down at her, laid his fingers on her pulse.

He said, "Mr. Hogarth should have made more haste. He said that your wife is prostrated, but he went to them. They should be here."

The meaning of the words reached Charles seconds after the doctor had gone from the room. He shook, still clutching Mary in his numbed arms. He began to cry, in loud, retching sobs.

She opened her eyes. "Charles, what is it?"

He looked down. He saw the gray, living eyes, he heard the pitying whisper. He knew that she would live. He kissed her forehead. He kissed her mouth. He spoke in a whisper like hers.

"Mary. You've been quite ill, dear."

"I know. Don't go away, Charles. You must have held me for hours, you must be tired. But don't . . ."

"I'm not tired, my dearest. Rest a little more."

He felt the triumph of victory, the strength of his own life pouring into her body. He was faint with the exquisite, incredible joy of knowing that she had turned back from death.

He had held her so in his arms for several minutes before he knew that she was dead.

The others, the jangling others who claimed some part in her, crowded into the room almost as soon as he knew. With an awful effort he shut them out for the last possible moment. The waxy face, the flat, empty, dull eyes at which he looked were not Mary; and still he knew that once the others had started their sobs, their outcries, Mary would be gone from him as she was not yet, not yet.

Suddenly he cried out, first of any in that room, "Mary! Mary!"

Her dead hand curled over his living hand. On her ring finger she had always worn a small gold signet ring. He drew it off, working it over the knuckle of the dead finger with gentle deliberation. He laid the body back upon the bed.

The room was full of noise, but Charles did not hear it. He did not hear Kate's hysterical sobbing, or the primitive, strange groan that burst from Mr. Hogarth, standing at his side, or even the epileptoid cry that Mrs. Hogarth gave as she fell unconscious to the floor.

He worked at the ring with his fingertips. Alone, in the boundless solitude, he looked down at it, as if it were not Mary's body, so quietly put away from him, but that small gold circle which had housed her life. He studied it in a long leisure of silence. He lifted it to his mouth, waiting for the full knowledge, the full grief.

But it was not grief that came first into his studious, patient, isolate waiting. After his first wild crying of her name, and the distant, puzzled quiet — the quiet of a mathematician reaching delicately, in pure mind, for the elegant solution which barely evades him — it was not grief that entered him, but release; release like joy, an anguished ecstasy of opening.

Mary had died, and set Charles free at last to fall in love. He gasped and threw back his head and felt his life break open as if a worm-blasted bud had sprung miraculously into flower.

Kate was flung across Mary's body, sobbing wildly. George Hogarth and the doctor knelt by her mother.

"We must carry her to a bed," the doctor said. "Mr. Dickens, will you put this sedative powder into a little water and get your wife to swallow it?"

"Yes."

Charles put the ring on the little finger of his left hand. He poured the water and prepared the draft.

"Kate," he said. "Kate."

Kate sobbed.

"Oh, God, Kate," he cried, "don't touch her, let her be still!"

She stumbled to her feet like a frightened child. He did not see the fear. He put the glass into her hand.

"Drink it, dear," he said. "You must lie down in your own room now. You must rest."

Kate said, "She's dead, Charles. Mary is dead."

He said, steadily, "Drink it, Kate. We must be as strong as we can, dear. God help us, we must give each other as much comfort as we can."

He led her into her room and drew the curtains. He took off her shoes, and covered her with a shawl. He kissed her forehead.

"Now rest. Try to rest."

Her hand reached up to his hand. Her fingers moved upon it and she said in a small, wondering voice, "You've got her ring on."

"Yes." The voice comforting, sustaining, quieting, not letting itself break upon the words that were so hard to articulate without weeping as he must not for her sake, for Kate's sake. "Yes, I shall never take it off again."

Her fingers still fumbled at it. He drew his hand away from her gently. He took in a short breath and spoke again, carefully, not letting his voice break, forcing it to be still steady, sustaining, tender. "Yes, dear," he said. "I shall wear it until I die. Until I die."

He kissed her forehead again, and got away quickly, shutting the door behind him. He covered his face with his hands to smother the noise of his weeping as he stumbled down the hall.

* * * * * * *

BOOK V

Enter Dickens

* * * * * * *

PART I

1

It is hard to believe; but it happened.

Charles held out his hand with Mary's ring upon it for Kate's puzzling fingertips to touch.

He let her fumble at the ring for a long moment before he drew it away and closed the hand that wore it into the other. "Until I die," he said.

And incredibly, he spoke to comfort her. And, incredibly, it never occurred to him as long as they lived together that she might take anything other than comfort from the daily sight of that ring upon his hand.

Mrs. Hogarth was still unconscious. Charles had her put to bed in the guest room. He spoke again to the doctor and sent the necessary messages to the coroner and the undertaker. He drank a little wine and tried to eat something, and went to Fred's room, lay down and slept.

When he got up, he began at once to write the first of those letters which, after months, he would still be writing, even to virtual strangers: the letters about Mary's death, and about Mary.

They were always the same letters, written compulsively and with that strange note of triumph, again and again. "She died in my arms . . . She died in my arms and the last words she whispered were of me." Again and again, agony and blessed release, no need now to hide from himself the truth they spoke: "the lovely girl who was the peace and life of our home . . . the joy and grace of our home." Release, unexamined outpouring of the heart so blessedly, terribly, finally committed. "The grace, the peace, the life of our home . . . Mary . . . Mary . . ."

He bought space for two graves in Kensall Green cemetery. His conviction of what was right and natural was so strong that George Hogarth himself never questioned it or guessed that his child was laid to rest with money borrowed in haste from Chapman and Hall.

Charles finished arranging it all before he went to bed that night. Kate, sedated, was already asleep. She was breathing through her mouth, and her cheeks were white and puffed with weeping. Charles looked down at her in an odd, impersonal pity.

Then he blew out the light and lay still in the dark, empty of feeling except for a dull fret of the mind, as if some forgotten task still nagged at its edges. After a little, he got up and lit the lamp again, and wrote the epitaph for Mary's headstone.

"Mary Scott Hogarth, young, beautiful and good. God in his mercy numbered her among his angels at the early age of seventeen."

He read it over slowly, as if the words, though they were unfamiliar, yet recalled to him some loss of his own suffered years ago.

Then, quite suddenly and noiselessly, he began at last to weep. He blew out the light once more, and sat on the edge of the bed. Over and over while the tears flowed his lips moved without sound: "Mary, Mary. My Mary, my love, my Mary."

Mary was dead. The young life that had known, judged, loved, and accepted his own essential life for what it was — Mary was dead.

The agony of loss was cleanly come at last. It was naked and immediate, altogether unlike anything that he had felt, that he would feel, as he wrote his endless letters about her. He lay with clenched hands holding its reality to him until at last he fell asleep beside his sleeping wife.

That night the dream which came nightly for so many months came for the first time.

He was walking alone by the sea when he saw her. Her face was lifted to the gray sky and she looked frightened and lonely. He called out, "Mary!" She heard him. She flung out her arms and ran to him. He held her, kissing her. "Mary, Mary . . ."

"She is with God," he said to Kate next morning, "we must know that, think about it all the time. She is with God."

Kate pushed aside the cup of tea that he had brought to her bed. She said, "Oh, Charles, what good does that do? I missed her even when she went to Mama's house for a day."

"I know, dear. But we will help each other through the years, they will go. And when we see her again we will forget that they were so long."

"Oh, Charles," Kate said, "don't talk so much just yet."

He knew that Mary would have spoken so, too. He bowed his head and closed his eyes for an instant. Then he bent and kissed her hair and walked out of the room with a humble, unhappy face.

Fred's room was empty, and the bed still unmade. Charles went into it and closed the door and lay down.

"Help me to wait until I die," he wept. "Oh, Mary, Mary, help me to wait."

The day of the funeral was sunny. The first fruit trees were in flower and the air was loud with birds. The clergyman took the words at a clip: "M'th'resurrection th'life s'the Lord . . ."

Only the two families were at the grave, without Mrs. Hogarth who still lay abed in her darkened room.

Mr. Hogarth stood staring straight before him like a guardsman on duty; his boys and baby Helen huddled at his side in an embarrassed, apologetic little group. Frederick, a little apart from them, wore an odd half-smile, as if it were all a hoax due shortly to be exposed. Mr. and Mrs. Dickens wept without covering their faces, as if they were in a darkened theater; Mrs. Dickens's bonnet was askew. Georgy, more like a witch-child than ever in black, had drawn close to the edge of the grave and teetered while she looked down into it.

Charles saw and did not see them. He held Kate's arm, supporting her.

Kate Dickens had no gift of expression. Her words were clumsy and her curious, static, animal beauty had no power to interpret them. But that morning her beauty was ruined. Her nose was red, her cheeks were pale, and the violet eyes beneath their swollen lids were dull, like the eyes of a sick child. And gratefully, gratefully, Charles loved her for it.

The handful of earth tinkled with pebbles as it fell on the coffin lid.

"Dust to dust . . ."

Guiltless, yearning like a groom for the bridebed, Charles looked at his waiting grave, and his hand pressed Kate's trembling arm to his side.

I will lie here, my Mary, Charles thought. They will put my body here in this earth, with you.

And he pressed Kate's arm against him, and thought with love of her grief-ruined face.

God help my Kate, he prayed. God, help us both. God . . . God . . ."

He had never loved her better.

He lifted his left hand to his mouth and pressed it there, hard, so that he could feel Mary's ring upon it, inside the glove.

❋   2   ❋

MRS. HOGARTH's collapse was shocking.

Kate sat beside the bed in the darkened room, and heard the endless, incoherent whisperings. "Our Father who art . . . my head will burst . . . talked before she was a year old . . . my head . . ."

"Mama." Kate caught one wandering, plucking hand. She spoke with a child's appalling innocence. "Mama, don't blame yourself, truly she thought you loved us all the same."

Weak as she was, Mrs. Hogarth went into hysterical screaming. Charles, running into the room, found Kate kneeling and sobbing by the bed. "Mama, I didn't mean . . . you loved her dearly, always, I know you did, Mama, I know you did . . ."

He put his hand on her shoulder and said, "What have you done now?"

She turned him a face stupefied with fear.

"I don't know. I was trying to comfort her and . . . I say things that come out wrong."

He said, steadily, "You'd better leave her for a little." He bent above Mrs. Hogarth's bed. "Try to be quiet, dear Mrs. Hogarth. God knows, we all understand what you're going through."

Kate got to her feet and went, slowly, toward the door. She spoke aloud, but not as if she spoke to anyone in particular.

"It's harder than you think," she said, "not being clever."

Charles did not hear her. He did not even hear her stumble over the doorsill as she left the room.

"I must get back to work at once," he was whispering under his breath. "I must get back to work."

He could not get back to work. For the only time in his life, Charles could not leap out of unhappiness into furious overactivity.

He told Chapman and Bentley to run notices that the stories would be suspended for a month. He had Mrs. Hogarth moved back to Chelsea and took Kate and the baby to a cottage in Hampstead.

Kate said that it was nice in the country, and that it eased the change wonderfully, didn't it?

And often, more times than Charles could count, she said, "Mary and I never had a cross word. Not even when we were small. It's so good to know that we never had a cross word for me to reproach myself for."

And every time she said it, Charles answered her smile and said, "Yes, dear, yes."

He wrote a great deal to his friends about the gallantry with which she had overcome her grief in her selfless effort of caring for her mother. "Kate, like the noblehearted girl she is, is now so calm and cheerful that I wonder to see her."

And he walked the countryside, crying. "Mary, Mary, my child, my life, my Mary. Oh, God, I miss her so, I miss her so."

When he wrote to Mrs. Hogarth he begged her to talk of Mary with the children as he and Kate did, so healingly and lovingly. And he shrank and winced in his heart whenever Kate said, "I wish I could fold Charley's napkins properly, Mary always got them so neat . . . Mary used to say . . ."

Her face was fresh and placid, her curls were smooth.

"Womanly, noblehearted, calm in her childlike faith . . ."

Charles whispered the words to himself again and again, like incantations.

And then, by the grace of God, Kate had a miscarriage.

Or so they both believed, though the doctor suspected that she had only skipped a period. Mercifully, however, he was young himself, newly married, and delighted with the prospect of city fees for a little aftercare. He kept his thoughts to himself.

"Ah, yes," he said. "A grave shock to the system. And caring for her mother, too, you say!"

When he left, Charles knelt beside Kate's bed, his closed eyes pressed against her extended arm.

"Oh, love," he whispered, again and again, "my love, my brave love whose body could not bear the burden of her suffering and grief despite her steadfastness, her noble, quiet cheer. My love, my poor, poor love."

To Charles's further good fortune, Kate believed him immediately. "Oh, Charles," she said, "thank you. Please don't cry."

He lifted his head.

They looked at each other with wide, wet eyes full of happiness that neither of them knew for happiness.

❄   3   ❄

JOHN FORSTER called the next day.

Their busy ways had not crossed since Ainsworth's Christmas party, but the letter about Mary's death had not surprised him with its intimate outpouring of emotion.

He came to Hampstead on the first day he could persuade himself that he would not be, as he put it, obtruding too harshly upon that lonely pain.

Charles saw him push through the gate, and ran out to meet him. "Forster, how good to see you!"

Forster looked down at Charles with eyes that yearned like a St. Bernard's from his large, flattened face. He laid one heavy paw upon his heart.

"You are good to let me come in this time of grief. That young life, so dear to you both . . . Forgive me if I say that I can read what you have suffered in your face."

The fine old tradition of talking of other and indifferent things as a means of conveying the fact that one knows and understands, was never a part of Charles's mythos. His heart, far from shrinking beneath John Forster's heavy onslaught, fell wide open.

"Oh, God, Forster, you don't know. Nobody will ever know. And my poor little Catherine is very ill. Her grief was too great for her body to bear, and yesterday she miscarried of our child. She loved her sister so — and I . . . oh, Forster, that innocent young life was like a part of my own. She died in my arms, Forster, a child and the closest friend that I shall ever have."

They stood in the door, forgetting to go in.

Forster looked at Charles's face, at the narrowed cheeks of pain, the

[201]

wide, fixed eyes. He saw the reality of that pain, he pitied it with all his heart, and the moment was precisely his cup of tea. He put out his hand.

Charles caught it hard.

Kate woke shortly before midnight. The two voices were still going, downstairs. They sounded angry. The loud, deep one roared so that she could even hear the words: "Lord Melbourne, you stupid fool! Who else, how else?"

A few minutes later, to her shocked surprise, they were both laughing. Charles was laughing. As if she were not there, in bed, made so ill by her grief, or anything.

The long evening's talk with Forster did Charles good. Like many writers, he was more extrovert than candid; yet from that evening he could be open with Forster to a remarkable degree, though the sweet salt sea of sentimentality which washed away so many barriers would still lie, a barrier itself, between certain final realities in them both.

On the other hand, a realist could scarcely have accepted the truth of what Charles felt for Mary Hogarth. The love so intense, the desire so curiously diverted to another bed, had been, to say the least, anomalous.

Not that Charles thought of that, of course. He only knew that he had found a close, good friend and that it had helped him, wonderfully.

He even wanted to get back to work again.

And he said to Kate, the next day, "And we must try, dear, to learn to be happy again, too. Not only brave, but really happy. A refusal of ordinary happiness is a refusal of God, I begin to see that now. Of faith in his strength when our own is not enough. Mary was always so busy — so full of — enjoyment."

Kate said, "My head aches. And Charley has diarrhea."

"Darling," Charles said.

He was smiling, his face absent and beautiful. He had heard neither the words nor the sound of her voice, which was wistful.

So he came back to work. And the work began to serve a purpose for him that it had never served before.

When he saw Mr. Pickwick's absurd and quenchless innocence dancing before him, his own heart leaped up, laughing and unfettered. And he had also begun to get a strange pleasure, a fury that was almost a refreshment, when he wrote at *Oliver Twist*. "It's taken on a shocking sort of life of its own," he said.

His visits to town became longer. He was increasingly convinced that Hampstead was bad for Kate, too. Despite her new pregnancy, she was often both tearful and pettish.

He said, "We must go back to Doughty Street again, Kate. And you must come to Fanny's wedding, and not wear black."

Kate stared at him.

"Charles, what would Mama think!"

But his feeling for Mrs. Hogarth was another part of his life which was beginning to come back more nearly to normal.

He said, "Oh, Kate, is that more important than your own good desire to wish Fan joy and spare her any reminders of grief on her wedding day? Think, dear, ask yourself, what would our Mary have done?"

Kate's dress for the wedding was a gray mull with the skirt handsomely overdraped.

Fanny, too, wore gray. As she came to the altar steps with her hand upon her father's arm, she looked smaller than Charles always thought of her; smaller and less dominant.

Burnett stood in his place to wait for her. His best suit, saved for concerts, was shiny at the cuff with much pressing. Fanny's dress was made in careful avoidance of high style, to remain presentably stylish the longer. Charles looked at them and swallowed.

"I, Henry, take thee, Frances . . ."

Fanny, the fortunate one, coming down the Academy steps on a Sunday afternoon, so long ago, so very long ago . . . You are still fortunate, Fan, still fortunate . . .

The slipper and the rice had been thrown and Burnett was handing his bride into the hired carriage when Charles ran and caught her in his arms again.

"Oh, Fan, God bless you. A good life, Fan, a good life. Oh, Fan, no great griefs and so many joys!"

She kissed him. "Charlie, all eyes and feelings, my old Tom Thumb that I teased so! Dear Charlie."

"Dear Fan. Take care of her, Burnett, as I know you will, thank God."

He spent the evening alone with Kate, and it was full of silences.

"I don't see why you act so restless," Kate said once. "Mr. Burnett is rather poor, but he's nice, and they're both musical. They should do well enough."

"You're altogether wrong, dear, I'm not at all discontented. They're wonderfully well suited . . . and fortunate."

"Nobody would think that you felt so to look at you," she said, "staring and twiddling at your finger ring."

Her voice was fretful, but only that. Objects that one sees day in and day out come to lose their connotations.

That summer they had a little jaunt to Paris and Brussels. *Pickwick* and *Oliver* pushed ahead. The *Miscellany* prospered, though Bentley, Charles had discovered, had no conscience concerning contracts drawn up under bargaining conditions that were wholly outdated.

However, Bentley would learn. For John Forster had turned out to be a blessing in more ways than one. He had taken the Macrone problem out of Ainsworth's hands and would carry it off handsomely, leaving Charles as free as air. Now he was eying the sleek, slick Mr. Bentley with the same purposeful energy.

Thank God for Forster. And whilst one was giving thanks, thank God for Anne.

Anne, hired simply as an extra domestic, had immediately made herself lady's maid, head nurse, and unofficial major-domo. She was dour, horse-faced, and ageless. Kate's incompetence she apparently saw as a patent of rank, quite admirably ladylike.

"I told them how you wanted the silver polished," she would say to Kate. "I've explained how you'd like the linens kept, ma'am."

The convention satisfied them both. Kate felt housewifely, Anne felt properly subservient, and the house ran quite well again.

Time pushed ahead. It was October, and *Pickwick* was almost done.

"I long to end it off, and I dread it," Charles said to Forster. "It was a world in itself." He turned the ring on his little finger and forgot to listen to Forster's answer.

On the afternoon that he set down the last word, he waited, and to his surprise he felt nothing whatsoever.

He reread the last page. It was done, it was good, he knew it. And he could only feel emptiness. He felt empty as a deserted beach at the ebb of the tide.

A double knock came at the door. He went to it before the maid could come, and took the letter.

It came from Mrs. Hogarth. She had sent him a lock of Mary's hair. It was drab in that single, finger-wound strand, the smooth, bright luster gone. Charles stared at it.

He folded back the bit of silk paper in which it was wrapped. His face was empty, like a face washed blank by extreme fatigue.

He went back to his study, shutting the door behind him. He fingered the edge of his work table. He spoke aloud, in the voice of someone who speaks to an incompetent servant.

"God, I can't go on so. I can't. She must be here, alive. I must have my Mary. My Mary."

He sat down and began to tidy the final day's work at *Pickwick*, stacking the pages with neat, angry hands. His eyes were wide and set, his hands moved with exasperated precision, like the hands of a woman tidying a room at too short notice for unexpected guests.

When the table was quite in order, he set his elbows on the edge of it and bent his face upon his hands. Then, at last, a shudder went through his body, and it was racked with noiseless, tearless weeping.

❋ 4 ❋

CHAPMAN AND HALL gave Charles a magnificent dinner party and a bonus check for seven hundred pounds. It was touching. It also pointed up Bentley's shabbiness.

Charles had left the *Miscellany* in September, to avoid the sight of the old bloodsucker as much as possible. It depressed him to think that after *Oliver* he still owed another novel under the same contract. But the book he'd planned to give poor Macrone would do, the one about the Gordon Riots. *Barnaby Rudge*.

For Macrone had become poor Macrone by dying, suddenly. The slate was wiped clean. Charles, all pity and energy, got together half the fast-selling names in London and brought out a book for the benefit of the widow.

"She's in straits, they say. And he, you know, gave me my first start."

Charley would be christened in December.

Charles asked Angela Coutts to be godmother, one day as he sat in her splendid drawing room, discussing her charities.

She was young, that triple-fortuned heiress; she was as handsome as she was rich. But even when her fine-cut, perfect face warmed to its theme of the world's need and her duty to it, she never lost a certain remoteness. She looked, always, like a princess who was both excessively shy and wholly conscious of her royal blood. Charles felt that the invitation was brash before he was done speaking it.

He was amazed to see her happiness.

"Oh, Mr. Dickens, how kind!"

She sat erect, and her voice was crisp; but her eyes shone, and her hands folded together, like a child's.

Charles said, "My dear Miss Coutts, the kindness is yours." His own voice was at once formal and a little unsteady.

That night, he told Kate.

"She was so touched. I never understood the loneliness of that great wealth before. Poor young girl, there is so little disinterested affection that she can ever hope to find."

Kate laughed. "Poor! Oh, but that is wonderful, Charles. Think of all that she can do for Charley."

"I daresay," Charles said, stiffly.

So Charles Culliford Dickens had the richest godmother in England.

The christening party had become very gay with champagne when Charles noticed that Angela Coutts stood beside Kate, alone on the edge of things.

He hurried to her rescue. As she moved away on his arm she said, "How gentle Mrs. Dickens is, how friendly! I enjoy her talk so much."

Charles glanced down, startled. She was quite sincere. She smiled up at him. Her classic young face had a look of direct innocence that was like Mary.

"You have made this day wonderfully happy for us, Miss Coutts. Proud and happy."

She glanced quickly away. "Have you given more thought to your new book, Mr. Dickens?"

It was not rebuff. She was only lonely in her cage of means, and shy.

Charles smiled. "In a large, wild way. It's come on me that I've been keeping my sun and shadow in separate pockets, and a good book wants both. It should be a fine tangled skein, all comical-tragical-romantical-melodramatical, and with plenty of elbowroom to disentangle it and weave it up again, do you see?"

He spoke eagerly, and when he broke off he waited for her to nod as Mary would have done, and say, "That sounds sensible," or to laugh, like Mary, and say, "So you've no plan yet?" He looked at the fine gray eyes and realized that they had been much in his mind lately. He waited.

And the fine eyes puzzled, as if they studied an inscription in some half-known language. A vertical wrinkle formed between the smooth black eyebrows.

"I'm afraid I don't understand *literary* problems, Mr. Dickens. What I meant to ask was about the *purpose*, you know — what wrong you'll be setting right."

The sudden letdown that went through Charles's body was curiously mixed with relief, release. He looked at the puzzling, desperately earnest young gray eyes. He smiled, in easy, unfeigned tenderness.

Yes, she was beautiful, good, intelligent — and born to evoke the not quite genuine in everyone. She was born so, as surely as Mary had been born to reach through sham and lay her finger on the central life.

He looked at the gray eyes that were so like and so unlike his Mary's. He made his own eyes grave, earnest, as she clearly wanted to see them.

"I want to expose the Yorkshire schools. Hells on earth, where unscrupulous men batten on the unwanted children whom they keep conveniently out of sight."

"Oh, Mr. Dickens, how I envy you your power to do good!"

Again he felt the strange throb of letdown and escape.

Yes, he thought, yes, some quality of being fully human is lacking in her.

He felt about for words that she would like to hear, swallowed down a small lump of distaste and spoke them firmly.

"We were both given powers that we want to use well, thank God. We're on an equal footing, dear Miss Coutts."

Her face lighted as it had on the day he asked her to be Charley's godmother.

"Oh, Mr. Dickens, what a beautiful thought!"

And Charles thought, Poor, beautiful, lonely little prig, God helping me, I'll see that your goodness is never exploited. You could not understand an honest man, but you shall have an honest steward, at least.

He gave her his most brilliant smile.

"And now we must lay aside our worries and be gay in Charley's honor," he said. "Come, you have no champagne."

Charles went to Yorkshire at the end of January. He used a false name and gave it out that he was hunting a school for some poor little bastard who had outgrown his first hiding place.

Mr. William Shaw of Bowes Academy had an act prepared for such prospects. The small supporting cast appeared as if at random, in answer to his hearty call, and went through their parts without a slip.

It was Charles who fumbled his lines as he saw the sickly, hunger-pinched little faces made clever by fear, and heard the anxious affirmations of plenty and cheer received at so reasonable a rate. He saw the chilblained fingers, the scrubbed faces, and the scurf behind the ears — mute evidence of frozen pumps and bug-infested beds. He saw, and remembered.

The smallest boy began to cough. Mr. Shaw patted his head.

"Cold. Throw it off in no time. Remarkable how they pick up here, with hearty food and country air. Only look at those rosy cheeks, sir, and you'll see."

Charles stared at the tuberculous flush, at the child's frightened, feverish eyes.

The village graveyard told him the rest, for few children at such schools were fetched home for burial.

That night in his hotel bed, Charles still saw the face of the consumptive child, and the row of small, cheap headstones slanting in dead winter weeds — *aged 9 yrs. . . . aged 11 yrs . . .*

The dying child, the children who were dead.

He told himself that their death had been kind, an escape from fear, loneliness, hunger, pain. But a horror of death was upon him, of those children's, and of his own, and last and worst, of Mary's. She had died, and he held her in his arms, not Mary but a corpse, a thing to be disposed of.

He shuddered at the memory as if he were caught in a waking nightmare. He knew that he had felt no horror then, only love; yet now his flesh shrank with it. He was sick with a loathing horror of death; of his own, of Mary's, of that which would come to all things living.

And then it was gone. He felt empty, blank and cold. He tried to pray, but he could not; not for those children, or for Mary, or for himself.

And he could not remember Mary's face. He could have described it, yes, but he could not make himself see it. He could see Mr. Shaw's face, the children's faces, but not Mary's. He struggled against the heavy tide of sleep that began to pull him down. He fell asleep at last, exhausted and despairing. He could not see her face, the dream would not come, the dream that had come every night since she died.

The dream came, more sharply real than any he ever had.

He thought that she had gone to Chelsea. He went into the room where he worked, full of the empty feeling of the house without her. And she was standing by his table, holding out her hands.

"I didn't go."

He caught her against him. "Never go again, say that you will not, say it!"

But her face had turned small and masklike, the gray eyes sightless, the mouth sagging open.

He cried out. "No, Mary, no, you love me, you are not dead!"

Then it was no longer nightmare, but the dream, the good dream again as it always ended. He felt her thin, straight back beneath his hands, he touched her smooth, fine, close-bound hair, he kissed the thin skin of her forehead, her narrow cheeks, her mouth, her living, breathing, gentle mouth. Mary, Mary, time without end, Mary . . .

The dream still possessed Charles when he woke, like the memory of a living experience. While he dressed, while he breakfasted in the hotel dining room, he thought over and over, But I saw her, saw her, touched her, kissed her. Alive, herself. In these months I had half forgotten her and I did not know it. I remember her . . . Mary . . . Mary . . .

He read the morning paper with his eyes alone. As he folded it, it came to him with an odd urgency that he must write to Kate.

He went back to his room and dashed off a long, chatty letter about coaches, accommodations, roaring inn fires, all manner of pleasant things. He did not feel like writing about Mr. Shaw's school yet; that could wait until he had seen a few more of them.

Charles had finished the letter, with a thousand loves to his darling boy; he had folded it and was about to seal it when, with the same abrupt, compulsive urgency which had sent him hurrying to write it, he laid it open again and added a postscript.

"Is it not extraordinary that the same dreams which have constantly visited me since poor Mary died follow me everywhere? I have dreamt of her ever since I left home, and no doubt shall until I return. I should be very sorry to lose such visions, for they are very happy ones . . . Love to all friends. Ever, my dear Kate, your affectionate husband."

Until he had posted it, he felt calm, loving, and confident. He even wondered at the senseless secrecy that he had kept about those dreams for so long, as if Mary, who was so incapable of secrets, could have wanted it, or as if Kate, who loved her, who loved him, would not have been interested and glad to know of them.

The sense of shock and foreboding did not come until the letter was out of his hand. At once he tried to shut his mind to it, to push it away.

But he knew that the dream would not come again; and it did not.

At first Charles told himself that it would come back when he was in familiar surroundings once more. Or when the book was started and his mind was quieter. Each night he tried to fall asleep in calm expectation and strong, evocative remembering.

Yet when he knew at last that the dream was gone for good, he had a single day of wild grief, and after that a day full of strange, alternating waves of undirected rage and causeless terror, and then, to his surprise, he slept heavily through one night and woke, as he put it, feeling more like himself than he had done in a long time.

Gratefully, unquestioningly, Charles accepted the sense of well-being, of liberated energy.

By the third week of February, *Nickleby* was off to a running start.

※ 5 ※

"Pickwick was nothing to this," he crowed to Forster. "Wait for April and the first issue. Ah, won't our Charlie be the toast of London! Lord, the people in it!"

Forster looked at him, reverent-eyed. "Where do you find them? All so unimaginable and inevitable. And immortal."

Charles laughed. "Look about you! It's only that in the world their wild essences get hid in a clutter of irrelevance."

"Bentley's mad to let you waste your powers on rewriting that life of Grimaldi."

"Ah, well, Grimaldi was a great clown, his name could almost sell anything. I'll have the money, it won't bear my name, and it takes only a few hours each day."

Forster gave a groan. "How many hours are there in a day? Or a lifetime?"

Charles shook back his hair. "More than you'd think for, as the waterfall said to the glacier. Come, it's slap-up weather. Shall we 'ire us 'osses and go for a canter?"

"Leisure," said Forster. "Nothing to do but to write three books at once."

Dickens, he thought, will always mourn that lovely girl, yet by giving his heart, his gifts, to the world, he has found peace.

It was a thought which often, those days, did much to make up to Forster for the vicarious grief which he had relished through so many months.

It was also, oddly enough, not far off the truth. Charles was come again with rejoicing. He was not shut off from his tears; in fact he could weep more readily than he had done for a long time. But he was come again, and bringing his sheaves with him.

"Dear Mamie, dearest monkey," he crooned to the new baby, "who was born at the turn of the tide? Who's her Papa's crowning glory?"

She was a tiny baby, phenomenally plain and utterly enchanting. In the months before Fan's wedding, Charles had said, "If it is a girl, dearest love, we will call her Mary. What comfort we will have in saying that name so often and lovingly." Now, with no thought that he had given her another name, Charles rocked small Mary and crooned, "Mamie, her Papa's Mamie-monkey-mouse."

Kate had an easy time. By the next day she was sitting up in bed, with her beautiful hair brushed out, and a lacy shawl about her shoulders.

"Oh, love," Charles said, "I'd almost forgotten how very, very beautiful you are when you feel all well and happy."

She pouted prettily. "You horrid boy, are you saying I've looked all ugly these past weeks?"

He stooped and kissed her.

"Lord, who gave you that Grimaldi thing to read, your mother? Toss it away. It's earning money, God knows why, but it's wretched twaddle."

Kate eyed him sternly. "Now, don't fish for compliments." But at once she smiled, a relenting, lovely smile. "No, I must tell you that I'm proud of you. I don't know when I've read a nicer book. There isn't a single silly or depressing thing in it, and the language is truly elegant!"

More expressions crossed Charles's face in a moment than commonly cross one in a lifetime.

"Thank you, my beautiful," he said.

When the runaway sales of Nickleby began, Charles was grateful for them, warmed by them, touched by them, but not surprised.

How could he have been? That amazing crowd, shouldering to be set down in the dashing, pointed hand, slip after slip — where did they come from, who had ever seen their like? "Look about you," he had said to Forster; but it was not so. They came from another world, walking, prancing, on an air of glory. Fanny Squeers, Miss La Creevy, Mr. Mantalini — God, Mantalini! — could he have doubted that the good, dear, laughing, weeping world would love them as much as he did?

"And furthermore, thank God," Charles cried to Forster, tossing back his long, fair hair and slapping his hands together sharply, "the money all goes to yours most faithfully and Chapman and dear, honorable little Hall; and that bastard Bentley can brood on the rewards of being a thought too sharp!"

Forster's flat, ugly face was knotted with happiness. He raised his glass with a baroque flourish.

"To the brave new world of Dickens," he said, "with such creatures in it as only Dickens and God can invent!"

"'Ere now, don't blaspheme," said Charles. "It's unlucky."

But the light in the huge blue eyes showed that he did not consider it at all unlucky.

The lionizing began at once. *Pickwick* could have been written off for a brilliant one-shot fluke, and *Oliver* for competent melodrama, a bit on the rantish side, but when *Nicholas Nickleby* came hard on their heels it was clear to those who cultivate the great that there was a new, fixed star in the sky.

By June, Charles had been elected to the Athenaeum Club, an honor coveted by distinguished men twice his age. Even before that, he was part of the London Season.

The old gorgon, Lady Holland, wanted to show him off repeatedly to the dazzling circle of fashionables who gathered in her gilt-walled, pillared palace. He was welcomed by the political group in Gore House, the home of that strange, gigantic dandy Count D'Orsay and his stepmother, Lady Blessington, who was, by rumor, his mistress into the bargain.

It was Maria Beadnell's drawing room once again. Charles was dazzled and at the same time deliciously, unexpectedly at home wherever he went. He found Count D'Orsay's vast cravats, his flowered waistcoats, his huge white sleevebands and primrose-hued gloves bold but intoxicating lessons in sartorial possibility. The tune differed slightly from great house to great house, from splendid group to splendid group, but Charles in a flash could carry it always precisely as it was sung.

More remarkable, he knew without resentment where the line was drawn. It helped to pick up the tune, but there were houses in which he could never be more than the lion on exhibition, a creature who, socially speaking, was not quite real. And what matter? One saw the show.

Kate could not learn a tune. However, the society of the day had a knack for overlooking wives without conversation. And Kate was lovely to look at.

Charles bought her several handsome dresses, and was pleased that she appeared quite dignified in her soft-eyed, monosyllabic way.

When she did not trip on rugs, that is, or scatter hairpins and bracelets like a deciduous tree.

Nonetheless, one London Season at a time is enough. Charles was glad to leave for the rented cottage in Broadstairs, by the sea. He felt sure, too, that Kate would be happier there. It was strange how little pleasure she had found in all the new excitement and success. But by the sea she need only be with people of whom she need not be shy.

Yet once they were there, Kate complained of too much company, as if a pleasant country place did not always mean guests, the guests who are half the pleasure of a summer holiday. She did not even show pleasure in being with old friends like Forster, or Ainsworth, or Macready and Maclise. Though once she did say, grudgingly that Macready (the greatest Shakespearean actor since Keane) was very gentlemanly, *considering what he did.*

"You're a dear little hostess," Charles assured her often. "Nobody expects you to babble, pet — only to sit by and look your own lovely little self. And when you're tired, you can steal away."

"And sleep above all that racketing too, I presume?"

Charles felt baffled. Sea air and happy company did not lift Kate's spirits at all. In a curious way, she almost seemed most content while they sat alone and she indulged those little habits of nagging and sorry sighs which were growing upon her despite anything he could do.

Yet far more baffling was the indubitable, inescapable fact that *Kate was bored by babies.* Charley and Mamie — Snodgering and Popem, Charles called them — were quite amazing babies, *altogether* aside from one's own natural partiality. But Kate did not play with them or sing to them; except for an occasional comment on the state of their bowels — and even that was always passed on at second hand from the nurse — she did not talk of them.

She was even indifferent to Charley's love affair with the balloons.

They were hot-air balloons, made of paper and carried away into the high, blue distance by the heat from a tiny candle. Charley lived for them.

"Boons, Papa?" he would cry in the morning, as soon as he was out of bed. "Boons go up, and be gone so far?"

Even Mamie laughed, when Charles held her high and pointed;

but Charley's face, watching the miracle, was an adoration, an innocent glory.

Charles loved the balloons too, and gathered all his friends into the game. With Forster and Beard he formed the Gammon Aeronautical Society for the Encouragement of Science and the Consumption of Spirits and Wine. Daniel Maclise, the lazy, laughing, long-faced young painter, was made a member, one Sunday afternoon. So was Leigh Hunt, that ageless professional child who could have passed for a dried-up thirty-seven though he had been the friend of Shelley and Keats.

"Wasn't it fun?" Charles coaxed Kate on the morning after that meeting. "Wasn't Charley incredible? 'Boon gone *Godding.*' I could scarcely believe my ears. Didn't you enjoy Hunt?"

Kate sniffed. "I only wish you could have heard him when he was pretending to talk to the flowers as if he thought I was four years old, or he was weak-headed!"

"Oh come, pet, nonsense preserves the complexion. Look at his!"

"Please don't be silly."

The sun was on her hair and she was wearing a white dimity sprigged with mauve flowers. Charles sighed.

"I daresay he does overdo it. I'm irked myself when he takes to being gay and childlike about never carrying a watch. As if it scarcely mattered who else might have to wait. And the winsome charm about his finances is vexing. Still, dear, I think it may amuse you that once, long ago, when he was in prison for debt . . ."

Kate started back. She stared. "Charles! He's silly and tiresome, like half your friends, but I thought that at least he was *respectable!*"

She had struck the one sure note that they had in common. The sexual bond between them was a one-sided affair, they shared no intellectual interests; but Charles and Kate had precisely the same strong and positive feelings about money.

For ten large, cold seconds Charles held his breath.

Then he went on, quite pleasantly and as if he had not been interrupted, ". . . he sent out and had his cell papered with red and white roses."

"He tells of it *himself?*"

And Charles started. "What a curious slip of the tongue! It wasn't debt at all, it was a political trouble! Odd, I knew that quite well. How strange that I should have said that it was for debt!"

[2 1 5]

Kate yawned. "He is old, isn't he? Living at a time when one could still go to jail for politics, dear me!"

She was neither pleased nor displeased by the correction. Clearly, the whole topic of Mr. Hunt bored her.

Charles fidgeted his ring. Then he said, "Ah well, enough of our chatting, dear. I must get back to *Oliver*. Tell Anne to fetch me a sandwich when you lunch. I've put off killing Nancy long enough. I'll make a day of it, and have it done with."

Charles sat down at his table and closed his eyes. He saw the sordid room; the cowering trull, the victim. He heard Sikes's heavy step outside, on the stair.

For almost a week the book had been at a block. "I can't stomach that murder," he had told Forster. "It's got to be such a literally bloody mess."

Now the block was gone.

He did not see Anne when she came in with the sandwich, though she saw him and was badly frightened by his face until she realized that he was, as she told herself, only pretending of someone wicked to be in a book.

When the murder was done, and Sikes had fled the blood-spattered room where Nancy's battered body lay, Charles put his pen down.

He said, "Finished, thank God. And with time for a dig on the sands with the Snodgering before tea."

At once he caught the pain in his side with both hands, and got himself to the sofa. It made him writhe and sweat for about an hour before it began to pass.

As it slackened he smiled, grimly. "Let's hope the public takes it half so hard," he thought. "I'll test it out on Kate after dinner. The acid test."

He did not, however, forsee anything like the fit of hysterics which sealed his success.

"Sweet, sweet," he cried, holding her, "it's nothing but a tale, a tale your own boy wrote to earn our bread. God, Kate, sweet, sweet, try to control yourself. Anne, Anne! Oh, God, where's Anne?"

Oliver was finished in November. It had never been burdensome; that wonderful old out-and-outer Fagin always carried it along like a breeze. Charles was surprised that being done with it made him feel so free.

He said to Forster, "It's truly strange that I should be so glad. For, you know, it's the last writing that I ever discussed with Mary. It was the last thread that still held unbroken."

Forster said, "We must always go forward. Thank God, you have your world of *Nickleby*."

He spoke in a richly relishing voice of tenderness, pity, understanding. He was too lost in his enjoyment of the moment to observe that its delicacies were needless, even irrelevant.

In February, on his birthday, Charles wrote: "The end of a most prosperous and happy year for which, with all other blessings, I thank God with all my heart and soul."

PART II

❋ *1* ❋

INDEED THE YEAR had brought tremendous changes, in income, position, everything. Simple gratitude to life, Charles told himself, as well as real prudence, demanded a corresponding change in their whole style of living.

In the first place, they needed a house in which they could entertain properly. It would give Kate that ease and pleasure with their friends that she still lacked. She was pregnant again, too. Doughty Street would soon be too small for them.

When he told her what he thought, her violet eyes flared wide open.

"But this house is nicer than Papa's. Charles, do you mean that we're *rich?*"

He had not seen her look so enchantingly young for a long time.

"Not as rich as we'll look, but you can trust me to avoid debt like the Devil, sweet. And we must spend all that we can afford, to make more flow in."

She hesitated, clearly wistful, wonderfully endearing.

"And not save it?"

"Kate, who's the most successful writer in England?"

"I don't know. Bulwer?"

"Why Bulwer?"

"Think how rich he is — how grand."

He gave a triumphant shout. "Now, do you see? And there's more to it than that. People love to laugh and weep in a crowd, that's why they love the theater. But when they read a book, they can only know they're laughing and weeping in company by the way the writer lets them see that pile of shillings they've paid him for their laughter and their tears, their love. They like to point at the splendid house that their love bought, and say, 'Dickens lives there, the h'author.' Do you see?"

She did see. She hung gravely upon his every word, and her face was perfect not only in beauty but in intelligence.

"You shall have a house," he said softly, "so magnificent that you'll scarcely be able to believe that it is yours." He broke off, watching her. His eyes, fixed full upon her lovely face, were blue lakes of light. "And everything in it," he said, "will be new, and rich, and splendid. And up-to-the-minute. There will be gaslight on every floor. And *flush water-closets.*"

Kate exhaled a long, trembling breath.

It was a moment of true communion.

And when Kate whispered, "Oh, Charles, how proud Mary would have been!" he only smiled, and nodded, and stroked her hand.

For the strange sense of freedom that had come upon him as he finished *Oliver* was still present. Charles had come into the gay time.

Perhaps our gay times are always shallow-rooted, like bright beds of annual flowers. Charles took the news of the Governor's new debts far less well than he ever had before. On the other hand, he had never before been forced to hear such news from a third party.

And the whole thing was senseless, senseless. He had not seen the Governor of late as much as he would have wished, but he had not neglected him either.

Charles stared at the carpet, in Hall's office. "But why did you not tell me before this? Why?"

Hall perched on the edge of his chair, so ruffled and obviously wretched that Charles, even in his own shocked bewilderment, pitied him.

"We feared it might distract you from *Nickleby.* Chapman agreed with me. They were small sums at first. He urged us not to tell you and assured us that he would be able to repay it all soon."

Charles wet his lips. "What changed your mind? Why do you tell me now?"

Hall fluttered himself again.

"There are — unmistakable signs. In our business one sees men in financial trouble, serious trouble. To be plain, I thought you'd rather get to his house before the bailiff."

"I see." Charles continued to study the rug. He controlled his voice with difficulty. "I don't understand why he did not come to me at once. I . . . I have helped him before this. And gladly. And when I was less well able."

Then he forced himself to smile. He was unaware that his forehead and upper lip were wet. "Ah, well, I don't blame you, you made the mistake in kindness. You'll hold back the full amount from my next accounting, then. I'd best see him now."

He shook Hall's hand, still smiling, and left the office with a firm step despite the watery quivering in his legs.

I'll not take a cab, he thought. I'll walk, and rid myself of this disproportionate nonsense.

But it was so ugly, and so baffling.

He had never been in easier circumstances. Flush or broke, he had never turned the Governor down. Yet he had gone behind his back. *"Don't tell my son."* Why, in the name of God, why?

Abruptly, Charles shut off his mind. He shut off the questions. He shut off the humiliation: what must Hall think? Too niggardly to help his father without shaming him into the bargain? Of necessity, along with everything else, he shut off the love.

He walked hard, feeling nothing but a sort of brisk, interior emptiness until after he had pushed past his mother at her door, as if he did not see her. He walked down the hall, calling out.

"Governor? Governor, I must speak to you at once. Alone."

John Dickens had been reading a novel of high life in the small, nondescript room behind the stair which he called "my haven of withdrawal." He opened the door to Charles and shut it behind them again, quickly.

His face was extremely small. There was clearly no need for preliminaries.

Charles hurried to get it over with.

"I know only what Chapman knows, Governor. No more. I must have the full accounting. Try to grasp that. The full accounting here and now, Governor, not simply a bit today and a bit tomorrow."

He was shocked to see how the Governor's face crumpled and to hear the answering quaver: "Dear boy, I . . . temporary . . . unfortunate . . ."

He shut his mind to sight and sound. "The whole of it. And why, Governor, why to outsiders, why to *them?* Let's grant that from boyhood I've had a distaste for debt, but have you ever found me less than helpful?"

John Dickens pulled out a large white handkerchief and sobbed into it.

"Dear boy, how could I trouble you in this time of happy triumph for you? A time, can't you see, which has imposed ob . . . oh . . . obligations upon me as well as you . . . a certain amount of entertainment . . . a style of dress which should not cast discredit . . . oh, dear me . . ."

And Charles, too, wept and shouted through his tears, "Stop that, Governor! For my sake and God's sake show some dignity!"

They both stopped crying then. Charles made his voice kind, understanding, reassuring.

But when he left, the Governor's linens still looked limp and his face was a size too small.

The mess, it turned out, was even worse than Charles had feared. It was not only that the bills were bigger; one can pay bills. The real shock came with finding that the Governor had been selling his signatures and pages of manuscript, peddling them about, Boz souvenirs.

"But it's not *like* him," he said hopelessly, when he learned that.

He could imagine the voices of the purchasers. "Bought it of his father? Wouldn't you think he'd be willing to keep the old man in funds himself?"

It was when he had made that discovery that Charles, tight-lipped, said to Kate, "He's not safe in London. We'll have to move him to another place."

He had spoken only on the impulse of hurt anger. As soon as the words were out, he knew it. His father loved London and he loved his father. Shoving him out of harm's way was both wholly sensible and wholly wrong.

Kate got up from her chair with a happy smile.

"Yes, yes, and you should have done it long ago! Oh, Charles, only think, if we'd not discovered all this *in time!*"

Charles saw the wide violet eyes, so full of unqualified approval, of relief at his belated show of common sense.

He told himself wearily that there were situations in which no solution was altogether perfect. He told himself that the Governor would be quite happy, once he'd swallowed the notion.

By morning, Charles fully believed it, and by the time he had all the arrangements firmly in hand, he was full of energy. The March weather in Exeter was clear and windy, the town looked far pleasanter than grimy London, and it was like a downright miracle the way he happened immediately upon the perfect little cottage, just the right size for the two of them and Shrimp. They'd been paying too much rent, amongst other things, with the girls married and Alfred gone away.

It was charming, and a bargain. And a pleasure to furnish, too, all at second hand, sensibly priced, and good as new. Poor Mother and the Governor would have spent four times the sum for half the result.

Charles bustled back to London, all benevolence.

Indeed, up to the moment he was ready to take leave of them in the parlor of the cheery little cottage where they would surely be so content once they had settled down, Charles was brimming over with zest, efficiency, and kindliness.

"Goodbye, then, my dears," he said. "I mustn't miss my coach."

His mother had forgotten to take off her bonnet. It was askew. Her eyes had a bright, unfocused stare; her lips were parted, but the usual flood of words did not come. Shrimp had his hands in his pockets and his shoulders were hunched.

The Governor stood erect, his fine-cut lips held in a courteous smile. His hand went to his eyeglass, hanging on its ribbon, fingered it, and dropped away.

Charles looked at him. He looked at them all.

He said, "Governor. Governor, you'll be happy here. You'll make friends. You'll visit us, often."

He ran from the room.

At home, he found Kate sitting by the drawing-room fire, with her small bronze slippers on the fender. She was playing with her bracelets.

He kissed her. He said, absently, "How sweet you look, my darling." He began to walk about.

After a little, he spoke abruptly. "Exeter is a delightful spot. They're vastly pleased with the little house."

"Pleased!" Kate said. "Let us hope they'll make some effort to *deserve* it!"

Charles sat down. He stared at his hands.

"Kate," he said, "if the Governor hadn't been in some way afraid of me, it wouldn't have happened. He'd have come to me for a touch when he needed it. I get into a hurry, I get absorbed in things, but . . . Kate, I hate the thought that people I love can be afraid of me, and without my knowing it. Kate, you could never be afraid of me, could you?"

She looked at him blankly. She laughed, an aimless little laugh.

She said, "When you're tired like this you get confusing enough to frighten anyone."

"Never mind," Charles said. "Has the Snodgering gone to sleep?"

❊ 2 ❊

THE EXPENSE meant putting off buying a new house until *Nickleby* should be finished and the new baby born. However, on the morning after his return from Exeter Charles went out, on an unexamined impulse, and bought a horse and a handsome little carriage.

"We really needed it," he said to Forster, "for convenience as well as for appearances."

He also said lightly, in the course of the same conversation, a thing that he would say many times throughout the years.

"My dear Prodigal Parent, what a time he is in growing up."

The sense of gay well-being, briefly disturbed, was already almost fully restored again.

Kate Macready Dickens, born a few days after *Nickleby* was brought to triumphant finish, was a beautiful redhead, with a two-months-old complexion and the strongest lungs in London.

"Her mother's beauty and her father's iron will," Charles told everyone, glowing.

They moved to Devonshire Terrace in December. Kate had actually paled when she first saw the house.

"But it's fit for a duke," she cried.

It was not, quite; but it was a fine house and furnished as it deserved. Charles had expressed himself.

There were full-length mirrors with leafy gold frames set into the walls. There were richly framed oil paintings, all with a cheerful or

[223]

an inspiring story to tell. There were flowered carpets and red-velvet curtains hung over lace; and beneath them were the newest mechanical curtains, enchanting as toys when one drew them down or let them up on their springs.

It was all grand, but it was all cozy and colorful, too.

There was also a library, as was only proper for an established literary man. The books from Doughty Street filled only one small corner; the rest of the splendid show was bought in job lots, shelf after shelf of standard books in handsome bindings, laced with a generous sprinkling of rare editions.

It was a stage library, and Charles loved it precisely as he loved the mechanical curtains and the flush water-closets. He had just done with arranging the show, dustcloth in hand, when Kate passed the door and he called her in.

"Behold! The place where the great man sits, surrounded by his elders and betters."

"Mercy me, it is fine! It might have cost a fortune!"

Charles bowed. Then he laughed. "And, surprisingly, I've read most of it. Senior Wrangler of the British Museum."

"What?"

"Look, I missed one out. On the chair, behind you."

She picked it up. "One of our old ones. Almost too shabby to keep."

"Jeremy Bentham! Come, old fellow, bless you, here you go into the corner with God's holy poor." He stood up, dusting off his hands. "Done! Orchestra rises, cymbals clash to indicate kiss of golden guineas. Wealthy author, front center, perspiring freely. Lovely wife moves forward. Kiss. Curtain."

"Oh, look, isn't that one of the good new ones under that chair?"

Charles stooped. "Tooled morocco! Let's hope the corners haven't got dented."

He reached and picked it up. He caught in his breath.

"Charles, what's the matter?"

He held a copy of *Don Quixote*, in one single, heavy volume, the covers tooled in gold curlicues and tiny ivy leaves. It was not battered, but that was the only difference. It was the same, the lost restored. It was his *Don Quixote*, from the miraculous box at the Brook; his, the dearest, the last to go . . . The Orfling whispered through the cupboard door: "You've got the insides of it in your head, anyways . . ."

He stared. He turned it in his hands, as if, like Thomas, he could believe by touch alone, not sight.

"Did you wrench your back, Charles?"

"Isn't this curious? A copy of a book that I owned as a boy, even identically bound. It was lost — in a moving. I was heartsick."

"Fancy remembering a book so long!"

"I loved it, for God's sake!"

"You needn't curse and bite my head off."

"I'm sorry." But he spoke mechanically, while his hands still proved, believed. Oh, but how much we forget . . . that garret room, and the sunlight making ripples like water on the wall . . . and the children shouting outside in the churchyard . . . the Orfling . . .

"Since you liked it so much, why do you look as if you'd lost your last friend?"

"Did I? How droll, I couldn't be more pleased. It's like an omen, dear. Ah, Kate, we'll be so happy in this house!"

"I hope so," Kate said, "after the money you've spent!"

He laughed, still full of the sense of Time relenting, of superstitious joy.

"Oh, practical-minded Mouse, dear beautiful, come, kiss your boy!"

Omen or no, a good time had begun.

It was also an innocent time, for Charles was still in love with Kate. Her clumsiness, her untidyness, her sulks, her naggings, her indifference to the babies all troubled and vexed him; and she continued to gain weight. On the other hand, the tastes of the period were for opulence, her skin was living velvet, and they slept in a double bed.

And Charles was happy there. It did not occur to him that their love-making was increasingly like the rape of a remarkably absent-minded stranger. Pure women are pure. He noted pretty girls, he liked to tell friends about how a set of eyelashes or an ankle had set him all of a misty tremble. But it was play, not genuine speculation.

Nickleby, in hard covers, continued to earn money. Forster hypnotized Bentley into selling his copyrights to Chapman and Hall, including that for *Barnaby Rudge,* still unwritten.

Charles bought a talking raven and loved it with such ardor that

Ainsworth said he had gone raven mad. Ainsworth and he and Forster were the Cerberus Club, three bad horsemen always ready for a canter across the heath and dinner at an inn. Maclise and Charles shared an endless game of being madly in love with the young Queen, staggering up and down before Buckingham Palace as they sobbed into their outspread handkerchiefs.

He often called upon Angela Coutts. He fanned her interest in the Ragged Schools, those first precursors of the free school system. She listened gravely, even eagerly, to all the notions that his other friends wrote off for visionary madness.

"Dear Miss Coutts," he would say, "your high example will bring a new world to birth."

Kate was often plagued by absurd little jealousies, but she was not at all jealous, ever, of Miss Coutts. Even she, apparently, saw in some wordless way, that touching doom of one born into other politics and another star.

There was time for nonsense, and for earnestness. There was time —and means and setting, too—for entertainment worthy of any guests, however fashionable. There was also more time for old friends.

Oddly, that was so. Beyond Wellington House Academy lay Potter's world, beyond that Maria Beadnell's drawing room, and Ainsworth's, and Gore House, Holland House, the great world . . . Devonshire Terrace gave Charles the sense of ease which a traveler finds at the end of a long voyage. Without ever noticing that he had ever neglected them, he now had time to see good old Beard and Tom Mitton often again.

But central to everything was the new book.
And central to the book was the child.
His child, his Little Nell.

Mary Hogarth would have winced to hear that tremulo stop full-drawn on Little Nell. One can almost hear her say, "Oh, mercy, Charles!" Yet Charles saw her once more a child in Chelsea and wept for love. And he was young; he still could only speak in the voice of his own time.

By July, Charles and his family were at Broadstairs; Nell and the old man had set out on their pilgrimage; and England hovered over a fictional child's journey to death like a mother at an awful bedside.

People read Nell, thought Nell, trembled for Nell. Briefly they relished a shudder at Quilp, embraced Dick Swiveller's inspired madness, gave the Marchioness more love, poor creature, than she had ever found in her proper person as the Orfling — and returned to Nell, sustained by the counterthreads of the tale as the mother goes back to her bedside ordeal stronger for a cup of tea and a taste of gossip.

It was as if they knew, before Charles himself knew it, that Nell must die. Knew, and like Charles, refused to know.

He had planned the book with a happy ending.

"She must die," Forster said. "You know it yourself."

"Oh, Forster, no. Let all these people who love my child close their book with quiet hearts!"

But Forster shook his head. "If Nell lives," he said, "she'll be a charming little character in one more book, enjoyed and forgotten. If she dies, every soul who is reading of her now will have her walking about in his heart forever, in all her gentle innocence."

Charles began to cry.

"Damn you," he wept. "I'm so afraid you're right."

By November, the postman was staggering to Devonshire Terrace under the weight of the letters. Letters, letters, begging like so many prayers to the God of life and death, "Don't let her die. Mr. Dickens, don't let little Nell die."

Charles read them all, and wept because there was no turning back. He could do no other.

The fantasy which had gripped that enormous reading public was incredible. A vast political upheaval, or the wildfire grown of some end-of-the-world religious frenzy, could have shaken the solid city of London no more than it was shaken by those last green-bound, monthly, shilling issues of The Old Curiosity Shop, by Charles Dickens.

In slums, the illiterates sat about the scholar as he spelled out, word by word, the latest news of their child. Cynical, worldly clubmen huddled apart from each other in reading-room corners, eyes fixed on print that blurred and enlarged, noses blown often and heavily.

And night after night, Charles paced the London streets, weeping. Sometimes he wept, "Nell, my Little Nell"; and sometimes, "Oh, Mary, my Mary, I can't live through it again, oh, God, I can't!"

But day after day he went back to his desk. And, false to our ears as it spoke in the living accents of his own time, the grief of those weeping, walking nights poured into the hearts of multitudes.

With the January issue, that which they feared was come upon them. Carlyle wept. Walter Savage Landor wept. A distinguished member of Parliament threw his book out of the train window — the Steam Age had begun — and thereupon wept his heart out, shamelessly, for all the world to see.

And except for Wellington and Victoria there was no better-known name in England than that of Charles Dickens.

And Charles, his face drained, said, "It's done, Forster. I lived through it. I wonder if anybody who's not done it can think what it's like to write a novel and give it all he has, all — and to *finish* it. I'm empty. I could be content never to write another word."

❊   3   ❊

BUT ALMOST AT ONCE the tide had swept him back to the world of things as they are. Mary was two years dead; Kate was vastly pregnant, but with all the celebrity and prosperity, she was far less mopish than usual in the home stretch. And prettier.

Charles laughed as he kissed her, and said, "'Appy to be the wife of the most celebrated murderer a-goin'?"

He accepted invitations right and left.

He marveled at the children as if he had been away from them on a long journey; at Charley, the four-year-old gallant, at Mamie, obedient and worshipful; at Katey, flashing fire, already the world's most enchanting antagonist.

"I'm free!" Charles said. "It's done! I'm come back!"

But by inbred habit, he sat down daily at his writing table. He was emptied; he had absolutely nothing to say. And, at long last, he found himself actually writing *Barnaby Rudge*.

The new baby was, somehow, less of an overwhelmer than the others, but still a fine boy; Walter Landor, a young lamb with an old lion's name.

Barnaby Rudge progressed. Forster had persuaded Charles to go to a public hanging; it left him sick with an unwanted knowledge of his fellow man, but at least the firsthand experience of mob blood-lust had brought the Gordon Riots close. He knew what the burning of the Newgate had been like as well as if he had stood by to watch.

"There'll be one great scene, at least," he said. "And one great character — my raven!"

Charles had grown so fond of his raven that he even let it into the house to watch him work.

"Ah, there, old girl. Don't mess on the chair or you'll go back to the stable where you belong. Thou wast not born for death, immortal bird. No, old Mad-Eye, Grip is what they'll call you, but it will still be you, to the life, in a book. *Wheeou-whit?* Pretty girl?"

In mid-March, the raven died. It had looked droopy in the morning. At noon, it staggered the length of the stable floor, said, "Ah, there, old girl," and fell over dead, claws up and curling inwards.

It was absurd, Charles told himself angrily, that a noisy, promiscuously defecating bird could fill a house full of people with the empty sense of death. Absurd. Why, even the children took it easily.

He mocked himself, lightly, charmingly. Volubly.

At the Garrick, Macready said to Maclise, "If that bird of his was a bore in life, what can we call it in death?"

Maclise smiled. "Oh, we'll weather it, bless him. But, you know, I could swear that everyone who's had a letter from him in this past week has had to hear about it. And that raven died a little differently every time."

Macready looked into space. "In my arms," he said, softly, "and the last words she whispered were of me."

"What?"

"Nothing. A line from an old play. You painters are a simple breed, Maclise. There's much you'll never understand about us old troopers, our friend included. Grant us your faith, dear fellow. We're quite like you, under the grease paint."

Maclise laughed, the lazy affectionate laugh with which he often embraced the world. He crossed himself.

"I believe," he said, "because it is impossible."

A few weeks after the demise of the raven, John Dickens was in debt again. Charles went to Exeter to put things right. But even after everything was cleared up, his father went on pleading, explaining.

"In a small town—er—one so rapidly finds himself obligated to those who—er—those many who worship at the shrine of the Muse. Your fame, dear boy, though I am—er—retired from it in this humble cot, still—er—seeks me out. And I . . . I . . ."

"Governor, I'm grateful that you're proud of me. But I've four children to bring up and educate, I'm sending Augustus to school in France, I . . ."

"Dear boy, I am too sensible of all that, I can only offer my profoundest . . . humblest . . ."

"Oh, God, Governor, don't. Can't we have a glass of the rosy and end our visit happily?"

Charles poured the wine himself.

"Charley sends you his dearest love, Governor. He loves to hear me tell of our Sunday walks and the splendid parties, when you used to let me sing."

But the ruffles would not regain their starch. At last Charles had to leave and get back to town.

He was dressing for dinner when Kate said, "It's scandalous. Why should he take advantage of you?"

Charles hit the dresser with his fist.

"As I have already told you, Kate, it was a small matter and easily righted. Please attend to your own concerns."

"Obviously it was worse than you say or you would not look so upset."

He turned his back on her. He said, "Oh, God, can't you let it alone? I'm tired."

She began to cry. "I only sympathized, and you begin to curse and swear."

"My little love, I don't mean to be unkind. Try to believe it, dear. Please. Please don't cry."

She sighed, submitting to his embrace. She said, "You can't help the way you're made, I daresay. But I wish that you sometimes noticed how people feel."

Charles said, "I must say good night to the babies now, dear."

He examined a rash on Walter's bottom. He held Katey's hands while she bounced on her bed, and tucked her away with a kiss and a prayer. He sat in the nursery armchair, with Mamie on his lap and Charley at his knee and told, at Charley's request, "the story about

the boy that had to eat pig food and went home and his papa gave
him a party."

He drank love and trust and fearless confidence, like a thirsty
sponge.

"Now prayers and off to bed," he said. "Whose Papa loves them
more than all the world?"

"Us's," said Mamie firmly. "Us's does."

He was still smiling when he passed Anne in the lower hall.

She said, "Good evening, sir, a pleasant trip, I hope?"

He answered warmly, "Ah, yes, thanks, Anne. Slap-up."

The gay time grew gayer. The attentions that society had paid to
the brilliant young author of *Nickleby* were scarcely more than the
cold shoulder, compared with the courting that came to the creator
of Little Nell.

"It's a stunning education," Charles told Forster.

Certain nuances, however, still escaped him. He did not suspect
that his top-flight tailor blenched to receive his ebullient instructions,
or that the clothes which gave him such happy confidence appeared
to parody Count D'Orsay's, as D'Orsay's with intentional, half-
homosexual wit, parodied those of society.

Charles trusted and loved his huge, voluptuous neckcloths, his
imaginative waistcoats, his flaring lapels, his dangling seals and his
scarfpins, as a young squire newly knighted might have trusted, rever-
enced, and loved his first suit of full armor.

The great Mr. Dickens, in hard fact, startled many people at first
sight. His clothes were a mouthful; he was unexpectedly small; and
he also appeared incredibly young, for at twenty-nine he still had
the skin of a boy, and his long, fair hair emphasized its youthful
freshness. Moreover (for the positive demands of a group are always
more quickly mastered than its taboos), a willing worshiper was often
startled to see Charles whip out a pocket comb and give that long,
fair hair a little casual tending on the spot.

Indeed, for the first minute or so after they had entered a roomful
of strangers, Kate, though he never suspected it, did better than
Charles.

But only for that first minute or so.

"Amazing eyes — like searchlights. And such warmth — so utterly unpretentious — and still, you know, not a trace of false modesty about his books. Exciting person."

Few, very few, retained a memory of the Mr. Dickens they had seen at first glance.

"Is he tall?"

"Not very, about five feet ten, I should say." (The advantage of inches given, unfailingly.)

"Cockney?"

"His parents came from Portsmouth, I understand. They live in Essex, now."

"The wife?"

"Silent, stoutish. Superb complexion."

Almost nobody remembered the pocket comb.

Charles, however, could have taken any one of them off to the life. When the city of Edinburgh gave him a ceremonial banquet, he came back to act out for Forster the whole show, the speakers, the gallery crowd, the fast-sailing waiters, "and my own cowerin', modest, endearin' little self."

Forster laughed like a wounded rhinoceros. Then he turned grave.

"But how did you really feel? Why isn't your head turned?"

"Because I don't know what comes next, I daresay. And *Barnaby*'s only warmed-over yesterday. Forster, what does come next?"

Forster's square, ugly face was knotted like a relief map of hero worship.

"God knows. Something incredible. Thank God you laughed it off when they asked you to run for Parliament."

"On the strength of Little Nell? Yes, that was a charming example of the workings of the English political mind."

"That's scarcely just. You've always had views and aired them, God knows. Weren't you tempted?"

"Tempted? I lay awake half one night changing the course of history. And God, how the Strangers' Gallery cheered and wept. I was better than Macready playing O'Connor. Before dawn, I was Prime Minister."

"You chill my blood."

"For the sake of society or of literature? I want exercise, Forster. Come out, let's look at faces and breathe some air."

❊ *4* ❊

CHARLES OFTEN FELT like getting out to breathe some air. He was bored by the winsome, playful little Dolly Varden, heroine of *Barnaby*, currently clasped to the heart of a public who should have known better. He was thankful for Angela Coutt's involvement in the Ragged Schools and all the travels and paperwork it cost him. He was thankful for the old friends and new friends and fashionable acquaintances who kept his bright, successful world so gay.

Sometimes the gaiety mounted until he was tipsy and outrageous with it, as he and Daniel had been in their glory as scholars of Wellington House Academy.

It was like that on a summer evening at Broadstairs when he pounced on a shy girl by the name of Eleanor.

"Light of my life!" he cried. "Oh, sweet, relentless empress of my soul!" And he whirled her in a waltz, not only to the water's edge but into it while she cried, "Oh, Mr. Dickens, no! Oh, Mr. Dickens, my silk dress, my only silk dress!"

"You're mad!" Kate said. "Charles, you should be ashamed!"

He dropped his dripping burden on the sands. He clutched his hair and smote upon his breast. "You talk to me of silk dresses! What of my tortured heart! What of my *new* patent leather shoes?"

"You shock me," Kate said when they were alone. "Getting tipsy in public with that champagne!"

He had not tasted the champagne, but clearly it would have been inefficient to say so.

"You're altogether right. I'm ashamed of myself. Will you forgive your stupid boy this once and give him a kiss?"

She eyed him, weighing it out.

"Ah, these stays, I can scarcely unhook them, Anne laces me so tight. Oh, dear. Ah, well, since you're so frank and sorry about it, Charles, it was disgusting but I'll not speak of it again."

She had looked well that evening and received many compliments, and it had done her good. Suddenly she smiled and shook out her back hair, and made a pretty, pouting rosebud mouth.

She said, "There!" and lifted it for a kiss.

[*233*]

It was Dolly Varden to the life.

The Hogarths came to visit, with Georgy who was growing up nicely, and adenoidal little Helen, a total blank. Charles's parents came, and Charles gave them a party flowing with the rosy and garlanded with highly droppable names to take back to Exeter.

Kate said, "I cannot feel it well advised in you to spend so lavishly while they are here."

"Oh, Kate, a fatted calf never hurt anyone!"

"What?"

"Where are the children?"

"On the sands, luckily for my poor head. Why?"

"I wanted to see them. Is that *also* difficult to understand?"

"You are so strange, Charles. One never knows what will make you cross."

"I'm sorry, dear. Perhaps we need a change. I've been thinking of a trip to America."

They would sail in January, with *Barnaby* done. He had all manner of flattering invitations from Longfellow, Irving, the lot.

The Macreadys would keep the babies for six months. He would miss them cruelly, but he would see the land of the free, the democracy in which all his dearest visions were living realities. Universal education! Universal suffrage!

However, at the thought of being separated from her little ones, Kate began to weep. Sometimes she wept for hours on end; and never, curiously enough, with them, but in her own room with the shades drawn and Anne instructed to keep them all quiet, especially Master Charley.

The grief was unmistakably genuine, and so baffling that Charles preferred to think about it as little as possible.

He was pushing hard through *Barnaby* one morning when Kate stumbled in upon him, weeping again. He glanced up, trying to conceal his vexation.

"Oh, sweet, still troubling for our babies?"

She said, "George is ill. He's very ill."

George, the least interesting of her brothers, was a dimly amiable sort of boy. While she lived at home, Kate had scarcely appeared to notice that he was alive. Charles stifled a sound of annoyance.

"Sorry to hear it, dear."

"You don't understand. He's very ill indeed."

She held out a note, crumpled in one hand. Charles laid it on the desk and got up. He put his arms around her.

Obviously, the old vulture, Mrs. H., was back at her favorite game. A dull week, a sore throat, and George has diphtheria. Or consumption. God, her poor husband!

"There, sweet, there, you know how readily your mother vexes herself over little illnesses. Go to Anne and have her make you ready, and I'll call the carriage. You'll cheer her in no time. Why, come, you know your mother, dear, don't cry."

Kate, however, was still weeping as she drove away. Charles felt a wave of guilt. Nonsensical or not, he knew that he would have been quick and tender to comfort such tears and fears in a child. He should have gone with her to Chelsea like a loving husband, comforting her.

"Brisk and sensible," he said to himself wearily as he sat down to write again. "Brisk and sensible at the wrong time again. Poor girl. Ah, well, it's done. Let's grind away."

The writing had been going well when Kate broke in upon it. Soon it went well again, so well that Charles lost the sense of passing time. When he heard the carriage come back, he thought that Kate must have changed her mind. Or had she forgotten her portmanteau? No, he himself had put it into the carriage.

He walked out into the hall, curious and mildly exasperated. The coachman was waiting there, and he did not need to speak. His face, and the way he held his hat, told Charles that young George Hogarth was not a little ill, or dangerously ill, but dead.

Charles found Anne, told her to tell the children that they would be back tomorrow, took his hat and got into the carriage without waiting to pack a bag.

George Hogarth (though nobody recalled the fact as one of any significance) had, like Mary, suffered in his childhood from "growing pains" — the cheery Victorian name for rheumatic fever.

Through the long ride to Chelsea, Charles readied himself humbly for Kate's reproaches.

God knew, he thought, for once he would deserve them all. Self-sheltering, brisk . . . laughing at her fear and grief, hurrying her off, weeping and alone . . .

In his mind, as the carriage drove on, he pleaded with her. "Try to forgive me, Kate. Try, only try."

She was waiting for him. She opened the door herself. Her face was tense, her eyes dry and bright. She said, "How quickly you got here, Mama won't lie down, she only sits and cries, and Papa barely seems to hear when I speak to him."

He caught her to him.

"Kate. Oh, Kate, my Kate."

"It was this morning, just like — when Mary — only quicker. He'd been cricketing, he was quite well. He came in, he ran up those stairs and . . . Charles, I'm so confused. It brings things back so, doesn't it? I feel all so confused and strange . . ."

"Lie down, dear. Here, come to your old room and lie down for a little. I'll do what I can and come back to you soon. God help them. God help us all."

She shuddered. She said, "You would have come with me if she had only put what really happened into the note . . . not only 'terribly ill.' "

Charles remembered that he had never thought to read the note, after all.

When the household had gone to sleep that night at last, Charles walked alone over half of London.

Strangely, the Hogarths owned no burial place. Late in that afternoon, as if someone else spoke with his voice, Charles had heard himself telling Mrs. Hogarth, steadily, gently, that her dead boy would rest beside his sister.

"Together. In time it will ease your loneliness to know that they lie there, together."

She had wept more easily then, in pitiful gratitude. And there was no going back. He had given away his grave.

He walked through the dark, tearless, and felt his body ache from holding Mary in his arms. Was she more than four years dead? And through all that rich, gay time of prospering, had a grave meant so much to him? Had he cared so much for the promise that he would lie there at last?

He tried to tell himself that nothing could matter less than where the castoff carcass lay, the life once gone. He tried to hear Mary's voice: "Oh, mercy, Charles!" Did she see him, on this torturing, idiot's walk? "Oh, mercy, Charles, go home and go to bed."

At last he turned back toward Chelsea.

Mary was dead. He had thought that the recurrent dream kept her with him, when it had only blunted the reality of her loss. He had thought that he lived her death again in the death of Little Nell, while he strode the streets crying her name in that huge luxury of tears, so unlike this dry-eyed knowing. She was dead.

She had opened her eyes, seen him, spoken. He had known that his own life was poured into her body, that because he loved her so much she could not die. He had held her, full of that knowledge, feeling her rest against him quietly, quietly, restored to life with his life.

She was dead.

She was dead, but by tomorrow he would not have to know it like this. Not like this.

He was near Chelsea again when he spoke aloud.

"There's a long pull of years ahead," he said. "I'll work while it's light. Death takes care of itself."

And a little farther along he said, "Oh, my Mary, if you are alive anywhere now, as I shall be so sure that you are tomorrow, God help me — please go on bearing with me. I'll do what I can with what I am. Mary."

Kate woke as he got into bed.

She said, "Oh, Charles, Charles, the things that happen. Our Mary and now George. How can we dare to leave the little ones? Oh, Charles, must we really go to America?"

As if it were Charley or Mamie who wept, Charles held her, crooning, patting her shoulder, until at last she was soothed and fell asleep.

✳ 5 ✳

In 1842, male Americans, except for an upper-class handful, were phenomenal spitters. For frequency, range, and volume they have scarcely been surpassed. The nation was fond, as it is now, of overheated rooms; the overheating was then produced by red-hot ornamental stoves. The penal and charitable institutions were generally advanced. Labor regulations were humane. In Massachusetts, a child was forbidden by law to work more than nine months in the mills; a full three must be given to education.

No country ever had such a gluttonous taste for lectures, for self-improvement.

And surely, Charles wrote home, there was no country on earth with less freedom of opinion.

"I do fear," he wrote, "that the heaviest blow ever dealt at liberty will be dealt by this country in its failure of example to the earth."

For America lived with the ugly fact of slavery. The newspapers ran columns of advertisements: "Ran away, Negro woman and two children . . . iron collar . . . leg iron . . . branded on forehead . . ." And it lived with it in a conspiracy of silence. Gentle, amusing, civilized, endearing people, like Irving, or the gay, sensitive young poet Longfellow, or dear Felton of Harvard, said, "Dickens, I agree with you utterly, but you must be careful of what you say. It doesn't help the problem, and it could do you endless harm."

The same excess of caution extended to all matters of controversy. "Dickens, I couldn't agree with you more about the need for international copyright. It's equally hard on me, in fact I sell better in England than I do here. But people are odd, it does no good to offend them."

At least, it forced one to think harder about his own politics. Yet six months of such treading on eggs would have made Charles homesick even if he had not missed the children so much. Kate always kept letters from home unopened until they could read them together. She was good to do that. Charles made himself think of it often, for her lassitude and lack of curiosity did not make her an ideal traveling companion. Sometimes, on a long pull by steamboat, coach, or rackety wood-burning train, Charles could have blessed poor Mr. Q. for the unvarying, prayerful adoration he held for Kate; faith, they say, is contagious.

Mr. Q., whose real name was Mr. Putnam, served them as secretary, courier, and awe-drunken worshiper. He was a cadaverous youth who wore a cloak like Hamlet's, and a very tall, limp, dusty hat. He sang in a bass voice and frequently asked them if they might not find a little music soothing. It was clear that he underwent torments of jealousy over every service that Anne performed for her drooping mistress.

Charles doubled his wages, said, "God bless you, we know *only* too well that you'd serve us for nothing," and smiled to hear his own choice of words, thankful that Mr. Q. lacked an ear for niceties.

That was the six months in a nutshell, except for the part of it that mattered most.

Charles wrote to Forster, "I have had deputations from the Far West who have come from more than two thousand miles distance: from the lakes, the rivers, the backwoods, the log-houses, the cities, factories, villages and towns . . . It makes my heart quieter, and me a more retiring, sober, tranquil man . . . I feel, even in the best aspects of this welcome, something of the presence and influence of that spirit which . . . has pointed upward with unchanging finger for more than four years past. And if I know my heart, not twenty times this praise would move me to an act of folly."

Nor did he write for effect, though he was, undeniably, affected by what he wrote.

They had both been so seasick on the voyage out that Charles's sole comfort had been the fact of Kate's being too far gone to talk and disturb the isolate perfection of his misery.

On the voyage home, Charles was the life of the ship. He had bought an accordion in America, and on the first day out he formed a trio with a violinist and bugler. (The bugler's enthusiasm was so great that he started practice at six in the morning.) He also had acquired a small white, shaggy, highly effervescent dog named Timber Doodle. It was not confined to the hold; the Captain still cried over Little Nell.

Sometimes between a game of charades and another concert, Charles would kiss Kate, and shout as if they were just released from some grim captivity.

"Kate, Kate, can you believe it? Home! Home, home!"

In the cab on the way to Macready's house Charles said repeatedly, "Six months is a lifetime to babies. If they seem indifferent don't be distressed. Their love will come back in no time, dear."

Eventually Kate said, "Oh, Charles, control your nerves. Any child *naturally* loves its parents."

Apparently she was right.

Walter snuggled in Charles's arms and made happy sounds. Katey jumped up and down. Mamie clung to his leg and said, "Papa, Papa, sing the *right* song. They don't know the *right* song!" Charley cried, "Mama!" and immediately had a convulsion.

The doctor, summoned in haste, said, "The little fellow's constitution was overthrown by so much joy."

Charley, already restored, said, "Go home, you old doctor! Papa, tell the story about they didn't have any picnic and Jesus magicked one with lots left over."

And Charles said, "Oh, Kate, how could we have left them for so long?"

The *American Notes* did poorly at home and infuriated America. Charles had praised much, but he had not whitewashed. "Thank God for fiction," he said. "People will hear anything if they don't know what they're learning until they've learned it."

One evening in October he said to the painter, Clarkson Stanfield, "Stanny, dear old Stanny, there's a great new book waiting to pounce on me. Before it starts, will you come on a very short vagabond's holiday? You, and I, and Forster and Maclise together?"

It was a holiday to go down in time. Wild northern country, wild endless fun, climbing crags, discovering inns, developing wonderful headaches and laughing them off at dawn with wonderful laughter.

Late one night at an inn, Forster rose, a brimming tankard in each hand. "A toce to our guiding spirits," he pronounced. "Oh, Beauty and Mirth, limpin' from compass—*hic*—comin' from 'Lympus to grace our so-society, accept our humble duty and service and receive these our prayers once offered."

"Book of Uncommon Prayer," Maclise annotated solemnly. "Amen."

Stanny raised a bemused and reverent face. "Man limps from compass," he said, "and he leaps into the light, without sharp north, without declining west. I don't know how you are, but I, as of now, am immortal."

Charles, the only sober member of the company, stood on his head.

It was too foolish to recount. It was tomfoolery that even Daniel of Wellington House would have rejected as only fit for the nursery. Charles said that it sent them back to the world four giants refreshed.

"And this little giant speaking is about to deal the world's hypocrisy a blow that will leave it staggering. And the joke is that they'll pay for it, too. It's odd, in the *American Notes* I made a few faint, faint, courteous hints that professions of Christianity and democracy don't square too well with the fact of slavery, and half a nation raged at me for a fool and ingrate. But if I write a *tale* to expose all our sanctimonious snivellings, they'll gulp it down and make me rich into the bargain. It's amazing, amazing what fiction lets one speak out. It's like a cloak of darkness and an armor of light!"

But the great new book played coy and cumbersome by turns.

It began to move in December. But still at what a price of carpets worn in tracks, of forehead knocking, of neglecting all normal, common human responsibilities!

Charles walked into the drawing room one evening, saying, "I hope Miss Coutts wasn't hurt today. I couldn't have broken off for tea with God."

Kate blenched. "Charles, oh, what makes you say such things?"

"It's all right, dear," Georgy said. "He didn't mean it literally, you know."

Georgy had come to stay.

"I wish Aunt Georgy lived here," Charley had said. "We would have been sad without her to visit, at the Macreadys'. She unlonesomed us there, a very, very lot."

"She's fifteen," Charles had said. "She'd be a companion for you, too, Kate."

At once, she had fitted in. Charles was enchanted by her bustling tidiness, amused by her skill at winning over Anne. "You have so much to do! Would it help you today if I had the books dusted and saw that they went back in proper place, do you think?"

Anne's own method, at that! Yes, quite delightful.

She was pleasant to look at, too. Sexlessly thin, but always so neat and fresh, and such an endearing, clever little smile with the small white teeth that overlapped a bit at the front of her mouth. And such a keen little mind!

The little mind, in fact, was extremely keen. In a very short time Georgy had grasped the fact that Charles was happiest when he could pretend that Kate was perfect and that he was never at all bored or vexed with her.

After that, she knew how to behave. And it was not long before she knew that she would never, never have to go back to Chelsea and Mama.

[241]

The knowledge became her. Happiness becomes us all.

And while nobody would ever be like Mary, it was, sometimes, Charles thought, in the strangest way like being back at Furnival's Inn again. Yes, sometimes when the children were abed and they sat, all three, quiet before the fire, a look would cross the child's face that was almost like a stir of the past; the plain little face had almost a look of Mary.

That haunting look, as a matter of fact, was quite simply one of unqualified adoration.

In the year that followed, Charles often needed it.

✳ 6 ✳

CHUZZLEWIT WAS A GOOD BOOK, Charles never doubted that. It was a good book and he had never been more obsessed with the need to speak directly to the hearts and consciences of multitudes.

And the damned thing did not sell.

Month after month, despite each new burst of comic invention, melodrama, romance, *everything* that anyone could conceivably look for in a novel, it pursued its awful way as a *succès d'estime*, admired by all except for the blessed crowd with their blessed, educable hearts and their blessed, blessed shillings-per-issue.

But it had to sell.

It had to sell because Charles had bought Devonshire House and gone to America, both, on the absolute assumption that it would sell like all the others rolled into one.

It had to sell because Kate was pregnant and five children are five children.

Furthermore, the Governor was up to his tricks again.

"But he's *happy* serving his friends all that damned vintage champagne," Charles said to Forster. "And ever since I sent him off to Exeter, he's looked so — God, I don't know — so pinched and woebegone when I clamp down on him."

Forster snorted. "Let him sink or swim. He's a competent newspaperman, he always has employment. Why should he leech upon your energies?"

Charles shouted. "Can't you ever attend to your own affairs?" And at once he was ashamed. "I'm sorry, Forster. But I do love the old boy, and he loves London. Don't you think that if he were on the outskirts, in a house that gave him some modest little sense of pride he might . . ."

"I most confoundedly do not! My God!"

In the upshot, John Dickens moved to the suburbs. He got a place on a paper, and Miss Coutts found Augustus a little job with an investment house.

And Charles wrote on. He marveled at Sairey Gamp, with her gin on the mantel to set to her lips when she felt so disposed, and her overarching angel, Mrs. Harris. At the end of a day he would look back over the close-written slips and whisper, "Oh, Mrs. Gamp, dear love, you're permanent, you walk with Falstaff. Fetch us in some cash, now, bless you, we needs it."

And precisely nothing happened.

Away from work he had never been more energetic or more gay, or kept a picture of soaring success more firmly fixed in the public eye.

He said to Kate and Georgy, sometimes, "I don't know how the days get so desperately full. Never mind, Broadstairs and the sea will set it all to rights."

But Broadstairs meant a rush of people, too. By July Charles was giving more energy to Miss Coutts's charities, and particularly the Ragged Schools, than half the world spends in getting its bread.

"God bless you," he said often to Miss Coutts. "The world will reverence your memory."

He meant it. He also meant it when he said to Forster, "The world is changing. When its conscience wakes, the day of the philanthropist will be past."

He meant it when he said to Kate and Georgy, "How good to have this quiet hour at home"; and when he said to Maclise, "Children, pregnant wives, flush water-closets out of order, confusion, bills — for God's sake let's have an evening like happy bachelors."

And month after month the bills kept piling up.

It was November when Hall suggested a Christmas book to be dashed off for the holiday market.

"You know — no Christmas dinner until little Mattie's innocent faith brings off the last-minute miracle."

"I don't . . ."

"Don't be hasty," Chapman said rather heavily. "The Notes didn't do well either, you know. We could all use a little profit."

Charles's head went up. His face was cold and tight.

"I feel that the firm has little to complain of in me, nonetheless. You were a small house when I contracted for *Pickwick*, I remember. I feel no obligation to interrupt my best book for drivel which would hurt my reputation and do little to help your purse."

He was fully as startled by his own angry ill-nature as his publishers were. Indeed it was he who broke the brief, shocked silence.

"I was rude. I'm sorry." He looked away, and suddenly he nodded. "More than that, a Christmas book, about the length of two installments, could be a good book. It could say something. I'll begin it now."

Chapman looked distressed.

"Oh, no!" he said. "Something light and pleasant! For the holiday, you know, for the holiday!"

Charles looked at him. His eyes were ice-blue and hard. He smiled, a smile that made little Hall edge away and Chapman clear his throat nervously. He spoke in a voice that was nastily, pettishly precise.

"I am delighted at the prospect of earning a little hard cash and I feel myself altogether capable of doing so. Particularly as my feeling for the holiday and its significance is, apparently, closer to that of the general public than it is to your own. Upon which I pin such slight hopes of salvation as I dare to entertain."

He got away as quickly as he could. It took him a good hour to walk himself into a decent frame of mind. Indeed, as he was halfway through that walk, a passer-by said to his sweetheart, "See that chap got up like Lord Guineabags? Face like a meat-axe, wot?"

His sweetheart sniggered. "Just murdered 'is dear old mother, if you asks me."

"Damn them," Charles was still saying, over and over. "Damn everybody, have they no reverence? Is everybody in this foul world ashamed to admit that he's *good*, and wants to be *better*? Are they ashamed of Christianity?"

It was highly disproportionate, hysterical, and an orgy of self-justification as Charles realized even before his legs were thoroughly tired. He had been, he knew it, for months in a state of mounting panic. He had believed himself safely out of the pot-boiling class forever, the public's infallible love. He was wrong, it was frightening, it hurt his vanity, and a deeper, growing pride — the pride of the artist. He had tried not to know it, Chapman had forced him to know it, and he had made a fool of himself.

He admitted it.

And suddenly, as he walked, he laughed aloud. "On the run for all these months and never knew it," he whispered. "Poor Mother's sheltered girlhood and the Governor's bottomless purse — Lord, what a fool. Chapman was *kind*. I'll drop him a note tonight.

"A Christmas ghost story . . . yes, the good old traditional Christmas ghost story . . . with advantages . . ."

His eyes became remote. He began to smile. He worked his tongue behind his smiling lips.

As he neared Devonshire Terrace he nodded. He spoke aloud again, affectionately.

"I've a surprise for you, old lad," he said. "You're about to slide straight through the needle's eye!"

He was, of course, addressing Mr. Scrooge, of Scrooge and Marley.

❋　7　❋

AND MARLEY was dead, to begin with.

He was dead, but, dear Heaven now his partner, and his partner's clerk, and the clerk's family took over the living world!

It was an extraordinary experience.

Not only the people, oh, good God, what people, but the words, the flood of those effortless, right, right words!

How or why he had started to write it, Charles had forgotten. It had come out of the void, taken him over, and that was all. The question of how it would do simply never rose. It had happened. It had to be put down. It was there, it made him laugh, it made him cry, and the right, right words streamed off his pen.

He wanted next to no sleep. Late, late, night after night he walked about the streets; it was the trial of *Pickwick* vs. *Bardell* and Little Nell and every triumph of fancy rolled into one. *Yes . . . yes, that's it! Oh, yes, yes, yes . . .*

He wrote all day; half the night he strode over London weeping and laughing like a madman.

And it was done.

God bless us every one, it was finished.

Even Kate laughed and wept as he read it aloud, and Georgy said, "Oh, Charles, I can't believe that it always hasn't *been* written, just like that! I love it so that I feel as if it always *was*. Does that make sense?"

Her face was full of that look that brought back Furnival's Inn, and Mary.

Charles took the manuscript to Hall the next morning in a blaze of glory.

"I know it's overlength, but I want it to go at a shilling a copy, I want everyone to be able to afford it. It will cut the profits, but we'll more than make it up by the bulk of the sales. And it must have truly good illustrations. They'll pay for themselves. Get Leech to do the plates."

Oh, Charles knew what he had, without the peradventure of a doubt. Now that it was done, he knew not only what he was giving to the world but what the world would give him in return.

He heard the news of the first fantastic sales with joy, but he had not needed reassurance. How could they have been less? Had there ever, ever been such a Christmas tale?

That year in Charles Dickens's house, Christmas to Twelfth Night was one uninterrupted festival.

Even small Walter came to the Christmas dinner. Georgy demanded it, and she was right. He sat in her lap, ate from her plate, bite and bite about, and was good as gold through all the laughter and the speeches and the toasts.

There was a positive glitter all over the Governor. God bless him, he shone as if he were spangled with gold dust. Everyone, even, by Heaven, Mrs. Hogarth, looked happy, loving, lovable.

And none of them, none of them suspected the necessary miracle that had happened. He was overdrawn at the bank, it would take contriving to see them through to February when the first accounting would be paid. But paid it would be, and paid in a golden flood.

Oh, Mr. Scrooge, God bless you! Six thousand copies snatched off the stalls the first day out, still thousands more each day. Letters, letters, letters, and all of them, from friends and strangers alike, full of such warmth, such love. Yes, yes, a miracle, as if Christmas itself had seized upon whatever gifts and powers he possessed, and used it to its own, own blessed ends!

Charles stood up, laughing, throwing back his hair, the wineglass high. He was small, overdressed, a little absurd; he was beautiful and his blue eyes were the eyes of a saint in ecstacy.

"A merry Christmas to us all, my dears," he said, "and may we truly, soberly, joyfully keep Christmas in our hearts on every day of all the years to come. God bless us!"

Except for his mother, who was lost in trancelike monologue, everybody began to laugh and kiss everyone else.

On New Year's Day, Charles said to Forster, "Think! The weary, weary year to end like this! The letters come in mountains, the new printings sell before they're off the press! God knows what went wrong with *Chuzzlewit*, yet the fault was mine, somehow, I know it now. How could I have doubted them, Forster, all those good people who long to be reminded in what Image they were truly made?"

Even Forster was slighty embarrassed.

Charley's Twelfth Night party crowned the season. Charles hired a professional conjurer to coach him, though his quick hands and patter already lifted him a peg above the amateur class.

When the sack of bran turned to a live guinea pig, Charley was the only child in the room who was not staggered. He bent a grave young angel's face above the scrabbling rodent and kissed it fondly, but with no surprise.

"But how did he do it?" the crowd of children were shouting. "Charley, Charley, how does your Papa do it?"

"Magic," said Charley. "How do you think, stupids? He's a man that can magic, that's all."

Charles kissed him.

"Well put, sir," he said. "Very, very well put."

Kate went to bed shortly after the children did. But nobody noticed, new guests came, guests who had fetched their children home returned. Maclise and Stanny were in stupendous form; Mrs. Macready put a holly wreath upon her husband's head, and they played the death scene from *Antony and Cleopatra* to wild applause. The effect was enhanced by Macready's alternate stage-whisper coaching and the passion of tragic projecting that came upon him with his own lines.

The party, as Charles observed, was half madhouse and half ball with all the finer elements of both. The guests were transformed, and, surely not altogether with champagne; no, he could have sworn it, the love he felt for them all and for the world was working in them like a liberation. Could champagne alone have ever set Carlyle, that crag-faced Ezekiel of the North, to joining him in a hornpipe?

That hornpipe, however, reminded Charles briefly of Kate's sense of the proprieties, and breathless from the dance he cast his eye about for that ultimate bluestocking, Jane Carlyle. She'll have a word to say tonight, he thought.

Mrs. Carlyle flew past on Forster's arm, a waltzing maenad with her back hair fallen half down. He swung her through a doorway, in magnificent disregard of such hard facts as doorframes, and she cried, "Oh, take care, you'll dash my brains out!"

Charles heard Forster's roar come back.

"Your brains! Who wants brains here? *Let them go!*"

Charles flung his arms about Mrs. Macready. He had gone the road sip by sip, but at last he, too, had arrived at the common goal.

"Allow me," he said. "I love you. You are proxy for your whole sex. Oh, come, not your *cheek!* In this kiss I embrace every one of you old enough to wear these devilish, frustrating corsets."

Mrs. Macready, though a gentlewoman, was quite used to theater people in their cups, and she had enjoyed the champagne herself. She hugged him close and laughed.

"Behave yourself, you idiot," she said.

Upstairs, Kate rolled over in her sleep and moaned. The noise made her dream of the ocean; she hated the ocean.

Frank was an excellent baby.

"You're a worthy addition," Charles told him. "Yes, you are. You're wholly approved."

He thought of taking Kate to the Highlands for a holiday. Her spirits still hung a thought on the droopy side. However, the first of February bills were stunners. Perhaps it might be well to wait for the statement. Yes, one should be a realist. The *Carol's* low price and those expensive plates might well have held its profits down to not much over a thousand pounds. One could drop by and inquire, to be sure, but such overeagerness is never good long-term policy.

The statement went out on the eleventh.

Hall had said several times to Chapman, "We should let him know in advance that by keeping the price and plates to his specifications we've published at just this side of loss."

Chapman said, "He's been above himself ever since he went to America. The sketches were poor, even aside from that irresponsible stuff about slavery and the like. *Chuzzlewit's* a sleeping potion. He needs a little shock to keep him spurred along. He's proved what he can do, only now, and it could have made us a fortune if he hadn't been so set on dictating his own terms. No, Hall, we've got a rich future or an expensive past in that fellow, and it depends on how we hold the reins."

"I don't know," said Hall. "You may be right. Oh, dear me. I don't know."

Charles ran, at the postman's double knock and snatched the statement. He carried it into the library, and forced his fingers to be slow, deliberate, as they broke the seal, as if the actual sum did not matter at all. Nor did it, really; a thousand pounds clear was all he needed, not one penny more. The rest was sheer lust of triumph.

Mustn't be greedy now.

He opened it. He stared.

He stared even though he took it for granted, almost at once, that a mistake had been made, a partial accounting had been sent off through a clerical error.

There was no mistake, as he learned by quick exchange of written messages. The amazing sales of the *Carol*, still continuing, had fetched Charles in precisely two hundred and fifty pounds.

And Charles, who had so movingly hymned the rich man's poverty and the poor man's wealth, hid his face in his hands and went to pieces. He wept as he had not wept since a day, long ago, when he hid in a broom closet weeping because *Don Quixote* had gone for a soupbone, bread, and a screw of tea.

John Forster, the only soul Charles ever told about that broom closet, and the Marshalsea, and Warren's Blacking, 30 Strand — Forster got him out of the panic, somehow.

"You're by no means as pushed as you think," he said. "Think of your assets. Think of what this house would bring in rental, furnished as it is and with your name thrown in. Do you realize how cheaply you can live abroad? And if you did that for a year, who would know unless you told them that you did it to economize? Writers as rich as Bulwer do it, why not you?"

He also said, "Bradbury and Evans would certainly be overjoyed to get you but I wish you wouldn't be hasty. I wish you'd reconsider walking out on Chapman and Hall. It's been a long, long good relationship."

"We won't talk of that."

"But really, now . . ."

"Forster, once I've closed a door, it's closed. No regrets, no backward glances. I'm made so. I can live no other way."

Forster had been turning over some of the papers that were on the table as Charles spoke.

He said, comfortably and fondly, "Oh, don't talk nonsense."

He lifted his flat, heavy face with the canine-tender look it so often wore when he looked at the man of genius who was his dear, dear friend. The look froze.

He was looking at a stranger, and a frightening stranger. There was none of the anger or wounded vanity or self-pity that he had looked up expecting to see in those set, still eyes. They held nothing, indeed, but a strange, inhuman perfection of casting out. One could imagine that look on the face of the angel with the fiery sword who guards the gates of Eden. But not on a mortal. Not on a friend, a tender, sensitive, gifted, close, great, good, good friend.

"Dear me," he said rather weakly after a long moment, "stubborn, aren't you?"

And the look, blessedly, vanished. Charles only looked extremely tired and perplexed.

"I don't know. Perhaps. Still, there it is."

Forster hunched his heavy shoulders and straightened them. Indeed, the picture, so incompatible with his whole notion of his friend's character, had dimmed in a few passing seconds to the range of the acceptable, the possible.

"Then let's pray God I never run against that stubbornness," he said. "I, or anyone else who's fond of you. Ah, well, then Bradbury and Evans."

Charles listened and Forster talked. The black tide, little by little, rolled back.

Toward the end of the evening Forster said, "And when you're abroad and saving all that money, don't be in a rush to earn more. The *Carol*'s magnificent, but it doesn't really reflect your politics. There's a sense in which it was outgrown before you wrote it. In any event, an artist wants time, occasionally, to wonder where he's come and what he is."

"Dear man, one finds that out with his pen in hand while he writes a tale."

"When you go to Italy, try a diary."

"And talk to myself? God forbid! There's too much in any life that can be enjoyed more if it's thought about less. Let's talk of something else. I wish that you were coming with me to Liverpool and Birmingham, you damned Conservative. It would do you good to hear what I've got to say to the mechanics' institutes."

"The hornyhanded sons of toil will adore you."

"And the dazzling sight of my new magpie waistcoat, black, white, and incredible. If they can get in. Standing room only is now being sold to gaze on England's glory stony-broke."

"I wish you were going to share in the proceeds."

"I shall do well enough." Briskly, curtly, almost as if it were he who had been helping Forster to pluck up heart, and not the other way about. And in almost the same flash his face sagged and his voice went tired. "In fact, now we've got things arranged decently enough so that I can tell Kate."

"Tell Kate?"

"No, I've not told Kate. Does that surprise you?"

Forster, in fact, had winced. A singular virgin romanticism bedewed his picture of Charles's marriage without in any way impoverishing his picture of a Charles eternally bereft, forevermore wearing his Mary's ring.

He was utterly wretched when Charles spoke again.

"No," he said, "my helpmate is still wrapped in the golden dream. I put it off. I didn't feel up to it. The sort of situation that could be handled more easily if my wife had a little more confidence in me and the blessed Governor had a little less."

But before Forster could think of an answer, Charles snapped his fingers sharply and shook back his hair.

"No notion why I said that. Tired, I daresay. Meant nothing. Try to forget it, Forster. Do."

❀ ❀ ❀ ❀ ❀ ❀ ❀ ❀

BOOK VI
A Man of Genius

❀ ❀ ❀ ❀ ❀ ❀ ❀ ❀

IN FACT, when Charles packed the magpie waistcoat and went to Liverpool, he was feeling extremely lonely. Fanny and Burnett were in Liverpool, too, at the time. He spent the afternoon before he was to give his speech with them. She and Burnett stroked each other's hands, absently, as they sat side by side.

Their well-kept clothes were far from new. They were in their middle thirties, but their faces had a young look of undimmed hope, shared hope. They looked alike, and when they talked to each other it was in a comfortable, allusive shorthand, the private language of married lovers.

Charles told himself that such happiness was wonderfully moving to see; that it lifted and opened one's heart.

If his heart was not precisely lifted, it was at least wide open; still yawning open as he walked out onto the platform to address the Mechanics' Institution.

There was a standing ovation as he took the chair. He bowed to it and ran his eyes down the written agenda in his hand. The evening would open with a piano selection. He made the announcement with a nicely timed break and a gentle overemphasis upon the performer's name.

"By Miss—er—*Weller*. Miss Christiana Weller."

The name, as he had hoped, brought down the house. Charles bowed to the roar of laughter, still keeping his own face grave, and turned, bowing again, his hand extended.

The girl who came toward him was slender; she had a look of almost ethereal fragility. She was flushing and trembling at the laughter and she lifted her face to Charles in a childlike pleading that was innocent of reproach.

So lovely, so frightened . . . How could he have been such a clumsy brute?

Charles stepped toward her quickly, whispering a few stumbling words of apology. He led her to the piano. She sat down, bowing her fair head for a moment and then raising it with a quick, bright smile. "I was silly to let myself be startled. We . . . all love Sam."

She wore a green velvet dress trimmed with dark fur. Her skin showed blue-white, transparent against it. It was not velvety thick like Kate's but delicate . . . delicate . . .

Spiritual, Charles's mind translated sharply. What a rare, spiritual young creature!

He heard himself murmuring some automatic, clumsy gallantry about a new name, which she would surely find soon. He went to his seat on the platform in a blur of emotion.

Christiana Weller played well, but Charles did not hear the music. He was consumed by the sense of sight. What spiritual depths were in that amazing young face, bent above the keys! What spiritual powers showed in those fluent, caressing, fiery hands!

The chairman of the evening heard not a single word pronounced by the dignitaries whom he introduced so gracefully. The ghost of Darling Daphne was revisiting the glimpses of the moon.

And still, when the time came for his own address, he gave a quick push to his hair, smiled, drew in the waiting silence, felt the audience stir, and knew his purpose with them, and nothing else. Perhaps the House of Commons had lost a useful member, after all. A born actor, with an obsessive horror of poverty extending beyond his own pocket to include those of his fellow men, a born optimist who had learned (like all newspapermen) that legislators are not per se wise — far less disinterested — Charles might, conceivably, have pushed his youthful demand for a brave new world to some genuine effect.

Now he spoke to shame the self-styled Christians who shut their eyes to the relationship between poverty and ignorance, ignorance and social decay. He spoke to wake the hope for an England in which universal education should enable England's laboring class, itself, to create a world in which the ordinary decencies, the minimal needs of health and self-respect should depend not upon philanthropic whim, but legal right delineated and enforced by universal suffrage.

He spoke from a radical dream, lost to himself. He was not even conscious of how well he used his actor's voice, and his flashing, actor's face. When he finished to cheers, he started, hearing them like a man waking.

Then his head flew back, his hands went out. He was Charles with his audience, Charles triumphant.

The group on the platform had risen. They crowded about him. "Brilliant!" "Superb!"

And a soft young voice said, "Oh, Mr. Dickens!"

He had forgotten her. Incredibly, he had forgotten her.

He took her hand. It was cool and smooth. He looked into the spiritual young face; he saw again the slender form, the translucent skin that spoke of, oh, such a pure, singular young spirit.

"Everything you said was new to me," she murmured, "but as you said it I felt that in a way I must always have known it. Isn't that odd?"

"No. I can see in your face that you were born with an understanding heart and an understanding spirit, Miss Weller."

The little fire in Charles's hotel sitting room had almost burned out before he went to bed that night. He sat before it thinking of Christiana Weller's spirituality. He thought of it until his lips and his body trembled and his palms turned cold and wet.

Tomorrow, he thought. Tomorrow . . .

For his friend, T. J. Thompson, as it had turned out, was slightly acquainted with Miss Weller's father. Thompson was a Yorkshire landowner, a pleasant thickish, middle-aged widower. He had come on for the Institution meeting and appointed himself Charles's guide and caretaker. He had engaged Charles's hotel suite for him and had supper served in it for them both, on the night of his arrival.

And now he had said, "I've suggested that we might drive out tomorrow and call at that little Miss Weller's house, if you've nothing you'd rather do with the afternoon while we wait about for the dinner and the ball. Quite the little charmer, isn't she?"

"A good thought, Thompson. I'd enjoy it."

Tomorrow . . . tomorrow . . .

Charles Dickens, the eminent novelist, father of five, went to bed in a quivering adolescent trance.

And the next day the dream still held. It was an astounding afternoon, yet so elusive in its bright, spiritual quality of understanding that when it was over Charles could scarcely remember a word that they had spoken.

He tried to remember, as he sat by Thompson's side in the carriage with his head bowed. He remembered clearly, almost painfully, the clear, translucent pallor of her skin. He remembered the changing expressions of her delicate face as it lifted to his own. He remembered how suddenly, how pitifully its light was always extinguished when she spoke to that wooden-faced old man, her father, or to the edgy, shrill young sister with the bitten nails, or the bosomy, genteel-pretentious mother, who were, so unthinkably, her family — her captors.

"You know," Thompson said suddenly, "I like that girl. She's not only got looks, she's intelligent."

"Thompson, I am only afraid that she is too intelligent, too spiritual. That house is a prison to her young soul, she belongs to another sort of world altogether. And her body is frail, so frail. Only now, as you spoke, it had come upon me like a certain knowledge that she will die young."

"My God!" Thompson exclaimed. "Don't say things like that!"

Charles touched his arm gently and changed the subject. It had been, he knew, a brutally tactless thing to say to a man still mourning a young wife. Yet the sense of strange foreknowledge remained with him. Christiana Weller was not of this earth, and she would soon escape her bonds. The thought was a tragic excitement almost undistinguishable from elation.

The ball lasted until three in the morning, and Charles flung himself into it with such a fervent gaiety ("I'm sorry, no, we don't go often to balls," she had said) that he reached Birmingham, next afternoon, with a severe hangover.

The welcoming committee took him to see the hall in which he would make his address. It was stupendously overprepared. There were banks of ferns. There were transparencies depicting, apparently, the triumph of God Knows What over Everything Else. There was a huge floral arch which spelled out *Welcome Boz* in red and white carnations.

Charles stared. His belly was seized with a queasy churning. He smiled his most winning, spontaneous smile.

"I danced until three, last night. You must take me to my hotel for a nap and a quiet meal alone or I'll fall asleep in company with my audience."

He had experienced perhaps half a dozen hangovers in his life, most of them incurred with that fellow man-of-the-world Potter. He had never felt stage fright before.

Alone, he examined the sensations with astonishment: the boneless legs, the quivering diaphragm. He lay down on the bed and was surprised to find himself falling asleep almost at once. But he dreamed that he stood on the platform with his throat frozen, while all the audience jeered except for Christiana Weller. She sat in the front row, wearing a severe little black and white bonnet. She was reading a book; reading calmly and indifferently, as if she were quite alone.

Charles woke sweating.

The magpie waistcoat when he had unpacked it looked appallingly of a piece with the overdecorated hall. They must have spent a small fortune on those decorations; money that the Institution needed, thrown about to flatter a man who was being driven into exile by the threat of debt!

Charles, before the looking glass, found himself combing his hair twice over, like a timid girl dreading an evening of quadrilles. With the sense of having hit upon a most singular and original notion, he rang for a pint of champagne and half a pint of sherry and drank them down. It was a singular and original notion, for him. His drinking was so exclusively a social gesture that he remained both startled and dubious until the large, bright peace began to flood him.

"My God," he whispered, "how astonishing, I feel *completely* like myself!"

If he was slightly tipsy at the start of the evening, none of his audience suspected it. Indeed, he had never had such an audience, weeping, cheering, and standing when he finished like one soul responding to his own.

"Bless you," he whispered as he bowed and held out his hands to them. "Bless you."

The fantastic transparencies and the huge floral arch had become tasteful and touchingly generous gestures of love.

Before he went to bed he wrote to Thompson. He wanted to write to Forster, for he was full of complex emotions that ached for a sensitive reader, yet he realized that to one who had not seen Christiana Weller the written word could not convey her quality. Thompson saw her through a glass, darkly, to be sure. Nonetheless, he had seen something, something of what she was.

And still, once he had dashed off his report of the evening's triumph on the proper note of light self-mockery, Charles hesitated. For who can express an experience wholly unique? How could one convey an emotion at once so tenderly aware of that fresh young beauty and still so utterly, utterly a response of the spirit?

"I cannot joke about Miss Weller," he wrote at last, "for she is too good; and interest in her (spiritual young creature that she is, and destined to an early death, I fear) has become a sentiment with me. Good God, what a madman I should seem if the incredible feeling I have conceived for that girl could be made plain to anyone!

"Well, well, there must be things of this kind in Heaven; and some of us are going there faster than we think for, perhaps. . . . The landlady is not literary and calls me Mr. Digzon. In other respects, it is a good house."

Charles had said what he could. He went to bed.

✻   2   ✻

IT WAS UNLIKE Charles to have hesitated over that letter. He always had a singular faith in the ability of others to see him as he saw himself.

So it had been when Kate's sad, questioning fingers fumbled at Mary's ring and he had said, to comfort her, "Yes, dear, I will wear it until I die." So it was, alas, when he came home from Birmingham.

For several days he talked incessantly of the lovely, spiritual young creature who had played the piano in Liverpool. Earnestly and at length he described her bright, delicate soul, and her frail body, and the lethal imprisonment of that strangely alien home in which she lived so gently, brightly, uncomplainingly.

Georgy listened intently, though Kate showed little interest. However, Kate seldom showed interest in talk about people who were behaving themselves; Charles's surprise was as great as his shock when, in the middle of the week, she cried, out of a clear sky, "Oh, for mercy's sake, will you never be done with talking about that artful, unpleasant little flirt? Can't you even see by *now* how she took you in?"

He made an enormous effort at self-control.

"My dear, if I ever were to feel the sort of unfortunate interest in a girl which you seem to imagine that I feel for Miss Weller, I trust that I should have the courtesy to conceal it."

"That's a pretty thing to say!"

Charles looked away from her face, which nowadays looked puffy and flushed when she was angry.

"Darling," he said, "don't you know that I love you more than all the world?"

Hurt though he was, he had no doubt that he meant it.

An hour earlier, he had been composing a brief note to Miss Weller in his mind, the note that he would enclose with the volumes of Tennyson which he was about to send to her; his own copies, not new, because he had fancied that she would like them the better for that.

Now, abruptly, he decided to send them to her father's care and write to him, instead. It might be better so, and for her sake, too, in a world that can misinterpret so utterly what it does not understand.

And, yes, he thought as he wrote, it is even possible that the word of a stranger may wake that old man to a new understanding of the rare life that has been given into his care.

He wrote, rapidly: "I cannot help saying that . . . I read such high and unusual matter in every look and gesture of the spiritual creature who is naturally the delight of your heart and very dear to you, that she started out from the whole crowd the instant I saw her, and will remain there always in my sight."

It was only after he had posted the letter that Charles realized how much more of his heart it had shown in it than he could have spoken to her directly. And there was no doubt that it would be read aloud in her presence.

His emotions, in that moment, were highly confused.

But he began to wonder when life would bring him a new reason to go to Liverpool again. Despite himself, he thought of it not less and less but more and more.

He had been at home for eleven days when a letter came from Thompson which bore a Liverpool postmark.

That's odd, Charles thought idly. He's not gone back to Malvern Abbey as yet?

He broke the seal and began to read.

A shock went through his body. He felt as though his blood had stopped flowing. His lips turned white.

Thompson had written for advice. He had not yet proposed to Miss Weller, because he had doubts despite the fact that she gave him reason to hope. There was a wide difference in their ages, and his first marriage had been extremely happy. Could he make her happy, too, as happy as she deserved to be? What did Charles think?

Charles did not think.

He saw a green dress that described a young body, not thin but slender and subtly curved. He saw clear skin that the eyes translated into exacerbated sense of touch. He saw a face whose mobile responsiveness was a promise of latent ecstasy.

Oh, God, not Thompson! No . . . no . . .

Othello, with the pillow in his hand, had at least the comfort of respecting what he felt, both as a man of passion and a man of honor. Charles could only know, desperately, that he did not feel what he was feeling.

It was impossible. Because of what he felt for Kate, because of what he would always feel for Mary, because of the singular, spiritual quality of his emotion toward the lovely, spiritual creature herself, it was impossible.

And it was impossible. For he was Charles. Thirty-five, perhaps forty seconds held him anguished and helpless in that startled hell of emotional honesty; and then it was over.

Maria's Charles had idly opened Thompson's letter. A stranger read it, a man tormented by lust and vengeful jealousy. And in a matter of moments that man had become yet another, Thompson's friend.

And Thompson's friend was identified in passionate empathy with all that Thompson felt for the young girl with whom he had so touchingly fallen in love after his long, sad, widowed time of loneliness.

Charles sighed, and put back his hair. He reached for his pen. The full, sensitive lips were grave and quite beautiful in their serious tenderness.

Thompson would understand the first strange intensity of shock which he described to him; would forgive the impercipience which had imagined that Thompson would soon forget that lovely memory which Charles's own heart would always keep green.

Charles's pen moved fast and faster, as he urged his friend to put away his needless doubts, to carry her away to some sunnier, gentler clime, to keep her free from care. Oh, how Thompson would reproach himself otherwise if, in later years, her memory dimmed even in his own heart, some careless friend should say, "You recollect her? She is dead."

Thompson had spoken of his first marriage, the old heartbreak. Charles knew at cruel first hand what such heartbreak was; yet he urged, urged his friend to win her.

And that was the whole story; no story, really, but only a blade of grass held up to the changing wind. There were a few more letters urging Thompson to make up his mind, lest he deal the sensitive young creature a deeper blow than he thought for. There was one of heartiest congratulations, bidding him ask her always to save the green dress trimmed with fur that she had worn when they saw her first.

In April, Miss Weller felt a few doubts, and Charles, at Thompson's request, wrote to her in his behalf. It was an absurd notion for Thompson to have had, and an impossible sort of letter to write. Charles could not, somehow, get the proper, serious note into it — only an unsuitably gay and charming lightness. "Whatever happens in this case," it ended, "I am sure that it will all happen Wrong, the undersigned being debarred from the competition."

In any event, Miss Weller put her doubts away again.

She came to London in June to play two concerts. It seemed to Charles that she was in better health than she had been in the winter. He sent bouquets to the concert hall, and took Kate and Georgy to hear her play, and invited her to dinner, with Thompson.

Kate disliked her, which was to have been expected. Georgy said that she was not quite, somehow, what she had fancied her. Charles had really no time to think about her much, one way or the other.

Chuzzlewit was finished, and he was up to the ears in preparations for the move to Italy. The courier was engaged, a bustling, bristling, madly efficient little brigand from Avignon, Louis Roche by name. Baby Frank would stay with Grandmother Hogarth, but the rest of them, thirteen including the servants, would travel *en famille* in their own coach, a mildewy monstrosity which Charles had picked up at a great bargain. An unthinkable coach, with ample room for them all, and their luggage, and Timber, too.

There was so much last-minute business to be settled, and so many last-minute social obligations to be fulfilled and farewells to be taken that it had been, in fact, quite an effort for Charles to fit Thompson and his sweet-young-bride-to-be into his overcrowded calendar.

❊ 3 ❊

THE SEA was glassy still for their passage to Boulogne. Only Anne was seasick, and Georgy said, "Isn't she marvelous, always knowing what's expected of her?"

Charles laughed and hugged her. "Oh, small person, you're my delight!"

The whole journey, indeed, was delightful. Little Roche, the Brave, as Charles called him, was superb, a wild unending storm of maps, compasses, stores of information, and psychic insight. Apparently he knew every road and hostelry on the continent.

It was worth the loss of time to watch him make high drama of a customs inspection, fiercely refusing to give the routine bribe and demanding that every scrap of luggage be unpacked and examined while he shouted himself into an absolute frenzy of virtuous defiance.

"Ah, these rascals 'ow they 'ave enrazhe me!"

Even the Brave was momentarily staggered when they reached Albaro and saw the house that Charles had rented sight unseen. The Pink Jail was not so much a house as a comic catastrophe, an isolated, inconvenient, mad pink monster of a house.

But at once Georgy was laughing at it and the Brave was rallying the staff.

"I will arrange, be cone-tent, soon it will be all other, all suitable."

And miraculously he had Anne, Charlotte, the cook, and the parlormaid all functioning as if they were in Devonshire Terrace, almost overnight. Soon their sole quarrel with Italy seemed to be that the natives stubbornly refused to understand English even when it was shouted, slowly, patiently, and at the top of the lungs.

Kate said that it was all very depressing, but beggars can't be choosers.

Georgy said, "Italy! I'm living abroad!"

She was dead in love with every manifestation of foreignness, even to the mildew on her bedroom wall. She said that ancient castles were always dank.

The children saw the Mediterranean and cried out in joyful surprise, "Italy's a Broadstairs!" Every night Wally, who was both remarkably small and articulate for his age, sighed from his toes and said, "Doesn't it pleasant, in a Italy!"

And fortunately their trial lease lasted only until October. With the sun so splendid outside, a few touches of mildew within scarcely mattered.

Charles grew a mustache and bought a bathing dress, that Continental inspiration which let a man swim in public unsheltered by a bathing machine.

He loved Italy.

He loved the shouting green of the trees and the vineyards, the haze of purple and lilac that swam against the distant hills; the sea, blue with the very color of forgetfulness, like Lethe water. He loved the days that leaped out of night and blazed, fiercer and brighter, until they exploded in climactic sunset and went out so suddenly in thick, black night again.

He loved to watch the people pouring their souls into every casual conversation, waving their arms as if each word were a threat of murder or a vow of undying devotion.

His delight in them was pentecostal. He learned fluent, bad Italian with amazing speed. When he went walking, he could talk to fishermen, coast guards, winegrowers, children. They were all wonderful.

On the other hand, the English colony was dull. In the long evenings he often ached to talk with Forster or Maclise or dear old Stanny. He told himself that at last he really had time to write; that writers went abroad for precisely this freedom from demands.

In August he made a desperate attempt to start the Christmas book, and it was like plowing sand.

Frederick came out for a holiday. He reported that the Governor was getting fat; not simply stocky, but fatter by the day. And that

Mother was, oh, Lord, Mother, you know. "And speaking of former affluence, could you manage, Charles, only until the first of the month . . .?"

The visit was far from unmixed delight, yet once he had gone, the evenings, after the children were abed, felt even emptier.

"This damned stage-set of a place," he cried one night. "This beautiful, picturesque, dead isolation!"

Kate sighed, the familiar sigh. "At least we don't have to give dinner parties all the time."

When October came, they moved into the Pallazo Peschiere, the Palace of Fishpools. It was both a magnificent place and cheaper than the Pink Jail.

The fishpools were in the formal gardens. The *sala* was fifty feet high and frescoed from designs by Michelangelo. Even the walls of the bedrooms were frescoed; Phaëthon plunged downward above Charles's bed. Yet despite its grandeur, the house was comfortable. Better yet, it was at an easy walk from Genoa, which had streets in it; small streets, thinly peopled, if one thought of London, but still streets.

Everybody was delighted. Even poor Timber, who had been beset in Albaro by fleas of nightmare size and appetite, could grow out his shaved coat and stop turning around and around in unhappy search of himself.

Charles arranged his writing table. He clapped his hands together.

"And now, at long last, the Inimitable begins a tale that will put the dear old *Christmas Carol* in the shade!"

The book would strike a real blow for the poor. Tragedy, starting in some small accident, and developed with awful inevitability by the harsh facts of English slum life. At the end, to be sure, there must be the Christmas-morning discovery that it had all been a dream. But even then he would introduce no opulent god from the machine. It must remain an indictment. As like the *Carol*, and as unlike it, as any book could possibly be.

And days passed, and Charles continued to stare at blank paper.

And the damned bells of Genoa rang incessantly, and loud, loud, as if they were no farther off than the fishpools. How could he see one character clear or hear one voice with the women whining and bickering, and those damned, damned bells? Oh, God, for a walk across London, for one hour of good talk!

Charles paced off Genoa until he knew every back alley, but the releasing power was not in it. He took to dropping in often at the De La Rues' apartment. Mr. De La Rue was a Swiss banker, very pleasant. His English wife was a friendly little creature with a small, quaint pansy face topped by a pile of shining coal-black hair. Kate, needless to say, did not like her. But they did not seem to notice that they were not invited to the Peschiere, and they were always glad to see him.

However, though they were restful, they were not people of ideas. They did not stimulate the book.

On All Soul's Eve, the people went about the streets, calling out prayers for the dead. Charles could hear them, near the Peschiere, as he fell asleep; he heard them fretfully, the anxious, sterile frustration of his wasted day channeled into anger against superstition, popery, the clutter of the Middle Ages blocking the way of progress.

"Disgusting," he was whispering as he fell asleep.

He dreamed that Mary stood before him, veiled in celestial blue. He saw her face, and felt his heart tear open in an anguish of release. He ran forward, arms outstretched.

"Mary! Oh, my dear, my dear!"

She shrank back. She belonged to another world, and one that he was unworthy to enter. He sank to his knees before her.

"Mary, Mary how can I know that this is not a dream?"

"Make a wish. It will be granted."

He must wish the noblest wish that a human soul could rise to.

"I wish that Mrs. Hogarth may be happy."

Oh, but he had overcome his earthly self too well. Her face shone with light, the moment was consummation and now she would vanish.

He pleaded, "Wait, wait. Tell me, are all religions good, or is the Roman Catholic the best?"

She smiled with unspeakable angelic tenderness.

"For you. For *you* it is the best."

Charles woke sharply. He could still feel the singular emotion of the dream, the yearning love, the awe.

Not since that night in Yorkshire. Mary. Can it be possible that the dead come back, and try to speak, and grieve when the living call it a common dream? Mary . . .

He sat up. Suddenly he caught Kate's shoulder and shook it.

"Wake up, Kate. Wake up. I just had such a strange dream about Mary."

It was hard to rouse her. She was sleeping heavily.

"What?"

"It was about Mary." He told it through, twice over. "I want to make sure that I will remember. Remember it just as it was."

"Charles, truly, a grown man waking people to tell his dreams!" But she was amiable, even laughing a little. She settled back into her pillow with a yawn. "Poor Mary. Catholic, of all things." She fell asleep again, almost at once.

And Charles did not wonder why he had wakened her, or regret it.

The writing went as badly as ever. Or, in other words, it did not go at all. And there was almost no time left. Charles began to be frightened.

Then, one night, the bells woke him as they had done repeatedly through the past weeks and he was sure that, again, he would not be able to get back to sleep.

He heard his own voice, muttering: "We have heard the chimes at midnight, Master Shallow."

And he had it. Like a miracle, he had it!

The Chimes. The chimes that he had tried to escape had been the soul of the book, waiting for him to know it! Their clangor was a flood of goblins, the Christmas spirits, who would speak to the poor old porter in his dream. His dream, more real than the wakening which must come for Christmas cheer and all the dear, needful shillings per copy.

The bells rang on, and Charles lay on his back, listening, his lips parted and his clasped hands tapping lightly against them.

They rang from a London steeple. Toby . . . Trotty . . . Trotty Veck . . . Yes, on the lean days he hears their voices . . . "Trotty Veck, Trotty Veck, keep a good heart, Trotty . . ."

Ring away, now, bells of Genoa. Charles has gone off into another place. The *Carol* was nothing to this!

Charles will change the laws of England, he will save the world from Kant and the Categorical Imperative and teach instead the specific instance and the spontaneous love. Singlehanded, he will defeat Malthusian inhumanity, he will break the world clean away from the Bad Old Times, once and for all; he will bring about a world as new as the morning or as the Sermon on the Mount. He knows it, he knows it!

See him now. He walks, he weeps, he is a giant armored in light. Or, as Charles puts it, he is really feeling like himself again!

❊ 4 ❊

BUT, IF ONLY Forster could be by to hear it as he wrote!

Georgy, despite her good little heart and quick mind, knew so little, so mercifully little of what it was all about. And the slashing satire packed into the characters of Filer and Sir Joseph and Alderman Cute was utterly lost on her. God, to see Carlyle listening to all that!

No, money or not, he would have to make a flying trip to London and read it to the elect. Stay at a hotel, gulp down that cup of joy, and be back in Italy for Christmas.

"I must read it to them," he told Georgy. "I should explode like a bomb, else!"

"Oh, to be sure you must. Oh, I wish that I could be there, to watch them laugh and cry!"

He hugged the bony young shoulders. He laughed, looking down at the parted lips, the small, crooked teeth. "Small person, did you know that you grow more endearing every day?"

"Oh, how they'll love it!"

Kate sniffed. "He's conceited enough as it is, Georgy."

Charles kissed them both. He had not heard Georgy's words or Kate's automatic response. His mind was already with the handful, the chosen.

And every one of those he wanted most was well, and in town. Macready had been due to open a play in Paris, and by a glorious fluke the opening was postponed for a week.

Dyce, Harness and Fox were there, Jerrold of the *Edinburgh Re-*

view was there with poor, luckless Laman Blanchard, needed because he had responses like a plucked harpstring. Fred was there, which was a risk, but even he, that night, was unashamedly moved, his growing cynicism for once overthrown.

And of course there was dear old Stanny; and Maclise, who sat sketching the scene for posterity, bless him, and putting a radiance around the reader's head.

Forster looked more than ever like God's own St. Bernard dog at the tenderest passages.

Carlyle, God bless him, sat upright throughout the whole reading, looking as if he'd written it himself and was more proud of it than of all his other work together. But it was Macready who crowned the evening; for halfway through he began to cry, and he wept, helplessly as a baby, right on up to the last word.

It was a long book to read aloud at one pull. Charles's voice held perfectly, but his throat had begun to ache just before Macready began to cry. The tears released that ache like a draft of wine. From that moment on, Charles, as he read, was two separate souls, the one lost in the passion, tenderness, and furious judgment of the written words; the other drunk with power, power.

It was an evening fit to crown a life.

Small Frank was flourishing. The Governor was, indeed, growing fat, but he carried it with a swagger. The sight, sound, and even the smell of foggy, sooty London were all that Charles had hungered after. He was more than content.

The children shouted when he got home. Charles swung Mamie up in his arms. The others loved him; Mamie worshiped him, and now that she had lost her first enchanting monkeylike plainness, Charles often felt a twinge of guilt that her obedient, humorless devotion bored him.

"Papa's own love," he whispered. "Papa's girl."

Georgy said, "I can't wait to hear about it!"

Kate said, "It's rained all the time you were gone. Is poor Mama as well as can be expected?"

"Yea, dearest, and Frank's as big as Goliath and didn't know me from Adam. Come, you haven't given me a kiss."

He still felt on top of the wave.

"And now for the Twelve Days of Christmas! Charley, old fellow, we must plan the Twelfth Night feast!"

Miss Coutts sent Charley a Twelfth Night cake the size of a doll's house. The magical show was superlative. The children of the English colony were as dull as their parents, but all the magic and forfeits and blindman's buff made a party almost as noisy and spontaneous as Charles could have had in London. Charley himself was in glory.

"What have you to say *now*, stupids?" Charles heard him demanding of two dazzled guests. "*Did* I make up the magic he can do? Did I, now?"

Then the holidays were over. The reports began to come from England. *The Chimes* was outselling the *Christmas Carol*, selling incredibly, and at a profit, too. Selling, whipping up sales on old books, even *Chuzzlewit*; melting away the debt.

"Oh, bless their good, good hearts!" Charles cried. "I knew it, Georgy, I knew they'd love every last word of it! The Inimitable is back in stride!"

His smile was brilliant, warm, triumphant. His wide blue eyes looked empty and uncertain.

He knew that he was being ungrateful to life, but he felt edgy, and lost, and heavily let down.

Objectively considered, it was small wonder.

Charles wrote *The Chimes* in a towering rapture. He had read it to such an audience as few actors find outside that corner reserved for such of them as get to Heaven. Charles's patchwork cloak of many loves had never wrapped him so warm as it did that night in London.

And, finally, the book sold. And when the immortal Sairey Gamp went for tuppence, Charles had learned the writer's hard lesson: *You can't tell how it will hit them.* No matter how good you think it, no matter what successes lie behind, a book is a gamble. Charles had not let himself think about it, but the knowledge was there.

And it sold. The power and glory, the love, and the hard cash were all his.

And suddenly it was all over. The exaltation and the simple relief alike belonged to yesterday. He was Charles, in his ever-consuming *now*.

He had nothing in hand. Genoa was depressing, the English colony was dismal. Kate had no interests. Georgy was a child. The children were getting to have no more notion of tidiness than their mother. Timber would doubtless live forever, and a man wants a *big* dog.

One night, to Kate's bewilderment, Charles looked up at the plunging Phaëthon frescoed on his bedroom wall and laughed.

"Wot yer might call a speakin' likeness," he said.

He spoke aloud, but he did not trouble to turn his head. The habit of uttering an amusing line is hard to break, but the effort of explaining it afterwards becomes increasingly painful.

Charles, briefly, was in the state of mind which leaves a man most prone to making a fool of himself.

Mrs. De La Rue's strange affliction and his miraculous power to heal it revealed themselves like a godsend.

* 5 *

KATE'S BITTERNESS over the De La Rue affair would actually have been better justified by the brief nonsense over Christiana Weller. Indeed, Charles never so much as thought of Mrs. De La Rue by her first name.

That was the simple truth. It is equally true that any woman in her senses would have found it as impossible to believe as Kate did.

In the first place, Mrs. De La Rue was small and well rounded. Her *belle-laide* little pansy of a face did not quite live up to her hair, which was that ultimate desideratum of the Victorian charmer referred to so often and lovingly in the literature of the day as "a wealth of raven tresses"; but that hair alone would have kindled a light in the wandering eye even if she had been downright plain. Indeed, a more worldly and percipient woman than Kate might have found yet deeper grounds for suspicion.

Certainly no man was ever more blatantly cast for the role of cheerful cuckold than that simple man of business, trustful friend, and doting husband, Emile De La Rue. Moreover, though he was not unhandsome, and had an unusually glossy and dashing set of whiskers, it was obvious that his placid disposition offered a wife little in the way of emotional excitement.

Mrs. De La Rue did not flaunt her taste for such excitement, but a sharp enough eye could have seen that, too. Charles found her delightfully responsive. She was indeed; she was responsive to a degree seldom found in any but the genuine, medically certifiable hysteric.

Kate was quite wrong, but one cannot blame her. The stage was set for a far meatier and less fantastic drama than that which actually took place.

The De La Rues were always delighted when Charles dropped in upon them.

"Dear friend, what a pleasure! *Ma petite*, we have Mr. Dickens with us. Come, a glass of wine!"

And Mrs. De La Rue would come forward, hands outstretched, lifting her shining weight of hair. "Oh, how nice! What did Emile and I do with ourselves before you came here?"

As Charles put it to himself, they were not stimulating but they were enormously pleasant; a dear, good fellow and an excellent, affectionate little creature.

Occasionally, however, De La Rue would open the door with his finger at his lips.

"Please, come in, let us have our glass of wine. But quietly. The little one is *souffrante*. The migraine, so severe."

The apartment was not large. Invariably, Charles only pressed the extended hand, whispered a few sympathetic words, and went away.

But one evening in mid-January, Charles was extremely dispirited and at loose ends. He felt a sharp throb of disappointment when he saw the lifted finger at the lips.

But De La Rue clung to his hand. "Dear friend, I am in distress of mind. Truly, tonight I long for a moment of your company."

"Oh, De La Rue, bless you. I was only afraid to intrude. Can we be quiet enough, do you think?"

He came in and sat down at once. De La Rue poured the wine.

Charles watched him, full of pity. Poor De La Rue, those gallant whiskers and that good simple face; how he must love her to agonize over a headache so. It's touching, one could almost envy it.

He smiled his thanks for the wineglass. He sipped in silence for a moment. A notion, a helpful desire had come to him, but he had doubts of how De La Rue would receive it.

"De La Rue," he said abruptly, "do you know anything of mesmerism? I believe that it could help your wife."

De La Rue stared blankly.

"I have seen it effect some remarkable cures."

"My dear friend, you suggest that I take my wife to a mesmerist? Surely a man of your education knows that they are all charlatans with paid accomplices who enact the supposed trance?"

"Do you trust me as a friend? Do you consider me a charlatan?"

"You?"

"De La Rue, I was a skeptic like you. I became a close friend of Dr. Elliottson, in London — a man of utter integrity who was expelled from the Royal College of Physicians and Surgeons for no other reason than his deep study and practice of mesmerism. It is not charlatanry, but a genuine healing force. I have watched his work, and he has taught me how to induce the mesmeric sleep."

De La Rue swallowed his wine and poured another glass. He looked, quite simply, bewildered.

Charles leaned forward earnestly.

He had been painfully at loose ends that day. Now, he quite forgot Mrs. De La Rue's headache. He only saw De La Rue as one in darkness to whom he must bring light; as an embodied purpose.

As he began to speak, the weary letdown, the uncomfortable sense of having nothing in hand, was swept away. Unconsciously he let his voice gain volume, little by little, until it was the voice which would always thrill audiences and evoke the willing suspension of disbelief.

"Please, De La Rue, hear me out. I must warn you at the outset that the treatment is not beneficial to everybody. I have cured a good number of friends of severe headaches and of neuralgic pain. Yet once I attempted the same thing for my wife, and she came out of the trance in such hysterics that a doctor was forced to give her an opiate. Her nature, however, is *completely* unlike that of your wife — or of any of the friends I have cured. It is — I scarcely know how to say it — more rigid, less trustful than that of any other person for whom I have ever felt a . . . an equally strong attachment. Your wife, with her responsive nature, is one of those, I'd be sworn to it, who would find the most prompt, healing benefit in the treatment."

De La Rue continued to stare. He looked incredulous and slightly stunned.

As abruptly as he had begun, Charles gave up.

"Ah, well, it's no matter. I missed my calling, you see, I was born for the pulpit or the hustings. I'd like to talk of this to you again one day, when you're not troubled, but now, poor fellow, let us take our ease."

Before De La Rue could answer, the air was torn by a long, eerie, quivering cry. It was not a sound of pain but of terror.

Charles started to his feet. He cried, "My God!" and rushed toward the bedroom door. De La Rue was there before him, blocking it.

"Wait." He was whispering. "Wait, you must know that we have not been open with you. The little one, it is not migraine that she suffers, but a cruel disorder of the nerves. She hides it from all; you see, people talk, tales grow, they would say madness, epilepsy — and it is only the nerves, you see. The nerves."

Framed by the jaunty whiskers, poor De La Rue's good, pink face was trembling like a baby's. Charles caught his hand in a strong grip.

"Oh, dear man, poor little woman! I wish that I had known before this."

De La Rue looked at him, swallowed, turned, and opened the door.

Mrs. De La Rue's hair, unbound and fantastically long, fanned out all about her on the bed. Her eyes were closed. Her nightgown covered her legs, but her feet were bare. A white shawl lay tumbled beside her.

She spoke, without opening her eyes. "Emile? Did I cry out, or did I only dream that I cried out?"

De La Rue spoke to Charles, very low.

"The worst is over. She comes to herself, now. It is better for her if you steal away and return tomorrow to speak with us of this cure."

She opened her eyes.

Then she started up, catching the shawl and pressing it to her bosom in a pretty show of modesty. Her lips parted, like a startled child's.

"Mr. Dickens! Emile! What . . . oh . . ."

Good heaven, Charles thought, what hair!

He began to speak.

"Dear Mrs. De La Rue, don't be troubled that I am here. Your husband has brought me to you, to help you. Come, it's all right, you've no occasion to blush. Lie back and let your husband arrange your shawl. I can help you, Mrs. De La Rue. Lie back while I tell you how I can help you. As I can. As I can . . ."

He listened to his own voice, light at first and full of gentle laughter, then deepening, soothing, hushing.

God, he thought, if Elliotson could hear me! He'd give over his practice and say he'd always lacked the touch!

It was the last objective thought that Charles would entertain about Mrs. De La Rue's strange affliction and his healing power.

She lifted her eyes. Oh, God, such pitiably believing, hopeful, humble, dependent eyes.

She whispered. "Can you? Is it true, Emile? Oh, Emile, it must be true."

Charles was a gone goose.

He was a gone goose, his long-treasured myth of a happy marriage was doomed, and the irony was unthinkable. Granted, the drama of suffering dependent and healer-priest which was played out under the awed and grateful eyes of Emile De La Rue was highly habit-forming to both principals; yet to Charles, at least, it was nothing if not chaste. A soul was in torment, his alone could save it.

On the tide of that fantasy, common sense and simple masculine appetite were swept away. Indeed, in that very moment, the moment of its inception, Charles even ceased to think about the wealth of raven tresses and the daintily rounded form which had previously given him a casual and uncomplicated pleasure.

"It is true, dear Mrs. De La Rue," he said. "We do not yet know why or how mesmerism heals. Yet it does. The one certain requisite in my own mind is trust. You must trust my desire to help you."

De La Rue interrupted. "Dear friend, I cannot rid myself of the thought that you are somehow deluded, but at the least I know the honest kindness of your heart."

"That is all you need believe in. Do you believe in it, too, Mrs. De La Rue?"

"Oh, Mr. Dickens, how can you ask?"

Charles looked down. The humble little face appeared to float upon a sea of tumbled black hair. Dear God, such suffering, and such pitiful faith!

He smiled. The mingling of true pity and sharp, sweet gratification made it a singular and beautiful smile. He lifted his head, tossing back his own hair, and stood quiet for a waiting instant. With his face raised, his hair shaken back, he looked as he felt, tall, quiet, certain, strong.

He bent above the bed. De La Rue was forgotten. So, in hard fact, was Mrs. De La Rue. Charles saw only weakness, suffering, lifted up in all dependent trust to his strength, his healing gift.

He was lost in the moment, no part of him separate and watching. He did not even hear his own voice, though it had never spoken more beautifully, compellingly.

"Lie still . . . let your hands lie loosely, open, loose . . . Ah, you are growing so quiet. Keep your eyes on mine . . . on mine . . . they are growing heavy, heavy, but look at me, while you fall asleep . . . asleep . . ."

Mrs. De La Rue's eyes flickered, broke free from Charles's eyes for a moment and then came back to their wide, rapt stare. A dim half-memory had stirred in her mind, a sense of something — what? — something that she should be doing. It did not matter, now. She let it go.

Charles's voice went on. Her breathing changed its pace, her eyelids closed. Sweetly, fully, Mrs. De La Rue dropped away into the trance which she had so eagerly planned to feign.

De La Rue's eyes were almost circular. His cheeks twitched until the handsome whiskers quivered like fans.

"I could not have believed it. I did not believe it."

Charles laid an affectionate hand upon his arm.

"We will let her sleep while we have another glass of wine. Then I must waken her and get back to the Peschiere. When she wakes she will feel quite calm and well, just as you heard me tell her so many times while she went into the trance."

He spoke with firm confidence, smiling brightly.

However, he wanted the wine. It had just occurred to him to wonder, sharply and for the first time, what in God's name he should do if Mrs. De La Rue, by any appalling chance, reacted, upon gaining consciousness again, as Kate had done.

But she did not. When Charles left she was still whispering, "It's like a miracle . . . a miracle . . ."

He walked home on air.

Kate was already asleep.

Georgy was first at the breakfast table. As Charles walked into the room her thin pink lips squared in a smile of delight and she clapped her hands.

"You've a notion for a new book! I can tell, Charles, I can tell!"

He kissed the top of her head and gave her waist a squeeze. "Not that, small person; but I've become useful. Ah, here's Kate. Sit down, sweet, I've quite a tale. You must hear this, too."

He told it well. Kate's face, drowsy-indifferent as he began to talk, was closed like a trap by the time he was done.

"I knew it! I knew she'd scheme some way to make an idiot of you!"

"Why, Kate!" Georgy's voice was genuinely shocked. "Kate, the poor lady didn't want anybody to know. It was her husband who told!"

Charles said, "I think that for the time, my dear, we'd better talk of something else."

Georgy was sitting very small and erect, trying to look as though she had not spoken. She looked, Charles thought, like a child unhappily trying to pretend away a quarrel between parents.

He looked at Kate. Her face wore the heavy, sulking look that made it appear so much older and fatter than it really was. A handkerchief, not very clean, a shawl, a bracelet, and an opened letter lay beside her on the table.

Charles got up.

"Will you excuse me, my dears? I want to look in on the nursery before I answer my letters."

He bent and kissed Kate's cheek as he left the room. She had never disappointed him worse, or put him more furiously on the defensive.

※ *6* ※

At first, Charles planned to mesmerize Mrs. De La Rue only once a day. But her disease of the nerves was worse than he had realized. She needed treatment at the onset of every one of her strange dreamlike attacks of terror if they were not to do further damage to her nerves, in a cruel circle of cause and effect.

Charles stressed the need, holding De La Rue's hand firmly as he spoke.

"You must never hesitate or fear to inconvenience me. Send for me at any hour of the day or night, when you even so much as begin to fear that she might need me."

The whiskers quivered. "Dear friend, dear friend, what can we say? Such goodness, such generosity of heart!"

But as the days passed, Kate became increasingly unwilling to admit her mistake.

"Try to see things as they are," Charles begged. "Try to understand their situation, their need."

She said, "I think that I understand quite well enough, thank you."

It was hopeless. She had shut her mind to him. And he could not ask Georgy to talk of it with her, for Georgy was too innocent to understand Kate's thoughts.

But he must not judge. He must try to forgive Kate, fully and from his heart. How could he lead Mrs. De La Rue to peace unless he also had it in himself, unfeigned? He must not let his mind be vexed and weakened.

It was increasingly important that he should be calm and free in spirit now that he was coming close to the source of the trouble.

In very light trance Mrs. De La Rue could talk of the dreadful fancy, strong as hallucination, which always came upon her just before her attacks. She saw a green hill crowded with faceless people.

"No faces . . . no faces . . . the green, green so bright all about them. . . . He made them like that . . . he will do it to me . . ."

He was the Phantom, a spirit of pure evil. Charles was sure that once she could talk easily of the Phantom in her waking state she would recover.

Now she could only do so for a few moments before her words would start to wander and grow wild. "Oh, forget me, don't anger him! You, you who are so good to me must not make him your enemy!"

At such times, to do her justice, Mrs. De La Rue was only marginally aware of using her affliction to purpose. That it served Charles any purpose never, of course, occurred to him. Yet it troubled him that he must leave her and risk her slipping back from the progress they had already made, if he were to set out with Kate, as planned, and gather the material for his promised book of travel sketches.

He did what little he could. He gave De La Rue lessons, though surely nobody ever had less gift for the healing art. He gave Mrs. De La Rue continued mesmeric suggestion that she would be well in his absence and respond to her husband's treatments as though they were his own.

Mrs. De La Rue, however, continued to dread the separation. Indeed, despite himself Charles began to suspect that she even resented it.

"Now, come," he said to her briskly, two days before his journey must begin. "I shall replenish my forces by this rest, and you will show your husband what a brave little woman you are, and we shall both be the better for it."

It was rather late in the evening. When he got home, Charles found Kate asleep, pointedly close to the farther edge of the bed.

Yes, and the tour will lift her spirits, too, Charles thought as he dropped off. Perhaps I have really let this sad business absorb me too much, of late.

He had been asleep for some hours when Roche knocked on the bedroom door. Mr. De La Rue had sent for him.

The summons was as unexpected as Kate's fury.

"If you have no shame, her husband should have! Oh, that woman, that creature!"

Charles stared at her. He forced himself to speak quietly.

"The need for shame, Kate, is scarcely on my side, or on theirs."

She did not answer. He flung on his clothes and rushed to the sufferer.

The seizure was shocking. Mrs. De La Rue's head was tucked out of sight, her body rolled into a weird knot like a circus contortionist's.

De La Rue, in his nightshirt was white and sweating.

"My God, my God, her heart, such strain, she will die! Touch her, she is iron!"

Charles put a firm hand on De La Rue's shoulder.

"There is no danger. Go into the other room, take your dressing gown. Try to be quiet. Your fear may work against the mesmeric force."

But though his voice was steady, Charles still felt nothing but a shuddering of distaste. The headless ball of nightgown and black hair was a dreadful, almost inhuman sight. The tender sense of strength, of sweet outflowing power would not come.

Briefly, and for the only time in the whole episode, Charles wondered whether the mesmerism might be doing more harm than good.

He shut his mind to the doubt; he mastered the revulsion. He lifted a strand of black hair and traced it to its source, forcing his hands past the rigid arms, between the rigid body and contorted legs. He twisted his wrist within that shocking vise until his hand found the sweating forehead. He drew a deep breath between lips that were rigid as Mrs. De La Rue's flesh.

He began to speak. "You feel my hand, you hear me. You know that I have come to you, that I can help you . . ."

And he could feel nothing that he wanted to feel. The inner shuddering only gave way to a strange embarrassment, a sense that the whole situation was ludicrous, artificial, distasteful.

He forced himself to listen to his own voice, the gentle, deep, thrilling, soothing voice; and it began to come with less effort, and less. But it was not until the very moment that Mrs. De La Rue trembled and went limp, lying upon her back and staring up at him with dazed, confused eyes, that Charles finally felt the floodgate open and the sweet, right power, the delicious intoxication come back again.

Charles welcomed it back without further question. He was still standing tall with it, still brimming with that trembling, wide elation when he went to De La Rue.

"She is quiet now. Thank God you sent for me. Bless you, dear friend."

De La Rue's eyes were wet. "How can I thank one who thanks me for the loss of a night's rest and — ah, yes, I saw your face when you looked at her — a true anguish?"

Charles took his hand. "You gave me the joy of being needed, of being counted upon as a friend. As for sleep — nonsense! Haven't we both danced this late times without counting?"

It was, however, nearly dawn when he got back to the Peschiere. He was so tired that he barely glanced at Kate when he lit the candle to undress by, and he fell asleep in the same moment that he lay down.

It was fortunate for his peace of mind. Kate was a singularly bad actress. Her pretense of sleep would scarcely have deceived a child.

❋ 7 ❋

CHARLES WOKE LATE, too late to eat breakfast, he thought, glancing at his watch. He rang for a cup of tea and gulped it down while he dressed. He gave a quick, final brushing to his hair and set off briskly in search of Kate. He had wakened with such a slap-up notion that it quite pushed aside the memory of their quarrel in the night.

He found her alone in the *sala*.

She sat upon a narrow, straight-backed chair which she overflowed with a dismal effect of having begun to melt and run. Her face was puffy with the night's weeping; the hair that hung down on each side of it was out of curl. Her shawl, two damp handkerchiefs, and a scattering of fluted paper cups from a box of sweets lay on the floor about her.

Charles saw and did not see her. Even the clutter on the floor failed to annoy him. He was too preoccupied with what he must say, and say effectively.

He drew up another chair. "I'm glad you didn't lie awake, I wasn't home until all hours. She'd had an appalling seizure."

Except that one plump white hand shut into a fist and the other cupped hard about it, Kate might not have heard him.

"Poor De La Rue was distraught, nothing I'd taught him worked. Perhaps a husband cannot mesmerize his own wife successfully. You remember . . ."

"Oh! Oh, oh, *dear!* Oh . . ."

Charles started. He stared; he bit his lip.

Why, good God, she was in a shocking state, she must have been sitting there half the morning, working herself into it. Dear Lord, but he must hurry or she could start on a scene which would make his good new plan impossible! Yes, quickly, he must appeal to her better feelings.

He began to speak. He spoke faster than he realized, the words rushing out like a patter of mountain hailstones.

"I've had a thought, dear, I know you'll find it good, too. It's clear that Mrs. De La Rue's anxiety over our having to interrupt the mesmeric treatment at this crucial point is making her worse again. Now, De La Rue is most pleasant company and she is really an *excellent* little creature as you would see if it weren't for your — prejudice. Now. Georgy wants to stay here for the Consulate ball and join us in Naples by boat. We'll be rattling about alone in our huge coach. Can't you see that the *kind, sensible* thing to do would be to ask the De La Rues to make the tour with us? Really, Kate, dear, when you think about it *impersonally,* can't you see how silly and unkind it would be to do otherwise?"

As he spoke, his eyes had been fixed upon his hands while the fingers of the one absently turned the small gold ring upon the other. As the rapid pattering of his words broke off, he glanced up, for the first time since he had begun to speak.

Kate's cheeks were colorless, and shaking in a strange, limp quiver. The violet eyes were set in such a hard, dead stare that the tears which poured from them appeared to wet her cheeks and yet leave the staring eyes themselves dry.

Charles whispered, "Kate . . ." He swallowed and found his voice and spoke foolishly and helplessly. "Kate, Kate, why, darling . . ."

She spoke in a low, dull voice. "Half-past four in the morning. Where was her husband? Visiting a friend of his own, I presume, like most foreigners. Don't tell me that he was there all the time, I can't bear to hear you say it again. I've let it go on and on, for all these weeks. But now . . . now . . ."

He felt his body give an odd jerk, like sudden waking. There was, indeed, something like sleepwalking in that eager preoccupation which had carried him into the *sala,* so set upon selling his plan. But he saw her now, and heard her, in spite of himself.

He tried to tell himself that her thoughts, her words were ugly, unworthy of a pure woman. He could not. He could only see her suffering. He stared at that suffering in a waking horror, his body wrenched with shame and with pity. Helplessly he clung to the meaningless, irrelevant words: ugly, unjust, impure. He snatched and fumbled for the protective, self-justifying anger. He could not find it.

Instead, he remembered her sharply, precisely, as she had looked, sitting there alone when he had first come upon her. He heard the sound of his own voice, rapid, high-pitched, as it had pattered out his proposition so quickly, quickly, before she should get a word in first.

Suddenly he felt his heart torn open by a more intense and genuine love for her than he had felt for many years.

"Kate, you fool!" he shouted. "I will not bear this insane, vile, ugly-minded jealousy! I have never so much as looked at Mrs. De La Rue in any way that the most jealous woman in the world could object to. You disgust me! Don't you know, God damn it, that I love you? Are you so stupid and cold-blooded that you truly can't distinguish between adultery and your husband's friendship for a happily married couple? Oh, damn, damn, damn, you shock me and revolt me!"

Not only were the words oddly suited to the emotion; their tone rose from a deep bellow of fury to a thin high shriek of frustration.

And still, they were a cry of love.

And the shudder that went through Kate's body did not come from anger, or fear, or even laughter; it was a shudder of hope against hope.

The quivering mask of despair fell from her face; she still wept, but she wept from wet eyes, and with the twisted face of a weeping child.

And Charles fondled her messy hair and kissed her twisting hands.

"Dear love," he said, "try to believe that you have been terribly mistaken. We'll start out for Naples alone, sweet. Please, put this ugly foolishness out of your heart forever."

She said, "It was half-past four."

But she said it pleadingly, and Charles continued to stroke and kiss her hands.

"Yes, poor love. Your boy understands, he forgives you, Yes. Yes."

Charles made his farewell visit to the De La Rues hearty and brief.

"And remember," he said in parting, "these forces are not limited by distance. You must sit down quietly every day, from ten until noon, and know that I will be concentrating upon helping you, wherever I am."

He hurried back to the Palazzo Peschiere. Kate said, a little stiffly, "You didn't stay long." But she had changed her dress and curled her shining hair. Charles smiled.

Her pride made her speak clumsily; it always hurts to admit that one has been deeply mistaken. Her curls and her pretty dress spoke, too. She understood, now. She believed him.

He kissed her red mouth and the side of her neck. He breathed the musky-sweet fragrance of her skin as if he had been away from her for a long time and almost forgotten it in his absence.

"My beautiful. My lovely, lovely girl."

Kate Dickens's face was capable of no subtleties of expression. The struggle between deep doubt and anguished hope, which still filled her heart, showed in her sweet, immobile features only as a shy, almost virginal confusion.

And Charles looked down at it, his own face tender and exultant as it had been on a morning long ago in Chalk, when Kate said, "That nasty old headache is quite, quite gone."

Though he had only exchanged a new fantasy, briefly, for an old one, even a change of dreams is seldom without tangible result in the world of fact. Charles's fourth son and sixth child was born nine months from that day.

Perhaps it could have made little difference to the story in the long run if Charles had not made his last-minute, impulsive promise to give Mrs. De La Rue absent treatment daily. Yet he and Kate were really happy in the big old coach on the way to La Spezia, their first stopping place on the road to Naples. They were both happy, until Charles fell into his remote, protracted silence and she discovered the reason for it.

Charles found her stubborn refusal to see the simple altruism of a service so patently chaste too shocking for words.

There were words, however. Unfortunately there were many words on both sides. "Mooning over her! Nobody would believe it if they were told. A man alone with his wife, and expecting her to keep quiet for two hours of every day while he moons over another woman! Two hours by his watch! Are you so much in love with her that you've gone mad? Mooning by your watch!"

"God damn it, will you *try* to hear what I am saying? This is not mooning, this is a procedure accepted by every open mind in medicine. Dr. Elliotson practices it! I am doing this for poor De La Rue as much as for his wife!"

Before Georgy met them in Naples there had been many other words; spoken in heat, not wholly meant on either side, and still, once spoken, spoken. Words sometimes denied as soon as they were spoken with tears and frightened caresses, but still opening an abyss which would have to be skirted with care for all time to come.

"Did you ever love me, Kate? Are you capable of loving anybody?"

"You've never known or cared what I felt; you only wanted to make love, as you still call it. Even on our honeymoon you hated me until you could do that, and now you'd even rather do *that* with her."

"You never loved me, Kate, but I think that you have only hated me since Mamie was born."

"If I'd died instead, you could have married Mary. You'd have liked that, wouldn't you? Nothing but flattery from morning to night!"

There are marital quarrels, even bitter ones, which serve to deepen love. Ambivalent emotions are released, temporary misunderstandings are straightened out, permanent incompatibilities are recognized and accepted as present in the relationship, limitations like those imposed by any medium upon any art.

There are also quarrels which can only be put out of mind as well as may be, because they have bared truths too cruel to live with; partial truths, as every truth of those complexities which call themselves a man, a woman, is partial; yet nonetheless truths.

After such a quarrel a man and his wife may kiss and make up, but something is finished.

Charles and Kate had said too much.

The possibility that was lost had always been a limited one, God knows. By mind and temperament, Charles and Kate were as unlikely a pair as a laughing fate could well have produced. Yet Kate was, in her own way, undemanding, largely content with long days full of naps and nibbled sweets and hypochondriac reveries. And Charles was still moved by her face, and her hair, and the texture of her skin; she had gained her weight ounce by ounce and he did not always notice it. And above all, he was a romantic, believing in love and the sacredness of marriage with the born mystic's flair for avoiding discomfortable fact.

Yes, before their quarrel on the road to Naples they might have had a chance. That handsome, overdressed young man with the blue eyes like tormented fire, and the taut-drawn cheeks, and the full lips bitten to bleeding — he and the sagging, fat young woman with the untidy, fashionable traveling clothes, and the sullen, tear-streaked face which was still, and movingly, the face of a beauty — they might have had a chance. The chance of a good enough, happy enough sort of marriage, for which, in their separate ways they were both still pitiably eager to settle: they might have had that, at least.

They lost it in a quarrel that said too much. A quarrel as to whether or not Charles should give mesmeric treatment by thought waves to a woman for whom he did not, in hard fact, give two pins; to a peg on which he had hung a curiously sexless fantasy.

They arrived in Naples smiling and holding hands.

"My little darling knows that her boy did not mean one word of all those ugly things he said?"

"Oh, Charles, I was very unpleasant too. I'm glad you have forgiven me."

"Dear, dearest sweet. My own dear beautiful."

✳   8   ✳

VESUVIUS WAS ACTIVE. The edge of the crater had risen a hundred feet in a week. Roche was frantic when Charles insisted upon making the ascent.

"Monsieur, I implore you, you do not know what you do!"

"Roche, be quiet or I'll put you into a cap with streamers like Charlotte's. The ladies will go in sedan chairs quite safely, and wait until I make the last little climb to the crater."

He laughed to Kate and Georgy. "How Roche loves to make drama of everything!"

They believed him.

There was ice on the way up. Charles was choked with sulphur and black with ashes as he looked down into the awful beauty of that seething hell. The footing was too bad for the chairs on the way down. Kate and Georgy made it afoot, their clothes torn to indecent tatters. Two men, a guide and a tourist, fell to death; the body of one of them was not found.

Charles did not wonder why he had not listened to Roche. And Georgy loved adventure, and Kate had the physical courage sometimes found in people of no imagination. It did not occur to them to be angry with him for having risked their lives.

"I needed that to blow off steam," he said. "One gets no proper exercise in Italy."

He felt better. Perilously better.

At first the promised letters from De La Rue were jubilant. Everything, thanks to their dear friend Dickens, was going splendidly. But soon came qualifications, then doubts, then mounting anxiety, then desperation. Ah, such cruel seizures and so many of them!

In Rome it was the Carnival season. The ancient ruins, the medieval religious processions, the modern masquerade folly were an incredibly textured richness.

"It's precisely what's wanted to call her out of herself and cheer her poor husband, too," Charles said when he had read the last of the letters to Kate and Georgy. "They must join us here and return by our coach."

Georgy cried, "Oh, to be sure! Oh, Charles what a kind thought!"

Kate could only stare.

Charles kissed her without guilt or misgiving. Even for him, he had done a singular job of no longer knowing what is better unknown.

He was genuinely surprised, as well as shocked by her subsequent behavior. On the whole long homeward journey Kate refused to speak a word to Mrs. De La Rue. Charles had never been more angry or more humiliated.

It made an impossible situation for them all, and a dangerous one, he felt sure, for Mrs. De La Rue — poor, blameless, defenseless, suffering little creature that she was. Often, along the way, Charles had the coach stop by some olive grove, so that he might take her aside and give her a brief mesmeric treatment. How otherwise could her very sanity have withstood those waves of senseless hatred that poured from Kate like a black flood? Even De La Rue and Georgy were obviously bewildered and wretched. Charles kept up a desperate brightness of small talk, but it evoked no response; it remained largely monologue.

At night, alone with Kate, he appealed passionately and in vain to her nobler, kinder feelings.

The rest of the story was only compulsive, painful repetition.

Charles, in fact, had turned the whole power of his unemployed genius toward selling himself a bill of goods. It made him miserable. Long, long before June he was yearning to be out of it and out of Italy. Even on that strange, angry journey with all the mesmerizings in the olive groves, the fantasy had begun to fail. He was dreadfully tired of the De La Rues long before the end, and he spoke accurately when he told Kate over and over that he continued the treatments for no reason but his duty to be kind.

Or almost accurately. For it was also, of course, a matter of pride. Of Charles's own furious, stubborn, self-justifying pride.

❊ 9 ❊

IF MARY HOGARTH had not died, she might have recalled Charles's angry disillusionment with that trusted friend, Macrone; Macrone who once so inconveniently expected delivery of a book bought and paid for. Or, perhaps, Charles's righteous fury toward Easthope quit without warning after years of mutually satisfactory association, quit in the moment that Mr. Bentley's contract was safely pocketed; Easthope who had written a letter of farewell that was less than abject in its appreciation for services past — and had even gone so far as to suggest a straightening of accounts.

She might have remembered, and said, "Oh, Charles, stop it!"

And Charles could have looked into the face of love, and forgiven himself by grace of that forgiveness, and laughed, and been grateful. Grateful for the knowledge that he was acting like a fool, that he was being cruel to Kate; that he need not be.

However, Mary was dead; and Kate was too frightened by her own lacks to be able to understand those of another.

Yet while Charles could not admit to the furious boredom and the furious shame which that once delightful dream of being strong and needed had now become, at least through those last long weeks Charles could talk of how he longed for England.

"Italy is all wrong," he said, again and again. "Its people are warmhearted, its landscape is beautiful, but it is *relaxing.*"

In common speech the word had not yet wholly lost its old opprobrious sense of *enervating;* but as Charles spoke it, it was the casting out into outer darkness.

And when the coach came at last to the top of the Simplon Pass, with the children shouting, and Timber barking, and the mountain-winey air in his lungs like a breath of freedom, Charles caught Kate in one arm and Georgy in the other and shouted too.

"London! London, Devonshire Terrace, home, home!"

Kate said, "What makes you so excitable?"

The pettish tone, however, was only pure habit. Charles's joy was so clearly unfeigned that she even began to wonder if possibly, possibly he had been telling the truth all along. He had certainly wasted no tears at parting from that creature. He truly seemed almost wild to be at home.

Kate was right; Charles was wild to be at home. A strange, wild energy, a purposeless sense of purpose, poured from him in a torrent. It rushed upon London, a flood stone-blind and on the rampage.

We all know times when love and creative direction lose their way. For most of us, these are periods of inertia. We put off obligations, kill time, take colds which hang on mysteriously. The literary among us take to writing diaries or otherwise picking old scabs.

Charles was not like most of us. With him, a loss of direction seldom meant a loss of energy. The eleven months which he now spent in London were among the most active in his life.

He had barely unpacked his luggage before he was organizing a tremendous production of *Every Man in His Humour*.

Stanfield would do the sets. They'd hire a theater, no drawing-room nonsense, this. The costs? They were worked out to the penny; two guineas from everybody in it would cover it all except for the costumes, which each of them would find for himself.

Charles himself would produce, direct, and star as the braggart Bobadil. Admission by engraved card, and the social event of the year it would be, too.

Indeed it was. Charles's own performance was magnificent.

"It's bloody well unfair," Macready said coarsely, "that a man who knows nothing of acting should act so superbly."

The repeat performance, given for the benefit of the Sanitorium was an equal success. So, too, a few months later, was the benefit for Miss Fanny Kelly, that aging actress-manager who had dramatized so many of Charles's books.

Thompson married Christiana Weller and Charles pitied him; the girl, on closer acquaintance turned out to be both spoiled and affected. Fred was at the wedding, making eyes at the young sister, Anna, whose nails and bosom had grown out within the year. She promised, shortly, to be as captious and tedious as her sister.

The new baby, a boy, was born in October. The red-faced, wailing accomplished fact was infinitely more acceptable than Charles, for the last nine months, had expected it to be. A wonderful boy, in fact. The christening was a very grand affair.

The baby's name, though Charles did not suspect it, occasioned considerable amusement here and there.

"Alfred D'Orsay Tennyson Dickens!" Jane Carlyle smiled, shrugged, and shook her head.

"You observe," Robert Browning said, "Alfred — for both his god-father and his devilfather."

Though Charles's knack of selective attention had not observed it — in cause or in effect — D'Orsay, with his stepmother-mistress and side interests in youth of both sexes, was becoming with many people something of a tedious joke.

Charles, however, enjoyed the mouth-filling cognomen and the elegant christening as much as his father did; and the Governor was in his element.

But Charles had less time for the baby than he wished for. He was involved with so many people: old friends, high society, literary people, underdogs. And causes: the abolition of capital punishment, for one, that soul-blunting, eye-for-eye atavism, which would have been justified if it worked as a deterrent upon crime — but it did not.

Miss Coutts must be won past her first virginal shrinkings to his plans for a home in which young prostitutes might be reclaimed, taught trades, and even given hope for useful life, marriage, and children of their own in other parts of the world, such as Australia.

The wild freshets rushed. The travel sketches came along handsomely, taking next to no time. He kept them light, leaving out Garibaldi and politics generally. Italy, after all, was irrelevant to England; no point in offending people as he had felt compelled to do with the American sketches.

He thought of starting a cheerful family magazine, *The Cricket on the Hearth*. The notion was lost in a whirl of other undertakings, but the title gave him the theme for his Christmas book. The cricket should be the little household god, chirping when things went well, silent in times of trouble. A pretty fancy, charming!

Charles wrote it at a clip, never suspecting that the most inspired parodist could scarcely have taken him off more neatly to the life. Oh, so inventive, playful, pitying, sweet! It outsold *The Chimes*. It made the critics ill. And Charles's fury with them was strikingly like his all but forgotten fury with Kate for her inability to perceive the selflessness of his service to the De La Rues.

Yet the quality of those eleven torrential months is most perfectly summed up in the singular fact that toward the end of them Charles established a long-lived, first-rate liberal paper, the *Daily News*, and quit it after eighteen days as its editor-in-chief, on finding himself at loggerheads with the backers over some matters of policy.

He conceived the idea, found financers, set it up, staffed it, and set its permanent political tone. He made his father the circulation editor; the Governor, God bless him, despite his growing, empurpled obesity, still had the old swagger and the old eyeglass and vastly relished his position of authority.

He stayed with the paper, and with Charles's tenderest blessing after Charles himself had stormed off the scene. Forster became editor, and Charles thereupon loyally tried to make it appear that he had only intended to found a paper, never to run it.

Yet the staggering fact remains that, single-handed, Charles had founded an excellent, long-lived newspaper and after eighteen days found it, abruptly, no longer worth troubling about. It was only one freshet of the divided flood.

Yet, also, as Emerson has pointed out, we often do not know where we are going, when we think that we most know. "A good deal of buzz," he says, "and somewhere a result slipped magically in."

For eleven months, Charles had been a marvel of outgoing friendship, vital activity, generous enterprise, and emptiness. In the rare moments when he was at home and not writing, he had never got along better with Kate.

And then, without warning, the waters found their course. Charles was full of the huge urgency of a novel — novel whose theme was the overcoming of pride by love.

It came upon him without warning, as he was walking home in an April evening after a talk with Miss Coutts about the refuge for unfortunate girls, which she was now all eagerness to make a reality.

He had been thinking of all that money, and the responsibility which she, and her father before her, too, had always felt toward it. Like a guilt at being on the receiving end in a society which allowed of such absolute extremes of wealth and poverty. A rare sort of guilt, unfortunately . . . A wicked system . . .

And without warning, in a flash, the novel was upon him; not as a vague theme, a rush of characters, but as a story with beginning, middle, end. The merchant prince, his harsh pride centered upon the child who will carry on his name, the name of the firm. And the neglected daughter, who loves him, and the boy. And the boy's death; ruin, pride destroyed, and love found, understood at last in the girl's long, waiting, enduring forgiveness.

Yes, yes, what a fancy . . . The strong, proud, wholly vulnerable, destructible man, the girl with the strength of the meek . . . Of love . . . love . . .

Charles walked through the early dusk, loose-jointed, slack-faced, only his eyes fully alive. His eyes, even in the twilight were so wide, so luminously blue that two young girls whispered together as he passed and looked back over their shoulders with love-stricken, adolescent stares.

He came into the house. He looked at Kate out of those wide, unseeing, so intensely seeing eyes. He said, vaguely, "I think I have a notion . . . for a tale . . ."

He went into the library and shut the door.

At breakfast next morning, he exclaimed, "A man can't live in London without wasting all his energies. Senselessly. Senselessly. We should go back to the Peschiere!"

"Oh!" Kate cried. "Oh."

"Or to any quiet place you may like. I can't write a novel here. What do you say to Lausanne? Tidy, not relaxing, mountains . . ."

Kate stared. "I truly don't understand you! Rush, hurry, do! I've scarcely seen you in all this year past and now it's more traveling!"

Georgy had sprung up from the table.

"Oh, Charles, a novel, how wonderful, how wonderful!"

She was on for eighteen. She would never be a beauty, but the witch face of her childhood had changed to a girl's face, pleasant and lively. And sometimes, rarely, when she was extremely happy, her green eyes looked almost gray — almost like Mary's.

She was happy now, touchingly, touchingly happy.

"Bless you," Charles said. "Bless you, small person."

His voice was tender, like that of a father speaking to his oldest, dearest daughter.

And Georgy gathered up her fallen crumbs, and was grateful.

❊ 10 ❊

A CHANNEL had opened, and Charles, so incapable always of self-examination, was in touch with himself as he had scarcely been since the days when Pickwick, Oliver, Nickleby, Little Nell and all their attendant host of witnesses spoke piecemeal for that very young complexity of hate, love, laughter, vaulting ambition, self-serving, and true reverence for the Christ of the Gospels and for his fellow man which went by the name of Charles Dickens.

He did not feel it so; he only felt that he had a story to tell. Yet it was so; and he had come in touch with a more considerable person than the torrential young genius whom the author of *Chuzzlewit* could neither quite remember nor quite forget.

If the fact was something less than notable in his daily life, it is scarcely surprising. The artist is rarely a wise man, or a saint; and the heart that can state its faiths, doubts, and hungers in good factual prose brings a less than consuming passion to paint, music, poetry, or taletelling.

Somewhere, in that year of buzz, a result had been slipped in. And Charles was in touch with Charles. But he only knew that in Lausanne he would start a new book.

There was nothing new, certainly, in the energetic subletting and winding off of affairs, the journey with Roche in his storm of maps and compasses, the discovery and settling of the perfect little house, the enthusiasm for Swiss tidiness and punctuality. The moment that launched the book was a boyish moment: Charles walked to the bookcase, drew down a volume at random — it was *Tristram Shandy* — let it fall open, and set down his finger, lo! on the oracle: *What a work it is likely to be — let us begin it!*

"BEGAN DOMBEY!" he wrote to Forster that night, and the upper-case letters were a schoolboy shout of triumph.

Yet from the start, the writing felt like nothing he had ever known. It was both more compulsive, immediate, and harder, harder, with an altogether new discipline of selection.

He saw Mr. Dombey look at his newborn child. He heard his voice: "Dombey and Son. Dom-bey and Son." A tide like a tide of vivid memory swept upon Charles; faces, voices, emotions. He could scarcely believe that he invented; it was all remembered. It was all true, live — and, damn it, chiefly irrelevant.

"The devil of writing a book," he said to Georgy, "is that one can't simply dash everything down only because it happened — I mean, might have happened."

It did not occur to him that it was a new problem.

Nor was he conscious of any newness in that sense of compulsive and yet sober immediacy in which he wrote, so unlike any enthusiasms, intoxications, or drudgeries of the past. But he knew that the bare thought of interrupting himself to turn out a Christmas book was agony.

"I was mad to have promised it," he said. "No man in his right mind could have planned to *begin* two books at the same time."

Kate sniffed. "How you love to make a fuss of nothing! Why, you wrote the lovely one about the cricket in no time, when you scarcely had a minute to call your own, and here you haven't a thing to do but write, and chatter at your new acquaintances."

Georgy looked at Charles's face. "Oh, I wish you needn't!" she said. "Have you thought of a story for it?"

"I don't know. I have some vague notion about a battlefield, all those young bodies buried so long ago that nobody thinks any longer of why the earth is so much greener there. . . . Quiet and green, in the sunlight . . . and the reapers singing . . ."

"Horrors," Kate said. "For Christmas?"

"In a word, Georgy, I've no notion as yet."

Kate shrugged. "Why not ask some of your new friends for one? They're clever enough, mercy knows."

He smiled, as if she had uttered some tenderly relished little family joke.

"They do chatter enormously, don't they? Ah, well, in a small spot we must take what company we find."

He loved the whole small English-speaking colony in Lausanne. Particularly, he loved the Honorable Richard Watson and his gentle, percipient wife. He intended to keep their friendship.

"Isn't Mrs. Watson lovely-looking!" Georgy had said to him after their first meeting.

He caught her by the wrist. "For God's sake, don't say so to Kate!"

He was shocked by his own disloyalty, and by her matter-of-fact, conspiratorial giggle, and tried to forget them both.

And in point of fact, that rare wisdom of walking delicately had been, for once, unnecessary. Kate found the Lausanne circle tiresome, but quite undisturbing. Mrs. Cerjat was almost as plain as Mrs. Carlyle; Mr. Haldimand's sister, Mrs. Marcet, was old. Mrs. Watson was well into her thirties, refined and pleasant; but clearly she would never have got such a handsome husband if aristocrats weren't always marrying each other, regardless.

Not that Kate hadn't been surprised to discover that the Watsons were aristocrats; they certainly weren't much like all those dreadful people at Lady Holland's house, and such places!

In that point, she was right. The Watsons of Rockingham Castle were gentle and civilized to a degree. Thackeray would always say that Dickens was incapable of depicting a gentleman; and so he was, until he knew Richard Watson and his wife, and was loved by them. Not afterwards. His quick ear had heard a new melody, and while it would never be his own, he loved it.

And Mrs. Watson said to her husband, "What a dear he is! Even his absurd clothes are touching, they're so much a part of all that gaiety and relish for life."

"I know. I could wish his poor wife weren't such a vast emptiness. The young sister is quite pleasant."

"She worships the ground he walks on. They all do. Have you watched his children fly at him? 'Papa! Papa!' Even the servants, that little courier . . . And, Richard, in her quiet way his wife is intensely proud of him, one can see that."

"Be odd if she weren't, wouldn't it?"

But while the Watsons and their friends loved Charles, among other reasons, for the work he had done, he was not a lion with them. He was a good talker about books, politics, people. He was magnificent company at pencil-and-paper games, and at charades. He was a dear.

And in their company, Charles unconsciously began to let the new assurance and restraint which had come into his work with *Dombey* flow over into his manners and his appearance. For a single, odd example, he forgot his hair. He never consciously learned that he had been violating a taboo, but the shop-girl urge to comb it in public simply melted away. And from the time of that stay in Lausanne, his clothes quieted down; they remained splashy, but they never again quite overstepped the line between the exuberant and the ludicrous.

Charles loved the whole group, but whenever some experience had moved him intensely, it was always to Mrs. Watson that he wanted to talk.

He hurried to see her when he had visited the jail, which imposed the same rule of silence as one he had visited in Philadelphia. The prisoners in Lausanne were better clothed, they were airily, brightly, cleanly lodged, their food was excellent, but they all had suffered the same awful falling apart of the personality as those poor souls in America. They refused their food, believing it to be drugged. They even picked at their hands in the same way. Charles hurried to Mrs. Watson, to watch her face; to feel that he was not seeing it alone.

He wanted to talk to her very much whenever he had been visiting the Institute for the Blind. There was a little girl who was also a deaf-mute; she spent her days in a curious crouch, her hands to her ears, and still sometimes, incredibly, she laughed aloud. Charles went to see her day after day, watching her begin to feel the world around her, the touches of the other children, in waking human response. And he had to tell Mrs. Watson about it.

"The director has given her two pebbles to roll between her hands. She seems to feel that it has a purpose, and she works and works at it, her task, her exacting, important task."

And Mrs. Watson's face saw the child, and he felt companioned and quieted.

On one of his visits to the Institute, someone was playing a piano, and a teacher laid the child's hand upon it. As she felt the vibrations she shuddered and flushed, and suddenly her face became like little Katey's, beautiful with sheer life — God, so alive.

He told Mrs. Watson about it that evening, and her head went up. Her smile was the smile he had imagined.

"What a thing the human soul is! Even in all that dark and silence, reaching out, wondering!"

"Oh, God bless you, yes."

When he read the first issue of *Dombey* aloud, at Haldimand's house, not only Mrs. Watson's face, but the faces of all the circle lived it even more fully than he had dared to hope for. And when he was done, old Mrs. Marcet gave her sharp, acid-sweet smile and said, "You demon, I'll not be able to bear it when that poor little boy dies."

"Whatever makes you think that Paul will die?"

"But how else would you begin to destroy the father?"

What worlds away from Genoa! No need to run to England, now, to find the listening hearts, the audience! When the reports began to come of *Dombey*'s huge, immediate success, Charles laughed. In effect, it was already old news.

In mid-September all of them, even Kate, made the rugged trip to the Grand St. Bernard on muleback.

Charles was amused by the airs of self-sacrifice with which the monks endured a glorious view, continual company, and a flowing alms box. But it was beautiful, a beauty not to have been missed, up there in the high, thin air among the gray, snow-patched rocks with their lean summer harvest of lichen.

He wakened before the bell for first Mass and dressed and went out to look at that view alone. Mrs. Watson was there before him, the dawn fog blowing about her and her face lifted to it.

She accepted him beside her in silence, as if they had come there together and had already been standing so, looking, for a long time.

After several minutes she said, "I feel like that child with her hand on the piano. Something quite new, and wonderful, and still recognized at once, you know. A size too large for us, and, still, not. Not only the mountains, something about the early morning, and the fog . . ."

"I know." It was an absent noise of happy assent to the blowing fog, the early morning, the peaks now starting to flush with light along their crests. "I know"; an absent, happy, companioned, married sound.

And he heard his own voice. He loved Mrs. Watson; he was not in love with her, nor even trembling upon the verge of it. Though Kate bored him, irritated him, rebuffed him, disappointed him; though he had moments when all that he felt for her was distinguishable only from hate by its odd admixture of unhappiness, Charles was still in love with the beauty that Kate had once possessed and, in some fluctuating measure, still possessed. He only heard his own voice and knew, with a sudden clarity, how much more of a marriage God, or chance, or life might have given him than he had got; the sound of his own voice overwhelmed him with such an admission of loneliness as he had never made before; no not even on the road to Naples, when rage sustained him and served to confuse the very view that it laid bare.

He could not bear that sight. He slammed a door of his mind shut upon it. He looked at Mrs. Watson, and smiled warmly, tenderly.

He said, "Thank God you married Richard Watson. I could not have borne it, to know you and see you married to a man who couldn't understand and rejoice in what he had!"

She reached out, closing her hand over his where it lay upon the parapet. "Oh, you dear, dear, person, thank you. Yes, I always know how wonderfully fortunate I am. We're very much alike, Richard and I."

He said abruptly, "Ah, there goes the bell. Come in, now, and help me mock the Pope."

And unfortunately, Charles could not go back to the place in which he might still have talked with Charles. It was now time, and past time, to leave *Dombey* for a while, and write the Christmas book.

The crippling, heavy depression in which Charles found himself once they had come back to Lausanne was caused, he was sure, by the atmosphere; the air of Lausanne had a lowering effect upon the constitutions of many people.

It could not have been more unlucky that he should have begun to suffer its effect now, of all times. The book was shortly due, he had not allowed enough time for it, and the harder he drove himself the worse it went. And every night, he got the same nightmare, about a maze of rooms through which he wandered, unable to find his way out. He developed giddy attacks. He developed a bloodshot eye. It was essential, completely essential that he get away from Lausanne.

"Mercy!" Kate said. "I'm sure I have no objection to a little visit to Geneva. You needn't curse and swear and get excited like a child!"

And as he had expected, once they were settled in their hotel, the red eye cleared, and his pen began to move along. Yet the dizziness and the strange depression hung on stubbornly, even now that their cause was removed.

One night he said, vaguely, "A pain in my side that I used to have, sometimes — for the last few days I've been expecting it back at any moment, I don't know why."

Kate was always interested in physical ailments. She said, "Your side is sore? It aches?"

Charles had no notion of why he should have felt suddenly furious and shouted, "No! No, nothing of the sort!"

Kate, not surprisingly, looked frightened; and he apologized, and kissed her, and made love to her.

Still, he forced himself to walk his regular fifteen miles each day, and to write steadily, and he assured himself that though it was hard to write when one felt ill, the tale was a deeply moving, an inspiring one.

He could scarcely have been worse mistaken. *The Battle of Life* was not, to put it gently, a victory.

It concerned two sisters who loved the same man. The sister to whom he was engaged pretended to elope with someone else and hid at a relative's house so that the other could get him on the rebound. Self-sacrifice. Even the comic relief was relentlessly uplifting. It centered upon a servant who could, as she said, only read a thimble and a nutmeg grater. These objects bore engraved mottoes: *Do as you would be done by*, and *Forgive and forget*.

Mercifully, Charles out of touch with himself was also, always, his own kindest critic. The task done, he felt much better than when he had come to Geneva.

By a further mercy, he was a reader who made anything sound good. Of his audience at the Haldimands' house, only Mrs. Marcet was distressed. She, indeed, suffered a definite sensation of nausea. However, she mastered it, reminding herself that Charles had six children to support while all his genius flowed into that magnificent *Dombey*. And the others listened almost as the faithful had listened to *The Chimes*.

Charles watched them all, and loved them, as he read. He saw in their faces the promise of the book's success — that singularly unmerited and astounding success which it actually had — and his heart was full.

"I wish I'd not planned my year abroad so well," he said. "I wish that house in Paris weren't leased and waiting. I shall miss you all more than you know."

Mrs. Watson leaned forward. "I know," she said, "for I know how we shall miss you."

His eyes filled with quick, emotional tears.

"Thank you," he said. "Thank you. God bless you all."

At once, uneasily, he glanced toward Kate. But she was only smiling, amiably.

She herself almost wished that they need not leave Lausanne. Charles's friends were talkative, but nice enough once one got to know them. And it was remarkable how contented he had seemed there, except the short time when the lake disagreed with him. Yes, especially since none of them were famous, or the sort of creature he got silly about, or anything like that.

❋ 11 ❋

THE HOUSE IN PARIS was fantastic, a sort of combined dollhouse, whorehouse, haunted castle, and mad variety of clock. The drawing room was approached by a series of chambers, each smaller than the last, like the sections of a telescope. The dining room was a grove, its ceiling bowered in branches stuck all over with broken bits of looking glass. The last tenant had remodeled it, redecorated it, and left at once. "Obviously, aghast at what he had done," Charles said.

Paris was Paris, wicked, brilliant, muddy, depressing, dramatic, beautiful, and full of people who knew Mr. Dickens or were eager to have the pleasure. And *Dombey* had been waiting since the trip to the Grand St. Bernard; waiting to make its compelling, consuming way toward the scene that lay ahead, months away at the end of the first volume, the scene already so clear in Charles's mind, which should end off poor little Paul.

One morning when they had been in Paris for a little more than a week, Georgy said, "Charles, do you miss Lausanne?"

He was thinking of *Dombey*. He said, "What?" absently, and then, as the delayed meaning of the words came through, "Not really. No."

He did not notice the smile of singular happiness that flashed across her face.

He wrote to the Watsons. He wrote to them almost as often as he wrote to Forster. Mrs. Watson was the letter writer for both of them;

her letters carried the sound of her voice, as few people's do. Charles loved to get them, and to read them aloud to Kate and Georgy. But that late autumn, winter, and early spring were *Dombey*. Once they were past, nothing else remained of them but a few bright, floating pictures: Katey and Mamie, curtsying to each other proudly in their new Paris dresses; Charley's face, small with pleading, lifted to his as they sat at table beneath those spangled branches.

"Papa, please, please don't send me away to school."

"It's a splendid school that will ready you for Eton, Charley, and Eton is the finest school in all the world. If Miss Coutts weren't such a loving godmother to you, you could never dare dream of going to Eton."

"You lived at home and went to a splendid school — Giles's Cats, and after that the one with Daniel, too. Oh, please, Papa!"

Pictures: old Victor Hugo in his stage-set drawing room, the great man so superbly played, and staged with tapestries, old armor, gilded lions, everything; the Morgue; a public ball crowded with *lorettes*, their faces haggard, calculating, wreathed in smiles.

Only a few floating pictures and one day, one isolated day that he could never by any subsequent effort forget in its least detail.

It was the day on which Burnett's letter came, the letter telling him that Fanny had consumption.

Shortly before he had left for Lausanne, their brother Alfred got married, and she had come on to London for the wedding. She was shockingly thin and coughing, and it had frightened him. He took her to Dr. Elliotson, and went back to him again alone to make sure that she had been told the truth and that her lungs were not affected.

"He was wrong as our own doctor had been wrong," Burnett wrote. "She may have a year left. Do not come to her, she still believes that she is not very gravely ill."

Charles was alone when he read the letter. He sat alone for about half an hour, finding his way to the knowledge that Fanny, Fanny would die.

Fanny, the denizen of the brighter world, coming down the Academy steps on a raw, gray Sunday afternoon, making ladylike conversation until they were almost in sight of the Marshalsea, and then, without warning, taking his cold, bare hand in her tight, gloved grip.

Fanny, the first beloved. Fanny the enemy, the rival, the friend, the sister, yes, in a real way even the mother, too. Fanny, to die.

The tease, in Chatham, teasing until he raged and wept, and then the kiss; "Oh, my Tom Thumb, all eyes!" And in spite of himself, she would make him laugh, they would be running and holding hands and laughing.

Oh, God, Burnett! Poor, poor Burnett, and their almost successful music and their almost believable hopes! No, pity Fan, not him, Fan so alive, so warm, so quick, so gay. He has had her love. When she dies he will have got more from life than most men ever find. Not poor Burnett, but Fan, my poor, poor Fan.

He had been sitting so, with his head bowed and his lips forming the words that brought the belief, for that half-hour before he started and thought, heavily, "Oh, dear God, now I've got to tell Kate."

She was enjoying a few after-breakfast sweets before her bedroom fire. She drew a small, exasperated sigh before she spoke.

"Mercy, you look as cheerful as an undertaker. What's happened, did you find a speck of dust on the mantelpiece?"

He spoke in a voice that he scarcely knew for his own.

"I had a letter from Burnett. Fan's consumptive. For God's sake, try not to act like your mother and sob and gloat and assume that there's no possible outcome but the worst. I am going out. I want to walk."

He left the room without looking back at her.

He walked, through the whole day and into the evening.

He was a child in Chatham, he stared across the nettle fields behind the house in Somers Town, he stood again in the cold wind, waiting by the Academy steps. He was Maria's Charles, betrayed and wretched and cold with implacable anger, saying quietly, "I will never forgive you, Fan."

He remembered how long he had held that foolish bitterness, and wept, remembering it, without knowing that he wept or turning his face from the stares of the curious. He even began to pray aloud, "Oh, God, please help me, change me. I get up and walk out and shut a door, I've always done, I did it to poor little Hall. . . . Thank God, for that once at least I went back. Fanny forgave me. She laughed, she said, 'Poor old Tom Thumb, what does it matter now?'"

And still he walked on, at the same steady, purposeful, unchanging pace.

He lost the thought of Fan in the thought of death itself. He stood by Mary's grave on a cloudy May morning, and promised his body its place beside it. He was dead, and it did not matter where they had laid him; he was nothing, only a few printed words left of him in a world where he had been child, man, brother, son, father, lover, friend, Charles, alive and now dead; he was a walking knowledge of the reality of death.

Then he could bear it no more. He walked with his chin lifted, and told himself that doctors are often mistaken, and that Fan possessed unusual powers of rebound, determination, vitality.

He was painfully tired as he walked the final mile of the way home, but as he drew near the house he suddenly began to run, and when he had come inside it he still ran, up the stairs to the bedroom, Kate's and his.

He called out her name as he ran, and as he bent over the bed his words poured out on each release of his gasping, labored breathing.

"Kate, Kate, oh, my darling. I don't know why I was so brutal, so unforgivable this morning. Kate. I was unhappy, I felt that I had to be alone, I couldn't bear the thought that anyone, anyone might talk or cry. Kate? Kate?"

She pushed herself up in the bed. She looked as if she might have cried herself to sleep; her face was swollen, sagging. He was full of self-accusal, pity, love.

"Oh, Kate, dear Kate, my own wife who wanted to comfort me. I knew it, I knew it even then. Oh, my darling, forgive me."

She said, "I might have known that you couldn't be content with a simple apology. That once you'd thought it over you'd have to soothe your conscience with a hysterical scene."

There was an odd, empty moment. Charles's face went dead.

Then he said, as evenly as if he had not been running, "You do tend to expect the worst always, like your mother, you know. But I was unnecessarily rude."

"It's not made a particularly pleasant day for me."

"I'm sorry, dear. I had a strange sort of day myself. I forgot to eat dinner, or lunch either. I should go and find a bite now. I . . . I forgot to come home to say good night to the children. They must be asleep."

Kate sniffed. "They went to sleep quite happily, I'm sure. Georgy read to them, I believe from their own New Testament that their

Papa wrote for them in such nice, simple words to teach them how to be as kind and considerate as he is."

Charles opened his mouth, and closed it again.

His body ached with weariness. He was too tired to want anything to eat. He tumbled a tidy bureau drawer into chaos hunting a nightshirt before he realized that it was the wrong drawer.

As he blew out the light, he spoke once more, but not to Kate or to anyone else.

"Fan has consumption," he said.

The words were meaningless, empty of emotion. When he lay down to sleep, he felt like a thin, aching shell around a total emptiness.

Kate managed to hold back her tears until he was asleep and then to weep quietly, not wakening him. She had wanted desperately to forgive him, and to be kissed and told that she was beautiful. Through the whole day she had felt frightened and inadequate; or, as she put it to Georgy, and to herself, most dreadfully insulted and hurt.

Georgy did not make it better, either.

She said, "Let's not talk of it, Kate. He was too sad to know how it would sound, and people often want to be alone when they are sad. Didn't you, when Mary died?"

Kate shuddered and did not answer.

She had remembered something terrible, a thing that she had not remembered since it happened; no, not even on the very day after it happened. Mary was dead; she had fallen down crying, across the bed that Mary was lying on, dead. Charles shouted at her, to get up, not to touch her — Mary, her own sister.

He did not care how she felt, only how he felt. Even then, when her heart was broken, he had not cared how much he hurt her, or insulted her.

She began to tremble, remembering it.

Kate seldom verbalized her emotions. If she had found no words for the sense of utter inadequacy, of lack, of fear felt and remembered, she might have gone to sleep in Charles's arms that night, after all. But she found her inaccurate words, hurt, and insulted. And she knew how one who has been hurt and insulted should act.

She lay still, and wept herself silently to sleep.

And Charles, the next morning, went back to *Dombey*, where he found sufficient speech for every unexamined passion which informed his life: the daily life which he was so determined to find good.

✳ *12* ✳

FORSTER WAS COMING to visit; he would take Charley back with him to England and the school which he still wept to think of. Coming next day, for the year had run its course, and it was almost February.

Coming next day, and how could a coming have been better timed? For, as Charles said to Georgy at the breakfast table, "Now approaches the hour towards which every hour of all these past months have been tending, small person. Catch your breath and pray! I leave you now, to slaughter little Paul."

The day, though Charles would not remember it so, was a day of singular joy.

"The golden ripple on the wall came back . . ."

It was altogether unlike the writing of the death of Little Nell — Mary's death relived so helplessly and still in that curious luxury of tears. Paul had been born to die; to die in a lyric passage foreseen, planned far ahead in each detail, the light upon the wall, the sound of the rushing stream reaching the sea into which all rivers flow. A poem, and immediately the poem was done, the voice of Miss Tox: "Dear me, to think that Dombey and Son should be a girl, after all."

Even that change of pace, that comic line after the hymn to death, had been planned, in Lausanne before he was forced to break off for the Christmas book.

Charles sat down at his table. He sat waiting, like a man who has come first to some appointed meeting. He sat with his head lifted, waiting with a half-smile for the knowledge of death to come upon him; and when it came he welcomed it.

He began to write, carefully, slowly, word after word reached for, listened for. He wrote according to plan and did not know any longer that it was according to plan. He was a dying child, a tragic girl, a man whose pride was centered in the ebbing life. He was all of them, in a room where light made ripples like golden water on the wall.

He wept as he wrote, and if any part of him had been free to question his tears he would have said that they were for the child who had become so real to him. But the tears, in fact, were tears of joy. Of joy in his own force, discipline, in the act of creation.

The day that he had walked the streets with death was far from wasted.

It was ten at night when Charles laid down his pen and once more walked out of the house. He walked without fatigue until it was morning and time to meet Forster's train.

"My God," Forster said. "Since ten last night? No wonder you look like a ghost with a gaslight in its head."

Charles laughed. "I daresay I must, but the curious fact is that I don't feel really tired even now. Ah, wait until I read it to you, wait!"

Charley left bravely, too proud to let Mr. Forster see him cry.

Kate cried. She said, "The first of them to go. Oh, dear, oh dear, how old it makes one feel!"

She was big with the child that was coming.

"Poor little love, we're not as brave as he was this morning, are we? Our dear Phenomenon, setting sail."

Later that day, he said to Georgy, "Between missing Charley and missing Paul, I'm in bad form to swing the public heart over to sister Florence. I feel as I always do at the end of a book, and I've half a book still to write."

"Don't you feel happy when you end a book?"

"Only emptied. Lonely, no matter who's about. Lonely . . . I hope Charley won't be too homesick at the first."

For a moment, Georgy did not answer. Charles thought that the closed, sad look upon her face was a look of sympathy, and he was grateful for it.

"He'll do splendidly," she said at last. "And the lease on Devonshire Terrace hasn't so very much longer to run. It will be quite different once you're at home again."

Charles raised his head.

"Small person, you're very wise. Do you know why you are always happy? It is because you are always useful — as I can't be, abroad. When we're useful, Georgy, we have no time to repine for our lacks and losses. We forget them, and only see the riches, the true riches that we all possess."

She said, "Am I truly useful to you, Charles?"

He laughed. "Small busy one, what do you think?"

He did not see the look of disappointment, either. He was far too moved by the words that he had just spoken, the formula enunciated so compellingly.

Despite a quarrel on the road to Naples, despite a morning of blowing fog and brief, harsh light on a Swiss mountainside, yes, even beyond the hard objective facts of Kate's waning beauty and increasing isolation, a tender greed and a romantic dream still fought for life. Charles was an optimist; but more than that he possessed a most stubborn will to joy.

He knew none of these things. But he heard his own words, and was immeasurably moved by them. The shape of eight singular years had begun to form.

A week later, Charley came down with scarlet fever. Charles, rushing to him in panic, found him beaming with self-importance.

"I might well have died, you know, Papa," he said. "*Many* do."

Charles hugged him close, forcing his face to mask the anguished gratitude, preserving the innocent relish of a danger not too disturbingly real; not fear of death, but relish of a game, like all boys' games of battle, violence, and sudden death.

"Ah, but not you," he cried, "not our indomitable Phenomenon!"

Charley sighed with satisfaction. "It wasn't as light a case as they say, Papa. I was very, very ill the first day."

Dear God, and what if he had truly been? Oh, God, keep us mindful of our blessings, never let us cloud the knowledge of all we have and owe Thee with idle broodings!

Charles closed his hand tight over Charley's. He spoke, and his words surprised and pleased him as much as they did the boy.

"You know, now that Mama and I are back in England — that cruel doctor, not letting her risk the infection now that you're doing so well! — now that we're here, we shall stay and send for the others. I can visit you often. Are you glad of that?"

It did not make sense. The other children had not had the fever, and Charley would convalesce at his Grandmother Hogarth's house. The tenant's lease on Devonshire Terrace had not elapsed. It meant house-hunting, subletting, two movings in place of one and double rent to pay, and much as he loved lavishness, Charles hated waste.

He would lose time and energy when *Dombey* had come to a critical point in its fortunes. For the week past he had been overwhelmed and near panic with the difficulties, both technical and emotional, that blocked him as he struggled with the task of persuading so many thousands of hearts to center on Florence the love they had given Paul.

It was wasteful; it was irrational. Yet in a flash, Charles knew without doubt or question that the year abroad was over.

Something new was beginning.

"KATE, I'VE DECIDED to stay in England. For any number of reasons, it's the thing to do."

For any number of reasons? Charles would have been hard put to it to name one. Something had finished, something was starting; and Charles must find a house, send Roche for Georgy and the children and the servants, and get them properly settled.

He saw it through in a double whirlwind of efficient action and anguished outcries.

"Forster, I've not got a single slip of the new issue done. You can't conceive of the wretchedness of struggling over this *crucial* turning point, the whole book to stand or fall in consequence of how I manage it — and doing it in the midst of all this wear and tear and expense, worrisome expense, and *utter* confusion. Everything in that house at sixes and sevens — and every bit of the task to be done over again in Devonshire Terrace before it's finished here . . ."

"But why, in the first place? Why not have written the issue in Paris, quietly, and come home when your tenant's lease was up?"

Charles could only say, "Forster, I could no more have gone back to that absurd little house than a soul can go back into its dead body!"

The past was past; a new day had begun. The emotion did not permit analysis or argument; it only overwhelmed him.

And in one of those odd strokes of underlining that accident is always tossing into our lives, little Hall, of Chapman and Hall, died unexpectedly.

At the news, Charles bowed his head, ashamed for once of his tears. "Poor little Hall. So many kindnesses, through so many years. I owe him very much, poor little Hall."

He wrote to the widow, humbly, asking if the services were to be kept private. Her answer was prompt and kind.

The funeral was in Highgate Cemetery.

Charles sat with Kate throughout the evening, thinking. He had gone far back in time, behind Doughty Street, behind Furnival's Inn, when at last he began to think aloud.

"He was in the shop under the offices. . . . He put the magazine into my hands, with that first piece that I ever had published. Long before *Pickwick,* before poor Macrone . . . so long ago. He was so kind; such a kind little man."

Kate inhaled sharply. "Oh, Charles, can't you stop acting as if you thought you were so noble! Anyone can let bygones be bygones if the person's dead!"

Charles looked at her for a moment, his face blank, and perplexed, and very like the face which she so often turned to him. He came back slowly, from Maria's world, and Mary's; from the world which began with *Nickleby.* He pushed through the shimmering curtains of time past, into the present.

Kate was hugely pregnant this time, a pyramid of Kate topped by a bored, impatient, emptyish, beautifully featured face, the jawline only slightly beginning to sag.

Charles saw her. There was no wild, sheer energy, no sense of beginning, no stubborn will to joy in the moment.

"You misunderstood me, dear," he said. "I was only indulging myself with some memories."

His voice expressed nothing but a tired indifference, as if the misunderstanding meant very little, one way or the other.

Yet by morning, Charles was saying that a man who lives abroad is only half alive. London, thank God, made him feel like Lazarus.

Sydney Smith Haldimand Dickens was born on April 18, 1847, somewhat bruised by a complicated delivery. Charles was lost in love-at-first-sight. That summer at Broadstairs, Charles named him the Ocean Spectre (shortened in time to Speck) from the wide, rapt stare with which he watched the sea; but from the start Charles was saying, earnestly, everywhere, "He's truly astounding! Thank heaven, I've leisure to enjoy him properly. Poor Alfred and I scarcely had a nodding acquaintance until he'd begun to creep about!"

Strangely enough, now that the new tempo was established, he did have leisure; and for the other children, too, and for all his friends; and for *Dombey*, with Florence riding high at last.

"But it's always so," he told Georgy. "An idle man is invariably pressed for time, and a busy man has time and time to spare!"

It felt so; it did, indeed.

Yet viewed from the outside, the year which added Speck to the nursery was remarkably like the year of Alfred's birth.

In the first place, Charles discovered almost at once that poor Leigh Hunt was in grave financial straits.

Poor Hunt, a man of genius, suffering want to England's shame? Up, Bobadil to the rescue! *Every Man in His Humour* must be produced again, but with improvements; oh, on an altogether grander scale. They should play *The Merry Wives of Windsor*, too, on alternating nights.

Huge Mark Lemon, the editor of *Punch*, as the perfect Falstaff and Charles as Shallow. Two performances in London, two in Manchester. Costumes, sets, theaters to be found, arrangements, arrangements, and then the rehearsing, directing — the glorious vortex was spinning at top speed when Lord John Russell announced that the government was about to pay Hunt a liberal pension.

"Shamed into it by hearing of us," Charles said, "and here I'm left, Georgy, with this welter of meaningless, expensive amateur theatricals on my hands."

His depression was brief. Hunt had debts, it turned out, which the pension could not begin to cover. And poor old John Poole, who wrote so many slap-up plays in his heyday was in need, too.

To be sure, the news of Hunt's pension might weaken the London audience; and with theater rentals so high, they could only afford to play to a full house. But they could drop *The Merry Wives*, and still take a smashing, proper overwhelmer of a production to Birmingham and Manchester.

Between the benefit and *Dombey*, the spring and summer went like a lightning flash. And autumn brought no letdown; for Miss Coutts's Home had at last become a joyful reality.

"Think, Georgy, Kate! Those hopeless, wasted lives made useful again, given another try!"

"I still don't see what Miss Coutts is thinking of to let you choose which of them they'll try to save," Kate said. "A clergyman might know, perhaps. But *you*, of all people, always taken in so readily by hair and eyelashes and artfulness!"

"Beauty is a terribly perishable possession in that trade, Kate dear. But, more than that, in their jails and workhouses these girls have heard a great deal from the gentlemen of the cloth about their state of hopeless degradation. As a result they could not show their own true natures in the presence of — of professional blamelessness."

"You mean that you try to make them think you're *bad?*"

"Only that they are good. Some can't be any longer, they're past all help. Some can. But the sight of a round collar with all its associations of humiliation and despair — what a mockery of Christ! — the bare sight would be enough to make them all what you call artful. It would rob them of what little courage and self-respect they still possess."

"Oh, dear, dear, I can only say that I'm sorry we owe Miss Coutts so much — Charley's education and possibly Wally's, too. What a depressing thing for her to have got herself involved in!"

Georgy leaned forward. She looked about to speak. Charles caught her eyes, and shook his head a little. He stood up, and then gave a light pat to her shoulder as he started from the room.

Still, at the door, he allowed himself one more word.

"The world would be a depressing thing to be involved in," he said, "if it weren't for the few like Miss Coutts who are willing to be involved."

Kate's evaluation was quite wrong. Where his own life was not concerned, Charles was far from easily taken in. He knew the born trollop looking for a free holiday at first glance; he could spot the helpless but compulsive troublemaker; he could tell discouragement from incurable inertia, and timidity from ingrained distrustfulness.

He would sit across a table from a girl, his blue eyes intent upon her face, his chin propped upon his thumbs.

"Yes, Lily . . . How old were you then?"

"Twelve, almost. Mum had this lodger . . ."

One girl said to another, "It's downright odd the things you can tell to him. Here he is, rich — don't he dress the swell? — and young-ish and handsome even if he is getting high in the forehead on the sides; he's the very kind you'd pick upon to speak to, walkin' — and for all it matters he could be another girl the same as you."

"It is odd. It's not like he don't blame you, neither, it's only this feeling like he don't blame you no different to how you blames yourself."

"I shouldn't fancy he'd always been no saint."

"P'raps not. He does get to preachin' on different lines to the hell and damnation lot, don't he? Did he start in on you about always on time and rooms picked up neat and fingernails?"

Charles wrote to Miss Coutts: "The design is simply to appeal to them by means of affectionate kindness, but firmly, too . . . establishing habits of the most rigid order, punctuality, neatness — but to make as great a variety in their daily lives as their daily lives will permit of. On the cheerfulness and kindness, all our hopes rest."

A good many worthy Australian families would owe their existence to the fact that Charles, beyond the confines of his own emotional concerns, was shrewd, realistic, and compassionate.

In March, Charles went to Brighton to be alone while he finished *Dombey*. He had never felt more triumph in ending a book, or more oppressive reluctance to let one go. Or more strangely empty, unreal, detached from life, once it was gone.

Dombey, gone? Two years, so blessedly centered, so purposed — were they gone?

But at least the new theatricals were snowballing into the best and biggest ever; and they had purpose, excellent purpose; he could go back to London not at loose ends. At least, he was of use.

The production would buy Stratford-on-Avon for the nation, and the poor old playwright Knowles would end his days in comfort as its custodian.

This time they would really play *The Merry Wives of Windsor*, and what sport to alternate two comic characters as unlike as Bobadil and Shallow, night by night! First London, then off to the north as far as Glasgow and Edinburgh! But how much time it took! Every soul in the blessed enterprise needed continual supervision, from the carpenters on up, and not a soul of them would do his best unless one kept him somehow persuaded that he was the single truly essential cog in the whole machine.

How did one find time for his friends, too, and his family?

And still not so much as one wished for. At least he had got poor

Fanny out of the foul smoke of Manchester. Hornsey was green, and pleasant, and nearby.

But, oh, if these weeks sped by so fast for him, how fast they must go for her!

Charles sat at his writing table, answering letters. He answered everything, always, with a line or two at the least. He would have been appalled at the thought of a secretary.

"No," he wrote firmly.

No, he would not contribute five pounds to a fund to pay Knowles's debts. Such kindly efforts do not work out. Hunt had not told of a fraction of what he owed; it never came out until the bailiffs started threatening all over again.

"It's shocking, isn't it, when you took such trouble for me? I've always been simply a child in these things, simply a child."

Then Charles compressed his lips. The lips fell open, and he raised his head. An elusive wisp of memory was stirring, somewhere. . . . Something that Kate once said of Hunt . . . something that made him angry. They were at the seaside, he was writing *Oliver Twist.* . . . Yes, how odd, he could remember the very day, that same evening he read her the murder scene and it gave her hysterics. But it must be a false memory; even in those days he couldn't have been angry over anything to do with Hunt. Far more likely she'd really said something about the Governor . . .

The Governor . . . Fan . . . Fanny . . . And her second baby, born with that crippled back . . .

"Ah, but I'm wasting time! Come, back to work!"

Fan lived until early September, but the terminal stage of the disease, the change, as it was always called, began in early July, after the triumphant London opening of the plays.

She knew her condition, by then. Charles went to say goodbye for a little before he should start off on the northern tour. She was quiet, grave, more openly tender toward him than he had ever found her; and still, like a stranger, she seemed to console him for some threat of loss which did not concern her directly.

She said, "It's hard to die at my age, but I'm not afraid. I expected to be, but I'm not. My poor Henry . . . Keep in touch with him, Charles, never forget him. We were always so happy together." Then she smiled, a strange, easy smile that was somehow part of her unconscious slipping into the past tense, and she said, quite casually, "It may be difficult to arrange, but will you try to have me buried in unconsecrated ground?"

For all the half-hour past, Charles had been wishing, wishing that she would not so certainly find it embarrassing if he said a prayer with her.

Now he took her thin hand, and smiled down into the eyes of secret blackness that dominated her wasted face.

"Yes, dear Fan, if you want it. I'll find out how it can be done."

"Good. What do you hear from Letty nowadays? Anything?"

He told her about Fred, still in pursuit of Anna Weller, and spending every penny that could give them any future comfort. He heard himself talk, and he heard his own prayer at the back of his mind.

I know that You love her. Nobody was ever unestranged from human love and estranged from Yours. Thank You for the mercy of that knowledge.

She was amused by the family gossip, but he could see that she was growing tired.

"I wish that the tour weren't starting now, Fan. If . . . if you want me at all, let me know by wire."

Unexpectedly, she began to laugh. The laughing made her cough. She hid the bloody handkerchief under her pillow, and then she laughed again, cautiously, but with the old, familiar, mocking fall.

"My poor Tom Thumb, I'm sorry. No, go with your Cats, all in your white toppers, bless you. And resign yourself, dear. There are some performances that you can't direct."

"Fan, I only thought . . . hoped . . ."

"Poor love, did I hurt you? My Tom Thumb and his eyes! I only meant, dear, what could you do here? I have Henry."

"I know. I know that, dear Fan."

He walked back to London.

Had he wanted her to ask him to cancel the tour? To postpone it until the autumn? He would have done, and gratefully. No, that was the wrong word, surely. He was grateful, deeply grateful that she could say, "I have Henry," and take it so wonderfully for granted that it was the total answer . . . her husband. Grateful . . . grateful . . .

[315]

Come, this won't do. Walk briskly. Let it go. It's a world of questions without answers. "I have Henry . . . It's hard to die at my
age . . . unconsecrated ground . . ." Let it go, we all have the only
necessary answer for our practical purposes: "Whatsoever thy hand
findeth to do, do it with thy might."

Fill the moment; know it, love it, fill it. Actively, usefully . . .
Yes . . . yes . . .

Nobody who went on that wild, triumphal tour ever forgot
Charles's gaiety.

Or forgot his absurd energy: the railroad stop at which he was
nearly left behind because he was dashing up and down the platform,
organizing everything and everyone else; the mad perfectionist agonizing over details which always, by some unjust miracle, emerged at
last in the breadth of a final bold, smooth, casual effect. But chiefly,
the gaiety.

Mary Cowden Clarke, their Dame Quickly, the only amateur
actress in the cast, christened him Young Gaslights, shortened at
once to Young Gas. She laughed and wept at the farewell dinner,
catching Charles's hand on one side of her and Mark Lemon's on the
other.

"Oh, Falstaff, oh, my glorious Young Gas, now that we've had our
taste of reality, how can we go back to the nasty, brutish, dull, short
life of dreams?"

Lemon kissed her right hand. Charles kissed her left and dropped
it as he got up, laughing, shaking back his hair.

"A toast! Comrades in arms, a toast to our own glory."

"That Mrs. Cowden Clarke," Kate said, "sounds to be the silliest,
most conceited creature who ever drew the breath of life."

Charles said, "Yes, dear. I see."

He had not heard her. His mind was in Hornsey, with Fan.

Fanny did not die peacefully, as Charles had both prayed and
somehow expected that she would. There was no merciful coma at
the end. She died of strangulation, fighting for breath right up to the
last hideous, gargling, choking noise of the death rattle. Until their
final glazing, her eyes were wild, turning from Charles to Henry to

Charles again as if they cried, "Help me, do something for me, something, stop me from dying, help me!"

And still they were not eyes of fear, only of desperate, desperate battle. She had spoken quietly of death, but even the long, protracted dying, day after day, the drawn-out torment, had not fulfilled its usual, merciful function. Up to her last wrenching breath, Fan wanted to live.

❋   2   ❋

ONE EVENING that winter, Forster, Lemon, and the young painter Augustus Egg sat talking about Charles's new Christmas book, *The Haunted Man*.

"It's bad," Lemon said. He shifted his tall corpulence unhappily in his chair and added, "Hate to say so."

Forster drew himself up. He looked, Egg thought, like a St. Bernard who got there with the cask too late, doing the next best thing. Prayers for the departed.

"Lemon," he said, "you pretend to a certain cynicism, but even you cannot deny the majesty of that book's theme: Grief, the source of human value; our sufferings once forgotten, naught left but a brutish indifference."

Little Egg turned his head abruptly aside. His lips, as if in delight at a sweet savor, formed a word twice. "Naught . . . naught . . ."

Then his face turned serious, and he leaned toward the room. "I don't know, Forster. It's always seemed to me that a parable should be about the length of an after-dinner joke. Biblical length, that is. This thing moans on and on. It's not like him."

Forster laid his hand upon his breast. Before he could inhale his full, preliminary breath, however, Lemon said quietly, "He was very fond of that sister who died, you know. I daresay we all have to sell ourselves a solution to the problem of evil, once in a way. Let's only hope it won't last long. God, think of getting a full-length novel like that!"

Lemon and Egg were worried needlessly.

Charles sat at home, rolling a pen back and forth between his fingers and his thumb. His tongue worked behind close-pressed lips. His eyes were wide, brilliantly blue.

That night, he was radiant. He said to Kate and Georgy, "But this book has been waiting, staring me in the face for months — for years! David Mag of Blunderstone House . . . David Blunderstone . . . Ah, what a good feeling. Two whole years ahead again, when some small part of it all will make coherent sense!"

Kate said, "Of what all? Sense?"

"The general muddle. This welter."

"If you must insult me," Kate said, "need you do it before Georgy?"

"Dear, what do you mean?"

"I may not be clever, but I've given you eight children!"

For a moment the surprise of the misunderstanding made Charles blink. Then he was angry.

"So you have," he said. "Given them lock, stock, and barrel."

He was sorry when he had said it. He told himself that Kate could not help the fact that she did not enjoy children; that she was really conscientious, as good a mother as she knew how to be. He waited for the denials and the tears.

Kate, however, only retrieved and clasped one of her peregrinating bracelets and said, "I'm gratified that you admit to so much, at least."

She had not miscounted, by the bye. Henry Fielding Dickens had joined the throng. He was fat. A good little moon-faced monster, though not in the class with Speck.

Few novels sound so joyfully, spontaneously written as *David Copperfield*. Few have gone harder.

"I can't understand it," Charles complained. "This tale comes directly from my heart, Georgy. I love it, I love every word as I set it down. But it leaves me *tired*."

"Doesn't any writing?"

"Only what's ground out to order or what goes badly. No, a book like this should leave me feeling like *myself*, each day." Then he laughed. "Particularly since it is myself!"

It left him very tired. And restless. In London, he was anxious to get away to Broadstairs. Broadstairs, once they were there, was all wrong too.

"There's no quiet here," he moaned. "There's no privacy."

He could not even wait about until the subrental was taken care of. The need for quiet and privacy drove him off, almost at once, to search it on the Isle of Wight, in the company of Kate, Georgy, the servants, and eight children. They ran into Thackeray on the way, who reported in London that he had met them, "all looking abominably coarse and vulgar and happy."

The Isle of Wight, Charles was writing to all and sundry as soon as they arrived, was the quietest place imaginable. He had converted a waterfall on the grounds into a shower bath a hundred and fifty feet high. "Do come, if it's only for a few days. You would find it wonderfully restful."

John Leech came, and hired a cottage nearby. Mark Lemon came and the children leaped upon him. "Oh, Uncle Porpoise, stay the summer, do!" Sooner or later, most of the faithful came.

And still, despite the quiet situation and the friendly company, Charles did not feel like himself.

The strange, shaky trembling in his arms and legs was peculiarly unpleasant. On some days, he had to sit down to brush his hair, and the weight of the brush made his hand ache. He marveled that nobody appeared to notice his condition. He took naps. Even in company he sometimes had to struggle to keep awake. Indeed, it was only at night that sleep went out of him, and left him tense and jangling until the dawn.

There was no reason for it! True, the first numbers did not sell quite so well as *Dombey* had, but he felt no urge to bait the hook afresh, as he had with *Chuzzlewit*. It went as it must, even the wildest strokes of invention sprung from the living root. It was fiction, but far more true than the autobiography that he had started — and destroyed, thank God. No, he had no doubts of the book; he was not so much of a fool, ill though he felt.

And still, the fatigue, the depression of the nerves, the curious, tense lassitude grew worse and worse. He had not felt so ill even when he made that abrupt change from the exhilarating high altitudes of the Grand St. Bernard to the edge of Lake Leman.

Lake Leman: But of course! Clearly, he could not shake off the fatigues of the winter because of this island air. Why it was obvious, now that he thought of it; one could see that even Georgy and his friends also felt its depressing effect to some extent. Yes, all of them.

Except, thank God, for the children. Their clatter and unending, joyful racketing made the whole difference, on the worst days, between nervous discomfort and downright meaningless panic, like being out of one's head.

Even when the hairbrush weighed heaviest, he could feel quite rested and well while he and Charley instructed Wally in the noble art of cricketing. And on the few occasions when he could summon the initial energy to give a magical show and become the unparalleled necromancer Rhia Rhama Roos, to their rapture and the awe of every child who lived for miles about, he felt well for a day or two.

Charles rocked the moon-faced monster. He communed with Speck, he sang, told tales, played games. He said, in a voice of awful judgment, "Wally, you did not hang away your coat! Katey, compare the state of your dresser drawers with Mamie's and ask yourself if you cannot do far better."

Katey, one day, only turned away her head, pretending not to hear him.

Charles said, "Dear little girl, Papa only wants to see you grow up without untidy habits that will make everyone else unhappy."

Unexpectedly, Katey rushed at him and pounded him with her fist.

It was such a small, inefficient fist that Charles laughed, in spite of himself. "Why, Lucifer Box, what's this?"

She raised the small, amazing face in which Kate's earliest beauty was transformed by vivid, passionate intelligence. Her eyes were glazing. Her voice sobbed, but with rage.

"I love my Mama! I don't care, I do, I do!"

Charles was bewildered. "To be sure you do, pet. We all do. Katey, sweet, don't cry! Papa's own dear, don't cry!"

"You wicked girl!" cried Mamie. "Hitting Papa. Hitting our *Papa!*"

Katey hit Mamie too, and ran away to hide in the shrubbery.

Katey was one of those unfortunates who always fall in love with their eyes open. She loved her father desperately. And though she was not old enough to understand what she felt and saw that summer, she knew hate when she felt it in the air.

As Charles did not.

Through the whole summer on the Isle of Wight, Charles spoke to Kate with automatic courtesy as void of feeling as if she had been a stranger. He fell asleep, night after night, empty alike of any impulse to touch her or to withdraw from her; when he could sleep at all, that is. On other nights he lay beside her as if she were not there.

And by day or night he did not so much as notice that it was so. His heart had gone into the life of David Copperfield. Ahead, to the knowledge that Dora, the child-wife would die.

David would love her; he would be defeated in his hopes of forming her young mind, of finding companionship. And Dora, with all her pretty, empty-headed rigidity, was doomed. David would walk out of the book and away, down the long road to the final darkness with Agnes at his side. Agnes, Dora's sister; his angel, with her finger ever pointing upward.

Past the depressing effects of island air, past David's early youth with its fantastic cloud of witnesses, Micawber, Steerforth, Aunt Betsey Trotwood, Mr. Dick, yes, past that touching deathbed on which poor little Dora breathed her last, Charles's heart raced on to its consummation of peace; to Agnes, Agnes.

A stout, short-winded, dim, complaining, clutter-spreading mother of eight who went by the name of Catherine was, to all intents and purposes, not there.

Indeed, she had vanished so efficiently that Charles always remembered that summer as a period in which he and Kate had got on remarkably well. And little Katey, too, forgot her first sufferings from the fierce, bright, two-edged insight which was her own form of genius. She remembered Rhia Rhama Roos, and the pudding that he cooked in a top hat, leaving the hat like new; but nothing more.

And, back in town, Charles told himself that the holiday itself had also done him good in a way that he had not recognized at the time. For the spring had snapped back wonderfully, he was full of energy. In no time, he was engaged in half a score of varied undertakings at once, with time and strength to spare for friends, the family, *Copperfield*, everything!

"Thank God," he cried, "I feel like myself at last!"

✳ 3 ✳

THE WATSONS came to London occasionally, and it was always a joy to see them. Betweentimes, they sent Kate flowers from the Rockingham conservatory, and venison from the Rockingham preserve. Invariably, when they came, they talked of a good, leisured visit to recapture all the old pleasures of Lausanne. And always, Charles was up to the ears in something or other, and it never quite came off. It was in November after their summer on the Isle of Wight that Charles, Kate, and Georgy first went to Rockingham.

Somehow, despite the flowers and venison, Charles had always pictured the Watsons at home in a large, chintzy-cheery country house, its name a smiling tribute to long ownership and good county family.

The reality of Rockingham Castle quite took his breath away. It also filled him with a sweet, unlikely sense of homecoming. Portcullisses, great, shadowy, candlelit, firelit, galleried hall, twenty-four servants and all, Rockingham was both breath-taking and right, familiar, good. It set the Watsons' easy, unmannered warmth in a new perspective, and still he had never felt more deeply akin to them, either.

It was, in fact, a kind of falling in love; it was snobbery, but a snobbery blessed by poetry. Charles did not forget that the beauty he saw belonged to a dying world whose values he still held to have been too dearly bought; yet he saw what those values were and loved them.

Nor was his heightened love for the Watsons a base respect of persons; with *Dombey*, Charles had arrived, and his friends were where he found them. The Brave, little Louis Roche, had died that year; Charles visited the hospital steadily, wrote long letters in French, and at the end wept not for a servant, but a bright human spirit, another kinship.

No, Charles loved the Watsons more for being a part of Rockingham, and Rockingham for being beautiful.

And Mary Boyle for being Mary Boyle.

The Honorable Mary Boyle was Mrs. Watson's niece, and, if anything, a little older than Mrs. Watson. She was a small, fair woman, her gestures had a quicksilver grace, her voice was flexible and musical, and she might have been gross, swarthy, and awkward for all Charles would have cared after that first gay evening in which she became at once his mock inamorata, and his true, lifetime friend.

She had, in fact, much of Mrs. Watson's sensitive intelligence — without Mrs. Watson's handicap of being a living symbol of happy marriage. She was also a born actress, full of that fluid empathy which the outsider will always see as something sentimental or dishonest, but which another actor recognizes, in leaping kinship, at first glance.

At first glance, Charles and Mary Boyle were friends.

If Charles remembered little of that first joyful evening at Rockingham, it was only because he could, so soon, scarcely remember a time when Rockingham and the Watsons and Mary Boyle had not been integral parts of his life, and all inseparable.

The Rockingham theatricals were born that night, too, when Charles and Mary Boyle put on a scene from *The School for Scandal* for their audience of four, and followed it up with a hilarious ad-libbed performance as Mrs. Nickleby and her madman suitor flinging the cucumbers.

Next morning, Kate did not go down to breakfast. She ate a few sweets with her morning tea, and told Charles that she had a headache.

Georgy ran upstairs to her, as soon as she had breakfasted herself. "Ah, you've dressed, you're feeling better."

"I'm not. I thought they'd never get to bed last night."

"Oh, what a pity! Why didn't you slip away, dear? Mrs. Watson is so understanding, and in this huge house you'd have been quiet as if they were all asleep."

"Twenty-four servants! For two people with three children! It's ridiculous."

"Oh, Kate, no. This house is like a castle in a fairytale!"

"Yes, with that silly old maid for the fairy queen."

"Miss Boyle? She's only lively, Kate. She's very sensible to talk with. Isn't it droll, her being Mrs. Watson's niece!"

"Mrs. Watson has aged, or I should say, begun to show her age shockingly. She'd be pleasanter company if she realized it. I daresay it's hard to come to an age when one's so *obviously* far older than her husband. I daresay I should have pitied her last night, and that Miss Boyle, too — some old maids never give up hope! — but I was too scandalized. Do they really think they pass themselves off for young women?"

"Dear Kate, your headache must be very bad. You like Mrs. Watson, you know you do! Did you feel too ill to enjoy anything, last evening? Not even the theatricals?"

"Would you enjoy seeing your husband behave like an idiot before all those servants?"

"Dear, if having servants meant that one had to behave like an undertaker's mute, who could bear to be rich? Truly, it was only your headache. I still ache from laughing at Charles. How does he do it with only his eyes and his hands? Miss Boyle, too. Both of them sixty if a day, mad as hatters — you could even *see* those cucumbers!"

"Everyone to her own tastes, I daresay."

"Mercy, you are in the glooms." Georgy looked into the fire. "I wonder why Miss Boyle never married? She must have been a wonderfully pretty girl, she's still pretty. I was surprised when she dropped something out quite easily, I forget just what, but it told me that she was in her late thirties, at least. I should never have guessed it; blondes are usually so quick to show their years."

"I see nothing remarkable in her lack of success. Girls with more aristocratic notions than money are always setting their sights too high and losing what opportunities they might have had."

Georgy got up and went to the window. She looked down into the garden for several minutes. Then she said, "It occurred to me, last night, that perhaps she fell in love with someone who was not free, and never got over it."

"No wonder you're always reading your silly novels! Sometimes I think that you have the mind of a fifteen-year-old child!"

Georgy did not answer.

Kate's next words came in a voice of such concentrated venom that she was startled.

"And I daresay you also enjoyed watching Charles and her pretend to flirt and be smitten with each other? I'm sure you found that *highly* dignified?"

Georgy was so startled that her answer burst from her before she could check it. "You don't deserve to have him so in love with you! Don't you ever know when he's serious and when he's playing at a game? With someone who likes to laugh, like him? A friend?"

And Kate burst into tears, sobbing into her hands with the abandon of a small child.

"Kate, darling Kate, I didn't mean it, Kate . . ."

But to her amazement, Kate's first, wailing words showed that she had not heard her, really; that she had been already lost in her own unhappiness.

"They were different, in Lausanne, they were different! I hate this house, I hate it, hate it! Ohhh . . ."

Georgy went to the bed and sat down on the edge of it. She studied the palms of her hands. At last she said, "Hush, dear, if the servants were to hear you, what would they think?"

She had hit the right note. Kate was quiet at once.

If Kate never liked the Watsons so well after she saw Rockingham, she had a point. It was a friendlier world than Lady Holland's drawing room; and its very friendliness deprived her of protective coloration. Grand settings always made her feel inadequate, but she could do quite well as Dickens's wife when the part demanded only a handsome dress and an uninvestigated silence. Rockingham, by being kindlier, was less kind.

She was alien to Rockingham, and it showed; Charles loved Rockingham, and she knew it. Her sense of inadequacy was overwhelming, and her jealousy a torment.

It was of the friendly, gay, kind, tactful, and utterly excluding world of Rockingham that she was jealous. Though she had phrased her jealousy of Mary Boyle in the age-old language of sexual jealousy, it was only because she had no other language at hand for it. The jealousy was only part and parcel of her jealousy of Rockingham.

In a strange way, it might even have been easier to bear if Miss Boyle had been young, with a high-arched instep, or an opulent bosom and a tiny waist, or a wealth of raven tresses; a gleam in a husband's eye is painful, but at least one knows where it hurts, what one lacks, how one is outclassed. Rockingham permitted of no such simple analysis.

Even the size of the house and the extent of the grounds and the number of servants were not what mattered; Kate mocked at them, but it did not really ease her heart.

What mattered was the secret language, so friendly in tone always, and still so incomprehensible. Whether the talk was deep and dull or childish and nonsensical — and it jumped from the one to the other without warning — one always had the feeling of missing something. And not only cleverness, something else.

It eluded her completely. She did not know what it was that she was missing, but she felt intensely that Charles loved it, and blamed her for not having it, too.

And she could only translate; and translate inaccurately.

"Hurt and insulted;" she had said once. Now she said, "Snobbish and silly." And, oddly, though she felt no sexual jealousy for Mary Boyle, her jealousy of every pretty young girl who brought a casual kindling to Charles's face began, from that first visit to Rockingham, to become not simply an enduring discomfort but an obsession.

Charles was vexed that she enjoyed Rockingham so little and that she concealed the fact so badly. On the way home he permitted himself some tactless words on the subject, which he regretted immediately, and set himself to erase as best he could.

His method of erasure was far from unusual; so far, indeed, that one might almost have called it coincidence that little Dora Annie, number nine, was born in August of that crowded year — a year which was the first of four so crowded that the imagination blinks at them.

Certainly few people in history have managed four years which contained so few minutes in which they were not being, as Charles put it, actively useful. He was quite determined to love Kate as she was, and ask no more.

Even a more intelligent and less unstable woman might have found it rough and lonely going.

* 4 *

THE NOTION of starting a magazine had been simmering for months, and by January, when the preliminary work was done, it had developed into a bold and unusual enterprise: a popular monthly founded upon the assumption that the public has intelligence, taste, and a native sense of responsibility.

In W. H. Wills, Charles found the perfect assistant for a work which remained only second in importance to his novels as long as he lived.

Wills was literal, humorless, drab. He was so thin that Charles said that he slept in a flute case. He never saw Charles's jokes; in response to Charles's waves of ebullience, depression, righteous or unrighteous anger, he only nodded, seriously, and went ahead with his work. And he gave Charles a dedicated loyalty which Charles repaid with love.

From the first, the magazine was overwhelmingly popular.

"We must never waste fire on the irremediable," he told Wills. "When we sight a possible cure for a specific ill, we shall fire away. But no fruitless unpleasantness, no fruitless grief. And no fiction that shocks or distresses, unless it also lifts the heart by being a work of art. Why dissipate our readers' energies in a sterile gloom, or alienate support that our causes need? But, Wills, remember that the age of patrons is over, thank God, and literature will receive its overdue freedom and dignity from the hands of the common man. Never forget that, Wills, and respect it, God bless you."

Wills gave a small, dry clearing of the throat and said, "Yes, Mr. Dickens. I follow you."

And Charles was neither embarrassed nor let down. He said, "You're a godsend, Wills"; and that was that.

Household Words was no part-time undertaking. Charles was vigorous editor, talent scout, idea man and steady contributor to an astounding combined *Ladies' Home Journal, Yale Review,* and left-wing *Time;* a magazine as unthinkable as it was unthinkably successful.

With Miss Coutts's Home, and *Copperfield,* and all the demands that went with London life, and the children, and the family — Fred, needing money as soon as he married, for one thing, and Shrimp, married, too, and promptly proving himself a cut from the same bolt — Charles felt adequately busy for ten months.

But in November, *Copperfield* was done. Done, and at the thought Charles did not know whether to laugh or to cry. Done, and to stand for generations; he knew it. Done, and leaving him feeling as if he had sent some part of himself into the shadowy world. Done — and leaving a damnable emptiness.

When Bulwer asked him to come to Knebworth and put on a play, Charles leaped at the invitation.

No place could have been less like Rockingham than the showy opulence of Knebworth; and Bulwer, heavens! his curls and his monumental, villainous nose, and his brocaded dressing gowns, and his Turkish water-pipe which he smoked, reclining on a heap of pillows! But, on the other hand, how good he was! No drop of jealousy, though he was the butt of so many jealousies, and always giving someone who needed it a little encouragement, a little money; he didn't talk of it, but one heard.

Fetch him a play for the Knebworth holidays? Charles would fetch him a play that would knock them in the eye!

They must hire a hall, rehearse it in London. And Kate must have a part. Since little Dora came she was falling more and more into a way of moping on the edge of things. She couldn't act, to be sure, but a walk-on, a few lines, wouldn't hurt a good production.

"It's short, dear, you could learn it easily and it would be a great help to me. Will you? Bulwer would be so pleased."

She was unexpectedly, touchingly eager.

She said, "I have an excellent memory you know. I hope it won't call for many *expressions?*"

She did, in fact, learn it with ease. However, at first rehearsal she managed, somehow, to fall through a trap door. Her ankle was badly sprained. Mrs. Macready took the part.

Charles was as vexed as most people who are frustrated in a kindness. The play, however, went wonderfully well.

It kept Charles busy until it was almost Christmas, Charley's Twelfth Night party, and another splurge of the delightful Rockingham variety of theatricals, all fun and nonsense.

Mary Boyle had the lead in *Used Up.* She wore yellow, as the country lass; her cool little stage kisses were oddly endearing. After that, they were never Mr. Dickens and Miss Boyle again, but Jo and Meery, and their meetings and partings were always a light stage kiss, wholly playful, wholly undisturbing, and still moving, and sweet.

One could talk to Meery almost as one had with Forster, when he was young. The fact that she was a woman somehow made it easier, not harder. It was good to have a woman for a friend.

The Watsons were in joyful spirits, too, during that visit. And, in the play, they had the unselfconscious verve of people at after-dinner charades. Georgy, too, covered herself with glory, and Charley, on holiday from Eton, played a liveried servant boy. The twenty-four servants were invited to attend, forgot their place beautifully, and shouted like all the visiting neighborhood.

[*328*]

"In Heaven," Charles said as they were starting back to town, "we'll have theatricals for every night of eternity."

Charley cheered. Kate pretended not to hear. Her face wore the puffy, reddish look that it had begun to get more and more often in the last year.

For some time after he got back to town Charles felt at odds with himself, though London was full of people and tasks, with scarcely an idle minute in a day. It was hard to understand.

He complained of it in his bread-and-butter letter.

"What a thing it is that we can't always be innocently merry and happy without looking out at the back windows of life. Well, one day — after a long night, perhaps — the blinds on that side of the house will be down forever, and nothing left but the bright prospect in front. . . . Ever, dear Mrs. Watson . . ."

It was like a gift from heaven when Bulwer had his inspiration. There should be a national endowment, a Guild of Literature and Art; if Bulwer gave part of his lands for a group of rent-free cottages and a permanent fund were established, there would be no problem of what to do for men like Knowles, old John Poole, Leigh Hunt. Artists of proven merit could be assured a life worthy of their achievements.

Ah, such a worthy project! And such a certain success, for Bulwer was making it a present of his new comedy, not yet produced. Yes, think of that, Kate, Georgy — London and the provinces with a slap-up new Bulwer comedy, *Not So Bad As We Seem!*

And what a fortunate time for Bulwer to have thought of it — *Copperfield* done, the new book still only a vague, vague haunting, nothing in hand but the magazine and a handful of charities and committees.

"Ah," Charles was saying shortly, "what a difference it makes to a man's spirits to be *fully, usefully* occupied!"

In February, little Dora became dangerously ill with congestion of the brain. There were convulsions and high fever, and she was so tiny, so helpless.

On the night she was at last out of danger, Charles said to Georgy, "She was the ninth, you know. It took this to make me know how much I loved her."

Kate, for the last weeks, had complained of headaches and giddiness, and kept to her room. The doctor had thought it best to spare her any knowledge of the baby's danger. But when the worst was over, Charles tried to tell her what the situation had truly been.

He said, "I should not have listened to the doctor, Kate. I should have let you share the suffering, too, as you would have wanted to, her mother. Not only the joy. Oh, dearest, I've been in such a pointless rushing about, of late. I only saw it when she . . . Dora . . . Oh, my darling, do you know, really know how much I love you?"

Kate drew away.

She said, "Even when you have your wonderful new play to be theatrical about, do you have to make scenes and exaggerate even a poor little child's illness? You may enjoy being morbid and hysterical, but I do not."

Charles went out to walk.

That night he said to Georgy, "I must get away from this wretched town for a few days, or I shall explode!"

He took a little spin to Paris with Leech. They ran into D'Orsay, who was looking ill, old, and pitifully meaningless. Changed, terribly changed, since the gay time of *Nickleby*, poor D'Orsay. Not that growing younger is a common habit with any of us, God be merciful . . .

"What a good jaunt we've had!" he said to Leech, heartily. "I'm remade. I even feel my new book looming close!"

It was odd, but almost as soon as he had said it, it was so. A book with all England's present for its world, a sweep to take in every part of it, from Rockingham to that vile, haunting slum, Tom-All-Alone's. The essential good in the human individual shown against the essential rottenness in the whole organized fabric of government, law, church.

It would come. One need not press and search; only always, throughout the fullest day, keep some separate, listening ear to the wind, some waiting inner sense alert. It would come.

But, Lord, what full, full days. How fast the time went, it was nearly March. If only Kate . . .

Kate was not well. Blood to the head, more giddiness, more weakness, and the doctor could find no reason for it. And her condition was disturbing in other ways, too. There was nothing new that one could actually lay his hand upon; but the familiar clumsiness and stumbling were strangely exaggerated, her normal vagueness of speech was more and more of an incoherent wandering.

And still, Charles reassured himself, it was not really new. Ever since that year in Italy, she had sometimes taken mysterious protracted fits of weeping, hinting at imagined neglects, half hinting at imagined unfaithfulness.

It was not new. It was always a miserable thing for them both when it attacked her, but it was not new. One did not like to remember their last visit to Rockingham — Meery and Mrs. Watson so gentle with her, so kind, so obviously bewildered and frightened by her strange, flushed face, her silences.

One did not like to remember, but he did. That warm, good moment when Meery smiled at him across the laughing, talking circle and suddenly exclaimed, "Dear Jo, you can always make me feel that this is a good world, after all. Ah, and that I'm one of its better features, bless you. What old, comfortable friends we've all come to be in so short a time, less than a year."

And Mrs. Watson laughed. "It's longer, Mary. Happiness goes faster than we think for, doesn't it?"

When they went upstairs that night, Kate cried until at last he imagined that in some unthinkable way she must be jealous, and when he questioned her, so gently, so reassuringly, she laughed as incomprehensibly as she had wept.

"Of those old things? I think I know your tastes, by now! Jealous of them? Ha . . .ha . . ."

It was all too strange to bear much thinking of. And for her sake even more than for his own, it was obvious that the best thing to do was to keep as cheerful, matter-of-fact, and busy as possible. Thank God, at least he did not want for employment these days! He could have been ten men and still busy if the play were to have the stupendous success it must to lay the foundations for the Guild of Literature and Art.

Charles kept busy, steadily. On an inspiration he took the swashbuckling step of asking the Duke of Devonshire to hold the opening performances in his town house, and to invite Her Majesty and the Court to attend.

"It's colossal impudence," he told his friends. "I've only said how-do-you-do to him once or twice in crowded drawing rooms, but he seems such a dear, deaf old boy, I'm risking it. After all, at worst he can only refuse."

The Duke did not refuse. He was enchanted. He knew that Her Majesty would be most graciously pleased. He himself looked forward to knowing Mr. Dickens better.

"Glory!" Charles shouted when the letter came. "Georgy, Georgy, come here, listen! Glory! Oh, glory to the Guild, to all who love it and above all to the Owdacious Inimitable!"

He was answered, not by Georgy, but by screams; dreadful, insane, heart-stopping screams from the upper hall.

For fully ten seconds Charles stood quite still and thought without emotion, But I knew it. She has gone mad and I watched her going mad. I knew it. I would not, but I did. My wife is mad.

Then, with a convulsive start like one waking, he leaped up the stairs crying out, "Kate, Kate, my darling, I love you, oh, my darling, be still, I love you. Oh, Kate, my poor Kate."

The hysteria had passed before the doctor came. Kate lay upon the bed, under a canopy of crinoline caught up so as to overarch and not to fall upon her legs, sprawled wide apart. Her face was thickly heavy, like the face of a woman drugged. Her eyes were open, and her head turned toward him, but their look was dead — or, rather, as if it stopped at a blank screen set between her face and his.

She would not speak, not even to the doctor when he came.

And still Charles knew, and did not know how he knew, that she had not gone mad; and that she would not.

The next day he began, by post, to arrange with Dr. Wilson, a specialist in nervous disorders, who administered a cold water cure at Malvern. The doctor, with almost fulsome eagerness, invited Mr. Dickens and his wife to consider his home their own.

Charles explained that Kate's nervous ailment had long been heightened by visits to other houses. She fancied strange dislikes to them; for the sake of the cure she must not dislike Malvern, too.

No, they would take a house. He thanked Dr. Wilson, but he knew that it would be better so.

❋ 5 ❋

Dr. Wilson made his diagnosis. Kate's nerves were badly diseased, but there was absolutely no disease of the brain. The confusions, incoherencies, depressions, and strange fancies were wholly due to an illness which affected the nervous system.

The treatment was simplicity itself. Regular hours, cold water, fresh air, exercise, and cheery conversation. "And a good iron tonic with a little strychnia is also invaluable in these disorders. And there you are! In a matter of weeks, a new little woman, stronger than ever."

Charles accepted Dr. Wilson's words like an absolution. It had taken him long to admit that Kate had failed him; that life had used her to cheat him of something, God knew what, that he might otherwise have had. That he might also have failed Kate had come to him as a quite new and altogether terrible thought.

But, yes, certainly, he could see now that it had been irrational anguish; for her unfortunate disposition was hereditary, and now her nerves, too, had become diseased.

The absolution set Charles free to feel a tenderness for Kate almost like that he felt for his children. He could even get through four productive days of editorial work, letter writing for Miss Coutts's charities and the play, there, each week, at Malvern; for he could be objective. He could meet with tenderness that cold upwelling of hate which came out of her to fill and chill the room in which they sat, Kate staring, silent, Charles careful never to write for too long without a smile, a friendly easy word or two, as if little Mamie had taken a fit of the glooms, or Lucifer Box in one of her furious moods sat beside him, needing cheer and love.

"Was it Anne who arranged your hair so prettily, or did you think of it by yourself? Did you know, you're quite Dr. Wilson's favorite patient. He's so proud that you're getting on so famously . . ."

And still it could not be denied that after four days of Malvern, three of London were an immeasurable refreshment and liberation.

"Ah, Georgy," he would say, "my dear little housekeeper, it is so good to be at home."

Yet in those scant half-weeks a certain discontent began to attach itself to Devonshire Terrace, too. A man with nine children growing up, and all of them home for the holidays, at least, for years to come, needed a larger house. He should start looking about. And, while he was at it, for one with a suitable room for theatricals. The children would love to have plays of their own, properly staged and lighted, real plays with real audiences.

He mentioned the need to Angela Coutts one day when he went to tea.

"Theatricals for your children, too? Mr. Dickens, I must be honest with you. Even for the sake of our long friendship I cannot pretend that I do not deplore this passion that you have for acting."

He smiled affectionately at the grave, noble-featured face. There were a few lines at the eyes, now, but how well she aged! A pure heart does more for beauty than any actress can get from her paint-pots, after a certain number of years.

"But, dear Miss Coutts, since the Queen does not share your dis-approval, you will make one of her company? I should be truly sad if you did not."

"Thank you. Now tell me how Mrs. Dickens does. This country rest gives you both such a happy opportunity to be together, does it not?"

Kate had been at Malvern for ten days when the Governor fell ill. There was an obstruction in the urinary tract which made immediate operation necessary. And without chloroform; it was too great a risk to use chloroform in so dangerous an operation on a man of his age.

He had not been looking well. Not — when was it, good God, could it have been a month ago that they had lunched together? Kate's illness, the play, the magazine, the welter in general sent time along so fast; so much too fast.

Poor Governor, Charles thought. God take care of him, he's kept within his income too well of late for his own good or for mine. A man can be so busy that it takes a bit of illness or bad behavior from his very dearest to catch his attention. Oh, yes, dear God, yes . . . they must fetch my Dora downstairs now for her kiss, before I go to the Governor.

Dora came down laughing in her nurse's arms, reaching out to him as soon as she saw him.

"Ah, Papa's gayest one! Nurse, if I'm not here at the children's bedtime, tell them that I'm with their grandpapa who is very ill."

The operation was over and the room not yet cleaned of blood when he arrived. It was a shambles, a slaughterhouse.

"Governor, are you in much pain now?"

"Dear Charles. Less than this, ah, dramatic setting would indicate."

And he smiled, and put out his hand. Charles caught it, and kissed him.

John Dickens could not talk after that. He closed his eyes and lay still, his lips working until he dropped off into exhausted sleep.

It had not gone as badly as the doctor feared. Charles quieted his mother as best he could, trying to pity her torrential talking. He went back to the Governor's bed. Asleep, the Governor looked only like a sad, fat old stranger.

But all through the crowded hours after he had left him, Charles still saw the smile, the extended hand; heard that single gallant flourish of words.

He asked Forster to eat lunch with him. Forster was in the play — and loud and bad in it — but Charles needed to see him alone. He had never told anyone else about his childhood.

And still, except for a curt summary of the situation and a cheery diagnosis, he could say nothing of what he wanted to say until the end of the meal, and the actual words, when they came, took him by surprise.

"Forster, I keep remembering those walks we used to take in Chatham. He was everything admirable, gallant, generous, magnificent. I don't know. Perhaps that was when I was dead to rights about him. Perhaps children are part of the Kingdom because they aren't fools. Perhaps what we come to call wisdom is only confusion."

It had been a long time since Charles had said anything so completely up Forster's alley. Yet he was not gratified by the suffusing of the square, flat face, the immediate response of sentimental tears.

In fact, he did not see it. He had forgotten that Forster was there.

The fever set in the next day. On the day after that, it was clear how the tide ran.

His father did not talk of it. He was not like Fan. Yet the courage remained, so few sounds of suffering, and again and again the fine-lipped smile flickering in courteous denial of pain and death. At last he sank into a coma.

Charles held the unconscious hand through the long night.

The Governor . . . My father . . . God, be good to him. Lives, made by lacks, and gifts, and accidents. Up on the table, to sing for the company. He loved to see me there, he's loved it since and forgiven me what it costs in haste, in neglect, inattention . . . God, forgive me, too . . . God, forgive us all . . . Let him go quietly. Not like Fan, quietly . . . quietly . . .

John Dickens died at dawn. There was no death struggle. He died as Mary had died; at one moment the hand in Charles's hand was alive, warm and relaxed in sleep, and then, oh, so quietly he was dead.

Charles kissed the dead hand and laid it down. He had the doctor take his mother away to be quieted with a sleeping drug.

He thought, When I have gone to Highgate and bought the ground, I must go to Malvern. Kate need not come to the funeral. Oh, pray God she will not talk about him. He did so well, before the end. He liked the *Daily News*, he liked that little position of authority . . .

God, please let Kate say only kind things of him.

Kate, in point of fact, was sympathetic. She wept and said, "How hard for you, so soon after poor Fan. At least, Charles, you have nothing to reproach yourself with."

She also said, "It's too much to hope, I daresay, that your brothers will share the support of your mother, but at least she can live with one of the girls."

That night Charles wrote a long letter to Mary Boyle, a letter that told her a great deal about his father, and about his childhood. And about his father's last years, and how he had faced death, and died, so quietly.

When he had finished it, he read it through, and tore it up.

❀   *6*   ❀

THE DUKE was prompt in telling Her Majesty of the necessary postponement.

Charles said to the cast, "In the meantime, we must not spare ourselves. We desperately needed a little more time."

Household Words also needed a striking, timely piece. A night at Scotland Yard . . . excellent possibilities there. Fact, drama, emotion, all three. "Wills, we must find time to . . ."

No, no, the Queen *could* not object to professional actresses playing in a private house; it was fantastic! After all, she went to the theater without qualms. So, here goes another letter: "My Lord Duke." Let him explain to Her Delicate Majesty that Mrs. Compton is a lady of the purest character. Pure as the snow! Every woman connected with the enterprise a nun, a lily maid!

What rush, what pressures, and always back and forth between London and Malvern. Mid-April already, and still so much to do! And tonight the dinner for the General Theatrical fund. First, home to see the children, and to change. Then the dinner, and back to the office at *Household Words* for an hour or two. No time to breathe, these days!

Mamie and Katey were in the drawing room with Georgy. He paused for a moment to kiss them all. "Did you remember your letter to Wally, girls? He still gets homesick, you know."

He ran upstairs to the nursery. The five little ones were waiting for their story and their prayer. Dora, too, was wide awake in her cradle. He swung her to the ceiling, singing, "Mamie's the good one and Katey's the beauty, but Dora's the Dora and Papa's own love." She crowed with delight.

Charlotte said, "Ah, she's brightened up, now. She was dullish this afternoon, sir. I made sure as she was taking a cold, but see her now, the love, bright as a penny!"

"She's the gay one," Charles said. "She's the one who'll be the companion for her Papa's spirits and foolishness."

His after-dinner speech was extremely moving, and he knew it. He was vexed when he saw a servant hand a message to Forster, halfway through it, and Forster bend his head, studying it. He hated to lose even one bit of his audience. With intensified fervor, he gave himself to the rest of the company. Their eyes watered like his own as he spoke of the players who come from their own griefs, from sickbeds, yes, even from death itself to bring the audience their nightly gift of laughter and of tears. He forgot Forster, giving the words he read everything.

When he finished, there were cheers.

But Forster had risen and come around the table to him. He took his arm, and said, "Come. Macready will explain for us, I've told him. Come, your baby. Dora."

Dora had died in convulsions while the dinner was going on.

Forster rode home with him. Charles sat with his head bowed, trying to believe it. Forster did not speak, and he was grateful.

As the carriage turned in at Devonshire Terrace, Charles said, "The children will be frightened. When she was so ill, before, we could not keep them away. There'd always be one or two, drifted near, frightened. Death . . . Since the raven, so long ago, we've not even had a pet that died in the house." He broke off, and laughed, a flat, conversational laugh. "No, and I begin to fear that poor old Timber is immortal."

"Charles." Forster seldom used his friend's first name. "Charles."

Then, at last, Charles began to cry. "I must stay with them, for the first day. I can't leave them. Will you go to Kate? With a letter to say that our darling is gravely ill — that I have little hope. That if, when she comes I must say, 'Our darling is dead,' she . . . she will be wonderfully brave, for their sake?"

"God bless you. I'll go tonight or tomorrow, just as you will."

"Thank you. Wait, then, and I'll give you the letter."

Georgy opened the door to them. She caught Charles's arms in her hands, hiding her face against him. Her body was racked with her sobbing.

"Oh, Charles, Charles . . . without any warning . . . that little baby thing . . ."

He put her aside, gently. "Yes, Georgy. Yes, poor child."

He dropped his hat and coat upon a chair.

"Let me go up to look at her. I . . . I shan't be long."

Georgy and Forster watched him walk away from them and up the stairs. He pulled himself along by the rail, like a tired old man. His shoulders shook heavily, but he made no sound.

Then Georgy turned and looked at the chair beside her. She spoke through sobs, and still in a sound of wonder, as if at an upset of natural law too great not to amaze her even through her grief.

"Look," she said, "he didn't hang his coat away."

[338]

Kate never went back to Malvern.

Her first shock over, she was no more unstable, no more remote than she had been for many years. Since Mamie was born, really.

Indeed, she took all the words of strength and comfort that Charles had prepared for her out of his mouth and spoke them for him. Their content, so spoken, was terribly changed; it was only with the greatest effort that Charles himself could still cling to them, hearing them spoken so.

"It is sad for us, but not for her, in Heaven with Mary." Or "We have been fortunate, Charles, with such a large family. We don't know anyone else with so many who has not lost at least one."

He tried desperately to be glad that she was so brave. He tried, after a little, not to speak of it to her unless she spoke of it first. Sometimes he did, in spite of himself.

"I wish that I had never bought that vault at Highgate. Perhaps even now I could get a little plot and have her body moved. I want to think of her under earth, and growing things, and the open sky."

"Charles, how morbid! The vault is so nice, so suitable and dignified. You wouldn't do a strange thing like that?"

"Not if it would disturb you, dear. No. No."

He kissed her.

That night he lay awake, in an awful clarity of insight.

"Dora. I named her Dora. He fell in love as I fell in love with Maria . . . but it was Kate he married . . . Kate, in Furnival's Inn, with Mary. God, God. I've been unhappy, sometimes, but I've never hated Kate. God, you know that. Oh, God, if I meant that, if I'd wished that Kate had died, could I have given my little pet that name, that ill-omened name?"

The next day, mercifully, was a heavy one with the magazine. By nightfall, Charles had re-established himself in the world of necessary confusion.

He wrote to Bulwer, "Kate is as well as I could hope, speaking of it tranquilly . . . so good and amiable that I hope it may not hurt her."

Kate, alas, did not even suffer a small miscarriage as once she had done in Chalk.

"Charles," Georgy said, "you'll kill yourself for this play. I've seen you almost like this before, but never quite!"

"You've never seen me produce a play for the Queen, small person."

"I love to see you in a romantic part."

"Do you? I prefer comedy. Wait until you see the farce. The poor Queen must miss it, you know. It has to wait the public performances. At Devonshire House we close with Bulwer's final curtain."

"If you can still hobble about by then!"

"Miss 'Ogarth, after five hours rehearsin' and five more teachin' the carpenters their trade, I couldn't pull the stockin's off my legs last night. As well as not bein' known by my own children through the sawdust on me from 'ead to toe."

"Did the Queen truly send directions for which windows should be kept open and how wide?"

"She did, God save her. Never mind, it will all go off in a glory, never fear."

Charles saw to everything. The sole incident which came close to marring the opening for him was nothing that he could have foreseen, and he was able to set it to rights.

On the morning before the first performance, Kate gave such an awkward pull to one of her dressing-table drawers that its contents were scattered on the floor. Charles, bending to help her, saw a letter in Mary Boyle's hand: "Dear Mr. Dickens . . ."

He picked it up. "Kate, what is this?"

"Oh. I opened it by mistake. I . . . I felt giddy, that spinning sensation, on the day it came. I . . . I must have dropped it there when I went for my smelling salts. I forgot it."

Mary, at first, had been forced to decline. The note said that, to her delight, she had found that she could be in town after all. Only that. A brief, impersonal note asking if she might still be part of the first audience.

"I forgot it. I'm sorry, but I can't see that it particularly matters. She'll have enough opportunities to see this wretched thing before you're done with it, in all conscience."

"But, Kate . . ."

"You need not stare at me as though I were lying!"

Her face had the uneven, mottled flush that it had not taken since Dora died. Her eyes — and they were still beautiful, those thick-lidded, violet eyes — were full of the Malvern look, the confusion that was like fear, the fear that was like hate.

He smiled at her. He made his voice tender, casual, almost bored. "Darling Mouse." The old pet name came back so unexpectedly for his help. "Darling Mousie, why should I doubt it? It only slipped your mind because it was so unimportant. Perhaps Devonshire can still arrange it for her, and if not, as you say, no real harm is done."

He glanced at his watch, kissed her, and hurried off. The cold, hopeless feeling in his belly stayed there all the day. If Meery had been a pretty girl of whom Kate was jealous, he could have understood. But she had not hidden that letter in jealousy, only in meaningless, gratuitous spite. And she did not destroy it, she hid it and kept it. It was strange; it was frightening.

He tried to feel angry. Anger would have been easier to bear than that cold hopelessness; but it could not come. He could not shake off the sensation until the very moment that he walked out onto the stage, and Bulwer's comedy was being played to a delighted audience and Her Most Gracious Majesty, in the magnificent production which was so utterly, satisfyingly his own accomplishment.

The success was tremendous.

And still, blessedly, blessedly, it was only a beginning. One more performance in Devonshire House, then the public performances, then a short time by the sea, to take breath again, and then a tour that would last, in its interrupted spurts, for a year, with any luck. Yes, yes, at least a year.

The first public performance went even better than those in Devonshire House; but it was not Bulwer's play, but the farce, Lemon's farce that Charles had rewritten, which had the audience so shouting with laughter that scarcely a line of it could be heard. Which did not matter; the lines were not the joke.

For Charles played six characters, including Sam Weller and Sairey Gamp. The changes took a panting corps of precision-drilled dressers working like hysterical machines. He was never once recognized at first entrance; the shrieks, "It's Dickens again, it's Dickens!" would break out after two or three lines, and the house collapse upon themselves, drowning everything out once more.

Charles, stumbling off stage from the last wild ovation, was laughing and clapping his own hands as loudly as anyone there, while he gasped, over and over, "My name is Legion, for their h'ain't no end to the crowd of me! Legion! That's our Charlie. Legion!"

[341]

※ 7 ※

As THE SUMMER BEGAN, it felt like a long wait for autumn, and the start of the tour. The Exhibition opened in the Crystal Palace. Charles went to London, glanced inside, said, "I hate sights," and went back to the sea, the young corn, and the skylarks. But they, too, left him restless.

A young Danish girl who believed from his writings that he could help her find her way in life wrote him a letter that he tried to answer as best he could. "I am but a poor leader, who do not see myself the way that I profess to others. . . . The great commandments of our Saviour are distinct and plain. . . . Your way . . . is sufficiently clear when you admit your trying with a cheerful heart and no discouragement to regulate your life's conduct by them. . . . And . . . it will make you more merciful and gentle . . . to those who lose their way and claim your pity. . . . You sit down too soon to brood on these matters by the way. . . . Take courage and try."

And he thought, May she believe it, and do better than I.

Yet setting it down in black and white had lifted his own spirits. He began to plan a water party on the Thames for Charley and a few fellow Etonians. A hamper of Fortnum and Mason's best, and, yes, surely he could risk including that ultimate flattery of sinful, splendid, genuine champagne.

And when the party was over — a stupendous success, with no worse effects than a slight temporary glazing of a few young eyeballs — the new book began, miraculously, to crystallize out, the people, the living people come at last. Though with it, as always at the start of a book, the restlessness also grew violent, a continual vague urge to go somewhere, anywhere. Away.

It helped that he had just bought Tavistock House. A new house gives one plenty to do. And such a house, four full stories of magnificence, not counting the kitchen basements and the servants' attics! The plantings of shrubbery must be moved from Devonshire Terrace, the great mirrors set in the new walls, and more added. Then, new curtains and carpets, on a scale of awful splendor and magnitude.

The proportions of the library would be improved by disguising one door as part of a wall of unbroken bookcases, with false book-backs.

"Georgy, listen to these. *The Quarrely Review. King Henry the Eighth's Evidences of Christianity. Morrison's Pill's Progress.*"

It helped to have streams of visitors too; and to visit Chatsworth, Devonshire's country place. He went alone; Kate was not yet up to it.

And then came the agonies of moving day, with the huge house still half ready for it, and the children still at Broadstairs, and Kate wandering about, getting covered with paint and assured by the fact of being, somehow, highly useful. She was also pregnant again. Thoroughly.

At least there was the advantage that she would not try to follow him about barnstorming with the play. She still could not even pay a visit happily. One had to see the Watsons and Mary Boyle in other people's houses, and then write letters to say half of what one would have said given a little friendly quiet together.

The touring began in November. There would be a few cities organized in advance, a whole hotel hired for the company. Then away in a laughing crowd, to the knife-edged grimness before each performance, the unfailing triumph, and the gay, wild supper parties afterwards, ending usually with all the men in a game of leapfrog around the table.

And then back to London to mop the brow, slash away at *Bleak House*; to work at *Household Words*, and straighten out the problems that arose at the Home at Shepherd's Bush, and tell Miss Coutts about it — dear Miss Coutts, so unfailingly kind to Kate while he must be ever off and away again.

There were holiday parties to christen the new house, and for Charley's Twelfth Night, and a dancing party for Mamie and Katey, their first. They were old enough for that, though one still had to run up to the fourth floor every day to see that their rooms were in proper order.

He read the first issue of *Bleak House* to Miss Coutts.

"You see, dear Miss Coutts, the Guild demands less of me than you seem to believe. Yes, Kate is doing magnificently."

Except that she had so many strange, bumbling, stumbling accidents that sometimes he laughed at his guests' confusion until the tears came into his eyes. Yet she was improving. If one treated her as if she were cheerful, competent, unsuspicious, it helped her, wonderfully. The encouraging note, always. Letters, to approve of her calmness, her competence while he must be away, and the same tone preserved, continually, when he was at home.

But, my God, another child?

Ah, well, now on to Birmingham!

"Speaking strictly for the good of the play, you know," said Lemon. "I must say that I give thanks daily that John Forster's onerous tasks as editor, critic, and guardian of the public conscience keep him in town. In London, the play could stagger along with the weight of his — one can't call it acting, what can one call it? Like a family joke, you know. On the road we face the humbling thought that Dickens, here, is the only one of us with any curiosity value for the crowd. And he can act, and we can make a good stab at it."

Little Egg grinned. "Oh, *strictly* for the good of the play."

Young Wilkie Collins laughed. He was a giant, with woman's hands, tiny; an infant's round face behind small, round spectacles; his disposition was cheerful, his cynicism absolute, and his reputation with the ladies of the theater remarkably well earned.

"Forster! You've all known him for years, was he always such an overbearing ass? Galahad, Dr. Johnson, and the less endearing aspects of Jehovah? I like him, mind you, I like him, but what a stifler! Whenever I talk to him, I get the most interesting sensation, as if Her Majesty had just sat down on my face."

Charles said, "You don't know him, Collins. Forster is the kindest soul who ever lived."

He would not give voice to a disloyalty of which he was ashamed. Yes, ashamed, though there was no denying that of late years Forster grew more and more like Miss Coutts. Dear, very dear, *wholly* admirable — and still, limited. Putting one oddly on the defensive where there was nothing to defend. As if a marriage depended on the hours by the clock that a man spent in his wife's company. As if moping useless about the house would not dull any active man's affection for his wife, his tolerance, his helpful understanding!

Forster was dear to him, he always would be; but Lemon and Egg and young Collins made better comrades-in-arms for the tour. They knew the world of the theater. They knew that a touch of gallantry toward the charming professional members of the cast was no more than it appeared to be. A pleasant, innocent game.

The baby was born in March. Edward Bulwer-Lytton. Charles said to Lemon, "I am still not sure that I wanted him, but, objectively considered, he's a fine boy."

The sales of *Bleak House* were enormous, far outstripping *Dombey*. The magazine was running easily. Life was too quiet, for a little. The restlessness came back. There would not be another tour for months; Kate was still abovestairs and entertaining must still be of the most casual, informal sort; every committee he sat upon ran with an appalling smoothness. There was no fight in anything, nothing that took half of his energies. Miss Coutts needed no persuading to his plan for clearing a slum and rebuilding it rationally; he was thankful, genuinely, deeply thankful to see it done and done quickly, but her quick mind, her good heart, her vast wealth made the whole task so easy.

He walked out to Highgate one afternoon to see that the Governor's grave was being tended properly. He went into the vault that held little Dora's body in its prison, while the quiet graves outside lay green, under the sky, the sun, the rain.

As he walked home, his face was drawn. He looked, for once, older than his forty years.

A prison . . . Is anyone unchanged, who has been kept in a prison? Yes, the Governor, I thought that something had gone out but it had not, it was unextinguishable. . . . "This, ah, dramatic setting." The hand, the smile. So quietly, thank God, like Mary . . . not like Fan. Dora, the Governor, one after the other. "So dignified, suitable. You wouldn't do a strange thing like that?" "At least, Charles, you have nothing to reproach yourself for." Ah, no, but she does her best as we all do. I'm only unfair when I'm idle, idle, half used.

He made himself walk faster, throwing back his head, squaring his shoulders. We all have griefs and joys, satisfactions and discontents. We choose whether we shall be happy or unhappy on our way. We choose. We choose.

When he came home he said to Kate, "Dear, I'm accepting Mrs. Watson's invitation for a little visit to Rockingham. Georgy can keep you cheery, here, just as she has while I've been off with the plays. It's not only unfair to our friends, dear, it's unfair to you, to encourage these unhappy, lonely ways. I'd rather you came with me, I'm confident, dear, that you soon will, but I believe that it would be wrong in me to wait for it."

And it was good to be at Rockingham, so good.

Mrs. Watson caught both his hands. "Oh, you dear, it's been so much too long!"

Watson hugged his shoulders. "Serpent in my bosom! Thief of my wife's heart!"

Mary Boyle came running, her arms outstretched. "Jo, faithless Jo!"

"You are here! My heart's torment, my delight!"

Laughing, all of them laughing. And still wonderfully, utterly at ease, united, glad to be together.

They forgot to ask after Kate. She drifted into the conversation only late in that evening.

"And so your wife is contesting for your laurels. We have her book here, you see."

It was true. Kate had actually written a cookery book. *What Shall We Have For Dinner*, by Lady Maria Clutterbucks. Charles had inspired the enterprise and encouraged her in it steadily until it was done. It would give her employment, pleasure, confidence. He leaked the authorship to the public and it did remarkably well.

Meery said, "Such a fascinating sidelight on your home. Do you *always* begin your dinners with milk punch, and end with toasted cheese?"

Mrs. Watson made a Gothic spire of her hands. "Ah, but he has variety as well as stability. Only think, broccoli cooked in four separate ways at one meal!"

Watson nodded, gravely. "But I'd never realized, you know, how simply one makes a rice blancmange. 'Boil a quantity of rice in a quantity of milk.' Amazing!"

"Ah, but Richard, don't underestimate our cook. The genius must be there, too. You and Landseer would strike a quantity of paint onto a quantity of canvas with very different results."

And suddenly they all looked guilty, and began to play at the new fad of analyzing character from one's handwriting.

And after that the talk was easy, almost lazy: the comfortable mutual exploration of old friendship.

"Do you ever feel . . ."

"Have you sometimes thought . . ."

"Yes, but what should you do if then . . ."

When Charles kissed Mary good night, lightly, as always, he

thought of the quiet, empty bedroom that waited upstairs with a guiltless sense of release.

"Good night, my Meery."

"Go night, Jo."

Mary was forty-two. She was as understanding a friend as he had ever made. And, oh, God, for one evening, one, it was good to be left free with the enjoyment of it!

❊   8   ❊

AND PERHAPS I was only tired, after the last tour, Charles thought. Perhaps I only needed a short holiday in the country.

For after he came back from Rockingham, life was brimful of pleasures, and demands. The baby also improved vastly upon acquaintance. Until midsummer at Broadstairs, Charles found it not at all too hard to keep in the proper mood for steadily cheering and encouraging Kate.

Watson visited him there, briefly, before he and his wife set off for a jaunt to the continent. He looked young, and wonderfully well, and he brought all Rockingham into the house with him.

He was a blessedly unobservant person. When he left he took Kate's hand and said, warmly, "How good to find you back in health again, and to know that next year you'll be with us for our Christmas theatricals."

He had turned to Georgy at once, and did not notice Kate's absence of response. And when he had gone, Charles was careful not to let himself mention it.

The next day, he had a letter from Mary Boyle. It was an amusing letter, flowing over with her quality, and it sent her love to Kate and to Georgy, but Charles decided not to read it aloud. Watson's visit had made the atmosphere unpropitious.

He answered it that afternoon, while Kate was taking a nap, and Georgy was on the sands with the children. The house was sunny and still. Poor old Timber lay across his feet, giving occasional small, arthritic groans. No more bitches, no more wars, poor old Timber; even meat bones were becoming a matter of indifference.

"Watson seemed to be holding as by a sheet-anchor to theatricals at Christmas. Then, O rapture! But be still, my fluttering heart."

Timber groaned again. Charles reached down to pat him. Suddenly, as if his fingers, touching the old dog's nearness to death, had made his own life more alive, the arch-bright, coy, laborious-charming tone went out of him. He sat quite still for an instant, listening to the silence of the house, looking at the sunlight on the floor; quiet, alive, unsure, and still open, open.

He went on with the letter, wholly unconscious of the change of tone, writing as if he had written it so from the start.

"This is one of what I call my wandering days. I seem to be looking at such times for something I have not found in life, but may possibly come to a thousand years hence. At all events, I won't put your little pastoral pipe out of tune by talking about it. I'll go and look for it on the Canterbury Road, among the bye-roads and orchards. Ever faithfully your Friend, Jo."

He did not find it on the Canterbury Road.

Charles was forty. He had fathered ten children, written nine long novels, four short ones, countless sketches and articles. He was editor of a remarkable magazine. He had more friends than most professional socialites. He made countless people think about universal suffrage, universal education, penal reform, public welfare. He administered Miss Coutts's charities with shrewdness and vision. That April had seen the erection of London's first blocks of flats, multiple dwellings for laborers; slums of tiny hovels without light, water, or sewage were considered the normal dwelling places of the city poor until Charles gave Angela Coutts the inspiration for Columbia Square.

As poor John Dickens would have said, he had, in a word, accomplished much for a man of forty.

He walked inland, past ripe fields where the skylarks shouted. He felt no pride in anything that he had done. It was hurry and accident, blundering on at top speed to more hurry and accident. He knew it, he was wide open, and the knowledge was out of keeping with his character and a threat to his fundamental creeds.

When he had walked for perhaps an hour, he suddenly stopped still in his tracks and stood with his blank face lifted to the sky.

Dora died, he thought. The Governor died. And I could not stop.

I could not let myself take time to know it. I could not even stop for them when they died.

He sat down by the roadside, and began to tug up small handfuls of grass, and toss them absently away. He was talking aloud, in a low, unemotional, uninflected voice.

"All with the best intentions, yes. Fill the moment until it's a box of clutter, serve your God with so much thumping that you can never hear the still, small voice. And don't forget to end each day with a nice little memorized prayer."

He stared before him. The wide, blue eyes, which never lost their beauty until they were closed in death, were young eyes, in a face of outworn youth. In a face still handsome, fresh-skinned, not dulled, not heavy, but somehow done for. Positively the last appearance on any stage; a new face in preparation for our next season.

Charles tugged the grasses, twelve or fifteen at a time. He threw them aside with restless, angry hands which were a life quite separate from the still young, still handsome face; the unhappy, unsure, open face.

Suddenly he said, "Oh, poor Kate. Poor Kate, my poor Kate. God forgive us all for being ourselves." And then he said, "I am tired. Tired."

And then he shook his head back, sharply.

A moment later he stood up and started homeward at a brisk stride. Before very long, he began to work his tongue behind his teeth. The wandering day was over. A new installment of *Bleak House* was shaping up.

It was a remarkable installment.

Charles's encounter with himself on the Canterbury Road had been too brief. A great deal remained to be said in the world where Charles whose name was Legion could talk to Charles who was, as young Mary Hogarth said, on a Sunday walk long past, not multi-form but an integrity: "What the people who love you love."

He thought, *Bleak House*, Lady Dedlock, Mr. Tulkinghorn . . . He thought with fury of Mr. Chadband's snivelling pieties, and with tender pity of the crossing-sweeper, Jo. He was all of them, and he was Charles, apart. The restlessness was gone. Though he did not know it, he was gentler with Kate, less blindly, brightly, appallingly kind and encouraging than he had been for a long time.

And Kate, though she could find no language in which to express it but the familiar language of self-pity, was happier for a fortnight than she had been since Mary died.

The letter from Mrs. Watson came one morning while they were at breakfast. He opened it with a smile. "Ah, news from the Continent! Shall I read it to you, dear?"

And at once he turned white and bowed his head.

Georgy cried, "Charles, what is it?"

"Watson's dead."

"What?" said Kate.

He sat still, reading the page over. Then he handed it to Georgy and said, "Read it to her, dear. I think I'll go down to the sands for a little and get myself in order. Watson. It's hard to grasp, isn't it?"

He had died of acute appendicitis, or in the language of the day, of a sudden internal inflammation. Mrs. Watson wrote to Charles first of all his friends. After the worst of the pain the end had come quietly, she said; he died in her arms.

Charles did not let himself stay too long upon the sands. He remembered vividly the selfishness of grief in which he had learned of Fan's approaching death. He came back soon to Kate, and kissed her.

"Dear love," he said, "how much we take our blessings for granted! Dear love, I want to be a good, good husband to you. Poor Mrs. Watson, in her loneliness."

Kate sighed. "Yes, it must have been a dreadful shock. But with Rockingham and all that money even a woman of her years needn't stay unmarried forever, if she'd rather not."

Charles completely refused to have heard her.

He said to Georgy, "I wish that you might have come on that last visit. It was such a happy time to remember. Such a happy time."

Five days went by before he could write to Mrs. Watson. He always wrote a beautiful letter of condolence, and she treasured the letter he wrote; but he wrote it as if he wrote to a stranger. He had loved Watson; it was long before he could think of him without tears. He loved Mrs. Watson. Yet he could not pity her grief without a strange, separate mourning, as if she, too, were dead. Past the grief for her loss, past the grief for the gay, gentlehearted friend who had abruptly, meaninglessly walked out of life lay the unworded ache of feeling that Mrs. Watson, and Rockingham, too, were dead; a friend, a marriage, and a world all gone together into the same black maw.

And strangely, like an answering bell, a letter came from Paris in that same week to say that poor D'Orsay, too, was dead. The jasmine-scented primrose-yellow gloves and the unimaginable waistcoats, and, yes, the young man who wrote *Nickleby*, too, and the new, bright world that he had marveled at — they, too, were gone off with Watson into the hungry dark.

Also, while he was still bewildered with the loving tears for Watson and the further senseless sense of loss on loss, a curious plea came from old Lady Lovelace. She had remained D'Orsay's loyal friend when many, most of his friends had fallen away, bored at last by his odd gigantism and foppery and strangely innocent, aging shabbiness of dedicated vice. Now she wrote that she, too, was dying, and would be grateful if Charles, whose writing of Paul Dombey's death had comforted her through many losses, would come to her.

How strange, how sad, how ridiculous, to be a symbol of comfort, of certain answers to all the awful unanswerable questions.

❋   9   ❋

BUT, THANK GOD, thank God, the play now took to the road for its last superlative whirl. This time Kate and Georgy came along. Georgy was ebullient, and Kate, by and large, was decently amiable. She kept too markedly apart from the actresses for strict courtesy, but luckily it passed off for shyness.

Nor really, Charles thought, could one blame her, since all of them and Mrs. Compton in particular, had bosoms and waistlines to put highly specific thoughts into any man's head.

On the final night after the final triumph, Kate only said, "Thank goodness! By now I should think that even you must be glad it's over and done with."

Charles, still panting from the farce, only laughed and said, "Not one of the six of me now present can bear the prospect!"

He spoke less to her than to those who stood about them, but he smiled at her pleasantly.

They returned to a city hung with crape. Wellington was dead, the grand old man, taking an era away with him, and the nation had flung itself into commercialized mourning, like a nation of undertakers' mutes. Greatness and death, hawked on every street corner: "Crape sleevebands, here! Sixpence while they lasts!"

At least the children loved it. Charley came down from Eton, and Charles wakened the nursery at three in the morning to get to the office of *Household Words* and let them finish their sleep on the floor while the streets were still passable. The great funeral procession passed directly below their windows.

"Your children will say, 'Tell us again how you saw Wellington's funeral.'"

Their faces were wonderful. "We should of bringed the baby," Alfred said.

Kate had not shed a tear for Watson, but she wept profusely over Wellington. She was also — perhaps on the impetus — extremely saddened when Mrs. Macready died a few days later.

"It's strange that I feel so little," Charles said to Georgy. "I really loved her. And poor Macready, only retired from the stage this year. Perhaps I'm getting used to it. What swaths the great scythe cuts all around us, when we come to be forty! Was it before you came to us, that Christmas party? Macready with the wreath on his head, Antony, and she was Cleopatra?"

"It must have been before."

But the words had brought an ease of stinging tears to his eyes, and he went away quickly, to write the letter while he still could.

"My dear friend, I have been so lighthearted with her, and have seen her ever so simply and truly anxious to be worthy of you."

Sharing your laughter, sharing your griefs.

I must tell Wills that he is *not* to pay that bill for the lace cravats that had to be replaced for the last performance until I've had time to check on it. Time! The book, the magazine, all the Guild business, that new girl that they should never have taken in at Shepherd's Bush, the holidays so near . . . And I talk of time!

Charley had decided to go into business. In January he left Eton to go to school in Germany.

January, 'fifty-three. Charley, as old as Potter was when we smoked our cigars and were so worldly-wise? Is it sixteen years since the day when Mary and I looked for the table?

Ah, Wills should have seen that we can't use this article on hereditary insanity. Purposeless. Amusement for the morbid, fear and grief for any reader who knows that the taint is in his own family. No, rejected.

We need a new tale from Collins. No depths, but what a knack. And what resilience, a real future there, once he shakes off his laziness. I'll lunch with him tomorrow, and stir him up. While he glitters behind those little round spectacles and licks his chops over his sins and speculates in courteous silence on mine, in the flattering assumption that all my obligations leave me energy to glance at a neckline, to make merry with it!

Charles smiled, but he liked Collins, increasingly. Collins was, in fact, what Potter had once fancied himself to be. His world was small, but he knew it, in and out. And he was good-natured; he saw through all he relished, yet with no diminution of appetite or zest.

Except for the spectacles and the tiny hands, his physical appearance was oddly like that of Forster in his youth; in character, one could scarcely imagine two more unlike. Collins had no pietisms, no sentimentality, no pomposities. For matter of that, he had none of Forster's genuine idealism, either, but his astringent honesty and his easy enjoyment of life made him highly refreshing company, Charles thought, in these driven days. A kind of dry champagne.

There was even something restful in his casual assumption that no married man is satisfied at home. It was false, but no more false than poor old Forster's dog-eyed romanticism; certainly it was more true than poor little Miss Coutts's melting picture of domestic bliss. Yes, it was false; he loved Kate, they really got on very well, all things considered — yet it was oddly comfortable, too. It made for a kind of ease, when one could take his ease — so seldom, in these days.

Wills fell ill in February. His eyes went bad for some months, and it left Charles with a crushing pile of work to manage singlehanded. *Bleak House* drove on; sometimes it felt like a culmination, the last novel he'd ever write, sometimes like a true beginning, the first time he'd ever known his way, but always it was urgency, urgency.

The Guild; Miss Coutts's Home; and an hour or so to be squeezed in every day for the *Child's History of England* that he was dictating to Georgy. She preened herself so upon being his little amanuensis —

she loved it. It gave her extra employment too; she was not formed for idleness herself, bless her.

Drive, rush, hurry.

Ah, but a good life, a fortunate life. What a joy the schoolroom had turned out to be, convertible to a theater! How the children had relished their first Christmas play, done in company with his friends! They must have one each year, and every child old enough to remember a line must have a part!

Rush, hurry, rush.

To Brighton for a great blow at *Bleak House*; back to town for committees, public dinners.

"Georgy, do you know how many speeches I've made this past month? Whenever they're not honoring the Inimitable, he's honoring somebody else. A vicious circle."

Early spring, late spring. Wills better, and at once a plethora of complications with the Guild. With a plagiarism suit. And old Miss Kelly was in straits again.

"Such a magnificent actress once, Georgy, such a good manager. What we did for her with the old *Every Man in His Humour* company was pitifully little. I'd no notion of how to run a benefit then, none, really. It's May, now, with the season beginning. Devonshire would be a patron, and so would the Duke of Leominster, and the Duke of Beaufort. Lord, I could draw up such a list to pack them in. 'Under distinguished patronage.' I must find a minute to stir up Lemon, for a starter. He'll help me work on the old company."

He had not foreseen Kate's reaction. Or that the reaction would grow stronger and stronger.

"Kate, Kate, try to see things reasonably! We'll be playing *only* in London. With an amateur cast, not actresses — nice young girls from good homes. It will take next to *none* of my time, I haven't much to spare as you know. I shan't be from home, you'll see as much of me as ever. Dear, do be reasonable. . . .

"Kate, stop this sulking. Oh, sweet, you'll surely not sulk with our friend Professor Felton here from America, and the happy party that Georgy's worked so hard to prepare for, only waiting for a smiling little hostess? . . .

"Damn it, damn it, Kate, you will walk down those stairs with a smile when the first guests come! You will not humiliate me! Have you no realization, no appreciation of what I have given you, your house, your means, your position in the world, all, all bought by effort that would have killed half the men I know? . . .

"Oh, Kate, Kate, I'm sorry. I'm tired, tired and tense. The legal fight with that man Dunn, the work for Miss Coutts, and the *History*, and *Bleak House*, and the magazine; and the cast meeting this afternoon was an unthinkable mess, with everyone behaving like children, unable even to settle on the play we'll do, let alone actually get on with it."

"Yes, Charles. You do it all for me, don't you? For me and the little ones. Yes, such a wonderfully unselfish life, no wonder you get all worn out and first curse and then start to whine."

Her face was mottled, and it looked swollen, but her eyes were dull and dry.

Charles stared at her. He began to laugh because Kate, Kate of all people on earth should accuse him, him of whining.

"Ha . . . ha! Oh, the absurdity . . . ha . . . ha . . . the . . ."

And the laugh broke off short. Charles had heard himself. He had always believed that Kate had a monopoly of the art of whining even while she laughed, but he was wrong. He had heard the sound of his own voice.

He was quiet for a moment, working his lip between his teeth. Then he said, "Try to be decently pleasant for Felton's sake if you can't for mine"; and went downstairs.

It was still early. He went into the library to wait.

On his table, along with the rest of the ritual paraphernalia, the bronze fencing frogs, the carved penholder, was a new acquisition. The Danish girl, after two years of suffering-by-post which, God knew why, he was always impelled to answer, had sent him a little statuette of Hebe. Goddess of mirth. With a note morose as all the rest of them.

And Charles had seen that he must shut her off. Real duty, real friendship left one no time for this sort of nonsense. Clearly, his letters did her no good; they only indulged them both. Yes, that week past, he had seen it at last and written firmly.

"The chances and changes of life deprive us all of many hopes and loves we have cherished. . . . But the journey is ever onward. . . . Whether yours shall be happy or unhappy rests mainly with yourself. I shall never forget you, but this is a world of action, where everyone has a duty to fulfill, a part to play . . ."

He could remember snatches of it still. He looked at the little Hebe and shook his head.

The self-evident truth, and the one she'd doubtless never grasp, poor child. Ah, well, at least she could weep on a new shoulder. Hans Christian Andersen's for example . . .

He glanced at his watch and went to the drawing room to make sure that the fires had been properly laid. Does any servant ever learn to lay a fire properly?

In the course of that evening, Kate laughed whenever anyone else did, whether she was near enough to catch the words or not. She laughed until she was flushed, gasping, wet-eyed. Until her stays gave slightly, until a comb fell from her back hair.

Once, once in Chelsea she had laughed like that. She was a beautiful young girl, and she laughed in such wild, wonderful enjoyment that he was wild with joy as he watched her, and baffled and angry when Mary ran to her crying, "Kate! Stop, stop it! Kate!"

Charles began to sweat a little.

He thought, Even then, back then. What shall I do now, what can I do? How can I quiet her without making an obvious scene?

He did nothing.

Felton, as he went away at the end of the evening said, "It refreshes my heart to see the mother of a large family who has kept all that fund of natural gaiety. Ah, but small wonder, Dickens, with the joyous company she always keeps!"

The next morning, Charles woke more tired than when he had gone to bed. He had an overfull day before him, but even before he was done with getting into his clothes he felt utterly spent. Spent, and tense, at the one time.

He told himself that once the benefit was over, they must get away to Boulogne for a holiday. He would take the book with him and oversee *Household Words* by post, but nothing else. By contrast it would be idleness.

After breakfast he wrote a few urgent letters. One of them was to Forster, and he was tired enough to allow himself a little luxury of complaint.

"Hypochondriacal whisperings tell me that I am rather overworked. The spring does not fly back directly, as it always did. What with *Bleak House*, and *Household Words*, and the *Child's History*, and

Miss Coutts's Home, and invitations to feasts and festivals I really feel as if my head would split like a fired shell."

He went for his hat. He would take the letters to the post box before he began to write. The walk, he was sure, would make him feel a little more like himself.

Katey was in the lower hall. She was looking unusually small and down in the mouth. Charles put his arm about her.

"My beauty seems remarkably morose for a happy girl at the start of a bright June morning."

She pulled away from him.

Her eyes blazed at him and she shouted. "Oh, Papa, stop always preaching, preaching, preaching!"

He laughed at the bright, furious, beautiful face.

"Aha, that sounds more like my Tinderbox!"

But she flung her arms up crossed before her eyes and went into a passion of weeping.

Charles was confused, almost frightened. "Dear, Papa's dear, his own dear little heart! What is this, dear? Little love, what is it?"

"Mama. Mama has a headache, she is ill, she is crying so . . . she . . . she . . ."

Charles's stomach went cold with rage. Kate had no right to play upon the children, to satisfy her moods. She must not, it must be put a stop to!

He put his hand upon the shaking, convulsed young shoulders. At the touch he thought, But she is grown, she is a young girl, not a child, not really my little Lucifer Box.

She dropped her arms. She looked at him out of the most hopeless face that he had ever seen on a child or a woman. And she said, in a torn, unchildlike voice, "I love you. Even when I don't want to, when I try not to, I love you, Papa."

He would pass it off lightly, as one must with children's curious moods, if the child is not to grow up a burden to herself and to others. He opened his mouth to speak the words that had already formed in his mind: "Isn't it fortunate, dear, that we cannot help being good? Now, give Papa a kiss."

The little lecture was already worded, the lips were parted, smiling, ready to speak. But instead of the words, Charles gave a cry and fell to the floor, clutching at the agony of pain in his side.

Within seconds, he had forced himself to his feet. He made himself speak evenly.

"Don't be frightened, dear. Papa's not seriously ill. It's only a cramp, a bad sort of cramp. I'll get to bed and we'll call the doctor and he'll have me to rights in no time."

He was appalled that he had actually let himself fall down. How it must have frightened the poor baby, the poor love.

He managed a sound like laughter. "I doubled over so sharply that I lost my balance. Like a clown in a pantomime. I'd best get to bed now. Truly, dear Huge Eyes, it's quite all right."

For six days of excruciating torment Charles lay abed, unable to think of anything but the pain itself. Occasionally he said between clenched teeth, "I swear, I cling to this damned pain as if I loved it!"

A kidney, the doctor said. Rest, sunshine, rest.

Charles said, "So, Miss Kelly won't have her benefit. Kate will be delighted."

He insisted upon starting out for Boulogne while he was still quite weak. He looked shockingly ill; far worse, he assured everyone than he really was. It was only that he had been unable to eat for so many days; it had taken the flesh off his face.

No, as he had to go, it was best to go quickly and convalesce in a good place for the task.

They must go now. Anne could come with the children as soon as they had found a house. Forster would find a courier, or go with them himself.

The Brave was dead.

A good many people were dead, if one came to that. It was only the weakness, certainly, but Charles had the strange feeling that something else was dead. Part of himself, one more world left behind. Nonsense, to be sure, one of the idle, nonsensical feelings that come with physical weakness; yet it was there.

At least the illness had slowed him down for a bit. The shell would not explode after all, and thank God for so much.

He refused Georgy's shoulder with a laugh as he walked up the gangplank of the channel boat. He thought, Now, Charlie, keep yourself propped upright. A nice, mannerly appearance of life, now, until the journey's done.

He thought, Years since I'd felt that pain . . . but never so badly, never, even as a child. At least it's done with now. Done with. Done with.

❊　❊　❊　❊　❊　❊　❊

BOOK VII
The Frozen Deep

❊　❊　❊　❊　❊　❊　❊

THEY FOUND the perfect house almost at once.

"Fallen on our feet again," Charles said. "Now, Georgy, dear, if you can manage to hover a little less, I'll be myself before you know it."

And indeed if it had not been for Georgy's hovering, and the gaunt-eyed stranger who looked out at him each morning from the shaving glass, Charles soon would scarcely have known that he had been ill.

The sense of a break in time, however, still remained. He tried, one day, to put it into words.

"These past five or six years, Georgy — they've been so full. And not only with all the striving and doing. Four children born to me, and my sister, my father, my baby, my dear friend, dead. And still it was all — I don't know how to put it — half-written. A sort of running synopsis." Then he laughed. "Running like the devil, in fact."

"I know. You've been terribly overworked."

He let it go. "Ah, well, in September when the book is done I plan to start a long, real holiday. A bachelor holiday, utterly leisured, wandering about for a month or two with Collins and little Egg, too, if he'll come."

"Oh. That will do you good."

Her face was full of that innocent, bloodsucking dependence of every woman living. How odd that not one of them, apparently, ever felt a man's absolute need to be footloose, once in a way; untrammeled, free.

It failed to strike Charles that he, himself, had never felt the need before.

It was natural. It grew as his strength came back, and he gained health rapidly.

"Thank God, I've begun to shave an old acquaintance again," he said, one day. "I feel more worthy of my surroundings. Do you know, I find myself thinking that I must have written this house and our landlord, both, back in the *Nickleby* days when the lark was on the wing, as friend Robert puts it?"

He might have done. M. Beaucourt was straight from Charles's pen, with his round, pink, world-embracing face, his welling generosity — "Ah, to be sure there must be more night tables; *mon dieu*, perfectly, another bedstead!" — and above all, with his overwhelming pride and joy in the place itself, "the property."

The house was an enchanting profusion of looking glasses, little stoves, fanciful clocks which ran, apparently, on Australian time, and more pictures, statues, busts, and bas-reliefs of Napoleon than one could ever bring himself to believe in.

The grounds burgeoned with roses, splendidly grown; they were also landscaped in a madness of tiny summerhouses, bridges, fountains (fourteen, none of which played), and ornamental steps. In the front hall was a map with fifty-five beauty spots marked out upon it, none of which Charles was ever able to identify: The Bridge of Jena. The Bridge of Austerlitz. The Bower of the Old Guard.

One set of steps was trickily placed. Charles suggested that a beam of wood might be laid down to prevent accidents.

M. Beaucourt slapped his cap to his breast. "Ah, *mon dieu*, this is not a portion of the property where you would like to see wood."

A handsome iron railing was installed next day. When Charles, taken aback by having provoked the extravagance, offered to pay part of the cost, M. Beaucourt changed the subject.

"In the moonlight, last night, the flowers appeared to be, O Heaven, bathing themselves in the sky! You like the property?"

"M. Beaucourt, I am enchanted with it."

"And I, sir," kissing his hand upward, "I, also!"

No, Charles thought, smiling, going back to his writing table; I flattered myself. It took a more gifted Author than the Inimitable to imagine Beaucourt. Even then. Even then, when I was too young to know that he could not exist. That such goodness is impossible.

After that, he did not smile.

He had a task that he had been dreading before him that day; a task which needed all of his recovered strength. But he did not weep, either, as he wrote of the death of Jo, the crossing-sweeper. The luxury of tears for Little Nell, the tears of joy through which he had once seen the golden ripple on the wall above Paul Dombey's bed, were equally far from him; he loved the dying child, he loved the young man who tried to help him die in some knowledge of God's love, but he wrote with dry eyes, and the emotion that tore his heart was anger, not grief.

" 'Jo! Did you ever know a prayer?'

" 'No, sir. Nothink at all. Mr. Chadband, he was a prayin' wunst at Mr. Sangsby's and I heard him, but he sounded as if he was speakin' to his-self, not to me. Different times there was other genlmen come down Tom-All-Alone's but they all mostly said the other wuns prayed wrong . . . We never knowed nothing. I never knowed what it was about!' "

Charles's jaw was set forward. He wrote on, tersely, toward the end, death, dear readers, and no little arms lifting happily to bright angelic visions while you fumble out your handkerchiefs and enjoy yourselves.

The child's sight begins to fail. He wants someone to bring a light.

" 'Jo, can you say what I say?' "

Phrase by phrase, he tries to repeat the prayer.

" 'Hallowed be — thy —'

"The light is come upon the dark, benighted way. Dead!

"Dead, your Majesty. Dead, my lords and gentlemen. Dead, Right Reverends and Wrong Reverends of every order. Dead, men and women born with Heavenly compassion in your hearts. And dying thus around us, every day."

Then, for a few moments, Charles did cry, with his hands clasped, and his mouth pressed upon them. It was harsh, dry, silent weeping, and when it ended he kept his head bowed for a little longer, while his lips and teeth worked at the ring on his little finger, absently, as a dog without appetite might gnaw at a bone.

After that he stood up, with the written pages in his hands and walked up and down the room, reading them over. When it was finished, he stood still and spoke aloud.

"I don't think I'll be asked to sit by a deathbed because of *this*."

The postal service was rapid; he could take care of the magazine as easily from Boulogne as he had from Malvern. With the book, it gave him all that he wanted to do, and the children were sufficient company. The Plornish Maroon, born Edward Bulwer-Lytton, was the best boy who ever rounded off a family.

And it was rounded off.

The fact that Charles could put it to himself as a contraceptive measure still saved the surface, and he still wanted to save it. But Charles kept to his own side of the bed.

"You never used to call Kate 'Catherine,'" Georgy said one day that summer. "And now you do, more often than not."

"I hadn't noticed," said Charles. "Grow a few inches or gain a few pounds and I'll call you Georgina, too, if you like."

He was thinking about the book and forgot to listen to her answer.

On the night that he finished *Bleak House* there was a great storm of wind and rain. It lasted into the next day. Charles came in from a walk battered and blown.

"Ah, what great courtesy in nature to oblige with the proper orchestration!"

Kate said, "What?"

"I wanted this weather."

Georgy said, "Do change into dry clothes or you'll get congestion of the lungs."

"I'm a big boy, nurse."

She gave a wicked grin. "Like Walter?"

He laughed. "Ah, but no, Georgy, I only wish I were as fundamentally amiable as dear Wally."

Two days before, Wally, home on holiday, had ended an argument with the children's nurse by flinging a chair at her.

Charles locked him in a bathroom for a day, on bread and water. At the hour of his release, he took the boy into his study. He looked at him, so handsome in his school blazer, with his face flushed and closed, waiting for the parental lecture to be over.

Charles said, "It's depressed me, Wally, to think of you cooped in that bathroom all day. Do you know why it had to be done?"

Wally answered promptly, in the voice of one very anxious to get things over and done with.

"For punishment, to make me good."

Charles picked up the little statue of Hebe and turned it in his fingers. "I doubt that punishment ever made anyone good, Wally. Only the loving kindness that is God's gift does that. But at least it can make us prudent. When we lose our tempers, we only make trouble for ourselves. It's not worth it. Do you see?"

"I said that I was sorry, Governor. Please, may I go, now?"

Charles thought, And what boy ever listened to the lecture after the caning? And what was I driving at, for that matter?

He set the little Hebe down. He hugged Wally's shoulders.

"It's too bad the chair missed her," he said. "Then you needn't have felt that your day was wholly wasted."

Wally heard that, at least. He laughed, returning the hug, and they shook hands in a manly fashion, forgive and forget.

Charles stood, dripping rain, smiling, remembering.

"Amiable!" Kate said. "Flinging chairs."

"I think he's learned, dear, that it can be a costly impulse."

He went upstairs to change. He was, in fact, most uncomfortably wet. But *Bleak House* was done. Triumph and release, for once no emptiness. For once? No, once before he had felt precisely so light-hearted at ending a book. At ending *Oliver Twist*, even though it had begun in Furnival's Inn, with Mary. *That* was strange. But this was natural, for now he need only wind his business off, and move them back to town, and then, until mid-December, he was off. Off, off, over the hills and far away!

❊   2   ❊

THERE WERE qualifications. Both little Egg and Collins coughed and spat of an early morning more than they needed to. There would never be another Louis Roche this side of Heaven. Once or twice, Charles found himself thinking of a brief whirl to the Highlands with Forster and Stanny and Maclise when they had all been, dear God, so young — or, he amended quickly, young in another way, for Collins and Egg were young, and he, at least was superbly fit.

Collins, indeed, was sometimes appalled by Charles's fitness. On the day Charles danced up and down the Mer de Glace, while the awed guides cried, "But he is an intrepid!" Collins waited below and greeted him with a weary moan.

It was by nightfall that Collins came most alive. He was a con-noisseur of urban gaities, and particularly the naughtier of them. And when they spent the night in a country inn, he was slap-up company with his witty, boastful, cynical, easy talk.

He loved to talk while he drank, and unlike most bibulous, loose-mouthed Don Juans, he was never a bore, for he found his own failures and misadventures as hilarious as his successes. Charles and Egg both led him on for the entertainment of it, while his hard, bright eyes danced behind his tiny spectacles, and his tiny, womanish hands made broad, Gargantuan gestures to illustrate some broad, Gargantuan tale.

He was unusually involved with two or three women at the same time, a fact of which he said, with genuine regret, "It's highly inefficient, I never plan it so." But he held a strong and serious brief for the sexual honesty of the French.

"It rots a nation's whole integrity to live a continual, simpering lie. Rots it for issues that are, God knows, more important than sex. I write to amuse. You try to go deeper, but how can you, when you can't represent a healthy young man as he is without drowning the poor devil in propitiation for his being human?"

"In the first place, Collins, whether you believe it or not, it's human for young men to fall in love, too; the whole desire running in one direction. It's a fact, and one of the more dramatic facts. Some men even love their wives."

Egg grinned. "Lad, save your wind to cool your porridge. When they were making up his lot they ran out of human hearts before the end, and they made do with a few they had left from the last lot of billy goats."

"So much the better for my second point. I want to change the condition of England's poor, Collins. You may find your own serious work in time; that's mine, and I can't waste the public indignation on some fellow's absent-minded whoring."

Collins could drink for a long time, but when it caught up with him, it caught up abruptly. He blinked a little, and raised his glass. "The French," he said. "*Vive la France.*"

Charles smiled and stretched. "Ah, well, I'm off to bed." Then he looked grave. "And as for the oldest profession," he said, "your obliging little periwinkles, Collins, are by no means so lighthearted as one likes to think them, in England or out of it. And a whore can die as wretchedly in Paris as in London, give her time."

Egg, in a small, sad voice, a voice that did not sound much older than the Plornishmaroontigoonter's, said, "Oh, *dear.*"

And Charles, quite startled and quite accurate, said, "Why, I'm drunk myself and never noticed it. *Bon soir, mes enfants. Dormez bien. Vive la France!*"

None of them had headaches next morning. Egg said blithely that it was an example of Divine Injustice.

In Lausanne they saw Haldimand, Cerjat, all the old group. The old group, grown a little older. The Thompsons were living nearby. Christiana had taken up landscape painting. The house was dirty. The little girls had their hair weirdly cropped with bows stuck on top.

Christiana said, "I thought it would be picturesque but perhaps I was wrong."

At the Institute, they could not remember the little girl who held her hand to the side of the piano, at first; then, finally, one of the teachers said, "Oh, *that* child! She proved to be an idiot. We sent her away."

"It was so good to see you all," Charles said, wringing Haldimand's hand, Cerjat's, Mrs. Marcet's. "So good, so blessedly good."

He was enormously glad to get away. So much, much longer than he had realized. At least they had talked mercifully little of poor Watson.

He also saw the De La Rues, in Genoa. She was the same excellent little creature, the Phantom still haunted her faithfully, and her husband still adored her. A gray hair or two had come in the glossy whiskers.

Collins and Egg laughed inordinately when he later described his efforts to exorcise the Phantom.

In his letter to Kate from Genoa he did not mention the visit.

In Naples, Vesuvius was quiet. They had run into Austen Layard, a fascinating fellow who had given over a brilliant career in archaeology to become a Radical member of Parliament. He and Charles talked Reform all the way up to the slumbering crater and back again.

The first week of December was nearly ended when they came at last to Turin. Now they would only go on to Paris, meet Charley, take him home for holidays. Ten weeks they had been wandering. Ten weeks. And now, back to London, to the children, to Kate.

Ten weeks had been too long. He should have settled for a fortnight. Ten weeks of easy, tender letters that wrote themselves as if they would be read with the heart, accepted, understood; and now, back to the loneliness of direct speech, to a lake of hate beneath its thin, bright ice of making-do.

It was that. It did not help to ask for no more, to lose oneself in usefulness. It made things worse, and for her, too. He had seen it and tried to forget it that day on the Canterbury road, in the summer before poor Watson died. But did it have to be hopeless? Even now, might he not reach out to her, reach her, say, "Let us begin now?" say, "This is what I am, look, see me, show me yourself?"

He sat at a small desk table in his hotel room. He worked Mary's ring on his finger. He did not think of Mary. He only wanted what she had given him. He wanted to be known and loved for what he was, his good rejoiced in, his sins and weaknesses seen, grieved over, regretted, but still known, part of his self — and that self loved.

And he began to write the letter that he had not written from Genoa. The letter about what had really happened, back then. Ideas possessed him; he must make her understand that; understand that once he was possessed he had to pursue them in a way that looked like madness, that would *be* madness if it were not also the driving force that gave him his value to the world.

The letter began in passionate self-justification, and ended with brisk appeals to common sense.

"Whatever made you unhappy in the Genoa time had no other root, beginning, middle, or end than whatever has made you proud and honored in your married life . . . Now I am perfectly clear that your position is not a good one, not a generous one, not worthy of you at all."

It ended with suggestions for a nice little note that Kate should write to Mrs. De La Rue at once, in appreciation for her messages of remembrance, and in sympathy for her sufferings and cheerfulness.

Unthinkably, that is what he wrote. Unthinkably, that is, in the sense in which we are all rather unthinkable.

❊ 3 ❊

So CHARLES STOOD in the entrance hall of Devonshire Terrace under an avalanche of children.

"Home, in the nick of time for our Twelfth Night play! Tom Thumb the great, and Harry to be the star."

Charley laughed outright. "At his age, Governor? He'd die of terror."

Charles swung Harry up toward the ceiling. "Harry, afraid? To wear a gold helmet and a sword, and stay up late, and say the words Papa will teach him, and hear everyone laugh and shout and clap their hands?"

He set him down and waited, making his face grave as possible. Harry appeared to deliberate.

"How late?"

"Very late."

"And a sword? And a party downstairs, only I'll *be* downstairs?"

"A promise."

Harry screamed. He ran at Alfred and whacked him. "You said I'd be too little! *Foolish!*"

Charles bent to Alfred and whispered. "Remember, Skittles, how it felt to be the baby? We'll let him relish his years, won't we, old man?"

Alfred nodded, with eyes of complicity, the elder brother, amused yet kind.

"Ah, Kate," Charles said, "how very good it is to come home."

Kate said, "I can't get used to you in that beard."

Georgy said, "I think I like it. It is distinguished."

He put his arms about them both.

"I can't believe that it was ten weeks," he said. "It feels like a fortnight."

His voice was happy.

Next day, out of the blue, Katey said that she did not intend to act in one of those silly plays.

Charles kissed her, and shot a warning glance toward Mamie as he rumpled the bright hair. "Yes, I'd thought of that. You're such a young lady now that it would help the evening wonderfully if you wore a fine, new frock and played the hostess for us with Mama."

She walked away, her lovely face half triumphant, half crestfallen. Charles put his arms around Mamie.

"Will Papa's gentle one keep it for our secret that Katey is not so old as she thinks for? Will his wise little love help him to keep the peace?"

"Oh, Papa, yes!"

Her drab green eyes said, Ah, he trusts me utterly. He loves me the best.

She was almost pretty.

Charles smiled. He felt no guilt.

Instead, as he walked away, he thought, Why is it only Kate with whom I cannot be open and simple like this? Even with casual strangers, I can talk, and show my heart and find a heart's response. Why, Kate, my wife, out of all the world?

For after a day at home he had forgotten the hope in which he wrote the letter from Turin.

At Christmas dinner, nobody spoke of the Governor. Mrs. Dickens, in a hugely ruffled widow's cap seemed only to feel that it became her vastly. Her streams of language had taken on a new, arch girlishness, aimed chiefly at Mr. Hogarth, who grew — comprehensibly enough, poor chap, dimmer with the years.

Charles tried not to look at Mrs. Hogarth at all, or at Kate, who was in less than Christmas spirits. The children were all at table, all noisy and wonderful. Even the Plorn was there, on cushions, and when the pudding came on, burning, his face was entrancing in its awe.

The Governor would have loved him. This was the Governor's moment, always, the moment when the pudding came on; this was the moment when the eyeglass swept out, when he got to his feet and the most splendid, orotund of all the toasts began. The first, hard year without him . . .

It is the third. Last year we had just moved into this house, we were so busy with it, still . . .

That night he said, "I kept hoping that one of the children would speak of the Governor at table, naturally you know, and happily as we older ones could not."

"Happily!" Kate caught in her breath. Then she said, "Wishing that one of those poor children would show such heartlessness! Your own father! Small wonder you've always pushed your wife aside!"

Charles said, "Even the Almighty has his off days. He may have outstripped me on M. Beaucourt, but you want rewriting from start to finish. You strain credulity."

Kate said, "*What?*"

The next day Charles went to the Midlands to give three Christmas readings for workingmen's organizations.

"Do you feel well?" Georgy asked as he left. "You look so white, and — I don't know how to express it — as if your face was too small."

"I may be taking a little cold. Keep the children at saying their parts, small person. Little Betty and Lally Lemon, too. Have you seen Lemon in his costume, the giantess? He's unthinkable."

He got away quickly. It amused him, in a sad way, to know from her description so precisely how he must be looking.

He came home with the gentled, bemused face of a young man in love.

He said, "Oh, Georgy, such full understanding, such response. They missed nothing, nothing. They cheered, so, dear, that I could scarcely thank them, for my tears."

She only said, "I'm so glad. You shook off your cold, too."

But he could tell from her face that she knew what it had been, that brimming cup of love.

"It's absurd, I daresay. Nobody puts his lacks and his wrongness into his writing if he can help it, and they are real as the rest of him, God knows. And still one feels *known* by an audience like that — truly known."

Georgy only swallowed and nodded. Her eyes were full of the happiness, more rare in them as she grew older, which made them sometimes look almost like Mary's.

"*Known*," Kate said. "Making up stories and reading them as if you were Mr. Macready, to a lot of ignorant poor people who get excited! *Known*."

In the last year her hair had lost its shining luster; she would have been better advised to give up the girlish side-curls which were frizzy, by morning, now, and half uncurled by nightfall, and at all times emphasized the thickening jowls and the growing double chin. The whites of her eyes were seldom clear any longer; they were sometimes yellowish, sometimes pinkish, though the singular purple-blue of their irises was unchanged.

Where had her beauty gone? Charles did not wonder, for he did not see her. He saw a sea of lifted faces, all, all responding as one soul.

And he, a balding, expensively yet conservatively dressed man, with a spade beard, fine posture, an aura of substance, importance, smiled past her with eyes as young as the young Romeo's, forever calling to us from our youth: "It is the east, and Juliet the sun!"

Kate laughed as she looked at him.

"You can't live without flattery, can you?" she said.

He shook his head, vaguely. His face was still lost in love.

"So moving," he said again. "So beautiful."

The heroic drama of Tom Thumb was a huge success. The adults played to the hilt, the children were bold and letter-perfect, and Thackeray laughed so hard that he fell out of his chair with a crash.

Charles squared his shoulders and looked ahead at the year. The blow that he had come home prepared to give was desperately needed now. A great strike had broken out in Preston. Workers were starving.

Charles went to Preston and came home with the book at his throat. He would not be handling a popular issue. The nightmare philosophy of justification by statistics had confused men's hearts. But only confused them, not perverted them; he could make them look at Mr. Grandgrind, and see the falsity for what it was.

Hard Times is a humorless book. Its characters spout ideas; the sound of life is not often in their words.

Yet it does not lack power. It might have said what it set out to say, said it to ears that heard, if the Crimean War had not broken out in March. But it did, and England fell dead in love with it. Industrial slums and the lives of textile workers, coal miners, and their like, did not catch the imagination. Charles wrote to an audience that was thrilling to the sound of the trumpet and the drums.

"They'll sing another tune next year when they find their income tax doubled," Charles said.

He wrote on grimly. In May, he moved the family to Boulogne.

"God bless Beaucourt," he said to Georgy. "I feel less isolated from the world when I can love at least one militarist!"

He shuttled back and forth, himself, from France to London; it was a strain, but necessary.

Life was a strain; yet that May, through all its pressures, Charles found himself remembering with a singular sharpness the May in which Mary died. He was cruelly, continually pressed for time; yet whenever he was in London he was conscious of a longing to visit her grave in Kensal Green, to touch the headstone and the grassy mound beside his own grave that he had given away.

[371]

He did not. He told himself with anger alien both to his own nature and to the gentle necrophilia of the times that the impulse was unhealthy, wrong. Yet it came back upon him continually, until a day of shouting, boisterous green — it was a beautiful May, rich as summer yet freshly young and with day after day of blue, blue skies — a day which might have been one of those days that he could not stop remembering, one of those days that he had come to think of as a falsifying, romantic memory, the weather pushed about to build the tale.

He walked out of Tavistock House into that morning, and he did not go to the office, as he had planned. Neither did he go to Kensal Green. He went to Highgate, and bought a freehold, and arranged to have Dora lie as she should have lain from the beginning. Under the grass, the sky, the sun, the rain.

He expected to have a hard time of it when he got back to Boulogne. He was more aware of Kate than he had been for months as he told her. He told her gently, as well as anxiously, pitying the moment of freshened pain that she should feel, as well as dreading her certain, shrewish protestings.

She said, "Oh? I must say that I never understood your prejudice against those handsome vaults, but I daresay they can sell the space to someone else and apparently we don't want for money nowadays, in any event."

He forced himself to believe that the flat, indifferent voice was one of kindness, of tender self-control.

"Thank you. I've wanted it for her so long."

"I remember that quite clearly."

She walked out of the room. When she recounted the scene to Georgy she said, "I got away as quickly as I could. I would not give him the satisfaction of seeing me cry."

That week Georgy had refused once more to marry Augustus Egg; refused for the last time. When she had heard Kate through she brought her hands together hard, and bowed her head and worked her lips for some moments before she could force out the difficult, honest answer.

"Kate, he did not want to hurt you. He was afraid that you would be troubled, he hoped that you would see her pretty grave, and be glad."

"So that's what he told you?"

"He did not speak of it to me, Kate."

"If he ever notices you enough, Georgy, to turn his cruelty on you, you'll sing another tune."

Georgy's lips set in a straight line. After a brief pause she said, "Think what you like. It's no concern of mine."

Charles, at his writing table, stared straight before him.

She had not thought of Dora; she had not imagined that he might still love that small body. She had imagined no motive but spite, and even that left her indifferent. She did not care, even enough to be angry.

He pulled the papers straight, in front of him. He read back over the last sentences. He said, aloud, "I'm so tired all the time. I'm so tired."

By mid-July, as the book drew to its close, he was speaking little more than literal truth when he told his friends that he was half mad and half delirious with work.

He had also taken to waking before dawn. Kate snored, toward morning. Like a drunkard sleeping off a stupor, like Stephen Blackpool's drunkard wife. For several years, Charles had reached out, in an automation of half-sleep, to shake her shoulder; she would roll to her side and sleep quietly, then, and he, too, would fall asleep again.

Through the first half of that July he got up, instead, listening to it as he dressed in the half-light and not knowing that he listened, because he was also Stephen Blackpool nearing the death that would free him from living death.

It is always like this when I come to the end of a book . . . I am like this, with no real life apart from it. Always like this, so that I cannot even really know how I love poor Kate, love her and pity her with all the inborn handicaps that are no fault of hers. It is always like this. This time, I am Stephen, rushed on, helpless, to the release of death. In cramped, tight, agonizing magazine installments that leave me no room to turn about in. Half mad with work. Delirious with it.

And then it was done.

"Thank God," he said, "at last. As soon as I'm back from England I'll take the boys to visit the French encampment. They'll love the uniforms and the noise and the dust. God knows somebody ought to get a bit of good from this damned war."

Kate said, "Now you're done cursing, I expect that you'll go to hear their prayers?"

London was hot as a steam bath. Collins picked him up after a driving day's work at the *Household Words* office.

"Where shall we go, Collins? I can't shake myself free of that book, even now it's done. Desperate diseases call for desperate remedies."

"No need to be all that desperate, old fellow. Even London has a few pleasant corners where one's not likely to be recognized."

"Harun-al-Rashid and his Vizier," Charles said.

The fantasy, somehow, made the evening palatable as it was diverting. The fantasy, aided by a good deal to drink, at dinner, and for an hour or so thereafter.

Next day Charles took Miss Coutts to hear Grisi sing *Lucrezia Borgia.* They talked of the black state of the world; of Kate's improved health and M. Beaucourt's refreshing oddities; of the children's enjoyment of their out-of-doors life in Boulogne.

He did not like to admit to himself the degree of relief that he felt as he bade her good night and went to sleep away the rest of his headache on the cot at the office of *Household Words.* The Hogarths had been mucking about in Tavistock House as they liked to do in his absences and had left it in the usual state of filth. There was also a letter from Mrs. Hogarth, a really lunatic letter, about a notion to insure her life, at her age and in her state of health. Oh, God.

Next morning he felt much better, got through a phenomenal day's work, and went alone to see the Spanish dancers. After the performance he took their manager, Buckstone, a good sort, off to the Haymarket where they talked theater and drank gin slings until dawn.

He wrote to Georgy, "I have been in a blaze of dissipation altogether, and have succeeded (I think) in knocking the remembrance of my work out. I never in all my days read anything like your mother's letter for its desperation of imbecility. Loves to all the darlings, from the Plornish Maroon upward."

Despite another headache he felt cheerful. It was hard to realize that less than a week ago he was still writing the book and so possessed by it. He looked forward to a long rest in the sun.

※ *4* ※

KATE LOST the beauty that Charles had loved, in the year that the Crimean War broke out. Most of those gluttonous, sedentary, many-servanted, ever-bearing Victorian women were fat; but they were not unattractive. A little light of intelligence, or of religion, or simply of placid animal content and motherly warmth can make a round, middle-aged face quite delightful. Charles's books are full of such endearing dumplings; but after that year, not even Professor Felton of Cambridge could have mistaken Kate for one of them.

There was no redeeming grace in the ruin of her looks. Her beauty was gone; and in the singular loneliness to which their marriage had condemned them both, Charles had loved it out of reason and past its term.

Charles's rage against the Crimean War was unending and obsessive.

England was set back a good five hundred years. The cholera that came back with the troopships to rage through England's slums took a greater toll of life than all of the casualties among the underfed, ill-clad, mismanaged troops — and their lot, poor devils, would not bear thinking of. The newspapers fluted about the troops' enthusiasm. Tennyson found it all most moving!

Satire boiled off Charles's pen. By a furious editorial miracle he managed to keep up the circulation of *Household Words* and still bring the voice of honesty into all those damned, smug homes, where it might or might not make some small impact.

The year went on, and they came back to England. The mounting scandals of mismanagement and military blundering brought down the Government, and Palmerston came in with another, as like the old as two peas in a pod.

Kate said that she loved to read of how cheerful our poor soldiers were despite all the sad and shocking things they had to bear. Forster, a full, ponderous size larger with his sense of military responsibility, fought the war with maps and pins and was not at all satisfied that the ships were being properly placed before Sebastopol.

It grew near to Christmas.

Charles, looking at the calendar, started. He thought, Since last July, how little time the black state of the world has left me for my own life. And wrongly, wrongly, for surely in the world's blackest hours we have the greatest duty to love our dear ones and to enjoy our daily blessings.

He was startled by the thought, and much as a man might be startled by hearing some favorite dance tune of his youth being whistled in an alien market place.

He set himself at once to make ready for a Christmas as merry as all Christmases should always be.

And he felt, humbly, that he had succeeded beyond his deserts.

That year, at the Christmas dinner, Charley said, "You know, I still miss Grandpapa." And Wally answered, "Oh, yes! Oh, so do I!"

The words were warm, without sadness. They drew everyone close in love.

Charles scarcely noticed that Kate did not smile once throughout the meal, or that his mother was a year older, madder, and more determinedly girlish, or that Helen Hogarth's lashless face and bosom both promised a shocking resemblance to her mother's, give them a little longer, or that Charley's handsome face had begun to show a too familiar weakness and slackness. It was Christmas. The bright forefront of his mind was all Christmas joy and family love.

He lifted his glass for the final toast, tossing back his head in a gesture that was still habitual though he now wore his thinning hair cut short.

"And so may our every Christmas be merrier than the last."

It was as if the charity readings had long been part of the Christmas tradition. He could scarcely imagine a Christmas, now, without that brimming cup of love, that utter joy of giving and receiving.

The children's play, too, had all the good feeling of time-honored tradition. This year it was *Fortunio and His Seven Gifted Servants*. The dragon, played by Lemon, had a tail that switched and awful jaws that champed. Plorn got it drunk on sherry and slew it.

The program announced: "First appearance on any stage of Mr. Plornishmaroontigoonter, who has been kept out of bed at vast expense."

And Katey, at fifteen, was once more young enough to perform. Radiantly.

That night, as he was undressing, Charles said, "Think, Kate,

Charley's birthday. Seventeen years ago he was born, our Phenomenon."

"Yes, I can count."

"And another Christmas gone."

"Thank goodness, yes."

"Try not to feel that, dear. It came on me only now that these twelve days have been a — a holiday into love. For me, it was like that, and it should not have been. This whole year past, I've fought the muddle and wrong in the world until I forgot the banner I fought under. I've let the hate possess me. Kate, this year can't we help each other to keep this Christmas living in our hearts until the next?"

She backed away. Her words came in a tumbling rush.

"Please, no, Charles — I'm tired, I don't feel well — I —"

"I didn't mean that, dear."

She got into bed stiff-shouldered, obviously frightened and unable to believe him.

Still, for almost a month Charles clung to that revelation of gentleness; to that determination to keep, as he put it, the blackness of the world out of his heart. Through those weeks, when he looked at Kate he pitied her and blamed himself because she could no longer make him feel all that she clearly feared to make him feel. He tried to talk with her. He said to himself, "She is timid. It was never enough to go halfway in friendship with her; one must go all the way, patiently, in absolute, unwavering love."

He had planned, before Christmas, to take a February spin to Paris with Collins. Harun-al-Rashid and his Vizier.

As the time drew near, he wished that he had not planned it. He sat before the fire one night with Kate, not looking at her, and fiddling restlessly at his ring before he spoke.

"This jaunt to Paris . . . Speck and Alfred are making all manner of plans for my visit to their school as I pass through Boulogne. Come with me, Catherine. You alone, or you and Georgy, if you'd rather. Collins won't care if I tell him I've changed my plans. He never lacks friends for a spur-of-the-moment holiday."

Ideas possessed him, as he had said in the letter about Mrs. De La Rue. Somehow, as he spoke, he fully expected that she would look happy, touched, moved; that even though she refused, as she well might, her eyes would warm with the happiness of being wanted; loved and wanted.

She stared at him as though he had lost his wits, and lost them in a most unpleasant and ludicrous way.

"In this weather? To sit by and listen to you talk French to people? I don't know what's got into you lately, Charles, that nervous way you can't let me alone. I'd think you had something on your conscience if I didn't know how little your conscience has ever troubled you!"

He turned the ring slowly, all the way around. His lips worked and compressed themselves.

After a long silence he said, "Yes, I expect it would have given poor Collins rather short notice."

He was amazed at the pleasant, even tone of his voice.

❋　5　❋

HE HAD a great deal to clear away before he could start; work for the magazine, Miss Coutts, a dozen committees. A young man named Sanders had written a good play, and Charles had persuaded Buckstone to put it on, but the whole business still had a few loose ends that he wanted to tuck away before he left town.

With the various runnings-about, his private correspondence had piled up more than he liked to let it.

All this accumulation, in two days? He shuffled through it, before he began to sort it out. A curious startling went through his body that he did not understand. It persisted, as he went on with the task, like a startled, nagging, half-conscious memory. Had he forgotten to see to something very important?

He dropped the letters, and tapped the edge of the table, trying to think. When the answer came to him, he was amazed at the workings of the human brain. Seen in one quick, abstracted, tidying flash, the handwriting on one of these envelopes had reminded him somehow of . . . How curious, what could have brought that back? . . . Our curious minds!

But even as he marveled and laughed at himself his hands were rushing through the letters, tumbling them loosely before him. And, oh, my God, it was there, actually there — the pretty, square envelope, addressed in that hand so utterly unchanged, so unforgettable. Maria Beadnell's hand.

Maria.

He stared at it, afraid to open it, because it could not really be from Maria. And because it was really from Maria, and he was a middle-aged man and it was impossible that the joy and pain of the morning should push so absurdly, livingly as this into life again.

Maria. Good God, the garden where we sat; the kisses, kisses, all that youth and passion before they sent her away, and ended it for her and not for me. Maria. Have I ever been so utterly directed upon anything else again?

He cut it open angrily at last, as if he were stabbing the body of a dream. He spread it out with quick, impatient hands and set himself to read what would surely be another letter from some gushing female who had belatedly discovered Little Nell, or the like.

The letter was from Maria. She was married, of course, the mother of two girls. It was a frank, gay, gentle, affectionate letter; it wandered lightly back and forth from present to past, full of bright memory, full of warm, generous pride in his work, and the place it had brought him.

Charles read it through, and again, and yet again. It was a happy woman's letter though it had the wistfulness that always comes when we recall the bright, untested dreams of our youth. How strange to know that she was as old as Mrs. Watson and Meery; and with two children. Maria.

Oh, God, he thought suddenly, I wish I weren't going to Paris with Collins.

Twenty-four years, gone like a dream. Twenty-four years, upon him heavier than he had ever felt them. It was like that for her, too, when she found herself writing a letter, wandering, line by line, from woman to girl, from present to past.

He wrote her a letter that she might read aloud to her husband. Mr. Winter, a merchant. Mrs. Beadnell must have been happy over that. Yes, thank God, it showed in every line. Maria was happy too.

He wrote:

"Your letter was more touching to me from its good and gentle associations with the state of Spring in which I was either much more wise or much more foolish than I am now — I never know which to think . . . We are all sailing away to the sea, and have a pleasure in thinking of the river we are upon when it was very narrow and little."

He was curiously sure that she would want to write again, and soon. He gave her the return address of his hotel in Paris.

Collins was getting over an influenza. He had expected to feel well and did not. Of an evening they dropped in upon a few theaters, picked up an act here and there, and came back to the hotel to talk over hot grog. It made Collins feel downright guilt-ridden.

"I fully thought I'd be back in form. Please don't waste this city of charming opportunity because of me. I'd *rather* you found a few livelier friends, really."

"Try to believe me, old fellow, I'm better suited so. Perhaps I'm feeling my years, but truly all I wanted from this trip was a taste of quiet."

Charles was, in fact, brimful of a sense of miraculous deliverance. Maria's Charles and Collins's boon companion could not have housed easily in one body.

The letter had been waiting for him at the hotel. As casually as she had once sent him out with a bit of blue stuff to match to a pair of gloves, she asked him to go to a shop she named and pick up two velvet collars for her little girls. It was a light, sweet, reminiscent letter.

Or, it tried to be. Its gaiety was clumsy, and too gay; an underlying sadness showed through all the light rememberings. And across the bottom, scribbled on some compulsive after-impulse were two lines: "No one but I ever reads my letters, or cares to. You can always write to me all to myself."

The sentences were oddly young, innocent, lonely. And in the body of the letter she said, "Once before I started to write to you, but I remembered how we parted in a misunderstanding and I was afraid you did not remember me happily."

Was she gray? Did that narrow, lovely face have lines in it? He could only hope so. It would mean that they could come together easily once more; that Kate would not care. How odd that once he had thought of her as a brilliant, gifted woman — Maria, who had only been another child. A frightened, ignorant, narrowly bred young girl with beauty that transcended everything. Beauty and passion . . . passion . . .

Would she write to me like this if she had ever found what our looks used to speak of, what her kisses promised? Those kisses that taught me so much more about her than her own young ignorance could let her know of herself?

"My dear Mrs. Winter."

A light letter, a friendly letter. That boy and girl are long since dead. I know it, I will remember it.

"I can never think that other young people are in such desperate earnest, or set so long upon one absorbing hope . . . I began to fight my way out of poverty and obscurity with one perpetual idea of you . . . I have never been so good a man since . . . There are things that I have locked in my own breast . . . But when I find myself writing to you 'all to yourself' . . . how can I . . . make a feint of blotting it all out?"

No answer came before he left Paris.

The snow was delaying the posts. He had said too much, his letter made him sound a tedious, sentimental old bore. He had said too much, she, too, was lonely, and she would not answer it because she knew that she must not. She was touched, her heart opened, she answered it at once, but the heavy snow was delaying the posts.

When they left the hotel he told the clerk that he was expecting a letter of urgent importance; everything that came for him must be forwarded without delay.

Kate said, "Everyone with colds. For all the peace I've had, I might almost as well have gone to Paris with you!"

Besides the velvet collars for Maria's children he had brought home lace collars for Kate and Georgy, fans for the girls, a regiment of lead soldiers.

Plorn said, "I wouldn't be a soldier. They get dead. Why does Wally learn to be a soldier?"

Charles hugged him. "By the time he's an officer the war will be over, and all the girls will see his splendid uniform and kiss him."

"Even if he tells them not to?"

"Perhaps not, if he's firm. Here, Harry, squeeze in on the other side. What story for tonight?"

There was general debate. "Jesus." "No, Robin Hood." Puss-in-Boots won.

Charles thought, Catherine will call on her; I'll show her the collars and the little brooches for her children . . .

His voice continued, arching the stream of thought: "But the cat said, 'Do not grieve, young Master. Buy me a pair of boots, and all will be well' . . ."

Maria's letter came back from Paris a day later.

"I felt for you all that you felt for me. I was so young, when they told me all those wicked falsehoods about you, I believed them. I acted wrongly, proudly. It was so long ago, but I am still ashamed."

It was an awkward, childlike opening of the heart. Its very directness told him how happy she was now, how innocent. But she remembered. And she wanted to meet him for one first time, alone. To talk, to set the old confusions straight, to speak to the boy he had been before they became casual, smiling friends in the world of what now is.

She did not put it in so many words. She had no art in her pen, her letter wandered timidly from children's collars to old dreams and back. Yet that was what she wanted. And as if it were as easy a thing to arrange as it was innocent she said: "I could make it look as though I were shopping through the open bookstalls in Paternoster Row. I would know your face and not only from your pictures, though I do not think you would know mine by now. I am so old and ugly it will make you laugh, but we can talk for that one time alone."

As if she had read his mind, and longed to reassure him that it was all right now. Maria. If her face showed all the long years, so much the easier for them both in the time to come. Her eyes would be her eyes, her voice would be her voice. Maria, the morning, the wellspring of all he had become.

So innocently she made her plan, never imagining the necessary caution, the ugly necessities of a cheap intrigue that would be upon any private meeting that they might hope for, ever.

He wrote to her, tossed about between the man's harsh anger and the boy's holy dream. ". . . though it is so late to read in the old hand what I have never read before, I have read it with the old remembrance softened to a more sorrowful emotion than I could easily tell you. . . . I could not . . . have so set my old passion aside as to talk to you like a person in any ordinary relationship to me . . .

All this you have changed and set right . . . so courageously, so delicately and gently . . ."

Would she hate what he must say now, find it ugly, cowardly?

"I am a dangerous man to be seen with, for so many people know me . . . You would not like better to call here on Sunday, asking first for Catherine . . . ? It is almost a positive certainty that there will be none here but I . . ."

The ugly stench of intrigue was in it, and there was no help for it. What he felt for her was good, God knew what she had shown him so artlessly was good. Only, we cannot fetch back the morning, clear and clean, into the afternoon.

She was only too good to have known it.

The thrill of wonder went through him again, and he turned from the letter he was writing and read a single sentence of hers over again. "I hope you will not misunderstand it if I tell you that there is a way I have never been able to feel differently about you than the way I did then and to think of you still remembering is something I can't stop thinking of."

He swallowed hard, and wrote, "Remember, I accept all with my whole soul, and reciprocate all."

No, she did not know what she had said. In those earliest days, she had not known that she taught him more than she knew herself. Unchanged, unchanged. Please God she is even so guileless in her guile that this hole-and-corner caution will not show itself to her in its full ugliness!

He sealed his letter and thrust it midway into a stack of letters waiting to be posted. He wrote a bright, brief note: "Dear Mrs. Winter." About the collars. Saying that Catherine would like to call upon her.

He had told Kate about the collars, and the old friend of Fan's. He took the note to her now. "If you're willing, dear. For I think that we should ask them to dine, at least once."

"I'd as lief. I started to tell you when you mentioned it before, but you were hurrying off as usual; she called here when Fanny died. She seemed pleasant enough. It may have slipped my mind to tell you at the time."

"She called here?"

"Yes, she asked to see where you wrote your books and everything.

Very amiable, though not an actress or an Honorable or young or anything you'd have been interested to hear about."

Yet she was clearly indifferent. The stabs were only habitual; she made them as vaguely as she might have eaten another sweet from the box at her side.

Charles thanked God quietly and changed the subject.

And through the long hours he waited for Sunday afternoon.

❆ *6* ❆

HE WAITED, knowing more and more fully all that he wanted. He waited, knowing that he would never ask for more than he was freely offered, and that it would be far less than what he wanted, and still a goodness, a richness, a miracle.

He waited, filling the time, trying not to think ahead or feel ahead. He thought and felt ahead continuously. And bravely, counting every one of the twenty-four years gone by. It did not matter that the bright hair might be gray, or that the proud young face would surely be softened, lined. His own was older, too. It would be as if they had both grown older together. He was glad.

Yes, he was glad. Her face would be vulnerable now, like the heart that had dictated her letter, her last dear letter, which like an incautious fool he still kept and could not bear to burn.

He waited, waited.

And it was Sunday afternoon, and Catherine and Georgy had gone to call on their mother, Mamie and Katey were at a friend's house, the children were on the nursery floor, the house was quiet.

And perhaps even now she would not come. Perhaps as she was getting ready it came upon her suddenly that she, too, wanted too much from it; that she was a happy mother, a happy wife, that she must not want too much from it; that she must not come.

He closed his hands into fists and pressed them together and sat with his mouth pressed upon his knuckles, waiting.

John tapped on the library door.

"A lady, sir. She came to see Mrs. Dickens but she says you'll do."

Charles stood up. For a single, absurd moment he felt nothing at all but a mad wish that he had shaved off his beard.

He took the card and glanced down at it.

"Show her in, John."

He heard a woman laughing in the hall.

It was high, shrill, nervous, silly laughter.

Charles had stiffened with the shock of it even before Maria swooped upon him, in a wave of powerful scent which mingled with a wave of brandy fumes.

"You dear boy! Oh, I know it's dreadful to call you that, but when I look at you I can't feel that a week has passed, truly I can't!"

"Maria, how . . . how pleasant to see you."

She ogled from an eye that was slightly glazed and held a finger coyly to one large, wine-purple cheek.

"Not the tiniest bit changed, and every bit as timid as he used to be!" She drew back, lifting a squared-off, ponderous breast in a frightening parody of remembered invitation. "You know I warned you, Charles, that you'd find me turned all old and ugly!"

He said, "Maria, you have not changed at all."

And he knew as he spoke that it was no more than the truth, the unbearable, stabbing truth.

She was fat as Kate, though more fiercely corseted. Her face was red, her bonnet would have been too desperately winsome for a woman of thirty. Her arch smile showed a black gap where she had lost an incisor. And she was Maria, appallingly unchanged.

The love that David bore his Dora had been the love of a besotted adolescent for a dismal, empty-headed little fool. The bud was now overblown, and yet the same. The rush of memory was more vivid and more shockingly objective than Charles could have imagined possible.

"Sit down, Maria. We must have our little chat, just as we planned."

She pouted sweetly. "You're disappointed in me. Yes, you *are!*"

"Maria, you are amazingly the same. Your voice, your little ways. I've aged and changed, but not you." She showed signs of pouncing from her chair, and he went on hastily. "I can still see your harp . . . and Daphne, too. How I used to envy that little dog, in your arms. I hope poor Daphne had a peaceful end?"

Incredibly, she reached for a handkerchief and wiped real tears from her eyes. To be sure, even at a distance the brandy was a palpable aura.

"She lived for sixteen years, our darling Daphne. Mr. Winter grew very fond of her. When she passed away, we had such a lovely piece of taxidermy done. Yes, dear Charles, you'll see her when you come to dine, the very first thing as you come into the house, right there in a glass case in our front hall. So sweet and natural, except for the eyes. The eyes, somehow, never satisfied me, though everyone else finds them *very* lifelike."

Charles's hands gripped hard on the arms of his chair. He prayed in anguish. God, don't let me laugh. If I were to start I could never stop until they came and took me away. God, don't.

He spoke in a voice that shook a little, and it was clear from Maria's face that his obvious emotion moved her dangerously.

"It's easy to understand that. She always had a gaze for her dear mistress that she never gave anyone else."

"Why did I never think of that? To be sure. But a famous genius sees all manner of things that we foolish little women miss, doesn't he? Oh, Charles, if you'd not written me those sweet, sweet letters I'd be afraid you'd only find me a little bore, you must know so many clever people now!"

He stole a look at the clock and prayed again. Maria had come late; was there no merciful chance that Kate and Georgy would come home early? In a few minutes?

He said, "No woman is ever a bore. You're the same fascinating little mystery that you always were. And now, do tell me about your parents? Do you still see any of that group, your friends, and your sister's? What gay little evenings we all used to have . . ."

She made a shy, charming play with the handkerchief and the face slightly averted.

"Those evenings, yes. And the garden — do you remember the garden, and the little bench? You naughty dear, I know you remembered it the first of all!"

The sound of carriage wheels was the everlasting mercy made audible. Charles rushed to the door ahead of John, calling out.

"Kate, Georgy, such a pleasant little surprise! Mrs. Winter dropped in to call upon you, and I persuaded her to wait. Here, we're in the library, shan't we all go into the drawing room? Coax her to take a cup of tea, at least, since I've made her wait for you so long!"

And Kate, all amiable smiles, blessedly, blessedly nodded her way past him.

"Oh, you must stay. Georgy and I were saying only now that we wanted our cup of tea!"

The tea came quickly. Kate was downright chatty.

Unfortunately, it was apparent that Maria had interpreted that mad rush for the door as a gesture of guilt for those hopes which he had not yet quite dared to make realities. Of guilt lest Kate should have found them so, alone.

Throughout the rest of the call she punctuated her conversation with sidelong glances — hideously well-remembered glances. Glances that pitied, languished, promised a happier morrow.

When she left, Kate said, "How amiable Mrs. Winter is. But she has a sort of squint, hasn't she?"

Georgy laughed. "A squint! She was trying to charm poor Charles!"

"Georgy, how rude and unkind."

Georgy said, "You can be wonderfully fair to anyone who isn't young and pretty, can't you?" and walked out of the room.

"Well!" Kate said. "Apparently it's coming on Georgy that she's not quite as young as she used to be. Making a mock of that poor woman, like a spiteful old maid! Do you think she could get Mr. Egg, still, if she tried?"

"I don't know. I keep on thinking of her as just past fifteen. The girls, too, I forget that they're nearly grown."

Kate shrugged. "So I'm the only one that grows old?"

Charles looked at her. He chose his words with more respect for accuracy than was usual with him.

"I find it hard to remember that in Chelsea you were in the least different from what you are today."

He knew that Kate never heard a sentence as it was spoken. He knew, and intended, that she should receive it as a compliment, however ungraciously. He was surprised and repelled by his own ugly, sly malice. But he was also too angry with life not to stab it somewhere.

At once he was ashamed and sad and humbled, for the violet eyes brightened beneath the puffy eyelids and Kate said, "Thank you, Charles. That's the nicest thing you've said in a long time."

In God's good time, Charles turned the reappearance of Maria to excellent comic use. But the time did not come soon. For months it was horror and emptiness.

A Maria fat and toothless would have been a shock; but if the soul which never existed had looked out of her eyes, Charles would have done quite well. He had a knack for pity, and love is not love which alters when it alteration finds. But Maria precisely what she had always been, a vulgar, mindless flirt, changed in nothing but the overlay of boozy middle age, was something yet again.

It is hard to doubt one's premises. Once Charles woke in the night, sweating, asking himself, Was Mary what I thought? Have I ever known what I loved?

It was disproportionate, yes. But so was Charles.

Mr. Winter was a tired-looking man, but he appeared to enjoy the dinner. He walked about, through the evening, handling the draperies and the vases and tapping the furniture with as much satisfaction as if he expected to have it up for auction, shortly, at a handsome percentage.

It was as well that he expected no other entertainment. Charles was not free. Maria trembled by his side in girlish invitation all evening. Incidentally, she did well by the wine.

When they had gone, Kate said, "I apologize, Georgy, you were right, she really *does* try to make eyes. Still, Charles, she was a friend of Fanny's, you might have been nicer."

Georgy was laughing. "He was as nice as he dared!"

Kate also insisted that they accept the return invitation.

Daphne was in the hall, as promised. "Did darling Daphne remember this silly boy who used to be so jealous of her? Aha, I *knew* she did!"

It went on longer than one would have thought possible. Maria gave up hope hard. She wrote to him every day, for days on end. She called, repeatedly. Charles hid out at his clubs, wrote brisk notes saying that he must be out of town for many Sundays to come, wrote desperate appeals. "A necessity is upon me now — as at most times — of wandering about in my own wild way to think . . . I hold my inventive capacity on the stern condition that it must master my whole life."

At long last she believed him, and he was free to turn his full fury back upon the Crimean War.

Layard's Reform Bill never had a chance against it.

He said to Miss Coutts, "Layard does not set class against class, that is done already. Only look, and you will see revolution smoldering. My only fear is that it will bring something worse than what it overthrows."

"I hate to see you so depressed, Mr. Dickens."

"We get older. I was a boy when I put my faith in the Cheerybles. *Dombey* and *Bleak House* showed better sense, but they were still confused with a fool's courage, I know that, now. This time I will write a book without false hopes and outgrown dreams."

"Does your friend Mr. Collins agree?"

It was an edged barb, but he would not be drawn. "He's a cynic, yes, but in days like these one who never expected better of his fellow man makes good company when the day's wasted work is done."

That had been too much. Charles saw it before he was done speaking, and at once he began to tell her about the babies, and how splendidly Kate did.

He left her smiling.

In a way, we may say that it was Maria who ended off the first of Charles's two lives. A dream leaped from the past and engulfed the heart of a many-friended, lonely man; with ludicrous finality, the dream was destroyed. And Charles, for a time of hiatus, embraced the illusion that man can live without illusions.

It was a forceful illusion. A poor foreigner, Karl Marx by name, was simultaneously feeling much the same way, in a shabby room in another part of London. *Das Kapital* suffered the fate of most prophetic writings, ignored by its own times and fiercely misapplied to others. *Little Dorrit* caused no disturbance, then or thereafter.

Charles's genius had never been in more towering form. He said his say, damned his society, demanded another — and created a host of people so moving, ludicrous, touching, that he had never been more popular. Except for a few critics, everyone loved it, nobody was disturbed, and it outsold *Bleak House*, which is saying a great deal.

❊   7   ❊

NOBODY'S FAULT, he called the book at first.

Nobody's fault. This England, in which the blame for every sin of war or peace goes squarely, always, to somebody else; the Russians, the Lords, the Commons, labor, management, someone; only not I, never I.

The first bare, furious thought became a driving restlessness worse than any he had ever suffered. The wild, wandering angry abstraction drove him through the days, and all the obligations that he steadily, competently fulfilled — as editor, committeeman, endlessly, damnably helpful friend, father, husband, son, brother (his mother and Fred and Shrimp with their wives, one an idiot and one endlessly ailing, were the worst of the lot) — all of them, everything, felt like a haze of senseless interruptions.

Reality centered in the Marshalsea, and William Dorrit, aging there; none of Micawber's lunatic gallantry in him as the shaking fingers kept rising to his face in that gesture of essential life destroyed, integrity destroyed.

Charles, broken out of life, lost in the illusion of clarity, realism, looked at William Dorrit; and thought, I lied to myself because I had to. But a light went out, I know it, I saw it go.

But the tension grew.

Collins wrote a melodrama, and in June Charles put it on in the children's theater, with *Mr. Nightingale's Diary*, the six-part miracle, for the farce. He played the lead, and he had never made an audience cry so hard. The two-night stand in the children's theater packed with cheering, sobbing friends made it the talk of the town, and they had to do it again for a benefit. When it was done with, he wondered what he had done it for.

He got into a furious exchange of public letters with the Prime Minister.

In August Anne, the generalissimo, the unchanging, unaging, horsefaced, blessedly dependable, magnificent, permanent Anne Brown gave notice. She wanted to get married.

Kate said, "How shocking, how dreadful! She'll get no wedding present from *me!*"

"Our Anne, our virgin meat-axe! There's hope for us all, Kate, we're not so old as we've been thinking!"

He sent the wedding check in a handsome silver box that she might show about: "It was a position of trust, like. You might say I was on a footing of friendship with the 'ole fambily." Good God, Anne!

They would winter in Paris. Shortly before they left the country, Charles got Wills to go to Rochester with him, for a walk. He showed him Gad's Hill.

"I've loved that house for almost forty years. Falstaff used to drink in the inn across the way there, where we'll take ourselves now."

"Beautiful old house. Nicely placed, too, on that rise. Yes, perfect house."

"You and my father were very unlike, Wills, but I always felt that you — appreciated what he was."

Little Wills nodded. "I was fond of him. You were very much alike, you know."

"Were we? I never thought of it like that, I only felt close to him. Loved him. I've been thinking about him very much, this summer."

"I know," Wills said. He heard himself with distress. If there were circumstances in Dickens's life that he wanted to believe that nobody surmised, how was that different from the rest of us? Micawber, Dorrit — they select and use, in that business, all of them; as you might say, one love in its time yields many parts.

Wills cleared his throat. "Think of him often myself," he said.

"We used to walk here, when I was small. He told me once — with a few under his belt, I daresay — that there was — no reason why this house should not be mine one day—er—in this world of, I forget what. But a world of something as rosy as those bricks, certainly. That was the one he lived in, then."

Wills said firmly, "Then? He never left it, nor could you."

It was a declaration of love and a stubborn profession of faith.

Dear Wills, Charles thought; all loyalty and no insight.

"I'm afraid the glow goes off for all of us before we die," he said. "Come along, it's time for chops and ale; or half-and-half, or something equally vulgar and heartening."

Wills disliked drink at midday, and his appetite was never good. But he was, as Charles believed him, faithful unto death.

He wavered a little as they came out into the air again and said, "Remarkably fine house. Yes. Beautiful."

Charles never told Wills anything about his childhood. He had always regretted telling Forster. The Governor's troubles had been the Governor's, not his, to mouth about. But in the years ahead he told him about Ellen Ternan. When the whole wretchedness had to be told, for practical reasons, it was dry little Wills, of all people, to whom he chose to go for help and for pity.

Why did he tell him? God only knows. Perhaps because Wills believed the truth at the start, when Charles sent Ellen a bracelet, a gift more wistful but no more actively hopeful than many another that he had given to a leading lady when a benefit play was over, and it was delivered by mistake to Kate, precipitating the scenes and the public scandal and the separation. Wills had believed the unlikely truth, that Ellen was chaste; an actress, the child of an actress, but younger than Charles's own daughters, and chaste. Collins could never have believed that, or Egg, or Mark Lemon, though he protested his belief so unconvincingly; but Wills could.

Wills could believe it. And Charles could tell him, five mortal years later — five unthinkable, secret, hungry years of small favors later — when he finally overcame Ellen's scruples. Yes, and his own, for his unquestioning acceptance of the double standard still drew the line at virginity.

He told Wills, and Wills took care of things when he had to be away; when the child had to be given up for adoption — the child for whose birth Ellen never forgave him; the child for whose loss he could not forgive her.

Wills took care of things.

And somehow, from that day, before it all began, it was settled that he should.

He took care of things. And he, alone of everyone who knew Charles, did not ask why he drove himself against doctor's orders, through those last grueling readings all over England, Scotland, Ireland, America, England again. Drove himself, collapsing, utterly spent, time after time, when one of them was done, and at once up on his feet, laughing, full of outrageous life and wild, schoolboy pranks.

Why did Dickens do it? people asked, when he was on for sixty, hugely rich, the golden touch in everything he did, every investment kissed by fortune. Why? A costly nonresident wife and nine remarkably dependent children, with or without husbands and wives, were scarcely a nick in that huge fortune. Why?

Wills never put the answer into words. But he knew it.

Why? Why in a world of loves lost, disappointed, half returned, mucked up; why, sometimes weak, and often self-deceived, but always loving except for those few years when the deep froze up —

why should he love so desperately at the end the love that never failed, the lifted, loving face that never changed, the audience who knew him better than wife or mistress or embittered little sister-in-law who precipitated the separation from which she got so much less than she had dared to hope; or than children — Mamie, the faithful spinster so dead in love with the Charles that never was on land or sea; Katey, who rushed from the breaking home to marry the man she would never admit that she did not love, because she could not bear to hate the father whom she loved so passionately; Speck, always plunging deeper into debt; Plorn, the dear misfit, gone off at last to tend sheep in Australia . . . why?

Wills knew, and Mary Boyle. They were not acquainted with each other; and they told nobody else.

Paris was heavy with deep yellow mud. In spite of the war, it was a time of insane extravagance. Eugène Sue lived like a prince in a shopgirl's dream. Rotten from Bourse and Threadneedle Street to slum; the whole damned fabric was rotten, rotted through. Dorrit would come into a fortune, and it would only finish off the task the Marshalsea began.

And the Governor was dead. And he would never know that the dream was accomplished, and his son owned Gad's Hill.

The day after that walk to Rochester Wills was laughing when Charles came into the office. He had a tight, dry laugh, and the unrestrained triumph that now forced it to its loudest make him sound like an angel with laryngitis.

"It was intended that you should have that house! Gad's Hill! Your father knew! It's up for sale."

Gad's Hill. The topper waving, going back to defy the pull of the earth — the forgiving, waiting earth. Yes, God, I'm thankful. Yes, the accomplished dream. Oh, but God, I wish it had been on the market sooner. . . . I wish he hadn't been living so damned well within his means when he died.

Kate was not interested. Georgy said that it was remarkable how dreams came true; she said it with an enthusiasm which unkindly overemphasized her look of being past her first youth.

Charles went to England for the Christmas readings, and he visited Rockingham. Mrs. Watson was her lovely self, the house was its lovely self and it was a hard evening. Through most of it Charles kept writing in his head the letter to Mary Boyle; the letter about what it was like. For almost a year he had only seen Meery in other people's houses, but their letters were like a reminder that good is still good though in this ugly world it has no chance.

In the morning, before he left, Charles and Mrs. Watson went up to the gallery. Watson had set a bay window into it, the year before he died. He had loved the beam of sun it let down on the hall; he loved to sit reading up there, like a boy perched reading on the branch of a tree.

Now Mrs. Watson and Charles sat there, and looked down into the great hall, that was full of laughing ghosts. They looked down, and they did not talk.

And Charles thought, When I write her letters she is real to me, again, and close, and dear, like Meery. And here, in her house, she stands away across a gulf of time.

She was still a lovely woman; she looked scarcely older than she had, so long ago, when she looked down through the morning mists on the mountain; when he first knew all that she and Watson possessed in each other. But now, when he looked at her, it was like seeing her through the wrong end of opera glasses — small and far off, and alone, alone.

He wanted to say something good, something right. He wanted to take her hand and speak warmly, gently, of Watson and the plays, and the good times past.

He looked down and said nothing. In the end he told himself that he had done what he should, that anything else would have made her unhappy.

But when he got to London he wanted to talk to Forster. Forster was ponderous, pompous, relentlessly noble; he hated Collins and rather disapproved of Lemon and little Egg. He was not the boy who wept with a boy in Chalk so long ago; Charles knew all that.

And he would not know it. He had to talk.

"Forster, can't you see what it was like? She'd been a banker's daughter and I was taking shorthand in the gallery. She was everything, rank, beauty, love — oh, Forster such love. The little garden. . ."

Forster's laugh was heavy and puffy, and still it sounded like Harry watching Plorn take a tumble. "Twenty-four years? And you still expected . . . Ha, no, but that's delicious! Nobody but you, ever!"

"Four years of my life, four burning years . . ."

"My dear fellow, has that delightful world which you inhabit so much, ah! to our enrichment quite blinded you to the world of common day?"

Two months later, Forster — with deep solemnity — announced his engagement, to the widow of a wealthy publisher. He was forty-four, a self-advertised virgin of whose claims Charles had never felt the least question. For once, at least, Kate could share his laughter and awe at the utter unpredictability of things.

The Crimean War ended at the same time. The world said, in effect, "Oh? Anything else happen today?"

"Oh, you must be so happy!" Georgy said.

"Why? Do you think that it will make a difference? I laugh when I think that once I was fool enough to hope for something from the suffrage, in a system rotted through. Collins is coming to visit, did I tell you?"

"I'm glad of that." Firmly. "You need to be gay."

Clearly she was not glad, though she wanted to be.

Charles himself looked forward less to the entertainments of the Caliph and his Vizier than he wanted to think.

He was restless. He was wretched with Kate. On his last jaunt to London he had found Tavistock House a stye full of Hogarths and his remarks upon his return had precipitated a scene that he could not let himself remember or forget. He also felt old, and hated it, and found more kinds of reassurance and release than one in being a gay young dog.

But beyond all that he was incurably domestic, romantic, and full of unwilling insights and unwilling pities for Kate and the little periwinkles, as Collins called them.

He was glad when Collins went back to London. He was glad that he, himself, was getting out of Paris and back to Boulogne.

On their last day in town he ordered a cabriolet and drove Plorn about the streets and listened to his grave comments on the social scene, and was blessedly diverted and refreshed by them.

The camp was deserted, a great field of blowing dust. "The property" was rented, but Beaucourt had another house, almost as charming.

His other tenants, however, were artists; ill, drinking and penniless.

One of their little boys did the cooking. The crockery and glassware were being smashed, months of rent looked to be dead loss, never to be paid, and Beaucourt was not rich.

Beaucourt smiled like the sun, and had the other child, the feeble-minded one, work with him at his endless gardening, his beloved roses.

"The fresh air, do you see, keeps his poor little brains cooler. Monsieur Dickens, I am so desolated for them all!"

"But for yourself, Beaucourt? Have you nothing to say for yourself?"

"Ah, monsieur, it's nothing, let us not speak of it."

The evening star was out, at the end of the avenue. Beaucourt backed away toward it, waving his cap.

Charles, watching him, began to write a letter in his mind: "As if he would back straight off into it without waiting to go through the formality of dying first."

Putting it into words did nothing to diminish that singular, anguishing impact of Beaucourt's goodness.

Suddenly, for the first time in some years, Charles began to cry.

He belongs to the world I made when I was young, he thought. To a world I pulled down out of the sky, a world that never was. But still is. Beaucourt, empirical proof of the existence of God. Of the God I still pray to like a machine, night after night.

Oh, damn you, Beaucourt, bless you!

When he asked Mary Boyle to visit, in Kate's name and Georgy's as well as his own, he expected only mild unpleasantness. There was no reason, he knew as soon as it was done, that he should have expected it to go off as that trip to Rockingham had gone off, after the Malvern episode; no reason except that he wanted it to so very much.

At least the nightmare was brief; on the first day, when the post came in, Mary said that she had learned that she must get back to England at once; an aunt who was very ill. Yes, she must go, by next morning, at the latest.

Georgy walked in on him, in the room where he had gone to be alone.

She said, "Charles, it is so wrong. You should not have to bear it."

He said, "Please don't, Georgy. You love her. She can't help it."

"But Miss Boyle is an old friend and — and an old *woman!*"

"Georgy, please."

She went away. For a curious, suffocating moment he thought, Oh, God, why can't she marry Egg? And at once he reproached himself. My dear small person, my dear little housekeeper. She can't help seeing what everyone sees now, she can't always be silent without being more of a sham than her honest little heart will let her.

("Aunty was not quite straight," Katey once said.)

That evening, after dinner, Charles said abruptly, "Meery, come out. Take a little stroll with me."

They walked off into the grounds, Meery keeping her distance and with her face troubled, though she had come with him quickly and without a word.

She said, "Dear Jo, you should have let me know that the old Malvern trouble was threatening again. I should not have come just now."

"Meery, it's not that. Meery, I've got to talk to you. You and I have always played that game of being in love that nobody, not even Kate, could ever misunderstand. But there is a strong, genuine affection under it, isn't there?"

"You know that, Jo. We've always understood one another."

"I've got to tell you what it's like, Meery. Things that I've not even told myself until this. I need your friendship. I need it more than I have ever needed any before, and after this I shall always need it in the same way, as much as this. I don't know why it's so or how I know it or what made me get you here. But it is so."

"I wish you wouldn't, Jo. Tell me, I mean."

"No, let me. I've got to talk to a friend, and that friend a woman. And not poor Georgy, not her own sister."

"Jo, dear, what is it? Have you fallen in love?"

He laughed shortly. "At my age? What girl would think of me for anything except my money, even if I were free? And do you think I'd ever be fool enough to fall in love again unless I were loved in return?"

She was silent for a moment. Then, unexpectedly, she took his hand and held it against her cheek.

She said, "Yes, we're neither of us as young as we like to play at, are we, my dear? What is it then, Jo? Tell me."

"Kate. From the very start, from the first she has shut me off completely. She shuts everyone off now, even the children draw away from her. But that would not have happened to her if she had not

married me. I don't know why it is. I can see that I would have been
difficult for anyone, often. But not like this. We were made to destroy each other."

"Jo, my darling Jo, you sound like a hysterical woman. What big
words, dear."

"Please listen. She used to be very beautiful. I imagined a person to go with all that beauty. And when I came to admit what was
really there, after Mary died, I tried to love her, I tried to be content. Until this hour, I've tried desperately, always coming back to
it. And the devil of it is that she wants to love me, and believes
that she loves me. And she hates me. And, Meery, it's begun to kill
my soul. It is turning me in hard fact into a man I can only hate
as heartily as she does."

"You're tired, dear Jo. Your book tires you, and the state of the
world discourages you. You're saying things that you do not wholly
mean and that you will be sorry for."

"All granted. And they have to be said. They have to be. Listen to
me. In April I went to my house and her damned mother and sister
and poor old father were camped there in filth, running up bills to
my account. With no thought that it was anything to be grateful for.
I had to stay at a hotel in Dover until they cleared out, and I could
start in with John to make it fit for temporary human habitation.
When I got back to Kate we fought about it. Fought."

"Fought?"

"Like a drunken stevedore and his trull. Minus the blows. Not a
full rehearsal, only a reading. But good expression and a superb
script. And that finished it."

"Because you lost your temper, Jo?"

"Not that. Because as I thought back to it and tried not to, and
thought back again it came on me that it was the first time for years,
years, that our lives, our real selves, our emotions had met at all. It
was the only real contact that we had had, the only words that
weren't sham or total empty nothings since a row on the road to
Naples, years before. And *that* had been more real than anything
between us since Mamie was born."

"Please, Jo, you're wretched and she's not well. It's not an ideal
marriage, but you do love her. Please, Jo, don't tell me all this."

"She thinks that I manage somehow to wriggle into bed with every
good, innocent, pretty girl I smile at."

"She's only jealous because she loves you. If you'd married a woman who — who enjoyed the landscape, let's say, as you do, Jo, I think you'd have been jealous yourself."

"I know that, too. Meery, Meery, I'm sorry to have been so disgusting, I shall never talk of it again. But can't you, for God's sake, say that you see what it's like for us both? That you pity her, and that you pity me? The only passion in my life, in my writing, now, is anger. I see old Beaucourt, living like a child of God, a saint in a circus clown's dress, I swear it — I look at him and think once I had a little, not much, never so much, but a little of that same sort of goodness, too. But it's dying, drop by drop. I can't even cry any more. Kate and I wanted to love each other. What's happened is more by my fault than hers, at the start I was too happy with too little, I failed her, too, I know it. But knowing it can't change the fact of the ugly, permanent hate. No longer. No longer. Or the falsity, so that a healthy row over her family and my house feels nearer to love than these days and nights of dead familiarity."

His hand was quite cold and unresponsive as she took it and lifted it to her cheek again.

"You'll find your way, Jo," she said. "You can't help but find it. You're a much better man than you think. You're deeply good, dear Jo. I love you. It will be better, in time, for you and Kate both. I know it."

He said, "Forgive me, Meery. Forgive me and thank you, dear. Let's go back to the house."

Kate was near the door with Georgy as they walked along the path, Charles with his arms swinging, Meery with her hands clasped behind her back like a schoolgirl trying to better her posture.

He nodded toward them. He said, "Watching. Even us, even you. God, I wish I could cry."

He took a long step forward.

"Ah, you've come out to meet us. It's a lovely evening."

Toward morning Charles opened his eyes and addressed the ceiling.

"For one who has always made so much talk about loyalty, and about not belaboring the irremediable, you did rather well, didn't you? Poor Meery, so faithful and courteous, to the last gun."

Sometimes a man goes on a violent bender to break a tension and succeeds so well that shame builds a worse tension in its place. Charlie felt very much like that until he got back to sleep.

But Mary Boyle, in the next room, lay on her face and wept.

"Oh, my poor Jo," she wept. "My poor, poor Jo. It will be some young girl, I know it. Some girl the age of the girl who died. And Kate will never divorce him, and he is so good. Sooner or later he will fall in love with some girl, and seduce her because she is good, and God pity him, what will he do then? How will he feel about her, about himself? That new play of Collins's, the Antarctic one that he can't wait to get home and put on . . . If it's a success, he'll start some benefit, he'll take it to the road, with girls in the company. And then, or the next time, or the next . . ."

She closed her eyes and lay still, like a prophetess in the trance. Not crying, any longer, only still.

Then she said, softly, "Oh, Jo, I wish that I could have been young for you. Like her. That one, so soon now. So soon now, certainly."

She was a remarkably unselfish and percipient woman, Mary Boyle, that closest friend of Charles's last years.

❋ ❋ ❋ ❋ ❋

Epilogue

❋ ❋ ❋ ❋ ❋

❋ Epilogue ❋

JUNE EIGHTH, eighteen seventy. The Crimean War is fourteen years past. Charles is fifty-eight.

Gad's Hill. Windows open on the lawn, and the sweet of syringa heavy on the bright evening air. The double doors of the new conservatory wide open, the slanting evening sun on its glass walls forcing back into the dining room the smell of hot, wet earth, spice of carnations, pungent richness of musk. Color and light, the scarlet of the carnations spinning with the blue of the lobelias in a carnival riot, innocent and tipsy, the gaiety of nice young girls drunk on champagne.

Bright, loud, delightful color dancing into the room from two sides, through the open conservatory doors and back from the dazzle of the big mirror over the sideboard.

One can't have too many mirrors all over a house to play cricket with the sun. The Chinese lanterns had been a good idea, too, a capital idea. Twenty of them, strung up there only last night, now swayed, bright and nonsensical, over the bright flowers, in the sun, in the moving air.

Light, color, fragrance, sound. The birds were ending off a day of it too, outside the windows; a whole crowd of thrushes and one lunatic cuckoo. The evening was almost too beautiful, sweet-scented, loud.

"Katey left so early this morning. Did you and she sit up late, after you'd lit your lanterns out there?"

"Very late, Georgy."

Until morning. Talking for the first time as they might have talked for years, if they had not been father and child. Talking their lives through, from that night he got out of bed in Tavistock House and walked the thirty miles to Gad's Hill in the dark, until now. Talking their lives through, in love that needed no retreat to special pleading.

"Have you forgiven me for what I am, Katey?"

"I always did. Even on the night I ran away."

A beautiful woman, in her straight, pre-Raphaelite gown, green-blue, the Madonna knot of auburn hair on the elegant neck. Thank God, poor little Mamie was in town.

"What did you talk about?"

Charles started at the question. An abrupt sensation like falling took him amidships. It was with the utmost effort that he kept his body erect and his face composed. As he must. For Georgy knew quite well all that they had talked of. Despite her singular determination to know nothing, ever, she had always known and he always knew that she knew.

His left side was quite numb again today, except for the foot, which was once more like a bag of pain. But one could ignore pain; not this wave of frightening weariness, or was it fear like a bodily exhaustion? Yet if he pushed back the chair and lay for a moment on the sofa in the bay behind him, Georgy would be upset.

He stared into the mirror over the sideboard. Unless he turned his head, the left-hand side of it showed nothing but dazzle and blur.

He said, "We talked of this and that. We talked."

The heavy quiet that filled the room told him that she knew everything that she refused to know.

The table had been cleared. They were alone. They sat quite still for several minutes, as if the photographer, hand closed on the rubber bulb, had urged them to breathe through their mouths, keep their eyes focused upon one point, not to blink.

It would have made an extraordinary picture for the collectors, Charles Dickens and his sister-in-law, Georgina Hogarth, in the dining room of Gad's Hill. The setting itself so amusing in its ebullient, full-Victorian opulence, everything that could be carved, draped or polished, richly carved, elegantly draped, highly polished. And on the sideboard that fantastic silver epergne that was an admirer's gift — Spring, Summer, and Autumn, allegorical figures lifting their hands to support the basket for the flowers, the fruit. Winter not there because, as the admirer had explained, winter had no part in him.

"I never look at it," Charles once said, "that I don't think of winter the most."

Still, he laughed while he said it, and it stayed there, conspicuously placed; what we would call nowadays an excellent conversation piece.

Yes, a delightful setting; and in it, face to face across the full-flowing white damask, the tidy little spinster with her look of dried and withered girlhood, and the erect, dying man, so handsomely tailored, his cuffs and fingernails so immaculate.

They look not at each other but past each other, and their faces are secret; composed, pleasant, shut away from each other.

She is a small woman but she appears even smaller than she is, through having fitted herself to that picture of her own smallness through all the years since she was fifteen — my little housekeeper, our little Georgy, your little Aunty, small person.

He, himself, though he is neither tall nor heavy-set gives an effect of bigness; but the reason for the effect is immediately apparent. It lies neither in posture nor mannerism, but in the huge, extraordinary eyes, which even now, bagged below and shaded by swollen lids, and looking past her and guarding their counsel, are still almost shockingly alive. Like searchlights, someone had said, and someone else, that they could be the eyes of an archangel or a demon. People exaggerate, but they are remarkable eyes.

But Georgy started, suddenly. She leaned forward.

"Charles, you're not well. Lie down."

"I've been very ill this last hour. Let us finish dinner."

"Charles, we have finished dinner."

He tried to pick up his napkin and dropped it. "I'll tell Roche about it in the morning. I mean, John."

He glanced around the table, empty except for the two of them. "I'm sorry, my dears, but I must get up to London immediately. Roche?"

He stood up and swayed. The servants were in the pantry, they were alone, she could not hold his sagging weight.

"Charles, you must lie down, you must."

He slipped from her arms to the floor. His eyes had been closed while she supported him, but now for a moment they opened and came around large upon her face, though not as though it was her face he saw.

His deep, moving, actor's voice spoke with perfect clarity.

"Yes," he said. "On the ground."

He closed his eyes. The outcries of the servants drowned out the harsh labor of his breath. They lifted him to the sofa.

He lay upon it unconscious through that night and almost all the next day.

Georgy sent for the children, and early next morning she sent word to Mary Boyle.

Mary Boyle brought Ellen. She had not wanted to come.

"You must. You must be there with him."

"I am glad you brought her," Georgy said, "for years she has been like a third daughter in this family."

Mary nodded and went outside and sat in her carriage. She sat there through the long day.

Kate was not told. Until after a tear rolled down his cheek, with that final dramatic effect, even in the unconsciousness which never lifted, and he had ceased to breathe, she was not told.

Not even Katey had felt any impulse to send for her. They all knew that when Charles walked out and shut the door at last, it was shut for good.